WHAT READERS ARE SAYING

"I loved this book... The story of Chad and Hollywood is so deep and intense... a total gut wrenching and emotional book... it made me cry... made me laugh... it was packed full of everything a book needs. ... One of the best M/M books I have read."
—Diane, *For the Love of Pimping* on *Lover on Top*

"WOW!! This book is going to be one of the best I've read this year. It was flawless in my opinion. [...] I went through so many emotions reading this story but I couldn't turn the page fast enough."
—Kathy, *KathyMac Reviews* on *Lover on Top*

"*Everything Bared* is a delicious and edgy walk on the wild side of beautifully crafted erotica. Another 5-star achievement from gifted writer Kristine Cayne!"
—Laura Taylor, 6-Time *Romantic Times* Award Winner, 2-Time Maggie Award Winner, & RWA RITA Finalist

"Highly flammable and unforgettable. My favorite erotic romance of the year. Cayne's debut erotic romance was **impossible** to put down."
—*MsRomanticReads Romance & Erotica Book Reviews* on *Under His Command*

"This baby gives new meaning to the word HOT! Insanely creative, toe curling and to top that, an amazing story as well! If this is Kristine's first erotic romance, imagine what she'll think of next!"
—Jackie Munoz on *Under His Command*

"Loved it! Really, really enjoyed this and I hope there are many more hot firefighter stories in what looks like a very promising series!"
—Laci Paige, author of the Silken Edge novels, on *Aftershocks*

"Kristine Cayne is one of my favorite writers! Her characters are so remarkable and real.... The relationship you see between this Dom and Sub is not unhealthy or over-romanticized. It's a real relationship with depth and passion and a side most BDSM books don't let you really see. I loved every minute of this and can't wait for more!"
—Xavier Neal on *Handle with Care*

ALSO BY KRISTINE CAYNE

Six-Alarm Sexy Series
Aftershocks (Prequel)
Under His Command (Book One)
Everything Bared (Book Two)
Handle with Care (Book Three)
Lover on Top (Book Four)
Baby, Be Mine (Book Five)
Stripped Down (Book Six – coming soon)

Seattle Fire Series
(Six-Alarm Sexy Spin-off)
In His Arms (Book One – summer 2018)

Men of Boyzville Series
(Six-Alarm Sexy Spin-off)
Going All In (Book One)
Wrangling the Cowboy (Book Two – coming soon)

Deadly Vices Series
Deadly Obsession (Book One)
Deadly Addiction (Book Two)
Deadly Betrayal (Book Three)

Other Works
Origins: The Men of MER in *Shadows in the Mist: A Paranormal Anthology*
Guns 'N' Tulips
Un-Valentine's Day

Writing with Dana Delamar

Total Indulgence Series
Her Two Men in London (Book One)
Her Two Men in Tahiti (Book Two) – summer 2018
Her Two Men in Sonoma (Book Three) – fall 2018

LOVER ON TOP

SIX-ALARM SEXY
BOOK FOUR

KRISTINE
CAYNE

ACKNOWLEDGMENTS

My undying gratitude goes to Dana Delamar at By Your Side Self-Publishing, for her class-A editing skills, for her unflagging encouragement to try a different genre, but most of all for her constant friendship. A friend like you only comes around once or twice in a lifetime, and I'm grabbing on with both hands. You're not getting away from me, girl!

To my husband and sons, for putting up with my crazy hours, my release-time panic, and my Facebook feed full of half-naked men. You don't always get the way my mind works, but you still love me. ☺

To my readers, my fabulous street squad, and my amazing beta readers: Nanee, Tina, Sharon, Patti, and Renee. Each time one of you shares my books on social media, posts a review, or sends me an email, it lifts my spirits and urges me on. Your love for my characters and your passion for my stories rivals my own. *You* are my inspiration.

To all the fabulous bloggers and reviewers who've supported me with this book in one way or another. Especially to Jay, for seeing what we all missed.

To Becky Mathews, paramedic with the Seattle Fire Department's Medic One Battalion, thank you for taking the time to answer my questions with such detail. The work you and your colleagues do makes you all heroes in my book!

CHAPTER 1

Nathanial "Hollywood" Wright surveyed the slim offerings in his fridge. It was his turn to host poker night, and the guys would be expecting food, not just chips and beer. Especially not after he'd ragged on the quality of Damian's food last week. He should have kept his fucking mouth shut. But no, he'd had to tease the guy about his wife being out of town. Now the joke was on Hollywood.

Rummaging in the freezer, he spotted a package of drumsticks. Fried chicken would be perfect. He'd watched a date make it for him a few years back, and it hadn't looked all that difficult. Some breading, some oil, and voilà, it was done. Besides, Google was a single man's best friend. A few minutes later, he'd found an easy-looking recipe online and began assembling the necessary ingredients. Once the drumsticks were seasoned and rolled in flour, he put oil in a heavy skillet and set it on the stove to heat, then glanced at the clock on the microwave to see how he was doing time-wise.

Shit. The guys would be arriving any minute. Racing, he got the vegetables out of the fridge and began rinsing some mini cucumbers and carrots. When the smell of heated oil tickled his nose, he dropped in the drumsticks, the oil popping and crackling around them, and then went back to preparing the veggies. Maybe he should have started a little fucking earlier. Whatever. Beer. That's what he needed. What was the big deal anyway? It was just poker night.

He cracked open a can of Bud Light—if it wasn't vodka, he didn't care about the brand—and took a huge gulp, grimacing when the cold liquid hit his empty stomach. Yeah, he probably should have eaten something *before* he began drinking. How many times was he going to learn that lesson?

1

As he cut the last piece of red pepper, the doorbell rang. Shit. After tossing the peels into the garbage bin under the sink and wiping off his hands, he downed the rest of his beer and took a deep breath. No big deal. He had everything under control.

He opened the door to a grinning Jamie Caldwell. "Honey, I'm home!"

"Asshole." Hollywood laughed and grabbed the twelve-pack of Redhook from his best friend's hands. Rules were: host provided the food and guests brought the booze. "Come in."

Jamie thumped him on the back. "Something sure smells good," he said, heading into the kitchen.

Hollywood snorted and pushed Jamie toward the living room. "You'll get some when everyone else does."

"Some friend you are," Jamie grumbled as he swiped a carrot and slathered it in dip.

Hollywood playfully punched Jamie in the stomach, swallowing a wince when his knuckles met the wall of steel that was Jamie's abs. "Only looking out for you, buddy."

"Yeah, right. At least give me a beer."

Hollywood grabbed one from Jamie's pack and used it and the vegetable platter to coax him into the living room. With a beer in hand, Jamie's mood was much improved.

"How's Erica?" Hollywood took advantage of their few moments alone to ask Jamie about his wife. She was expecting, and there'd been complications.

Jamie shot him a shit-eating grin and plopped down on the couch.

"That good, huh?"

"That good." Jamie's eyes gleamed. He was in rare form tonight, and Hollywood couldn't be happier for him, even if he was slightly jealous. They'd been in the fire academy together and both were now lieutenants in Seattle's Technical Rescue Team, but that's where the similarities ended.

Jamie had met Erica, gotten married, and had Chloe. Sure, Jamie and Erica had gone through some rough times—they'd even almost gotten divorced—but they'd come out of them stronger and happier than ever.

As for Hollywood? He had a bit more money, a few more pounds of muscle, and a tougher attitude, but that was it. He was still alone.

"What about you?" Jamie asked, crunching on a piece of green pepper. "How are things with Jessica?"

"They're not." They never were. Hollywood had no problem getting dates, or bed partners for that matter, but things always fizzled after a few weeks. Jamie peered at him with an intensity that made Hollywood squirm. "What?"

"Nothing." Jamie shrugged. "It's none of my business anyway."

"Come on, man. You can't start something like that then clam up."

"Fine. I'm just wondering if this is enough for you?"

Hollywood grinned and waved his arms expansively. "I'm the all-American bachelor living the all-American dream."

"A girl of the week, random hookups with fire bunnies, parties, and poker nights?"

Hollywood frowned. Jamie made it sound like his life sucked. "I like poker nights."

"I do too. And I like them a lot more now that I get to go home to Rickie when they're over."

Hollywood smiled. No one else was allowed to call Erica "Rickie." Hollywood had learned that the hard way. "If I need companionship, I know who to call."

Jamie quirked a brow.

Hollywood sighed. "I'm not saying I don't want what you and Erica have. Hell, I'd love to have a kid or two. But I'm thirty-six. That ship has sailed."

"Why, though? You'd think, given all the women you've been with, one of them should have worked out."

Hollywood stared out his living room window, taking in the view of Puget Sound. "Don't know. Since Isabel, there's always something... missing."

"Maybe you're too—"

The ringing of the doorbell cut Jamie off. Hollywood jumped to go answer it, the excuse allowing him to get away from Jamie's analysis of his pathetic existence. Fuck him, anyway. Jamie thought he had it all figured out, but who really did?

Throwing open the door, Hollywood greeted Gabe, one of Jamie's platoon members, and the rest of the guys who completed their poker group. Classy as always, Gabe thrust a bottle of Southern Comfort at Hollywood and barged in, his nose twitching like a rabbit's. "Something's burning."

"What?" Hollywood said, catching a whiff of charred chicken. "Oh shit!" He tossed the bottle back at Gabe and ran to the kitchen. As soon as he crossed the threshold, there was a loud *whomp*, and the skillet of too-hot oil reached its flashpoint and went up in flames.

Heart hammering in his chest, Hollywood took in the fire curling up the sides of his cabinets, igniting the red curtains a previous girlfriend had installed above the sink. Black soot was already marking the walls and ceiling, and smoke danced in the lights over the counter.

Holy fuck. He'd set his apartment on fire!

The blare of the smoke alarm jolted him into action. Grabbing the lid, he angled it upward and placed it over the skillet. Without oxygen, the fire would die out. That taken care of, he reached over to turn off the burner. Flames from the burning cabinet licked at his skin. He swore and yanked his arm back. *Goddamn*, that hurt.

"Where's the extinguisher, Mr. Firefighter?" Jamie yelled.

"Fuck you!" Hollywood flipped him the bird without turning around. But Jamie was right. He had to put out the fire before it engulfed the entire kitchen and spread to the rest of the apartment. Reaching under the sink, he yanked out the general-purpose fire extinguisher he kept there for emergencies.

Muscle memory took over. Calmness coated his mind as he aimed the extinguisher above the flames. He was a firefighter, had been for years, and no kitchen mishap was going to get the better of him. As the last flame went out, he looked up at the ceiling, closed his eyes in thanks, and received a shower of icy water on his face. *What the hell?*

Blinking to clear his vision, he realized that the building's sprinkler system had gone off. "Jesus fucking Christ."

Laughter and applause erupted behind him. He turned to find his so-called friends all looking like half-drowned rats, except for their red faces and dancing eyes.

"Thanks for the help, assholes."

Damian, who worked on his platoon, smirked and used his hands to squeegee the water out of his hair. "Looked like you had it handled, LT."

Hollywood swiped a hand over his face to rid himself of some water. "Can someone find the super and get him to turn off the fucking sprinklers before all my shit is ruined?"

Jamie was the first to recover, the smile slipping from his face as he took in the mess of Hollywood's apartment. "I'll go."

In the distance, a fire truck siren wailed. By the snickers the others made, they'd heard it too.

Hollywood swore again. He was never going to live this down.

৪০ 🚒 ৫৪

With a groan, Chad Caldwell stretched out his legs in the cabin of Medic 11, one of the ambulances he'd been manning with his partner, Liam Parker, for the past year. They were only halfway through their twenty-four-hour shift, and to Chad it already felt like a forty-eight-hour one.

Liam glanced his way. "Partied too hard last night?"

"Fuck you. Just because Anna put you in the doghouse, doesn't mean I have to be in there with you."

"Relax, dude. All I'm saying is that maybe you shouldn't be hooking up in clubs when we have a shift the next day."

Chad rolled his eyes at his buddy, but let him continue thinking whatever he wanted. It was better than telling him the truth. That he hadn't hooked up with anyone last night. That he'd spent the night with the CockyBoys on his laptop, a tube of lube, his hand, and visions of a certain straight blond who hated his guts.

Liam squeezed his shoulder. "Just messing with you."

"I know."

"You can talk to me."

"I know."

Liam had stuck by him since the day Chad had hopped into Liam's ambulance full of excitement for his new job, and decked out in defensiveness against what could have been an uncomfortable pairing. But Liam hadn't cared that Chad was gay. He'd even gone so far as to stand up for Chad when Deputy Chief Wright had gotten on his case last August after some homophobic vandals had tagged their ambulance with the word *cunt*, then beat the shit out of Chad. If it hadn't been for Liam's quick thinking that day, Chad might have been killed. He'd certainly be without a job now.

Although... there'd been rumors that the straight blond of his dreams might have intervened on his behalf with the chief, who happened to also be said blond's father.

Maybe he ought to ask Jamie if the rumors were true. Though even if they were, it wouldn't change anything. Hollywood was Hollywood, and he sure as shit wasn't interested in Chad. Wrong equipment.

Chad's phone rang. He dug it out of his pocket and checked the display. Unknown number. "Hello?" he said, curious to find out who it was. There was no answer and a moment later the line went dead.

"Huh."

Liam looked over. "Everything okay?"

Chad shoved the phone back in his pocket. "Yeah. Just a hangup."

They turned onto SW Alaska Street, which would take them to the West Seattle Bridge and back to downtown. Given the light late-evening traffic, side streets whipped by until the familiar sight of fire trucks caught Chad's eye. Ladder 13 and Engine 11 were stopped in front of an apartment complex. Was that where—

"Isn't that the building where Lieutenant Wright lives?" Liam said, voicing Chad's question.

He glanced at the street sign and swallowed hard. "Yeah. It is. And tonight is poker night."

Liam raised his brows.

"Jamie's there."

"Let's go in."

Liam parked Medic 11 behind Ladder 13. They jumped out and

Chad grabbed the medical kit in case their assistance was needed. As they entered the building, some of the firefighters were filing out, huge smirks on their faces. "What's going on?" Chad asked Martini, a guy he'd attended the academy with.

Martini laughed and shook his head. "You have to see it to believe it. Apartment 314."

Chad exchanged a look with Liam. "Should we? I mean, we weren't called or anything."

"Oh you should. You definitely should." Martini smiled. "Besides, I think the *vic* burned his arm a bit. He might need you."

Chad nodded and headed for the stairs while Liam transmitted their location to dispatch. Chad had an uneasy feeling in his gut that they were indeed on their way to Hollywood's apartment. Not that Chad had ever been invited over, despite the fact that Hollywood and Chad's brother Jamie had been best friends for years, or that Hollywood probably attended more Caldwell family functions than Chad did.

Upon reaching apartment 314, he knocked on the half-open door. "Paramedics. We were told someone had burn injuries."

The door was yanked open and Jamie grabbed Chad's arm. "Perfect timing. Fucking idiot won't let me treat him."

Hollywood had been hurt, and all these assholes still thought it was funny? "What makes you think he'll let *me* help him?"

Jamie grinned. "He won't have to let you. I just can't hold him down and do the bandage at the same time. Hollywood's a big fucker."

Chad chuckled. Hollywood couldn't be that bad off if he was refusing Jamie's help. "Lead the way."

As they entered the living room, their boots squishing in the soaked carpet, Chad took in the state of the apartment. "What the hell happened here?"

Jamie's lips thinned as though he were struggling not to laugh. "Chef Ramsey here was trying to make fried chicken."

"For poker night?"

"Yes," Hollywood barked from his position on the coffee table. "For poker night. Something wrong with that?"

"Nope. Just wondering what's wrong with chips and beer. Or nachos. Or wings." Chad bit back a grin. Hollywood's feathers were definitely ruffled, but then again, his home was a waterlogged, soot-filled mess.

Hollywood narrowed his eyes. "Is that what you'd serve?" he asked, leaning forward. The movement caused his forearm to brush against his jeans, and he winced.

Chad immediately crossed the room and knelt on the wet carpet in front of Hollywood to get a better look at the injury. He opened the med kit, placing it on the coffee table and grabbed a fresh pair of gloves.

Keeping the conversation going might make Hollywood more receptive to treatment. "My friends are more the wine and cheese type."

"So that's what I should serve?" Hollywood threw a questioning glance at Jamie, who crossed his arms and shook his head. Hollywood sighed. "These assholes only like shit that has enough cholesterol to see us all dead in ten years."

Chad lifted Hollywood's arm to examine it. There were several small patches of red, lightly blistered skin, indicating mild second-degree burns, and his arm hair, what little he had of it, had been fried off. Nothing that would send him to the hospital. Continuing to chat about party food, Chad cleansed the affected area, applied an antibiotic cream, and bandaged up the arm.

It was too bad though; his one chance to touch Hollywood, and he was doing it while wearing nitrile gloves. Still, the steeliness of all that muscle transmitted right through to his fingertips as he smoothed down the medical tape, and he didn't dare look Hollywood in the eye. He forced his hands off Hollywood. "You're good to go. You'll need to change that tomorrow."

"Thanks," Hollywood said, twisting his arm right and left as though testing the dressing for comfort. Seemingly satisfied, he stood. Unfortunately, he didn't wait for Chad to get out of the way, and since Chad was still on his knees at Hollywood's feet, the change in position put the man's generous package right in front of Chad's face. For a moment, he was torn between wanting to squeeze the lieutenant's tight ass or swallow his dick, but with his brother looking on, neither action was recommended. Besides, Hollywood was straight. Even hinting at his desires could earn Chad a busted lip.

Turning quickly, he busied himself with packing up the med kit. Never in his life had he chased after a straight man, or even a bi-curious one. They were nothing but trouble. When he was done collecting the equipment, he stood. Hollywood looked so fucking lost as he scanned the damage to his apartment.

"Where are you going to go?" Chad asked gently.

Hollywood's eyes widened as though he hadn't realized he couldn't remain in his home. "Why?"

Shit. Why had he asked that? It wasn't as though he cared.

Liar.

Sucking in a breath, Chad waved a hand around the scene of the fire. "Because your place needs to be dried, all the damaged materials removed and replaced. You don't want mold to set in here. That shit kills."

With a grimace, Hollywood closed his eyes. "Fuck. I don't have anywhere to go."

7

"What about your dad's?" Liam suggested.

"Hell no. I'll go to a hotel."

Chad met Jamie's gaze. He got why Jamie wasn't offering Hollywood his spare bedroom, but the pleading look in Jamie's eyes held a suggestion that Chad wasn't prepared to make.

"A hotel is expensive, and God knows how long it will be before you can live here again," Jamie said, his eyes on Chad even though he was addressing Hollywood.

Chad shook his head. Was his brother insane?

"Who else has a spare bedroom?" Jamie mused, his gaze narrowing.

"You owe me," Chad mouthed.

"I know," Jamie mouthed back.

This was going to be bad. So very bad. Chad would hold this over Jamie's head as long as they lived. "Uh, Hollywood?"

Hollywood opened his eyes.

Oh God. He was going to do this. He was really going to do this. Chad cleared his throat. "You can stay with me. You know, unless you think of somewhere else to go."

"No." Hollywood closed his eyes again.

Chad felt the word like a punch to the gut. The fucker had some nerve. "Afraid to catch my gay cooties?"

Hollywood's hands went to his hips. "I already told you I don't have a problem with your being gay."

"Oh, I remember now," Chad spat. "You have a problem with *me.*"

Hollywood's lip curled into a snarl. "That's right."

Chad threw his hands up. "Whatever. Thought I'd return the favor since I heard you helped me out with your dad. But if you'd rather sit here and die of pneumonia or mold poisoning than stay in my spare bedroom, then have at it."

He grabbed the medical bag off the coffee table, turning for the door. He didn't need this shit.

A large hand gripped his arm. "Wait."

Stopping, Chad took in a deep breath, then let out all the humiliation Hollywood's rejection had stirred up in his chest.

"I didn't mean it like that. My problem with you is that *you* hate me, and I don't know why."

Chad dropped his gaze to the floor, afraid the man would see the truth in his eyes. "I don't hate you." *Not even close.*

Jamie came up between them and wrapped an arm around each of their shoulders. "Maybe this will give you a chance to work out your differences. I hate that my best friend and my little brother don't get along."

"Maybe," Chad said, risking a glance past his brother to Hollywood.

8

They had a huge difference to overcome. Chad was gay. Hollywood was straight. And Chad wanted to tap the man's ass so badly it was making him crazy.

Could they actually live together for several weeks without Hollywood noticing Chad's attraction to him? Fuck. He'd be lucky if Hollywood didn't end up killing him.

CHAPTER 2

Chad's back ached and his feet dragged as he turned the key to unlock his condo. The eight-AM end to the shift hadn't come fast enough. Last night, Jamie had given Hollywood his key to Chad's place so Hollywood could come over as soon as he was done with the insurance adjuster. Had he actually taken up Chad's offer, or had he bailed?

Stepping into the quiet hallway, Chad immediately sensed the presence of another—of Hollywood. His heart started to race like it did when Medic 11 was sent out on a particularly involved call. What would he find when he got there? It was the same question that consumed him now.

He rounded the corner into the living room and tripped over a large duffle bag. With a muttered curse, he caught himself on the back of the couch. And froze.

Hollywood lay sprawled out before him, his long legs angled over one end of the couch while his head rested on the opposite arm. The couch was wide, but his shoulders were wider. Chad sucked in a harsh breath as he took in the man's muscular body, covered only by a pair of tight black boxer briefs. Good God. Hollywood was a vision. Chad wanted to lick every inch of his amazing body and nuzzle the light dusting of blond hair on the man's chest. He wanted to spend hours worshipping the twin pink nipples that had perked up under his gaze.

Oh shit! He shouldn't be here. Shouldn't be ogling his new roommate like he was a tall, cool drink and Chad a man dying of thirst. He really ought to go, but his feet stayed glued to the floor. Hollywood shifted in his sleep. One foot fell to the floor, displaying the man's very sizable bulge in all its morning glory.

Heart pounding, Chad dropped into a crouch and fled to his room. His face flamed like that time he'd gotten a chubby in the locker room in junior high. Not that he had anything to be embarrassed about in that department. But it had been embarrassing all the same. Just like now. He rubbed a hand over his hardening crotch. Embarrassingly arousing.

A cold shower. Yeah, a cold shower in December was exactly what he needed to get that image of Hollywood out of his head. Undressing as he went into his en suite bathroom, he turned on the water, determined to keep the man out of his thoughts and his hands away from his junk. A shower, some food, then rest. That was his plan for the day, and he intended to stick to it, new roommate or not.

Ten minutes later, he emerged from his bedroom, a little damp, but arousal squelched. On his way to the kitchen, which was separated from the living room/dining room combo by a long breakfast counter, Chad peeked over the side of the couch to see how his guest was faring. Hollywood was still sleeping, his long pale lashes casting tiny shadows on his cheeks. Chad could get a blanket and cover the man up. That would help them both. But... he rubbed the back of his neck and turned away. Better to let sleeping dogs lie.

In the open-concept kitchen, he quietly set about making chamomile tea to help him sleep and toast to quiet the growling of his stomach. Usually, he and Liam had time to grab a meal around four or five in the morning, but not last night. Following the incident at Hollywood's place, it had been go-go-go until sunup. The worst had been the shootout between two homeless men at City Hall Park. There'd been no deaths, but a lot of injuries. And while they'd been treating the victims, they'd come across several cases of hypothermia, frostbite, and festering sores. Name it, they'd seen it.

All he wanted to do now was sleep for the next eight hours. When the toast popped up, he slathered it with peanut butter, his stomach, like some symbiotic alien, screaming to be fed. A grunt behind him made him jump and drop the knife he'd been using. It clattered onto the granite countertop as Chad spun around, his fists up in the defensive stance he'd perfected in high school.

"Easy there, kid," Hollywood drawled from his position against the counter. Dressed only in those damn boxer briefs, he lazily drew a hand up to his bare chest and scratched. Chad watched, mesmerized, as Hollywood's fingers pulled through the golden hair.

His mouth watering, Chad turned to pick up his plate and mug of tea. He had to put some distance between them, but to do that, he had to get past the man first. He plastered a smile on his face. "Good morning."

Apparently, he'd done a shit job of appearing welcoming because Hollywood immediately lost the mischievous grin and the sparkle in his amazing green eyes. And that was a damn shame. "Help yourself to some breakfast," he said with a bit more sincerity.

Hollywood moved into the kitchen, freeing up the space between the fridge and the breakfast bar so Chad could squeeze by. Once on the other side of the breakfast bar, he drew in a deep breath and forced himself to relax. *You can do this.* He could talk to this living, breathing Adonis without giving any indication that the man did it for him. *Really* did it for him. But for fuck's sake, couldn't he have at least slipped on a pair of jeans?

"Got any coffee?" Hollywood asked, no hint of a smile in his voice. *Damn it.*

"Sure." Chad retrieved the rarely used Keurig from the pantry, a gift his ex-boyfriend Quincy had bought and left behind when they'd split up. Chad preferred his triple venti nonfat latte directly from the cute twink at the Starbucks on the corner of Pike and Third, where he and Liam often stopped for their mid-shift break.

After setting up the machine, Chad returned to sit on his stool and eat his now-cold toast and tea. *Suck it up, buttercup.* It wasn't Hollywood's fault that Chad was bent out of shape after having seen him almost naked. "How come you're up so early? Did I wake you?"

"Nah. This is late for me. I'm an early riser."

Based on the eyeful Chad had gotten when he'd arrived home, he could corroborate that fact. He swallowed a bit of toast with a healthy dose of tepid tea. "Why didn't you sleep in the guest room?"

Hollywood opened cupboards until he pulled out a frying pan. He placed it on the cooktop to heat while he mixed eggs and milk in a bowl. He shrugged before answering. "Wanted to give you a chance to change your mind before I settled in." His tone was flat, humorless. Clearly this wasn't a joke.

"Why would I change my mind?"

Hollywood speared him with a look, his lip curled in a smirk. "We're not exactly the best of friends."

Chad looked down at his plate. No, they weren't. The friction between them could light a fire. And not the good kind. "Maybe we could work on that while you're here. You know, for Jamie's sake."

Scooping his scrambled eggs onto a plate, Hollywood grabbed the four slices of toast he'd made and came to join Chad at the breakfast bar. He heaped some egg on a piece of toast and stuffed it in his mouth. Chad squirmed under the man's thoughtful gaze. Hollywood swallowed his mouthful and slowly nodded. "Maybe once you get to know me, I won't irritate you so much."

Almost spewing his tea, Chad kept his head down to hide his reaction. It wasn't irritation, so much as an ungodly amount of pent-up sexual frustration that kept him on edge whenever Hollywood was in the room. The man was testosterone personified.

Unfortunately, a consummate playboy, he was also the very definition of heterosexual. Hollywood wasn't now nor would he ever be attracted to Chad, and that's what bugged the shit out of him the most. Maybe living with the man would expose his flaws, and then Chad could move on. Maybe then he would stop using the big blond lieutenant as the standard by which he judged all other men.

When he looked up from his plate, Hollywood was staring at him, an uncomfortable, even vulnerable, expression on his face. Chad chuckled. "If anything, I'm pretty sure I'm the one who irritates you."

Hollywood's shoulders unhunched, and he nodded. "For some reason, you always blow my fuse."

෨ 🚃 ෬

His cheeks turning an alarming shade of red, Chad choked on his toast. Hollywood stood ready to perform the Heimlich on his new roommate. Jamie would have his balls if he managed to kill his little brother within twelve hours of moving in.

It was only when Chad met his gaze, mirth swirling in those Caldwell-blue depths, that realization of what he'd said struck. And it struck like a two by four. "Oh, fuck me!"

Chad's eyes widened even farther, and he roared with laughter. Well, it would have been a roar if Chad hadn't still been coughing.

Why the fuck couldn't he control his own mouth?

Hollywood scrubbed his fingers through his hair, as he went to get Chad a glass of water. When he returned, Chad had managed to catch his breath and was drying the tears from his dancing eyes.

"Don't get all Freudian on me, you little shit," Hollywood growled. "Give me a few days to figure out what to say around you."

Chad sat up, a frown marking his brow. "What the fuck are you talking about?"

Hollywood turned and paced in the triangle of open space between where Chad sat, the dining nook, and the living area. "This"—he slashed his arm between the two of them—"knowing what to say. If I'd said that to Jamie, he wouldn't have thought I meant I wanted to have sex with him."

Chad rose and tossed his napkin on the counter. Sparks were flying from his eyes. *Oh shit.*

"Contrary to popular belief, just because I'm gay doesn't mean I want to fuck every man I see." Chad stepped closer. "It certainly doesn't mean I want to fuck *you.*" He punctuated the word with a sharp poke to Hollywood's chest.

Knowing when he was just digging himself deeper, Hollywood held his hands up in surrender. "You're right. I'm sorry. It's just that—" He broke off. Nothing he could say would make this better.

"Just that what?"

Hollywood closed his eyes, praying for divine intervention. He didn't want Chad to kick him out. He really didn't want to have to turn to his dad for a place to stay.

"Tell me," Chad insisted.

"It's just that we're both good-looking." Chad's brows flew up at that. "And… well, when I see a good-looking woman, I *do* want to fuck her."

Chad's lips twisted. "That's 'cause you're a horndog, man. Some of us have more class than that. I, for one, am a man of discerning taste."

"Oh yeah?" Hollywood sat down again and shoveled his cooling eggs into his mouth. Now that Chad had calmed down, maybe they could talk a bit. He didn't feel like dealing with his apartment repairs just yet. "What's your type?"

Chad turned away, but not before Hollywood caught the blush staining his cheeks. Hollywood decided to help the man along. "You're what? Six foot? Six-one? I bet you get hit on all the time by those girly guys. What do you call them? Twinks?"

"I've… I've had some twinks." Chad picked up his plate and rinsed it before placing it in the dishwasher. Hmm… Hollywood would have to remember not to leave his own in the sink.

"Was your last boyfriend a twink?" he asked.

Chad looked up sharply. "Why do you care?"

Why *did* he care what type of man Chad liked? Quickly he scrambled for a response that might make sense. "If I know, I can help you find someone."

"I don't need a fucking wingman!"

Hollywood had to laugh at the outrage on his new roommate's face. "I'm sure you don't. I'm only trying to get to know you so we don't kill each other before my place is ready."

Chad blew out a breath, tossed the dishrag into the sink, and leaned back against the counter. "Okay, fine. Let's see. When it comes to relationship-material, I prefer a man who is tall, dark, and handsome."

Hollywood sneered. "Very funny."

"What?" Chad asked way too innocently.

Hollywood narrowed his eyes. "You described yourself."

"Oh? Did I?" Chad grinned and wiggled his fingers goodbye as he sauntered off to his room, leaving Hollywood wondering what the fuck had just happened.

CHAPTER 3

Not bad for someone who's already a quarter of a century old.

Chad inspected himself in the bedroom mirror. His new skinny black jeans and gray jersey shirt showed off his build, and the royal blue of his Chuck Taylors added a much-needed splash of color. They weren't exactly club clothes. He kept those for when he was performing.

His nails were clipped, buffed, and painted blue to match the Chucks. His twin sister Tori had been right about the color. Oops. He'd forgotten the guyliner. He stole a quick glance at his Swatch. Fuck. Austin would be here any minute, and the less time Austin spent alone with Hollywood, the better. Dashing into the bathroom, Chad quickly applied a narrow line of black kohl under his lower lashes and added a last-minute swipe of lip gloss. When he was done, he grabbed his leather jacket off the desk chair and left his room. He could hear Hollywood in the living room, watching some show about flipping homes.

Chad's new roommate had moved into the spare bedroom, and the fridge and pantry now held some unfamiliar food items. The few times they'd both been home, they'd talked, but Chad had been careful to keep the conversation very straight, with no more discussions like the one they'd had the morning Hollywood had moved in. Tonight was actually the first evening they were both home.

When he entered the living room, Hollywood looked up and stilled. Only his eyes moved as they lasered up and down Chad's body. Chad cocked a hip and said in his campiest voice, "Like what you see, sugar?"

A muscle jumped in Hollywood's cheek and he pointed to Chad's hand, the one he held in front, limp-wristed. Shoving it in his pocket, Chad scowled. "What?"

"That blue shit."

Chad wanted to clock the man. He didn't give a fuck if Jamie got pissed about it later. He pulled himself to his full height and puffed out his chest. "Nail polish." He'd put up with enough homophobic bullshit in his life; he wasn't going to take it in his own home. He angled his head toward the entrance. "You have a problem with it, the door's right there."

Hollywood stood up, towering over Chad as his long legs ate the distance between them. It was amazing how much difference four inches and twenty pounds could make. Next to Hollywood, he felt small, something he hadn't experienced since puberty. Something he hated.

Do you really, Chad?

Shut up. Yes, really. Chad gasped as Hollywood's warm breath feathered his cheeks, his gaze focusing on Chad's eyes.

"Haven't you ever seen eyeliner before?" Chad shoved at the bigger man's chest. It was like pushing against a cement wall, and he had to fight the urge to curl his fingers around the man's incredible pecs and parkour his way up that hard body.

Hollywood's gaze shot down to Chad's mouth. He'd forgotten about the sparkly lip gloss Tori had given him for his birthday. "I've seen makeup before, just not on a man," Hollywood said, his voice low.

Was that a hint of curiosity or repulsion Chad heard? Fuck. Hollywood was driving him nuts. He forced a sultry smile. "Be thankful I'm not wearing a dress."

Hollywood's head snapped up, his brows low. "You do that?"

Chad spun and walked around the breakfast bar, anything to get away from the infuriating blond god who'd taken over his condo. Unfortunately, the man followed him. "Well?"

Chad sighed. "Dresses aren't my thing. Not that there's anything wrong with a man wearing one."

"There isn't?"

"No." Chad glared. "There isn't."

"Okay." But Hollywood didn't sound certain about that. He turned to stare out the windows, his back to Chad.

"Whatever. You're free to believe what you want." But as Hollywood continued to silently pace in front of the floor-to-ceiling windows in the dining area, the pressure in Chad's chest grew. God, it was bad enough when he'd thought Hollywood hated him on principle. What if he was actually disgusted by him? "What do you believe?" He needed to know.

Hollywood shrugged. "Dresses look better on women."

"Oh, honey. If you think that, then you haven't been to the right drag shows."

Stopping mid-pace, Hollywood turned away from what was a great view of Elliott Bay during the daytime. At night though, all they could see were lights from the surrounding buildings. His lips were pursed, like he'd swallowed a slice of lemon. "I've never been to one."

Chad's eyes bugged. "Never? Not even as a gag?"

Hollywood shook his head, and once again his eyes were riveted on Chad. Why did he keep staring? Did the makeup and nail polish disturb him that much? "What's your experience with gay men?"

"You and... uh... Dickens."

"The guy in Platoon B?"

"Yeah. Real name's Charlie."

"He's gay?"

"Mm-hmm."

"How do you know?" Chad had met him a few times when they'd been called to the same scene, and he'd never suspected a thing. His gaydar must be out of whack.

Hollywood's cheeks turned a delightful shade of red. His face screwed into an expression of extreme discomfort, he walked back into the living room and dropped onto the couch.

"Well?" Chad insisted.

"My dad. Okay? He makes sure all the lieutenants know if someone is gay."

Chad's gut tightened. "Why?" All the officers sitting together discussing who was gay and who wasn't.... It was fucking creepy.

Hollywood stared into the dark without answering. Chad waited him out. Whatever this was, he needed to know. Hell, they all needed to know. Finally Hollywood spoke. "In case any of us don't want to work with them."

What the *fuck?* Jamie had never even hinted at these secret powwows. Chad crossed over into the living room. "That's discrimination."

Hollywood's gaze shifted to the blank TV screen. He was clearly avoiding looking at Chad.

Heat blasted over Chad's face and chest. "What happens when no one wants to work with someone?"

"They get transferred."

"Is that what happened with me?" Chad took a deep breath and perched on the arm of the recliner.

Hollywood cleared his throat. "Most of the lieutenants were fine working with you, but when Deputy Chief Conroy found out what was going on, he reamed my dad a new one and demanded you be moved to his battalion right away."

Chad stared numbly in front of him. "I had no idea." He couldn't believe that this type of thing was going on, but really, why was he so surprised? Tolerance toward the LGBTQ community had grown, which was great. On the other hand, that "progress" could make discrimination insidious, popping up when you least expected it.

"My dad's a dick." Hollywood stood up and crossed his arms.

Chad snorted. "I bet he's thrilled you're living here. After all, my gayness could rub off on you."

Hollywood laughed and playfully shoved Chad's shoulder, only, Jesus, the man had no concept of his own strength. Chad went toppling over the arm of the recliner and landed in a heap on the carpet.

"Oh fuck!" Hollywood darted over and lifted him off the floor with a hand under each arm. Seemingly without effort, he supported Chad and sat him on the couch. "You okay?"

Everything had happened so quickly, Chad was a little disoriented. "Yeah, I'm fine." He rubbed his shoulder. "Just don't do that again."

Hollywood stuffed his hands in his pockets. Chad was still getting his bearings when the doorbell finally rang. "I'll get that," Hollywood said, moving toward the entrance.

From his spot on the couch, Chad couldn't see the entrance foyer, but he could make out Austin's sexy-as-fuck drawl. Austin and Chad's friendship dated back to their senior year of high school when Austin had moved to Seattle from Texas. They'd tried having sex when they'd been going through a mutual dry spell, but quickly decided they were better suited as friends than as boyfriends.

Hollywood came back first, a new expression on his handsome face. Chad was getting whiplash trying to keep up with him. "Your... uh... friend?" Hollywood's eyes searched the room as though looking for a better word. When he didn't find one, he settled on, "Yeah."

The smile on Austin's face was as big as the Texas sky as he eyed Hollywood's ass. "Hey, Austin," Chad said, more sharply than he'd intended.

Austin's smile increased a few more watts. "Hey, Chad. Gonna introduce us?"

Chad sighed and rolled his eyes. "Austin, this is Hollywood, Lieutenant Wright, my brother Jamie's best friend."

Hearing Jamie's name, Austin's smile slipped. He'd always been more than a little in awe of Chad's oldest brother.

While Hollywood and Austin shook hands and sized each other up, Chad put on his jacket and collected his keys. Both men were gorgeous and of similar sizes—Austin was a couple inches shorter than Hollywood, but his shoulders were just as wide. Where Hollywood was blond, Austin was dark, his shoulder-length hair coming down in natural waves Chad would kill for. Because of his job, Chad had to keep his hair short or put it up in a bun. Yeah... he didn't need to give the guys any more ammunition.

Chad gave a small sigh. Earlier, he'd let Hollywood believe he was into twinks, when in reality, these two men were exactly his type. They were also the story of his life—one man he didn't want, and the other he couldn't have.

ଚ୦ 🎬 ଓ

"So, where're you guys off to?" Hollywood asked Austin. The man was a walking, talking stereotype. It wasn't Hollywood's fault if he'd had to squeeze the cowboy's hand extra hard.

Austin glanced at Chad as he stretched out his fingers. Hollywood hoped like hell they were numb. "Boyzville. Right, Chad?"

"Yep." Chad zipped up his jacket.

Hollywood's gut clenched. Boyzville. It sounded like a gay meat market. Were Chad and Austin together? They were obviously close, but they hadn't kissed or even touched since Austin's arrival. Was that for his benefit? If they were together and they were going to Boyzville, it had to be to pick up a third. Bile rose in his throat. That fucker Austin had better keep Chad safe. "You got money for a cab?" he asked, reaching for his wallet.

Chad laughed, his expression disbelieving. "Yes, *Dad*."

"You've got my number. Call if you need anything."

Eyeing him curiously, Chad waved goodbye and headed for the door.

Hollywood's thoughts were all jumbled. What the hell was wrong with him? And why was he suddenly acting like Jamie and being all overprotective? Chad was Jamie's little brother, not his.

Christ, he was really wound up. And for no fucking reason.

Maybe it was that discussion about his dickhead father. Chad had seemed really thrown by those secret meetings.

Those meetings made *him* sick, and he wasn't in Chad's shoes.

Fuck. He needed to get his mind off this shit. He glanced at the TV.

No. No more TV. What he needed was to get laid. That would be just the thing. Since moving in, he'd been dry, and that shit was going to end. Going without sex for a week fucked with a man's brain. "Hey, Chad," he called out.

"Yeah?" Chad's voice echoed from the entryway.

"We never discussed guest privileges."

Chad came back into view, poking his head around the corner into the living room. "What did you have in mind?"

"Nothing much. One or two people."

"As long as you don't trash the place, I'm fine with you having friends over."

Friends? Not likely. Tonight's lay would be lucky if he knew her name.

ଚ୦ 🎬 ଓ

"So," Austin said as they approached Boyzville. "Why's your brother's

19

gorgeous friend stayin' at your place? And is there any chance at all he's gay?" He batted his lashes at Chad and grinned. "I'd love a piece of that ass."

Chad snorted. "He's as straight as they come. He accidentally set his kitchen on fire trying to impress his poker-night buddies and needed a place to stay until his apartment is livable again."

"Why stay with you though? Why not stay with family or your brother?"

"If assholes had a king, his dad would be it. As for staying with Jamie and Erica, well, she's pregnant and it isn't going too well." Not to mention that Hollywood's constant presence might put a damper on their experiment with a 24/7 BDSM service relationship. He didn't know how vanilla Hollywood was, but Chad could almost smell the bean on him.

"You're absolutely sure he's straight?"

"Don't you dare get any ideas!" Chad hated the practice some gay men had of going after straight guys until they broke. You were either gay or you weren't, even if some guys were so far back in the closet, they couldn't see the door to get out.

"I'm not the one you should be worried about."

Chad frowned. "What are talking about?"

"You." Austin blew out a breath. "I'm just sayin' that if I lived with a man who looked like him and who looked at me like—" His jaws snapped shut.

Alarmed, Chad shook his elbow. "Looked at me how?"

"Nothing, darlin'."

"Come on, man. You can't start something like that and not finish it."

Austin put his hands on his hips and tipped his face up to the cloudy night sky. "He was lookin' at you like a hawk eyein' a mouse."

Laughter bubbled up in Chad's chest, erupting into the quiet street. "So he looks at me like he wants to kill me?" They irritated each other, but that was going too far. They were firefighters, for Christ's sake. They lived to help others, not hurt them.

"You got me wrong, my friend. The good lieutenant wants to eat you right up." He waggled his eyebrows suggestively. "Only he doesn't know it yet."

"Bullshit." This just got better and better. "Now I've got my very own gay-for-me macho firefighter. When did you start writing fairy tales?"

Austin bumped his shoulder. "Fuck off, Caldwell. I know that look when I see it."

"Such a fucking romantic. Hollywood loves pussy as much as I love cock. You should see him drooling whenever a Victoria's Secret commercial comes on."

"So he's bisexual."

20

Could it be possible? Nah. Austin was getting to him, that was all. Hollywood had never looked at him in any way suggesting that he liked what he was seeing.

You sure about that, Chad?

Yes, I'm sure. Jesus. He slung his arm around Austin's shoulders. "Forget him. Tonight we're on a mission."

"To findin' the perfect man." Austin raised his hand for a high five.

Chad shook his head. He was pretty sure the perfect man was sitting in his condo watching football. "How about we settle for finding Mr. Right Now?" They clapped hands and grinned at each other.

As soon as they entered Boyzville, music, sweat, and the smell of sex assaulted Chad's senses. They dropped their jackets off at the coat check, then sidled up to the bar. A slim young guy covered only in the tiniest gold briefs slid across the bar top, stopping directly in front of Chad.

"Tequila shot, sexy?" the cute blond asked with a wink.

Chad chuckled at the younger man's theatrics. "Why not. What's your name?"

"Harry."

Eying the twink's hairless body, Chad arched a brow.

"Yeah, yeah. The irony." Harry grinned.

Holding up a shot glass, Harry pointed to his stomach. Chad bent over him and plunged his tongue into Harry's belly button, lapping up the salt. When he lifted his head, the guy's gaze had clouded over. Chad pressed his lips together as he reached for the tequila. He downed it quickly, then went for the slice of lime between Harry's lips. He bit down on it, sucking in the tart fluid that cut off the tequila's sting.

While he was there, he let his tongue play over the blond's lips. The guy grabbed Chad's head and lifted him off long enough to spit out the wedge of lime before pulling him back down. Harry was an expert kisser. His tongue slid into Chad's mouth, exploring his teeth, his palate, his gums, before twining around Chad's tongue and stroking it rhythmically.

Chad let him have his fun before taking over. In a swift move, he splayed his fingers behind the guy's head and neck to bring him into a sitting position. Harry wrapped his legs around Chad's waist, pressing his hard-on into Chad's stomach while his hands roamed under Chad's shirt. Christ, how long had it been since he'd last held a warm body in his arms?

Too fucking long.

Blunt nails raked up and down his spine, sending goose bumps across his skin. Breathing hard, Chad pulled back and stared into the brown eyes that seemed so out of place. Shoving that thought aside, he pushed a blond curl out of Harry's eyes. "If we don't stop right now, I'm going to fuck you on this bar."

Harry arched his back and let his head fall. "Not that I'd mind."

Chad laughed uncomfortably. Was this what he wanted? Austin elbowed him in the ribs. "It's those damn blue eyes, Caldwell. Gets 'em every time."

When Harry finally noticed Austin, his eyes widened and darted between the two of them. "Are you two...?"

"Hell no," Austin said, with more conviction than Chad felt the question deserved. He scowled at his friend.

Austin smirked. "Y'all go on now. Have fun." He picked up his beer and pointed toward the pool tables at the back. "Somethin' over yonder's caught my eye."

Looking over his shoulder, Chad spotted a curly-haired redhead and grinned. Occasionally, Austin liked to indulge in his favorite snack—what he called "gingersnaps."

Harry writhed against Chad, riding his abs. His attention back on the slim blond, Chad grabbed the guy by the wrist. "I'm taking you to the backroom. Any objections?"

Harry shook his head and gripped Chad around the neck. He couldn't weigh more than a hundred and forty pounds, if that. Chad barely felt the burden in his arms as the guy sucked on his neck.

"No hickeys."

An impish grin brightened Harry's face. "Too late."

"Fuck." Hollywood was sure to notice it. Well, tough shit. He wasn't going to live his life according to what Hollywood liked or didn't like. He didn't need anyone's approval.

"I really like your makeup. The guyliner makes your eyes pop."

"I like yours too." Chad nipped the guy's bottom lip.

Harry blushed. "It looks better on you."

"Nah."

"It does," Harry said. "Usually butch guys like you wouldn't be caught dead with makeup or nail polish. I think it makes you even hotter."

Ah, this guy was so good for Chad's ego, which had been left a little battered by his last breakup. Chad had made the mistake of telling Quincy about some incidents he'd experienced at work, dating back to when he'd first joined the fire service: whispers behind his back, slurs spelled into the fog on his car windows, dick pics sent to his phone or posted on his Facebook timeline. The fake Grindr account that had made him sound like a slut who'd take it from anyone. Quincy was the only one he'd ever told.

Then, on the day Chad had been beaten up, he'd come home from a meeting with his brothers, Drew and William, and Hollywood to an empty condo. Quincy had packed up his belongings and taken off. Other than the Keurig, the only thing he'd left behind was a note that read, "I'm

22

not strong enough for this."

The cops had caught the guys that time. But now that the phone calls had started up again, Chad was sticking to one-night stands. Quincy had been right about one thing—Chad had to be sure he didn't make anyone else a target.

Arriving in the backroom, Chad scanned the darkness, looking for an empty spot along the wall. Grunts and groans echoed through him like the beats of a bass drum. Christ, he needed this. Needed the release. Maybe afterward, he'd be able to deal with Hollywood without letting him get under his skin.

"What do you want to do?" he asked Harry.

"Told you at the bar. I wanna fuck."

"I only top."

"Figured as much." Harry pulled off his gold briefs and turned to face the wall.

Chad got out the condom and the packet of lube he'd stuck in his pocket before leaving home. He unzipped his pants and suited up, then applied the lube to Harry's asshole. If he bent his knees and Harry turned his head just right, Chad could imagine it was a different blond in his arms.

Harry rolled his hips, and Chad's semi rubbed up and down his crease. Chad squinted at the guy's profile, picturing him several inches taller and broader, with green eyes. His cock hardened. Okay, that was better. Removing his fingers from the guy's well-prepared ass, he slipped inside. "That's it, breathe out," he crooned. "This is gonna feel so good. You're gonna want to be gay-for-me for always."

"Oh yeah. Like that."

"No talking." The guy's voice was all wrong. Instead, Chad imagined a low growl, made even deeper and more gravelly by lust. Leaning forward, he pressed his face into the soft blond hair, inhaling the scent of Hollywood's shampoo. Reaching around, he gripped the firm erection that he instinctively knew didn't match the one he'd seen the other morning. God, he was being an ass, using Harry for sex. The cute little blond was a poor substitute for the man he really wanted.

Hollywood.

Christ, he might be a user, but he wasn't a selfish one. He'd make this good for the guy if it killed him. Ignoring the reality that kept intruding on his fantasy, he jerked his fist up and down in time with his hips, pegging the guy's prostate with every thrust.

Closing his eyes, he plunged back into the fantasy. Any thought of doing this with Hollywood would make him come fast. It was the only way he could keep going, because right now, he felt lower than he'd ever felt before.

"You love my cock in your ass, Hollywood?" he asked, pumping his hips ferociously.

He got a loud moan in return.

Chad gripped the slim hips beneath him, plowing into the tight ass as though it were his last chance to fuck the man. And it was, because this was imaginary Hollywood's last guest appearance in Chad's fantasies. Soon, jets of warm cum coated his fingers.

Letting go of his restraint, Chad whispered Hollywood's name into the guy's neck as he came. When he pulled out, the blond gasped. "You okay?" Chad asked.

"Yeah. I've just never been fucked so hard. You must really have it bad for this guy. Hollywood."

Chad closed his eyes. He'd treated Harry like a nobody, like someone not even deserving of his own name. "I'm sorry."

"You wouldn't be the first guy to come in here and pretend he's with someone else," Harry said.

Chad wasn't stupid. He could hear past the false bravado to the hurt in the guy's softly spoken words. He ripped off the condom and tossed it into one of the many trash bins scattered around the room. Once they were both clothed, he put his arm around Harry's shoulders and led him back to the bar. "Come on, let me buy you a drink."

If he was going to feel like shit about the furtive fuck he'd just had, he'd make damn sure Harry didn't.

CHAPTER 4

With his arm around the tall, busty brunette, Hollywood stole kisses as they stumbled down the dimly lit hallway to Chad's condo. When he nipped her shoulder, she squealed and tried to evade his teeth, causing the two of them to land against Chad's door with a thud.

"Ooi, the woman said on a high pitched giggle,

He smiled down at her and squinted. Her features were lost in a haze of vodka shots. "You okay, hon?"

"Yeah. You're a big guy though."

Smirking, he rubbed his hips against her stomach. "All over, hon. *All* over." He fished his keys out of his front pocket and, a few fumbles later, managed to shove open the door. "Want a drink?" he asked, tossing their coats in the general direction of the closet.

She hiccupped out what sounded like a positive response and weaved into the living room, flopping down on the couch and closing her eyes. Hopefully she wasn't too drunk. He didn't fuck women who were too far gone to know what they were doing.

In the kitchen, he opened the freezer, hoping Chad had some alcohol stashed in there, and smiled when he saw the bottle of Grey Goose. Pulling two glasses from the cabinet, he filled one with vodka, then topped it off with orange juice. In her glass, he put only juice. She'd never know the difference.

Soft music filtered in, the sweet tones sensual and erotic. Whatever her name, the girl could pick great tunes. He handed her the orange juice and sat beside her, sipping his vodka. Her red bandage dress had crept up her thighs, giving him more than a glimpse of taut, creamy skin. He loved women's legs, whether long or short, slim or muscular. It was the shape and texture that drew him, made him want to follow them to plunder the treasure at their apex.

The dress also highlighted the woman's ample tits. They were large and firm like grapefruits. He hoped they were real and couldn't wait to find out. After downing half his drink, he set the glass on the end table and patted his lap. "Hop on, hon."

Giggling, she tugged her dress higher, offering him a peek of the black lace covering her crotch. He swallowed hard in anticipation. Once she'd straddled him, she cupped his cheeks. "What's your name, big guy?"

Hollywood closed his eyes and sighed. What was he doing? What was *she* doing? She had come home with him, was willing to fuck him, and she didn't even know his name. Was this what he wanted out of life? A series of meaningless one-night stands? Opening his eyes, he gave her a slight smile. "Hollywood."

She swatted his arm. "No, silly. Your real name."

"No one except my father uses my real name."

"Well, I can see why the nickname stuck." She smoothed her hands over his hair. "You're gorgeous."

It wasn't anything he hadn't heard thousands of times before, and usually from women who didn't care to know more about him than that. Christ, he sounded like a teenage girl. "What's your name, hon?" Not that he cared; he just wanted to change the subject.

"Sandy."

Barely hearing her response, he drew her into a kiss, waiting for her to sigh before pressing his tongue inside her mouth. He wasn't big on kissing, but he knew women enjoyed it. He'd give her that before they moved on to the fun part of the evening's program.

His hands went to her breasts, shaping and molding them through the tight, slippery material of her dress. Since it was a strapless number, he rolled the bust line down to her waist. His playground was now free of any obstructions. He toyed with the dusky nipples, pinching and tweaking. She moaned, and the arch of her back pushed her tits more firmly into his hands. They were one-hundred percent real.

Hallelujah! His mood soared, as did his desire.

"Undo my pants," he told her, holding her away with his hands splayed across her chest.

Breathless and dazed, she reached between their bodies and undid the snap and zipper. He raised his hips so she could push his pants and boxers to the tops of his thighs. His cock sprang free to stand up straight between them. He sat back against the couch.

"What do you want me to do?" she asked. With her eyes glued to his cock and her tongue poking out to lick her pouty lips, he had a pretty good idea what she wanted to do.

"Suck me."

Nodding, she slid off his bent legs and dropped to the floor between them. She rose on her knees and captured his cock between her kiss-swollen lips. Like the rest of him, his dick was big, and try as she might, the poor girl couldn't take him in all the way. But she more than made up for it in suction and nibbling.

"Oh God."

The sound of Chad's voice surrounded him. He glanced up quickly, but didn't see anyone. It must have been his imagination. Or the fact that he was in Chad's home. Maybe he should feel guilty about having sex on the man's couch. Nah. He thrust up, managing to get her to swallow him a little more.

But it was no use. The mood was broken.

With his hands under her arms, he brought her back onto his lap and wrapped her small hands around his cock. Even without words, she got the message loud and clear. Gripping him, she moved her hands up and down his shaft, the friction eased by her spit. He leaned his head back against the couch and focused on her dark hair, on her blue eyes... Pleasure coiled in the base of his spine. "Yeah, hon. Just like that. Don't stop."

Distantly, he heard a door closing, but his blood was pounding too hard for him to do more than register it.

Then, "Don't let me interrupt."

Hollywood looked up into the much prettier blue eyes of another brunet. "Fuck."

80 🎬 timeline

Hollywood is fucking a woman on my couch.

The thought banged around in Chad's head like a bullet ricocheting off the walls of a metal box. He tried to catch it, to annihilate it, but to no avail. Not with the evidence staring him in the face. And what evidence it was.

Jesus. Hollywood sat on the couch with his jeans at his knees and his long, thick, mouth-watering cock standing tall and proud. The woman, a half-naked brunette who looked a little bit the worse for wear, winked at Chad. "Join us, handsome?"

"Yeah. Uh... no. I don't think so."

"Yeah, Chad. Come join us. I'm sure Candy doesn't mind. Do you, hon?"

"It's Sandy."

"Right." Hollywood grinned and she simpered. "Sandy."

Hollywood didn't even know the woman's name. Chad closed his eyes and pinched the bridge of his nose, trying to stave off an impending headache.

A moan from Hollywood had his eyelids shooting open, the sound going straight to his balls. The woman had restarted the up-and-down motion on Hollywood's gorgeous red cock. Chad could tell her grip wasn't quite tight enough to get his roommate there. He was about to tell her when Hollywood's big hand covered her own, guiding her movement and pressure.

Chad's heart rate spiked at the erotic sight before him. If Sandy weren't in the picture, it would have been perfect. But she was. Goddamn it.

As though sensing his thoughts, Sandy looked at him over her shoulder. "Grab a seat and enjoy the show."

Chad rolled his eyes. "Sorry, honey. You don't have what I need."

"He does though, right?" she said, winking again.

Fuck yeah. Hollywood had everything Chad needed in all the right proportions.

Hollywood's hands cupped Sandy's large breasts. "She's got boobs. Even gay guys like boobs, don't they?" He pressed her nipples together before taking them into his mouth. His eyes closed and his face melted into ecstasy.

Shit. He should leave. It wasn't right for him to be here, to see this. Not with the way he was starting to feel about Hollywood. But it was as though his feet had been bolted to the floor.

He couldn't fucking leave.

His eyes darted between Hollywood's face as he worked the woman's nipples and his cock as the woman's hands slid up and down. The urge to get on his knees, to shove her out of the way and take that big cock into his mouth, to savor the pre-cum leaking from the slit, was a physical ache deep in Chad's belly. He'd never wanted anyone this fiercely.

Hollywood opened his eyes, green lust-filled orbs that locked on Chad. He groaned and thrust into the woman's fist. When bliss came down over Hollywood's expression, his eyes dilating, his lips parting, Chad thought he was going to die. Hollywood groaned long and low, and came all over the woman's hands. The whole time, his eyes never left Chad's face.

Holy shit! Chad gasped and took in a deep breath to fill his air-starved lungs. Shock, bewilderment, a deep sense of hopelessness threatened to suck him down into a dark hole. But as he watched Hollywood's self-satisfied grin, anger filled his chest. Had Hollywood known what he was doing to Chad? Did he have any idea that Chad had feelings for him? Feelings that weren't so platonic? Was this some big watch-the-fag-squirm joke? Whatever the reason, it had been a shitty thing to do. Especially to someone who'd opened his home to him.

He pushed away from the wall he'd been leaning on. There was only so much he could take.

"Chad!" Hollywood called out.

"Fuck you, man. Just fuck you."

Sandy's giggles followed Chad to his room. He slammed the door even though it made him seem like a five-year-old, and dropped onto his bed. God, why did he let this fucker bother him so much? He'd seen other people have sex, whether straight or gay. For fuck's sake, hadn't he just banged a guy in the very public backroom at Boyzville? In comparison, what Hollywood had done had been far more honest. So he didn't care about Sandy. So what? Chad certainly hadn't cared about Harry when they'd walked into that backroom and sucked face. The only reason he'd fucked the guy in the first place was because of his resemblance to—

No. he wasn't going there.

A few minutes later, there was a quiet knock on his door. "Chad?"

Maybe if he ignored the man, he'd go away. Chad couldn't take another go-round tonight.

"She's gone," Hollywood said, quietly.

Chad groaned and got up. He opened the door, then went to sit on the edge of his bed. "I'm tired, Hollywood. Can't this wait until morning?"

Hollywood stepped one foot over the threshold, then froze. Despite his dark mood, or maybe because of it, Chad laughed. "Don't worry. I won't assume you want to fuck me because you're in my room."

The guy's face became a curious mix of pale and pink. Did the thought gross him out that badly? Chad sighed and dropped his head. "Say whatever you came to say."

"Look, I knew you were gay, but I didn't think you were one of those guys who hates women."

At that, Chad's head snapped up, and he glared at his roommate. "I don't hate women."

"But their bodies disgust you."

"I wouldn't say that. They just don't turn me on."

"Why did you get so angry back there then? Most guys like to watch."

"Would you want to watch me having sex with another guy?" he shot back.

"I wasn't having sex."

"You know what I mean."

Hollywood rubbed the back of his neck and winced. "Are you going to tell Jamie about this?"

Chad frowned. "What does Jamie have to do with anything?"

"He wants us to get along, and with this"—he waved in the general direction of the living room—"all I did was piss you off even more."

Chad shook his head. "I'm not pissed off." *I'm hurt. Disappointed...* The list went on and on. He really had to close the chapter on this

29

infatuation he had with Hollywood. The man was straight. But then...
why had he been looking at Chad that way when he'd come? Chad
pressed his palms to his eyes and let out a long breath. He had to let this
go. Had to stop inventing reasons to hang on. Had to stop imagining
what could never be.

It had already gone on too long.

"Well, whatever. I won't bring women here anymore." Hollywood
turned to leave.

Shit. Hollywood had every right to bring women home. The guy was
young and hot-blooded. He had a stressful job, and apparently booze and
broads were his way to de-stress. So be it.

"You can bring women here, just take them to your room for the
heavy stuff."

So I won't have to see you come apart for someone else.

CHAPTER 5

Thank God he had two days off in a row. After the run-in with Chad last night, Hollywood's pleasant buzz had turned into a wicked hangover. He still felt like shit, and not simply because of the alcohol or the brightness of the rare December sun smacking him like a thunderbolt between the eyes.

How could he have done that to Chad?

When Candy—or was it Sandy?—had suggested that Chad join them, it had seemed like a great idea. Now though, in the glaring light of day, he had to ask himself why. This kind of heavy duty introspection required coffee. Lots of coffee. And food.

He sat up in bed, listening for any sign of activity in the condo. Nothing but quiet stillness greeted him. Chad had already left. He glanced at the alarm clock by the bed. Seven thirty. Where the hell had the guy gone so early on his day off? He hoped he hadn't driven him out of his own home.

Feeling like even more of a heel, Hollywood flung the blankets off and headed to the kitchen, scratching his balls through the thin material of his boxers. A shower. Breakfast, then a shower, that's what he needed. He yawned then rubbed a hand over his chest. An image flashed in his mind of long, strong fingers not his own, curling in the short hairs, tugging sharply in a mix of pleasure and pain.

He stumbled and braced himself against the wall. That hadn't been a woman's hand. Blunt square fingernails, calloused pads...

His chest rose and fell, pumping like a bellows, as blood roared in his ears. He closed his eyes and forced himself to slow his breathing, to calm the fuck down. What was wrong with him?

Coffee.

31

Coffee would make it all better. It was early and he'd barely slept. His mind was fuzzy. That was all. Pushing away from the wall, he entered the kitchen and shoved a pod into Chad's fancy single-serving coffee machine. While it brewed, he got out the fixings for a few eggs, which he quickly scrambled.

As he was about to spoon them onto a plate, the sound of the front door opening froze him in place. Chad had seemed so upset and... disappointed when Hollywood had tried to apologize. Had he totally fucked up any chance for a friendship?

There was a loud clang, then Chad appeared in the living room. His face and arms gleamed with a thin sheen of sweat. He jogged up and down its length, shaking out his arms and singing to the music playing in his earbuds. "Uptown Funk." Heat pooled in Hollywood's abdomen at the sound of Chad's raspy voice, at the sight of Chad's muscled thighs outlined by the tight black running pants.

Shit. Why the hell was he suddenly noticing the guy's muscles? He had more than enough of his own.

Slowly, he lowered the pan onto the stovetop and hoped Chad wouldn't see him. He wanted—no, he needed—to sneak out, get back to his room, get away from Chad. But his feet weren't moving. It was as though he were paralyzed. Mesmerized.

Chad stripped off his T-shirt and dried his face with it before tossing it onto the coffee table. Facing the patio door, he rolled his shoulders and stretched, his skin golden in the early morning sun. The muscles rippled in his well-defined back. Hollywood's gaze tracked every flex, every contraction. He took in the Celtic knots twining around one bicep and the large-pattern tribal design on the other.

A bead of sweat trickled down the side of Hollywood's face, distracting him. He quickly wiped it away and returned his focus to the man in the living room.

Chad turned, and Hollywood sucked in a breath. His chest and abs were works of art—perfectly proportioned pecs shifted with Chad's stretches. He counted the ridges on Chad's stomach. Six. And that was *above* the waistband of his low-riding pants. Pants that exposed the thick-lined tattoo swirling just below his belly button. Oh God. Although the tattoos on his arms were high enough to be covered by a T-shirt, he'd seen them before at Caldwell family parties when Chad had worn a tank top. But this was the first time he'd seen the one low on Chad's belly. His mouth watered.

What was happening to him?

His gaze followed the deep V framing Chad's abs and the enticing tattoo, moving along the thin line of dark hair that disappeared into those very tight, very formfitting running pants.

Fuck. He couldn't look away from the bulge, lovingly cupped by the elasticized material. What did Chad look like beneath those pants? The rest of him looked like a model or a movie star, one women salivated over. As did, quite obviously, some men.

Chad twisted his torso and groaned. A tingling started in Hollywood's groin. He could feel his cock lengthening and filling.

What the fuck?

He dropped the spatula he'd been holding. As it clattered to the stovetop, Chad's gaze zeroed in on him. Hollywood stood statue-still, watching Chad saunter up to the breakfast bar, a mischievous grin breaking out over his face the closer he got.

Reaching his destination, he leaned against the counter and winked in Hollywood's direction. "Is that for me?"

80 🚋 08

"So, how are things going with your new house guest?"

Liam's question startled Chad out of his reverie. He'd been asking himself exactly the same thing.

Feeling suddenly confined in the cabin of the ambo, he tugged on the seatbelt to loosen it. The streets of downtown Seattle were typically quiet this early in the morning, making the final few hours of their shift torturous. He and Liam often used this time to chat and catch up on each other's lives. "Okay, I guess."

"Uh-oh. I know that tone. Tell me what happened. Did Lieutenant Wright leave his tighty-whities on the bathroom floor?" Liam grinned.

Yeah, Chad could be a little OCD about his home, but that was no reason to be mean. "Actually, he wears boxer briefs." *Skin-tight ones.*

Liam's eyes rounded in surprise. "And how exactly do you know that? No." He shook his head. "Never mind. I don't want to know."

Chad narrowed his eyes at Liam and told him about his encounter with Hollywood and his date, Sandy, leaving out the gorier details. "And yesterday morning, he was cooking breakfast in nothing but his undies," he finished lamely. Remembering Hollywood's hard-on sent his heart into overdrive. Had that mountainous erection just been morning wood, or had it been something more? God, he so wished it were the latter.

Liam frowned and shot Chad a quick glance before returning his eyes to the road. "I can understand you not appreciating the live sex show in your living room, but why does how he dresses bother you? I'd have thought you'd enjoy the view, if nothing else. Even I can see the man is gorgeous."

An involuntary sound of agreement escaped Chad's throat.

Liam's mouth opened in a shocked O. "Fuck. You've got a thing for the LT?"

Schooling his features, Chad stared blindly out the windshield.

Liam sighed. "Does Jamie know?"

Why did everyone keep asking about Jamie? The guy wasn't his keeper, for fuck's sake. "What the hell does my brother have to do with this?"

"He's the one who suggested Hollywood stay with you. Maybe he did it for a reason."

Huh. Chad shifted in his seat, the stiff pleather groaning beneath him as he faced Liam. "A reason. Like what?"

"I don't know. He and Hollywood are best buds, right? Maybe he knows something we don't?"

Chad shook his head. "Hollywood's definitely into women." But there had been that stare while he'd been coming, then the hard-on yesterday morning. It had been kind of funny watching a very flustered Hollywood shove a plate of eggs in front of Chad with a muttered, "Sorry about last night," before scurrying off to his room. Chad hadn't seen him again after that.

"All I'm saying is, if Jamie knew you had a thing for Hollywood, he wouldn't have pushed you two together unless there was at least a chance of it working out."

"It's not like that. Jamie doesn't know about this"—he twirled a hand in the air—"infatuation. No one does, except you and Austin." And maybe Hollywood. "Besides, the whole thing's pretty clichéd—younger sibling falls for older brother's best friend." He laughed, and it sounded bitter, even to his own ears. "It could be a Harlequin romance or a Lifetime movie. In fact, I'm pretty sure it is."

"A what?" Liam feigned confusion. "Don't be throwing your gay lingo at me, man."

"Fuck off." Chad laughed and lightly punched his friend's arm. "I know you and Anna watch those Lifetime Original movies on Sundays when you're not working. Speaking of which, how is Anna doing?" Liam's wife was twenty weeks pregnant, and both were thrilled about the upcoming birth.

"She's so happy, she's fucking glowing. Oh, hey." He fumbled in his back pocket while keeping one hand on the wheel. "We had an ultrasound yesterday."

He handed Chad a small black-and-white image. Turning it sideways, Chad could make out the curve of the child's head, the tiny hands, and the legs spread wide. Smiling, he passed it back to his friend. "Your son's going to be perfect. Let's just hope he takes after Anna."

"Now it's your turn to fuck off, Caldwell," Liam joked.

They spent the rest of their shift answering one call after the other. At seven forty-five, Liam took them back to Harborview Medical Center.

They went inside Medic One Headquarters, their firehouse that was located inside the HMC complex, and finished up all their paperwork before completing the handoff to Margaret and Tonio, the two paramedics taking over for the next shift.

After saying goodbye to Liam, who was racing off to have breakfast with his wife, Chad took his time showering and shaving before he left. It wasn't like he had anyone waiting at home for him. Instead, he was going to surprise his mom with a visit, and maybe take her out if she didn't have other plans, an idea she'd immediately kibosh if he showed up scruffy and dirty from his shift.

The weather had turned cold and dreary, so he bundled up and hurried out to his car. Rain drizzled down, making the roads slick. Margaret and Tonio were sure to have a busy day. In a place that rained so much, you'd expect drivers to be used to it. But—

The thought stalled in his brain when he spotted his car, parked a half block down the street from the station. It was covered in graffiti, the same slur that had been spray-painted on the ambo last August when he'd also been beaten up. The memories hit him hard, making him stumble. Phantom pain punched into his gut, his kidneys, his face. Fuck! He'd thought that shit was behind him.

He approached the car cautiously, scanning the area nearby for the culprits. Sometimes they liked to hang around to see their victims' reactions. Or to beat them up.

That's when he noticed that the car was riding low. Too low. "Goddamn." All four tires were slashed. Turning in circles, he shouted, "Where are you?" He wasn't in the mood to fight, but he wasn't going to run away either. He was a lot of things, but a coward wasn't one of them.

Liam was already gone. Should he go back to the station and get help from the guys? A dark doubt niggled after what Hollywood had said about the secret meetings. What if it was one of them who'd done this?

He could call one of his brothers. They'd be pissed off and go into overprotective mode, and he wasn't in the mood to be coddled. That left Hollywood or Austin, but Austin had some big work meeting today.

Reluctantly pulling out his phone, he dialed the officer's line at Station 44. Hollywood answered, "Lieutenant Wright."

The gruff, tired voice drilled through him, stealing Chad's breath.

"Hello?" Hollywood said.

Chad cleared his throat. "It's Chad. You busy?" He blew out in relief when his voice didn't betray the slightest tremble. His knees? Well, that was another matter.

"Just finishing up some paperwork. Why?" Hollywood sounded guarded.

God, why was this so hard? Oh right. Because he *hated* asking anyone for anything. Chad straightened his shoulders and stared at his hobbled car. "I need your help."

A chair scraped. "What's wrong?" The concern lacing Hollywood's tone warmed Chad's treacherous heart.

"I'll tell you when you get here."

"Tell me now."

He leaned a hand on the hood of his car and closed his eyes. The authority and confidence. It sent chills down his spine.

"Chad."

"I thought we were friends," he said. "Friends don't interrogate."

"Chad."

Christ. Couldn't the guy stop saying his name that way? Each time, he imagined Hollywood wrapped around him, repeating his name as Chad pounded into his glorious ass, over and over. He shook off the fantasy. "You know what? Forget it."

He ended the call, wishing he had an old-fashioned phone that he could have slammed down in a nice tension-relieving hissy fit. He had too much pent-up frustration to deal with all this shit at the end of a twenty-four-hour shift.

His phone rang.

It was Hollywood. If Chad didn't answer, Hollywood would call Jamie, and then his little car problem would become a family mission.

As soon as he answered, Hollywood barked, "Where are you?"

"On Alder."

"I don't remember a parking garage there."

"I rent a spot from a guy." Chad gave him the address.

"That's not the best—"

"Area. Yeah, yeah. I know that." *Now.*

"I'll be there in ten."

Chad stared at his phone. Had he just jumped from the frying pan into the fire?

CHAPTER 6

Hollywood turned onto Alder Street and immediately spotted Chad's flashy two-door Nissan 370Z roadster. The fire-engine red convertible, with its shredded soft-top and fenders tagged with black paint, stood out in the quiet neighborhood. The vulgar slurs—*cunt, fag, cocksucker, abomination*—spelled out in bold strokes made his stomach churn.

He slid into the empty spot behind the roadster and got out. Chad stood, shivering in the cold drizzle, the hood of the sweatshirt he wore under his leather jacket soaked through. His eyes were narrowed and dark. Even from a distance, Hollywood could see the tic in Chad's jaw and the curve to his shoulders as he seemed to hunch into himself. Someone so strong should never look so alone, so vulnerable.

"I thought this shit had stopped."

"It had." Chad gave a casual shrug of his shoulders that didn't mesh with the hard edge in his voice.

"Why do I hear a 'but'?"

"But there've been some little things lately."

Hollywood walked to the side of the car, taking in the state of the tires. He arched a brow. "Little things? Like this?"

Chad looked away, cupping his hands to blow on the reddened skin.

Hollywood shook his head. "Have you at least told anyone?" Jamie hadn't mentioned anything, and there hadn't been any talk around the fire station. He rounded the car, getting up onto the sidewalk beside Chad.

Abruptly, Chad raised his head, an angry sneer on his lips. "Like who? The Chief? The cops? None of them give a fuck. Besides, I don't trust anyone except my family and Austin."

Hollywood's pulse skipped a beat. "Then why am I here?"

Chad's expression morphed into a shy smile. "You're kind of like

37

family too."

They stared at each other in silence. Hollywood started to sweat. His gaze slipped from Chad's amazing blue eyes to his perfectly shaped lips.

Jesus. Fuck. He closed his eyes and turned away. "Why didn't you call a tow truck?"

"The less people who see this, the better."

That he could understand. The car was like a billboard advertising Chad's sexual orientation. It was attention he definitely didn't want or need. Hollywood walked toward his car. "I'll take you to Les Schwab."

The trip to the tire store was uneventful. Chad remained quiet, drawn into himself. Hollywood wished they had more of a friendship. Maybe if the guy let out some of the thoughts tumbling in his head, he wouldn't look so wrecked.

At the store, Chad walked up to the counter and placed his order. Luckily, they had the needed tires on hand. The whole time Chad was talking to the clerk, Hollywood couldn't help hovering. If anyone gave the guy trouble, they'd have to deal with him.

The clerk told them to wait in the designated area while he went to get the tires from the back. Hollywood headed straight for the popcorn machine. It was his favorite thing about Les Schwab, and he indulged ravenously.

A few other people were scattered around the waiting area: a young guy in his late teens, an older couple, and a businesswoman. Chad had picked a seat far away from the others. Dropping into the chair beside him, Hollywood popped a few kernels into his mouth. Chad stared grimly at the television mounted on the wall in front of them. It was playing an inane morning show that wasn't even mildly interesting. Hollywood got that Chad was pissed about his car, but was there more to his sullen mood? Hollywood wanted his fun-loving roommate back.

Before he could think better of it, he threw a piece of popcorn at Chad, hitting him in the cheek. Chad's only reaction was to quirk a dark brow.

Hollywood wasn't going to settle for that. He threw another, this time clocking Chad in the forehead. The guy's eyes widened and his lips pursed. Nothing else. He tossed more in quick succession, pelting Chad's head. He didn't stop until Chad broke down.

"Fucker." Laughing, Chad scooped a handful of popped kernels from his lap and dumped them over Hollywood's head. The battle continued on for several more minutes. When they'd quieted down, Chad rose to get some napkins. His eyes sparkled and there was a wide grin on his face that had Hollywood's gut doing strange things. The man was beautiful.

And why was Hollywood suddenly noticing? Why did the sight of Chad kneeling on the floor, picking up the mess they'd made, have his pants tightening?

He wasn't gay.

He'd never thought of a man as being attractive. He'd certainly never gotten hard for one... At least not until the other morning when he'd caught Chad dancing... *Christ.*

While Chad cleaned up their mess, the older couple rose from their seats and walked past them. The woman sneered and the man muttered under his breath, "Damn fags."

Hollywood's gaze shot to Chad. His eyes had gone dull. Dead. Chad gathered up the napkins, dumping everything in a nearby garbage can, then crossed his arms and stared out the large picture window at the front of the store. Hollywood wanted to go to him, to tell him it didn't matter what two strangers thought. But deep down, it *did* matter. Chad would risk his life to help the same people who'd see him dead because of who he was attracted to. And they'd never see that, never acknowledge it. And that was fucking awful.

Five uncomfortable minutes later, the clerk arrived with Chad's tires on a cart. Hollywood folded down the back seats of his RAV4 and they loaded all the tires inside.

The drive back to Chad's car was a short one, but to Hollywood it felt like ages. Chad's unusual silence was one of the most oppressive things he'd ever experienced

Working together, only exchanging words as needed, they replaced all four slashed tires with the new ones An hour later, as Hollywood was putting his jack away and Chad was doing the same, he knew he couldn't leave things the way they were. Today had obviously been a big blow to Chad, and Hollywood wanted to be there for him. After all, Chad had chosen to reach out to him for help.

Not his brothers. Not his fucking cowboy friend.

Hollywood.

"I know someone who can give you a cheap paint job, if you're interested," he blurted out.

Chad slammed his trunk closed and leaned a hip against it, folding his arms across his chest. "Is that right?"

"Um... yeah?"

"Why are you helping me?"

Hollywood frowned. "Because you asked."

Chad pushed off the Nissan and stepped close to Hollywood. "The more you hang out with me, the more you'll be subjected to shit like what happened back at the tire store."

"Like the popcorn fight? That was epic," Hollywood joked, even though he knew exactly what Chad was talking about.

A slight smile curved Chad's lips. "It was great. What happened after?

Not so much."

"Who cares what some old farts say? It doesn't change who you are."

"Huh. So you don't mind people calling you gay? Most straight guys go ape-shit over it."

Hollywood's breath caught. "Wait... what?"

Chad's gaze softened. "The man, he said, 'Damn fags.' Plural. They thought we were together."

Nothing Chad was saying made sense. It was like only half of Hollywood's synapses were firing. "Together?"

"A couple."

"Oh." How had he missed that? Oh, yeah. He'd been too focused on Chad's reaction to really register the exact words. But did he even care? He shrugged. "Whatever."

Chad stuck his hands in his pockets and smirked. "What if the guys at the station start whispering when you walk by?"

"Why would they do that?"

"Because we live together. Because sometimes we hang out together. Because I *am* gay."

"But I'm not."

"I get that. Others might not. Anyway, as long as you know what you're doing."

"I don't give a fuck what other people think. You're my friend." Hollywood got in his car. None of the guys in his platoon could ever be more bigoted than his father. He rolled down his window. "Follow me."

He pulled out and drove up the road a little to wait for Chad. As they drove to Andy's garage, Hollywood's mind jumped ahead to dinner later that night with his dad. The subject of where he was living was bound to come up, and Hollywood couldn't put off answering anymore. His dad would be anything but subtle in his indignation. Fireworks were guaranteed.

$\wp$ ♟ ϖ

After Chad had arranged a paint job with Andy, Hollywood ushered Chad through the entrance door and surreptitiously appraised Chad from behind. The guy's worn jeans were soft and snug, showcasing every contour as he walked. He had a great ass.

Jesus. What the hell was it about this guy, and why was he looking at his ass?

"Hollywood, I hate to ask you for another favor, but would you mind giving me a lift to a car-rental place? Andy said it would be a week or so before I got my car back."

Afraid he'd been caught staring, Hollywood jerked his head up. "No problem."

Lucky for him, Chad had his head down as he zipped up his coat. When Chad finished, Hollywood nodded toward a diner across the street. "But first we're getting something to eat. I don't know about you, but I'm fucking starving." The growling of his stomach punctuated his words.

Chad grinned and something in Hollywood's belly fluttered. Had to be hunger pains.

A cute hostess led them to an empty booth. The diner was busy, but their section was relatively quiet. When she handed them their menus, she leaned in close to Hollywood. So close that her breast rubbed against his arm as Chad's cologne tickled Hollywood's nose. Hollywood squirmed out of his jacket and stretched his legs out while, as inconspicuously as possible, adjusting his semi into a better position. His knee bumped Chad's under the table. Electricity raced through him. He pulled his leg back immediately. "Sorry," he said, his face burning.

"Tight fit?"

Fuck yeah, his pants were tight. He gulped. Shit. That's not what Chad had meant. At least he hoped it wasn't. The guy had better not be eyeing his crotch. Hollywood wasn't gay.

Then why are you suddenly springing a boner, asshole?

It was the feel of the hostess' tits on his arm that had gotten him going. Yeah. He picked up the glass of water in front of him and downed it completely, trying to ignore Chad's amused expression.

A waitress, an older woman this time, brought them coffee and took their orders. As soon as she left, Chad asked, "So, what are your hobbies?"

Hollywood took a sip of coffee, then sat back. Should he tell Chad the truth?

"Honey, don't tell me you pole dance, because I don't think my heart could take it," Chad said in a campy falsetto.

Chad adopted this queeny affectation whenever he was uncomfortable. It was an effective way to break tension or divert the conversation, but at the same time, it was like he chose to laugh at himself before others could. Well, Hollywood wasn't going to laugh at Chad, and there was nothing about being gay that he found funny. Maybe if he opened up a little, Chad would relax. It was a small price to pay for Chad's hospitality. For his smile.

He cleared his throat. "I draw."

"Really?"

"Yeah."

Chad chuckled. "I'd have bet my last dollar you were going to say football or rebuilding old cars."

"Not manly enough for you?"

"If you know anything about me, it's that I don't judge."

Hollywood took another sip of his coffee, a big one this time, and nearly scalded his tongue. Biting back a wince, he said, "But you do assume."

"Point taken." Chad's cheeks flushed and he fiddled with the roll of silverware. "Could I maybe see your work sometime?" He stirred some milk into his coffee, then took several sips.

Tapping his fingers on the edge of his cup, Hollywood grinned. "I'll show you mine if you show me yours."

Coffee sprayed from Chad's mouth, hitting Hollywood from head to waist. After recovering from a coughing fit, Chad started to laugh. He handed over his napkin and said, "As much as I want to help you clean up, you'd better do it on your own."

Chuckling, Hollywood wiped up what he could of the coffee spray with the two napkins they had. Yeah, he'd deserved that, but he'd made Chad laugh again. It was worth it.

The waitress arrived with their orders and promptly dropped an inch of napkins in the middle of the table. Her schoolmarm posture warned them to clean up their mess. Hollywood winked at her. She huffed and turned away.

"Damn, I haven't laughed this hard in a long time," Hollywood said, digging into his eggs.

Chad's expression was pitying. "You say the dumbest shit. What did you actually mean?"

Hollywood had known the double-entendre would set Chad off. The hit to his reputation was so worth the show. "I've heard mention that you sing... and seeing as I'm almost family and all..."

Chad blushed again. Not a dark flush, but an honest-to-God pink blush that spread over his high cheekbones. He could have made a fortune in Hollywood. "I'm performing at Bar None this Friday. You're welcome to come—if you're not working, that is."

Even if he was scheduled to work, he'd switch half shifts with someone. No way would he miss the chance to see Chad on stage. He hadn't been able to get "Uptown Funk" out of his head since he'd caught Chad singing that he was too hot and needed to call a fireman. Because yeah, apparently the guy was too hot, even for this fireman. If he closed his eyes, he could hear Chad's smooth notes, see his back muscles rippling, his tight ass flexing—

He gasped and a piece of toast went down the wrong way, sending him into a coughing fit. Chad watched him, something knowing in his expression. Had he somehow figured out what Hollywood had been thinking? Christ, he hoped not. After dinner with his dad, Hollywood needed to get his ass to a bar. And this time he'd fuck someone. Someone female. Someone with big round tits and an ass to match. Someone blonde with brown fucking eyes.

As they left the restaurant, Chad pushed up onto his toes and kissed Hollywood lightly on the cheek. The guy's lips were soft and firm, the scrape of his stubble on Hollywood's skin startling.

"Thank you," Chad whispered.

His face burning as though he'd had an acid bath, Hollywood blinked at Chad. "What for?"

"For being a good friend."

CHAPTER 7

Chad stopped the brand spanking new Toyota Corolla rental in front of his parents' West Seattle house and took long strides up the driveway. The place looked as immaculate as ever, despite the dreary weather. His mom had even found some hardy winter flowers to line the porch. The result was warm and inviting, much like the woman herself. Why had he stayed away so long?

Using his key, he let himself in. "Mom?"

"In the kitchen, sweetie."

As he wandered through his childhood home, memories of growing up in the crowded house with three brothers and a twin sister swamped him. They hadn't had a lot of money back then, but they'd been happy. Even after he'd come out. Somehow, his family had always known. He wasn't effeminate, and he didn't often act it, but still, most people figured out his sexual orientation after being with him for more than an hour. He'd never tried to hide who he was. He'd never had to. And he didn't take that unconditional love and acceptance for granted.

It was why he supported the local LGBTQ youth center in any way he could. Some of the kids, hell, most of the kids, had it bad. When he'd learned that as much as forty percent of homeless kids identified as LGBTQ, he'd known deep in his bones that he had to do something. So, at least once a month, he spent a day at the center working with the kids, teaching them about firefighting, about first aid, and about life as a paramedic. He donated the proceeds from his performances to the center as well. It wasn't much, but as Betty, the transwoman who ran the center, always said, "Every show of acceptance helps."

He was going to make sure the fundraiser was a hit. That Hollywood might show up made him nervous as hell, but excited him too. His stomach flipped. Shit, he was even more anxious about it than when his father had come to watch him sing the first time.

Before entering the kitchen, he ran his fingers through his hair and forced a smile. No need to worry his mom with the shit that had happened this morning. As soon as she saw him, his mother pulled him into her arms and peppered his face with kisses until he laughed and gently set her back. "Mom."

Ignoring him, she cupped his cheeks and smiled. "I've missed you."

He smiled back, a real one this time. "It's only been two weeks." That had been the big Thanksgiving/birthday party bash.

She gave him one more quick kiss, then went to pour him a cup of coffee, adding a bit of the vanilla creamer she kept on hand just for him. "What I meant," she said, setting it on the table in front of him, "is that I miss having one-on-one time with you." She sat and looked at him fondly. "So tell me, what's been going on in my son's life? And don't try to get out of it. I know something's happened. I can see it in your eyes."

He blinked, hoping she was bluffing. "Well, you know Hollywood's been staying with me," he offered.

Cupping her coffee mug, she brought it to her lips and blew on it. "Erica mentioned it. How's that going?" The concern in her eyes touched him. The whole family knew about the tension between him and Hollywood. They just didn't know the cause of it — at least for Chad. And they never would if he got his way.

"As well as can be expected. Our shifts have been different, so we've hardly seen each other."

"That's good. If he gives you any trouble" she narrowed her eyes meaningfully—"you let me know."

Chad chuckled at her momma-bear glare. "Seriously, it's fine. He even helped me out this morning with some car trouble."

"Oh? What's wrong with your car?"

Damn, he'd walked right into that one. "Some uh… parts need to be changed. He drove me to a car-rental place."

"I see." She cocked her head to the side. "Are you sure that's all it is?"

"Absolutely." He shot her his most charming grin. The last thing he wanted was to set her off on another mission. When he'd gotten beat up a few months ago, she'd tried for weeks to get him to move back home with them and Tori. Luckily, he'd managed to put a stop to that. He loved his family, but he loved his privacy too. He'd gone through enough years of sneaking in and out of the house. Sure, he was out and proud, but that didn't mean he wanted his sexuality to be the topic of every conversation, no matter how well-meaning his family.

"There's something," she insisted. "I can see it. Have you met someone?"

Jesus. Did the woman have a crystal ball? *This*. This right here was why he'd avoided being alone with her lately. His mother had the annoying ability to see right through him.

"If so, we'd love to meet him," she added, placing her hand on top of his. Would she still think that if she knew it was Hollywood he was pining over?

Pining? Christ, now he sounded like a Victorian damsel. Whatever. Hollywood had a reputation, and his mother would know Chad was setting himself up for a world of hurt, even if Hollywood was interested in Chad. Which he wasn't.

He gave her a lopsided smile, one that had gotten him out of trouble numerous times when he'd been a kid. "There's no one, Mom. But thanks."

She stood and ruffled his hair. "We just want you to be happy, son."

While preparing a plate of grilled ham and cheese sandwiches, she caught him up on all the latest family news. Tori had gotten a job at Vicenzo's, the restaurant owned by the famous Chef Ivy Turin, wife of their equally famous football-star cousin, Sam "Knute" Rockney. She'd work there a few shifts a week, not enough to interfere with her studies though. She was well on her way to earning a PhD in Psychology.

"When did she get hired?" He frowned.

His mother pulled a napkin from the holder on the counter next to the stove and carried the plate of sandwiches to the table, then followed up with two bowls of homemade tomato soup. This had been a surprise visit; still she had all his favorites on hand.

"Three weeks ago," she said, joining him at the table.

Three weeks? Tori hadn't mentioned it. They talked all the time. Or did they? Granted, with all the chaos at Thanksgiving, they hadn't had time for more than a quick hello. And now that he thought about it, the only communication he'd exchanged with his twin since then was a single Happy Birthday text on December first, their actual birthday. What was going on? Chad wiped his suddenly sweaty palms on his jeans.

"Tori's worried about you, honey. She says you've withdrawn, and I have to agree with her. You have."

He closed his eyes and pinched the bridge of his nose. Had he purposely been staying away from his family? Maybe subconsciously he'd known they'd sense something was going on with him, something he really didn't want to talk about. But shit, he couldn't avoid his family forever. He was hurting them, and that wasn't something he'd ever intended to do.

"I'll call her soon." When she arched a brow, he added, "I promise."

They ate their soup and sandwiches, chatting about Chad's work. She asked him about Liam's baby, then she said, "Everyone will be at the show on Friday."

Bomb. Dropped. And she didn't seem aware of it.

"Everyone?" he barely managed to croak. His family had heard him sing before and they'd attended a few fundraisers, but nothing close to what he expected this one to be like. In an effort to be even more inclusive, the youth center had switched venues from the gay club where they traditionally held the fundraiser to Bar None, which, as its name implied, welcomed everyone. He thought it was a great move on the center's part, but it could be a shocker to some people. And God, why hadn't he thought about that before inviting Hollywood?

"Yes. It's going to be so much fun. I haven't heard you sing in ages."

He suddenly felt a little light-headed. "You know, some of the acts are going to be pretty campy..."

"Come on now. Don't get squeamish on me. It takes more than a man in a dress to scare anyone in this family." She tossed her head back and laughed.

Chad loved his mother, loved all his family, but sometimes their support was overwhelming. Clearing this throat, he spoke around the tightness choking him. "Hollywood said he might come too."

"Oh good. We haven't seen him in a while."

"You'll have to keep an eye out for him. I'm sure it will be way out of his comfort zone."

"What's out of whose comfort zone?" Drew asked, barging into the kitchen through the back door, their father right behind him.

His mother got up to kiss them both, lingering in her husband's arms. Chad loved that his parents were still so affectionate, still so obviously taken with each other. He hoped to have that someday.

"Hollywood's coming to Chad's show," his mother informed the new arrivals.

She didn't notice the slight flare of alarm in their gazes, but Chad did. That flare was in his gut. Why the fuck had he invited the guy? It was going to be bad. His father patted his shoulder. "We'll make sure he sits with us."

"Thanks, Dad."

"Now get off your butt. You and Drew have some boxes to move."

"Okay. But... uh... why?" He was more than happy to help, but any mention of his parents moving had his dander up. They were his security blanket, and he wanted them right here. Always.

His mother smiled. "We're converting one of the spare bedrooms into a nursery. That way we can have a place for the babies to sleep when they come over."

"Babies? Plural?" Chad's gaze shot to his brother's equally questioning one. No help there.

"Calm down, boys. I just meant you're all reaching the point where

47

this sort of thing happens more often," his mother said, eyes dancing.

"I'm single, Mom." Drew crossed his arms, looking like he'd rather be anywhere but here.

Chad laughed. "I'm gay, so I've got you beat, bro."

"Nonsense," his mom said. "A lot of gay men have children through surrogates or adoption."

"Sure, but I'm single too." What was it about women and babies? He snared Drew's eye, angling his head toward the stairs.

Drew caught on quick. "I've got plans, so let's hurry this up."

The two of them practically trampled each other, racing out of the kitchen and up the stairs to the second floor. Behind them, his father's laughter echoed. "That's one way to get those boys to work."

"I think we've been had," Chad grumbled.

"No kidding. Mom knows us too well." Drew led the way into the spare bedroom. "What's all this crap?"

Columns of boxes were piled high, filling most of the room. Each was labeled with a name. Chad saw a whole column of his. He walked over and opened the top box. It was packed full of clippings of him at Pride events, starting with his first when he'd been in tenth grade. In each one, a member of his family stood with him. Tears pricked his eyes. This was exactly why he hadn't told them that the harassment hadn't ended after he'd been attacked last summer.

Drew came up behind him and threw an arm around his shoulder, tugging him against his side. "I've always been so proud of you. We all have."

Chad sniffed and leaned into his brother's solid presence. "Why?"

"You've never pretended to be someone else, never lied. You are who you are, and anyone who doesn't like it can go fuck themselves." Drew shrugged. "Not all of us are that strong."

"What are you talking about? No one in our family hides anything."

"You sure about that? Jamie's never come clean about being a Dom, even though we all figured it out a while ago. William's kinks were outed by the media—" He pursed his lips. "Yeah. And they're twice as old as you were when you came out, not knowing what kind of a reception you'd get."

"You know, I never thought of it that way." He turned to face Drew. "For me, coming out wasn't that hard. I didn't know if you'd all accept me, but I figured at least Mom and Tori would, and there'd be a safe place for me to sleep that night. Later, when I came out at school, you all had my back. Not everyone has that. Not everyone is so lucky. And if someone's into kink, well… you've seen what's happened to Dani and William."

"Maybe you're right."

"I hope someday Jamie and Erica feel comfortable enough to not hide that part of themselves from us."

"They seem really happy now," Drew said, his eyes going distant.

"Definitely."

Drew picked up a box. "But you're not. I noticed the rental outside. Yours?"

Chad closed the lid on the box he'd been rummaging through and followed his brother out to the garage where they deposited the boxes. "My car's at the shop," he finally replied, keeping it short, sweet, and neutral.

"Oh yeah? What happened?"

"A flat tire."

"A flat required you to get a rental." Drew stopped and very slowly pivoted. "Yeah. And I'm the tooth fairy." He was an inch or so shorter than Chad, but about fifteen pounds heavier. All muscle. Muscles which were now rippling as Drew crossed his arms.

The image of all that in a tutu with wings had Chad bursting out in laughter.

"Ha-ha. Tell me the truth."

Drew advanced and Chad backed up a step. "It's nothing."

"Chad." Drew let out a long, slow breath, and put his hands on his hips. "I've heard that there's been other incidents."

Chad couldn't keep the surprise off his face. "From who?" He hadn't told a soul.

Drew ignored his question. His bulldog face was on. "Was what happened to your car related?"

When Drew set his sights on something, he'd push until his target caved. No point dragging it out. "Okay, okay. My tires were slashed and the car was grafittied."

Drew punched the drywall that lined the inside of the garage, putting a dent in it. "Fuck. Why didn't you call me?"

"*This* is why! You, Jamie, William. I knew you'd react like this, and I don't want you guys getting into trouble—or hurt—because of me. I can defend myself."

Drew scrubbed his hands over his cheeks. "You don't have to go through this alone. We're here for you."

"I know."

"Did you at least call Austin?"

Chad shook his head.

"Anyone?"

Drew waited him out.

Chad blew out in exasperation. "All right. Jesus. I called Hollywood."

"Hollywood." Drew's tone was flat as he headed back up the stairs.

They worked in silence, bringing the boxes down to the garage for the next ten minutes. When they picked up the last two boxes, Drew asked, "Why him?"

"He's my roommate."

"Uh-huh."

Chad huffed and stomped down the stairs, Drew close on his heels. Inside the garage, Drew whispered, "The guy's straight."

Weeks of frustration came to a boil. How did brothers always manage to find exactly the right buttons to push? "I fucking know."

Drew set his box down and gave Chad a considering look. The guy was even rubbing his chin as though pondering the secrets of the universe. "I'd noticed the strange vibe between the two of you the night you got beat up, but I didn't realize it was because of a crush."

Chad bowed his head. It was time he owned up to the truth. "Oh God, Drew. It's so much worse than a crush."

Without a word, Drew opened up the back door and pulled Chad through it. Chad tasted bile in his mouth as they sat together on the bench that overlooked his mother's frozen flower garden.

"What're you going to do about it?" Drew asked, his voice hard.

"Nothing. What can I do?"

His expression softening, Drew leaned forward and clasped his hands between his knees. "You could find someone else."

"Easier said than done," Chad bit out.

"You've tried."

"Oh yeah." Harry's hurt face floated to the forefront of his mind. He owed the guy more than a drink to make up for that monumental clusterfuck.

Drew turned his head and looked back at him. "Have you told Hollywood?"

"Are you crazy? That would go over real well, wouldn't it? 'Hey, Hollywood. I know you're straight, but I really want to bang you. So here's my number. Call me maybe.'"

Sitting up, Drew nudged him in the shoulder. "Drama queen much?"

"Yeah, well. I am what I am."

Drew grinned, then looked away, sobering. "If you're not trying to get him into bed, then what *are* you doing?"

"I'm trying to be his friend."

"How's that working out for you?"

Not good, Dr. Phil. Not good at all.

⁂

A six o'clock on the dot, Hollywood stood on the front step of his father's house, bracing himself for what was certain to be a stressful evening, if not an all-out Wright-family battle. He was going to have to come clean about his living arrangements. A bead of sweat snaked its way down his back, making him shiver.

Better to get this over with.

Straightening his spine, he raised his hand to knock. Right before his knuckles made contact with the wooden door, it swung open. His father stood, feet spread, shoulders square, a drink in his hand, and evidence of many others on his red and puffy face. He stared at Hollywood with angry, glazed eyes. "So, you a fag yet?"

"What?" Hollywood could barely breathe, yet anger stirred within his chest. Anger that even at thirty-six, he still allowed his father to bully him.

"Marvin, from down the road, came over this afternoon. Told me all about that Caldwell fudge-packer. Said he saw you two at Les Schwab all cozy-like. He your *boyfriend* now?" With a final snarl, his father turned and staggered into the living room, where he promptly made for the bar to refill his glass from a half-empty bottle of cheap rum.

Jesus. The old man already had quite a head start. Not sure he could survive World War III sober, Hollywood grabbed a glass and filled it with ice and the shit his father was drinking.

After his father had sunk his mean ass onto the ugly recliner he favored, Hollywood sat on the sofa. "Chad is Jamie's brother. I helped him out like I would have any of the other guys in the fire service."

"What'd he offer you in return? A blow job?"

"Christ, Dad. Seriously? Whatever." He started to rise, determined to leave the conversation and his father behind, but then changed his mind. "On second thought, no. You need to hear this. Chad's tires were slashed this morning, all four. His car was spray-painted with slurs, all your favorites. And guess where this all happened?"

His father glared at him and slowly raised his glass to his lips.

"A half block from Harborview. How likely is it that no one saw anything? Huh? Zero."

"Just what are you implying, boy?"

Boy. The word raked down his back like a giant claw, causing the hairs on his nape to rise. "SFD needs to protect him, Dad. You can't keep looking the other way."

His dad stood and took an unsteady step toward Hollywood. Although his father was shorter than Hollywood's six four, he'd been a football player in high school and still had a linebacker's build. Hollywood forced himself to stand his ground.

"The service is for men. If that sissy can't take the heat, he needs to get the hell out!"

Spittle hit Hollywood in the face.

As casually as he could, he wiped it off. He'd heard his father deliver his sexist and bigoted tirades before, but never with so much vehemence. "Whatever you may believe, Dad, the fire service is doing fine as is. Hell, over eight percent of our firefighters are female."

"Bah!" His father spread his arms wide. Rum sloshed onto his hand and arm unnoticed. "Those broads are nothing but trouble. I'd have fired that Harris bitch's ass last summer, but I was outvoted. The way that bastard Starling stood up for her, he's gotta be banging her."

Hollywood rolled his eyes. "She's engaged to William Caldwell. Have you seen the man?"

His father sneered. "Yeah, *all* of Seattle has. That slut ruined him, and the dumbass is too stupid to see it."

This fucking conversation was going nowhere fast. "Listen, Dad. I'm just going to go."

"Oh, is your boyfriend waiting for you at home? You two got a hot date planned?"

Goose bumps erupted on his arms. "Excuse me?"

His father got right up in his face, the fumes from his drink overpowering. "You thought I wouldn't find out you're living with that cocksucker?"

Hollywood swallowed half his liquid courage in one shot, barely biting back a grimace at the harsh taste. "I'm not *living* with him. Shit. He offered me a place to stay while my apartment's being repaired. I had some water damage."

"You couldn't stay somewhere else? You own the damn building."

"All the apartments are rented out, and well… Jamie suggested I stay in Chad's spare bedroom—"

"So Caldwell's setting up tricks for his brother now? I knew something was off about that guy." He reached for something in his back pocket. When Hollywood saw it was a phone, the blood drained from his head.

"Dad, what are you doing?"

"I'm calling Mayor Maddocks. I want every one of those motherfucking Caldwells and their 'fiancées' fired."

"On what grounds?" Hollywood lunged and tried to grab the phone, but his father spun around, nearly crashing into the coffee table. His glass went flying and he barely managed to right himself using the couch arm for support. He wagged his finger at Hollywood. "I'll invoke the morality clause. I'll get a PI on them. Those sex-club photos were the tip of the iceberg. I feel it in my gut. That whole family is sick. Evil. And if you don't stop hanging around them, you'll end up like they are—sick and depraved."

Every word out of his father's mouth took him back to the painful years living in this house after his mother's death. The years before he'd met Isabel and moved out. The years when he'd been the sole focus of his father's hate.

But he wasn't that scared boy anymore. The teenager terrified of his father, of being beaten and thrown out on the street, was long gone.

Hollywood was shaken back into the present by his father's fingers digging painfully into his arm. He'd have bruises in the morning. A common occurrence when he'd been a kid. His father shook his arm. "You go there. You get your things, and move into your old room. And you do it tonight."

The hot breath hitting the side of his face with each word made him shudder. "No fucking way."

His father's closed fist arced through the air as if in slow motion. Although Hollywood saw it coming, could have moved out of the way, he didn't. Every muscle in his body froze as adrenaline flooded his system. Bone crunched on bone, his jaw absorbing the impact as he fell to the ground.

"You will." His father stood over him, and Hollywood was ten again. "If you want your friends to keep their jobs, you'll do as I say. Got it?"

The taste of blood in his mouth was a familiar one, the ache in his jaw even more so, bringing back memories he'd blocked out for so long. The drunken, belligerent, abusive prick towering above him had been a far more frequent visitor to their home than the loving, nurturing father he'd had before his mother died.

Pushing to his feet, he clenched his fists and faced his father, determined to fight him for the first time in his life. "I'm a grown man. You can't control me like you used to."

A blob of spit landed on his boots. His father's lip curled. "I should have known."

"Known what?" The twists and turns of this conversation were too sharp to follow.

"Something wasn't right with you, even when you were little. Your mom said you'd grow out of it. She was wrong. When I caught you with that Henderson boy, I should have known. I should have sent you to one of those church camps."

"What the fuck are you talking about?" He didn't remember his father ever going to church. And what was that crack about Bobby? They'd been best friends until Bobby's family moved away in fourth grade.

"One of those gay-conversion camps. Maybe they could have cured you."

A sick feeling, a sense of dread, swamped him. A fragment of memory floated through his mind. He and Bobby, his dad barging into his room...

Hollywood's heart pounded against his ribs, so hard he was starting to feel dizzy. "I don't know what you're talking about." Reaching behind him, he felt for the couch and dropped onto it as his legs gave way.

"I knew from the moment I set eyes on that Henderson kid, he was a fairy. And when I caught the two of you touching each other"— something flickered in his gaze—"well, thank God your mother wasn't alive to see it."

What? Had they really gone that far? "All kids are curious—"

"*That* wasn't curiosity! You think I'm a fool? That I'm stupid?" His face reddened and his eyes had a hard glint. "You were jerking each other off, and it didn't look like it was the first time. You were both naked, in a sixty-nine for fuck's sake, and I swear to God, if I hadn't interrupted, you were about to suck his fucking cock!"

No, no, no. That hadn't happened…

Hollywood jumped to his feet. "I don't know what game you're playing with this shit, these lies, but it isn't going to work." He grabbed his glass off the side table and threw it in the fireplace hearth, where it shattered into a million satisfying pieces. Turning on his heel, he stormed out of the house, trying to ignore his old man as he continued yammering behind him.

"You know it's the truth, Nathan."

Hollywood stopped on the stone pathway and turned. "I don't remember anything like that ever happening." He pounded his fist over his heart. "Isabel and I were engaged. I loved her. I'd still love her today if she were alive. We'd have a passel of kids and we'd be happy." Tears burned his eyes as memories of Isabel and their brief, intense time together flooded him. "I don't know why you're saying this."

"I don't like being lied to, especially by my son."

Hollywood stiffened. "*I'm* not the one who's lying."

"Ask yourself something, Nathan," his father said, his voice softer, patronizingly placating. "What do I have to gain by admitting I have a gay son? I'm trying to help you before things go too far, before you make the wrong choices. Stay away from that Caldwell fag. He's just like that Henderson boy. He'll corrupt you if you give him even the slightest opportunity."

Hollywood gave his father his back, and got in his car. The memory of Chad in his running pants, his tight ass and even tighter abs, rose unbidden. Was his father right? Had Chad already changed him? Corrupted him?

ℬ 🎬 ℭ

Hollywood sat in Chad's living room, working on his sixth beer. He hated beer, but what the fuck. He'd forgotten to replace the bottle of Grey Goose that he'd finished off the other night with—Candy? Sandy?—and right now he needed something to help him forget.

The lights were off, and only the flickering of the muted television kept him company. But even the alcohol couldn't take his mind off what his father had said. Was it true? Had he and Bobby touched each other? And even if they had, so what? A lot of boys experimented. Based on what his dad had said, the incident had happened when he'd been in fourth grade. That was a few years after his mother had died of ovarian cancer. As they'd later discover, she'd been the glue that had held their family together. Hollywood barely remembered her smile, the sound of her laughter, her voice when she sang him to sleep. How happy his father had been then, so different from the bitter drunk he was today.

Downing half the beer, Hollywood stared at the bottle, fully aware of the irony. Every day, he was becoming more and more like his old man, unable to move beyond the death of the woman he'd adored.

His and Isabel's love had been so pure, so full of ideals and dreams. She'd been his best friend, his high-school sweetheart, and they'd been so in sync they'd finished each other's sentences, loved the same movies, the same food, the same music. The sex had been great too. He smiled, remembering their first time together. Isabel had been a virgin, and he'd been honored to be the one she'd chosen. It had been awkward and a little painful for her, but afterward, they'd been closer than ever before. He hadn't looked at another woman again. Not until several months after they'd buried her.

His dad had to be lying. He'd never been attracted to men, certainly never gotten hard for one.

Liar.

The voice in his head had acid burning his throat. Oh God. Just the thought of Chad, his silky dark hair, his deep blue eyes, and his killer body had Hollywood hard enough to batter down doors.

But what did he want to do with Chad? Was this a look-but-don't-touch deal? He couldn't imagine taking Chad's cock in his mouth. Had he really done that with Bobby? On the other hand, he could more than imagine Chad's mouth on him.

Pre-cum leaked, wetting his boxers. He palmed himself, squeezing hard to force his erection down. He was having a goddamn crisis here. It wasn't the time to get off.

Sitting up, he finished the beer and cracked open another from the fresh six-pack on the table. He took a long drink before placing the can against this forehead. The cold eased the pressure building in his head. He had to try to remember.

Leaning his head on his steepled hands, he thought back to fourth grade, to Bobby. They'd often done their homework together in his room while the babysitter prepared supper. Had anything out of the ordinary ever happened?

His mind went back to those days. To *the* day. The day his dad had beaten him so severely he'd thought he should have gone to the hospital.

Bobby had been there... at least before the beating had begun. They'd been alone, and Hollywood had been excited to show him something... the *Playboy* he'd found under his dad's bed. That day, when Bobby had come over, they'd looked at the magazine together.

Hollywood swallowed hard, his face burning. He remembered it now—the shy giggles, the embarrassment of his cock hardening at the photos of men and women in various sexual positions. He'd glanced over at Bobby and seen that he was hard too.

"You ever touch yourself? You know... down there?" he'd asked.

Bobby's face had turned red and he'd stuck his chin out defiantly. "Maybe."

"You want to now?"

"Maybe."

"I'm gonna. You can look away or go home."

But Bobby hadn't gone home, and he hadn't looked away. He'd watched Hollywood lower his shorts and take out his dick. His breathing had sped up when Hollywood had started stroking himself.

Thinking back on it, he'd gotten off on being watched. His movements had turned frantic and he'd shot off in record time. There hadn't been any ejaculate, but there'd sure as shit been an orgasm.

"Wow," Bobby had said, his voice laced with awe. "Can you go again?"

"Sure." Hollywood had taken off his shorts and then his shirt. Bobby had disrobed and they'd sat face-to-face, stroking themselves. After a minute, they'd lain on their sides, head to feet, so they didn't have to see each other's faces. And they'd gone to work on each other's cock.

Hollywood remembered it all now. The sight, the smell, the feel of the other boy's hard dick in his hand. He remembered being fascinated by Bobby's slit, wanting to know how it tasted. He remembered leaning in, being drawn to it.

His memory ended there. Abruptly. That had been when his father had interrupted.

Holy fuck.

He leaned his head on the back of the couch. How could he have forgotten that incident? All these years, and he'd convinced himself he'd never done anything with a boy. Why?

Another glimpse of the past hit. His father's angry face. A belt. Fists. Feet.

The words, all those horrible words. The threat to throw him out on the street... the fear that his dad was going to kill him.

It had been the first time his father had beaten him, and it had been bad. Hollywood had missed a week of school, and when he'd returned, he'd learned that Bobby and his family had moved away. He'd never heard from his best friend again. No doubt his father had had something to do with that. And the old man was obviously hoping to repeat history. He wouldn't be able to scare the Caldwells away, so he was trying to scare Hollywood.

And he's doing a damn good job of it.

The memory of Bobby was real, and the hard-on in his jeans at the memory of Chad in his running pants was also very, very real. What the fuck was he going to do?

A noise at the door caught his attention. A key in the lock. The squeal of metal on metal. And then Chad was standing in the living room, outlined by the light of the television.

Hollywood's body overheated and his pulse drummed in his ears, his chest—his cock. Fuck.

"Hey, Hollywood. How's it going?"

Hollywood stared at the man who'd rocked his world and didn't even know it. Who'd turned it head over fucking heels. Who'd turned him inside out and upside down. He swallowed; his mouth opened, and out came his worst fear. "I—I think I'm gay."

CHAPTER 8

Chad couldn't have held back his laughter if his life had depended on it. Hollywood gay? The idea was too ludicrous to even consider. And that more than anything broke Chad's heart. But he couldn't let his new friend see that. Those words were exactly what Chad had wanted to hear, for months now. But they weren't true. It was time to put Hollywood out of his misery.

"What you are, my friend, is drunk."

Empty beer cans littered the top of the coffee table and several lay on the carpet where they'd no doubt been knocked down by Hollywood's size thirteens. Hollywood grunted. "Maybe."

Chad collected the empty cans and dumped them in the recycling bin under the sink before grabbing two bottles of water from the fridge. As he took a seat beside Hollywood on the couch, he eyed the rings of spilled beer and what was left of Hollywood's dinner: a bag of Doritos and some powdered donuts. He'd clean the mess up in the morning. Something else was a bigger priority.

He rested his elbow on the back of the couch and took in Hollywood's disheveled appearance. His shirt was half tucked into the waistband of his jeans and his hair looked like he'd been through a hurricane, but it was the shattered look in his eyes that had Chad pushing. "Want to talk about it?"

When Hollywood went to toss back the contents of the can in his hand, Chad took it and replaced it with one of the bottles of water. Not even acknowledging the switch, Hollywood completed the motion and drank deeply. Once the bottle was drained, he tossed it in the general direction of the table and watched it slowly roll off the edge. He didn't move a muscle to pick it up. After a minute, he broke the silence. "Saw my dad."

"Ah. I take it that didn't go too well." Hollywood rolled his head toward Chad, bringing the left side of his face into view. Chad gaped at the ugly bruise that was forming on the man's jaw. "Jesus. He hit you?"

Hollywood half-shrugged, the movement seeming almost more than he could manage. "'S'nothin'."

Anger and a strange sense of protectiveness welled in Chad's chest. "Like hell it is. What happened?"

"Had a fight."

"No shit. What about?" Hollywood lay with his head on the back of the couch, blinking slowly at the silent television screen. Why was Chad even asking? He already knew the answer: Deputy Chief Wright hated Chad with an unusual passion. He'd known this was coming. He'd just never imagined Hollywood and his dad would come to blows over him. "It was about me, wasn't it?"

Hollywood's head lolled to the side, his gaze landing on Chad's face, searching for... something. "Ordered me to move out."

"Okay," Chad said quietly, but it wasn't okay. He'd miss having Hollywood around, seeing him when they weren't both at work, seeing his belongings scattered around the condo. He'd miss the chance to get to know him better, even if it was only as a friend. His chest ached at the thought. Going for some much-needed levity, he smirked. "He does know you can't catch homosexuality by drinking from the same cup as me, right?"

Hollywood smiled—and God, was it a great smile. His sensual lips curved upwards, his eyes crinkled at the corners, and his hazy green gaze sparkled. "Thinks it's from the toilet seat."

Chad barked out a surprised laugh, and Hollywood's smile got even bigger. "Was that a joke, Lieutenant Wright? Did you actually make a funny?"

Hollywood swatted at his arm, but he overshot and hit Chad's chest instead. Hollywood's hand went lax and fell to Chad's thigh. His cock punched to life, filling his jeans, and just like that, he was on the verge of coming. Chad's lungs seized.

Fuck! His couch companion seemed oblivious.

No. No. No! Think of bad fires, dirty adult diapers...

Anything other than the hot guy with his huge hand inches from his throbbing cock.

When he could finally focus again, Chad realized that Hollywood was still staring at his face. Chad nudged his shoulder. "Hey."

"Mmm?" he said in a sexy rumble.

Chad felt the vibration right down to his clenching asshole. "What are you going to do?" he choked out.

"Nothing. Don't know... kiss you?"

"What?" Chad jerked back and gripped the top of the couch, certain he'd misheard. His mind had made him hear what he so desperately wanted Hollywood to say.

"Never done that before." Hollywood's face scrunched up. "Y'know... Not sure. Didn't think I'd ever touched a guy, but tonight I found out that wasn't true."

Maybe Chad really was the drama queen his brother had accused him of being, because his entire insides suddenly froze. He couldn't move, couldn't breathe. Hollywood had been with a man before?

"W-what"—he licked his lips—"do you mean?"

Hollywood straightened and he hugged a throw pillow to his chest. Like a scared little kid. "Bobby. When I was ten, we fooled around and my dad caught us. Funny, I didn't remember it at all until my dad threw it in my face tonight." He raised pain-filled eyes to Chad. "He said I was gay."

Chad's stomach bottomed-out as the faint hope he'd held evaporated. He couldn't let Hollywood keep thinking, believing, the shit his dad had put in his head. "Most boys experiment at one point or another. It doesn't have to mean anything."

When Hollywood remained silent, Chad pushed gently. "Have there been other times?"

Hollywood's hand on Chad's thigh tightened, gripping his flesh. Chad had to fight to keep his eyes and his attention on his friend. Had to fight to keep his hands where they were, because he really, really wanted to take Hollywood's hand and show the guy what he did to him. How even a small touch from Hollywood made him crazy. But he didn't. Because the confused, tormented expression on his friend's face told him it would be the absolute worst thing he could do right now.

What Hollywood needed was reassurance.

Hollywood's eyes cleared, and he shot Chad a crooked smile. "Really like boobs."

Chad chuckled, relieved to hear the humor in his friend's voice. "Yeah, I think we've established that."

"And pussy." His eyes took on a dreamy look. "I love the taste of it. How one lick can make a woman helpless in my arms."

Jesus Christ. Chad felt green. Green with motherfucking envy. One lick on his dick from Hollywood and he'd be fucking helpless too. Hell one kiss would do it. That's all it would take for him to be at this man's feet. Thank God the blond Adonis had no clue.

When Hollywood had moved in, Chad had hoped he'd prove to be such a macho prick that he'd see Hollywood wasn't for him and get over his… feelings for the guy. But other than that one night with Sandy, that hadn't happened. Instead, Hollywood had been a great roommate, and even better—or worse, depending on how he looked at it—Hollywood was turning out to be a really good friend.

A friend he didn't want to lose. He poked Hollywood softly in the ribs. "See? Nothing to worry about. You're as straight as… an arrow," he finished lamely.

Hollywood arched a blond brow.

"What?"

"My arrow's at least a little bit bent." His gaze dropped to Chad's lips.

Oh no. Oh no. Trying to tamp down the sudden racing of his heart, Chad swallowed and asked as calmly as he could, "Why do you say that?"

"Think you're sexy."

Chad's eyes widened. Holy shit! Had Hollywood really just admitted he was attracted to Chad? Was it the alcohol talking, or was it Hollywood talking because the alcohol let him?

Again, Chad went for a joke. He forced a laugh. "Honey, you don't have to be gay to find me sexy."

Hollywood's gaze intensified. He shifted, pulling one leg up onto the couch, which brought his face closer to Chad's. "Keep wondering what you taste like."

With his eyes glued to Chad's mouth the way they were, it was no secret what he was asking. Unable to stop himself, Chad leaned forward until the warmth of Hollywood's breath fell on his lips. And the smell of alcohol reached his nose.

Goddamn. Why did he have to be the bigger man? Why couldn't he be like so many and take advantage of the situation to get what he wanted?

Because he's your friend.

Resigned, Chad slapped a hand on the other man's shoulder, holding him at bay.

"Want a kiss." Hollywood's disgruntled frown was the cutest thing Chad had ever seen. But the circumstances weren't right.

Chad closed his eyes and shook his head. "We can't." Denying Hollywood, denying himself… it fucking sucked. Something tightened painfully in his chest.

"Why not?" Hollywood asked, tugging on Chad's neck. The heat of that large hand on his bare skin would be forever etched into Chad's memory.

"Because you're not gay."

"How do you know?"

Dropping his head into his hand, Chad searched for an answer. How did he know? Truth was, he didn't. But he did know he wouldn't be Hollywood's drunken experiment. Anyone getting involved with Chad, especially when he was still being targeted, had to be fully cognizant of the potential consequences. Hollywood already knew about the attacks, obviously, but given his current state of mind, he couldn't be expected to make a clear decision with full knowledge of how it could impact his life.

"I'll make you a deal," Chad said after a moment.

"Listenin'."

Chad raised his head and held Hollywood's gaze. "If in three days, you still want to kiss me and you're sober at the time, I'll let you."

"And if I want more?" Hollywood rubbed his lips, sending another wave of arousal through Chad. He barely resisted rolling his hips, trying to move that hand on his thigh closer.

Shit, was he really going to do this? He stared into Hollywood's eyes. He couldn't refuse this man anything, not if he was sober and aware. He wanted Hollywood, wanted to taste him, to touch him, to worship his body the way he deserved. His heart beating triple-time, Chad nodded. "Then I'll let you have it."

And God help them both if Deputy Chief Wright found out.

80 🚋 CR

The following morning, Hollywood trudged into the officer's room at seven thirty, a full thirty minutes before the beginning of his shift. *Give the man a medal.* His eyes were bloodshot, his head hurt like a bitch, and his mood was in the crapper. All he wanted was a cup—or ten—of coffee and a little peace before he started work. A Styrofoam cup hit him in the head, pulling him up short.

"What the hell?" he bellowed, then grimaced at the pain lancing his brain. Christ, even the sound of his own voice hurt. It was going to be a long motherfucker of a day.

"Advil and water are on your desk," Jamie said, his voice laced with humor.

Hollywood ignored his friend as he downed the miracle drug, emptying the bottle of water. He could drink a river right about now. "How'd you know?" he grumbled, easing into his chair. Best to keep sudden movements to a minimum.

"Chad. He texted me fifteen minutes ago."

On hearing his roommate's name, Hollywood's gut clenched and something a little lower stirred. Really? He turned his back to Jamie and stared down at his crotch, willing it to behave. "What'd he say?"

"Just that you'd had an argument with your dad and then drowned your sorrows in beer."

"Should've stuck to Grey Goose." Beer jammed up his sinuses.

"Want to talk about it?" Jamie asked.

"Not at seven thirty in the morning."

There was the scrape of a drawer closing, then footsteps behind him. A pile of folders landed on his desk with a thud. Personnel files. "Shit. Evaluations already?"

"Yep." Jamie cackled evilly, or maybe that's just how it sounded to Hollywood. Jamie squeezed Hollywood's shoulder lightly. "If you want to talk later, call me. I'll come back during your break."

Hollywood glanced over his shoulder. "Thanks, man." He wouldn't call Jamie though. What would he say? *I think I'm gay for your baby brother?* Yeah, that would go over real well.

Jamie was protective of all his siblings, and he'd lose his shit for sure if he knew what was going on between him and Chad. Hollywood wouldn't blame him. He was no catch for anyone—male or female. Groaning, he dropped his head onto the desk.

There was the squeak of their shitty office chairs. Damn. Did Jamie just—

"On second thought," Jamie said, answering Hollywood's question. "I'm not leaving here until you tell me what the hell is going on."

"I'm hungover."

"Besides that, asshole. How'd you get that bruise on your jaw?"

"Like Chad said, I had a fight with my dad, then got drunk. End of story."

Jamie swung Hollywood's chair around and scooched his own forward until their knees almost touched. They'd often sat close when discussing painful issues, and never had Hollywood felt any stirrings for Jamie. He loved the guy like a brother. That was it. So why did Chad light his whole body on fire?

"Talk to me, man. You know you can tell me anything. I wouldn't have made it through my problems with Rickie without you."

He couldn't tell him everything, but maybe he could tell him this.

"Have you ever felt like maybe your whole life was a lie?"

Jamie frowned and rested his elbows on his knees. "I'm not sure what you mean."

Hollywood watched his friend closely. "What if you thought you were one thing, but then it turned out you were something else? Or if someone you knew turned out to be different than you thought?"

"I still don't get it."

"Like when Chad came out. All those years, you'd thought he was straight, but he wasn't."

Jamie smiled slowly and shook his head. "I think I always knew."

"How?"

"It's not like he was into dresses and dolls or anything like that. I'm not sure what it was. He just seemed… different."

Okay, well this conversation wasn't going anywhere. "Forget it. I'm being stupid."

Jamie stood and crossed his arms, peering down at Hollywood as though debating something in his mind. Finally, he spoke. "There's something I've never told you. It might help with this discussion."

The seriousness of Jamie's tone had Hollywood sitting up straight. "I'm listening."

"Last summer, after Rickie and I got back together but were still having trouble, you and I talked. Do you remember?"

"Yeah." The conversation was clear in his mind. He'd felt certain he'd crossed some line that day and ruined their friendship. "I suggested that some women… Erica… might like it rough."

Jamie smiled. "Turns out, we do. We're into BDSM."

BDSM? Hollywood's brows popped. "Like whips and stuff?"

"We haven't tried whips yet, but yes."

"I assume you're the…" He trailed off, unsure what to call it.

"The dominant, yes."

"And Erica is submissive? I never pictured her that way. She's so proud and independent."

"Oh she is. But she also likes to give me control. That way she can relax and do the things she enjoys without feeling pressured."

"Only in bed, right?"

Jamie scrubbed his cheek. "We've recently begun a 24/7 service relationship."

"Service? Like some sort of servant or slave?"

"Not exactly. We have an agreement about things she needs to do—how and when—and consequences if she doesn't do them."

"Wow."

"Yeah." Jamie rubbed the back of his neck. "Is this a good example of what you were asking me?"

"Definitely." Never in a million years would he have thought that his best friend and his wife would be into this kind of thing. He'd heard a little about this type of kink. Still, it was hard to imagine anyone wanting something like that in this day and age. "What does she call you?"

"'Sir.'" Jamie's lips quirked, and his face took on a dark gleam. "Sometimes 'Master.'"

"And you both like this?" He didn't care what people did to get off, as long as it was consensual.

"Love it." Jamie blinked and the gleam disappeared. "Does this change how you see me? How you see Rickie?"

Hollywood chuckled. "No. As long as you don't expect me to call you 'Sir.'"

"Ha-ha." Jamie sat in his chair again. "So, now can you tell me what's bothering you?"

Could he? He really wanted to tell Jamie all his thoughts, his fears. They could hash it out together and figure out if Hollywood was gay or not. As long as he never mentioned Chad.

"Did you ever experiment when you were little? Play doctor or something?" Hollywood asked.

"Sure. Don't all kids?"

"With girls?"

"Yeah."

"What about boys? Ever play doctor with them?" Hollywood pushed. If Jamie, who was as hetero as they came, had experimented with boys, then maybe there was still hope for Hollywood's case.

Jamie's eyes narrowed and flicked around the room. "I'm trying to remember. I had brothers, so other boys' bodies and the mysteries of the erection weren't so mysterious to me. Hell one of us was always popping wood. We just laughed about it. Girls, on the other hand? Now they fascinated me." He shrugged. "What about you?"

"I hadn't thought I'd played at all, but it turns out I did."

Jamie suddenly burst into laughter. "Oh my God. I'd forgotten all about the day I caught Chad and Tori hiding behind the shed with the kid who lived next door. They couldn't have been older than five or six. Chad and the boy had their shorts around their knees and they were having a contest to see who could get their penis to rise fastest. Tori was shouting and clapping. It was her cheering that caught my attention."

Hollywood snorted. "Who won?"

"Chad, of course. The kid's a Caldwell through and through."

"What'd you say to them?"

"To pull their pants up, and that stuff like that wasn't supposed to be a spectator sport. Although, now that I think about it... I was wrong about that." Jamie grinned. "Anyway, it was funny as hell."

Hollywood got up and smacked Jamie on the back good-naturedly. "Thanks for the talk, man. I feel a lot better now," he lied.

Last night's conversation with Chad replayed in his mind. Chad had promised to let Hollywood kiss him in three days if he still wanted to. That day couldn't come fast enough. Every time he thought of Chad's words and the look on his face when he'd said, "I'll let you have it," his cock hardened.

So, yeah, maybe all kids were curious and experimented. It didn't have to mean anything. But lusting after a grown man? That *did*.

And there was no denying it.

CHAPTER 9

Slow days are the absolute fucking worst.

Give him a rash of calls, a shift where they barely set foot inside the fire station, and Hollywood was a happy man. He needed to be on the move, focused on saving the next victim, instead of focused on Chad.

Why couldn't he get the guy out of his head? Could an aneurysm make you suddenly attracted to your best friend's little brother? Maybe he should go see a doctor.

"Arrrgh!" He threw the tennis ball he'd been lightly bouncing off the wall with as much force as he could. It careened off his office wall, hit the ceiling, and ricocheted toward the wall behind him.

"Shit!" There was a shout and then a grunt as a gorgeous dark-haired guy grabbed onto his arm.

"Chad?"

Of course it was Chad. Who else would have his pulse revving like a probie's at his first fire? He gripped Chad's other arm to steady him. "Sorry about that."

"Do you greet all your visitors with a tennis ball to the head?" Chad asked.

Seriously, did the guy have to look so damn good in his paramedic uniform? Those navy pants, crisp white shirt, and navy jacket had never fit so well on anyone else. Had they been tailored for him?

"Hollywood." Chad snapped his fingers in front of Hollywood's face, and realizing he'd been staring, Hollywood quickly moved away. He pulled out a second chair.

"You okay?" he asked.

Chad rubbed his brow where a red mark had already appeared. "I'm fine. I think I should be asking you that question though."

"I—I was just letting off some steam." Hollywood looked through the window in his office door. "Where's Liam?" Chad was clearly on shift, so his partner couldn't be too far off.

"He's in the beanery with the guys." Chad held up a bag from a fancy downtown restaurant. Hollywood had heard of it, but had never visited. "I figured since I brought you dinner, he could have your share of whatever Sawyer's making."

Hollywood's stomach rumbled at the mention of his team member's cooking. "Oh man, I love that spicy chicken chili."

Chad pushed the second chair back to its place. "Oh, I didn't mean to keep you away from Sawyer's whatever."

"No!" Hollywood gripped Chad's wrist. "Stay."

Chad arched a brow and looked down to where Hollywood held his arm.

Hollywood let go. "Shit, I didn't mean it like that. Stay. Have dinner with me. I could use a break."

"You sure?"

He nodded. "Please."

After a moment's silence, Chad set the bag of food on Hollywood's desk and pulled up the second chair. They sat and Hollywood breathed in the scent of Chad's cologne while the guy chatted away about the Chinese food he'd brought. The words flowed over Hollywood like a warm breeze, flavored by the dark woodsy fragrance Chad wore.

He'd always hated the cloying stench of perfume, but what Chad had on really worked. He found himself leaning closer to the guy and inhaling deeply. His pulse sped up.

Chad stopped talking. He tilted his head to the side, a crease between his brows. "You sure you're okay? How's your head?"

As casually as possible, Hollywood sat back, putting as much distance as was polite between him and that intoxicating scent that was doing such strange things to him. "Better. Thanks for giving Jamie a heads-up. That Advil was exactly what I needed."

Drawing his paper plate closer, Chad expertly wielded his chopsticks to pick up a piece of General Tso's chicken. "How much do you remember about last night?" He put the chicken in his mouth, his full lips closing around the wooden sticks. Hollywood barely managed to stifle a groan.

He focused on piling food onto his plate from the take-out cartons on the desk. What had Chad asked? Oh, last night. The disjointed memories came back to him, and there was no way to hide his embarrassment as the skin between his T-shirt and his hair started to heat up.

Chad's sigh was the loudest sound in the room. "Look, man. You were drunk. It was nothing."

But it wasn't nothing. He'd asked Chad to kiss him. He'd really wanted it. Even now, Hollywood had a fluttery feeling in his stomach. What was that? Butterflies. Fuck. He had butterflies in his stomach. For a guy. For Chad.

Or was he just hungry?

Determined to ease the tension in the room, he grinned at Chad and began scarfing down his food. If he ate, the odd sensations in his stomach would go away, right?

Chad ate much more slowly, shooting concerned glances at him. After a few minutes, as though having made his own resolution, Chad began talking about Liam, and about the guys on Hollywood's platoon that he knew. Light banter. Inconsequential stuff. Hollywood appreciated the effort to distract him, even if all it did was increase the swarming of butterflies in his stomach.

The food wasn't helping either. Chad had left him a chance, an opening to laugh the whole night off as a drunken mistake. Or he could man up and tell the truth.

"I meant what I said last night. I want to kiss you."

Chad set down his chopsticks and fixed his gaze on the remnants of food in his plate. "You do? Even now?"

Hollywood eyed him up and down, took in the uniform, the width of his shoulders, his strong arms, his narrow waist and hips. His throat tightened and his cock filled. When he spoke his voice was strained with desire. "Hell yeah."

Chad's throat worked as he drank deeply from a bottle of water, his Adam's apple sliding down then back up. Hollywood had the weirdest urge to lick it, to follow its movements with his tongue.

Whoa! He swiped his plate off the table and got up to toss it in the trash bin next to the door.

"I won't kiss you drunk," Chad said quietly.

Hollywood stayed facing the door. "I'm not drunk now."

Shit, why had he said that? He was at work, for fuck's sake. Leaning forward, he banged his head on the wall. A hand on his shoulder pulled him away. "Hey, stop that. You're going to hurt yourself."

The worry and concern in Chad's voice warmed him and made him feel like shit at the same time. And now that he thought about it, as incredible as it sounded, maybe Chad wasn't attracted to him. Maybe that's why he kept putting off the kiss. What an arrogant fool he was.

Chad must have seen some of his thoughts in his expression. He punched out his hip, traced his hand down Hollywood's chest, and tossed him a saucy smile. "Honey, you are one hot-as-fuck fireman. Who wouldn't want to kiss you?"

Deciding to play Chad's game, Hollywood blew on his nails and buffed them on his SFD shirt. "Well... that would be no one. The fire bunnies actually line up."

Something flickered in Chad's eyes. He blinked and it disappeared.

"Thanks for coming by," Hollywood said, meaning it. He'd put Chad in a tough position with this whole kissing thing. He was acting like it was some sort of dare, but to Chad it was real. It was his life. "I'm sorry about last night. About pushing you."

Chad raised his hand, hesitated, then pressed Hollywood's shoulder.

"I've never even thought about guys that way. Well... not since Bobby, and it's fucking with my head."

"I have to ask, Hollywood. Are you sure you've never gotten even a tingle before? Never looked at an actor or a rock star or any guy and wondered what it would be like? Never found another guy attractive?" The doubt in Chad's voice was as clear as a fire-station alarm in the middle of the night.

Hollywood shrugged and went to sit on the edge of his desk. He'd thought about this during his long boring shift. "Not really. I mean no more than anyone else."

"What do you mean?"

"You know. There're some people everyone agrees are hot. Like..." He paused, searching his memory. "Like Hugh Jackman... or Jake Gyllenhaal."

"Jake Gyllenhaal, huh? What movie did you see him in? Bet it wasn't *Brokeback Mountain*," Chad said with a chuckle.

"You'd be out some cash then."

Chad looked so stunned, Hollywood thought he'd have to pick the guy off the floor.

"What? It won three freaking Academy Awards." Hollywood raised his hands and rubbed his head. "A lot of people saw it."

"Okay." Chad widened his eyes in some twisted mockery of an innocent expression. "What did you think of it?"

"Didn't like the ending, that's for sure. Those guys deserved to be happy."

Chad crossed his arms and paced back and forth between the two desks on either side of the room. Hollywood watched him warily from his perch. "You *really* don't have a problem with gay people? Marriage equality?"

Hollywood blew out a breath. "I already told you no." Why didn't Chad believe him? As far as Hollywood knew, he'd never done or said anything to contradict that. But then he remembered how Chad always used to get nervous around him. Chad had even admitted he'd thought Hollywood hated him for being gay, which couldn't be farther from the truth.

What was the truth exactly? Why had he always felt so off around Chad? Had he always been a little attracted to the guy? Fuck. Chad was eleven years younger than him. When they'd first met, he'd been in fifth grade. Still a kid. The age difference, although big, didn't matter so much now. But then? It would have been statutory rape. He swallowed down the nasty taste in his mouth.

Chad stopped in front of him. "How did watching Jack and Ennis kiss and have sex make you feel?"

That question had him squirming. How had he felt? Certainly not disgusted. Both men had been attractive, rugged cowboys, and seeing them fall in love had been... fascinating. But the hell they'd gone through had turned his stomach, for reasons he hadn't fully understood at the time. But now.... He could totally understand not being able to have the person you loved for fear of retribution. Fear of having your ass kicked or even being killed. But that was a little too much honesty for this conversation. "I felt happy for them."

"Did it turn you on?"

Hollywood looked down at his feet, anything to avoid Chad's probing gaze. "I don't think so."

"You don't *think* so?"

"It was a long time ago. I don't remember."

"Had you been drinking?"

Hollywood glared at him. "No, why?"

Chad rolled his eyes. "Why else wouldn't you remember? Or do you watch a lot of gay movies?"

"Fuck you, Caldwell."

"Only if you're lucky, Wright. Really lucky."

Warmth pooled in regions south of his belt, but Hollywood played it cool and rolled his eyes. Chad's suggestion sounded good, but the positions were reversed.

Chad tapped a finger on his chin. "Here's a test for you. Tomorrow, when you get home from work, watch a gay porn video. After that, if you still want to kiss me, to see if you like it, I'll keep my end of the bargain."

The previous night, Chad had told him three days. That would put the kiss on the night of Chad's performance. God, he couldn't wait to know one way or the other.

Hollywood smiled. "Deal."

80 🚊 ०३

Tired and hungry, Hollywood inspected the renovations to his apartment. The kitchen had been redone with new cabinets and floor tiles. The water from the sprinkler had ruined the wall-to-wall carpeting, which had to be changed, along with about twelve inches of drywall throughout the entire apartment.

The company he'd hired to do the initial drying and removal had done a great job of rescuing his furniture, clothing, and artwork. Thankfully, his books and vinyl albums had been in a cabinet with doors and hadn't been touched by the water or smoke. Every curtain, every sheet, every bit of upholstery, and article of clothing had needed to be professionally cleaned to get the stench of smoke out.

Most of the hard work was now done. Tomorrow, a team would come in to paint the entire place, and on Monday, he'd be getting his new carpeting. The super would oversee the work while Hollywood was on shift.

Thank fuck he had good insurance, or this fiasco would have set him back several years in savings. He made decent money at the SFD, but not decent enough to have tens of thousands of dollars lying around. Especially when he was still paying the mortgage on the sixteen-unit building he'd purchased six years prior. Rents took care of most of the expenses, but every year there were emergencies, things he had to pay out of pocket, like the sizable deductible he'd had to shell out before the insurance company ponied up a dime.

He was looking forward to having his apartment back, his privacy. Not that Chad hadn't been a great host. The guy had gone out of his way to make Hollywood feel at home. They'd hung out and watched movies a few times and had eaten some meals together. And as incredible as it seemed, Hollywood was getting used to it. Used to seeing Chad's shoes by the door, his *Men's Health* magazines on the coffee table. Even his dumb single-serving coffee machine on the kitchen counter with the silly rotating pod holder next to it, a holder that had become progressively more filled with the brand of coffee Hollywood preferred.

Maybe if he got away from Chad, put some distance between them, he wouldn't feel so conflicted and confused. The guy did things to him. Made him feel things he shouldn't—not if he were straight as he'd always thought he was.

That brought him right back to the damn test Chad had proposed. For the past twenty hours, he hadn't been able to think about anything else. What if he watched some gay porn and liked it?

The very idea of a positive response to that question had him shaking. It would knock down the foundation of his existence, destroy everything he knew about himself. He loved women, loved their bodies, their voices, their smells. But what if he liked men too? What if it wasn't only a fluke thing with Chad? What if it was?

God, he had to get out of here. Scooping up his jacket, he opted for the stairs and raced out to the parking lot, sucking in deep breaths of sea-scented air. His building in West Seattle was just far enough from the

71

main downtown core to be affordable, yet close enough to the bay that he could easily go there to jog on the waterside paths, and be only ten minutes away from Station 44, located in the heart of the SoDo district.

Chad's condo was a short drive from Hollywood's place, but it was a world away in terms of style. Located in Belltown, it was in a newer building that also housed a fitness center, rooftop garden, and swimming pool. Not to mention that Chad's place had large picture windows that encompassed one entire wall of his living room, bringing the bay to his doorstep.

Hollywood knew from Jamie that thanks to William's skill with investments, the whole Caldwell family was now very financially comfortable, which explained how a twenty-five-year-old paramedic could afford such a nice place on his own.

After circling around to find an empty parking spot on the busy street, Hollywood finally let himself into Chad's condo. The place was silent, beautiful, and empty. Perfect. He took a quick shower while heating up some frozen lasagna, then settled in to watch the news on CNN as he ate.

Once his belly was full and the news had circled into a repeat of the day's headlines, he knew it was time. His cock stirred, and he slapped at it in irritation. "Let me make up my own fucking mind, you dirty bastard," he said out loud. Great, now he was really losing it.

Like most men, he enjoyed watching porn. And so what if he sometimes spiced things up with a two-girl–one-guy or even a two-guy–one-girl combo? Regardless of the combination, there was always at least one guy in those videos. A guy who wasn't him, and that had never been a problem. If it was, every man in America would be considered gay. Truth was, guys liked to watch. They liked to see women getting fucked, and it had nothing to do with who was doing the fucking. This would be exactly the same thing. Someone would be doing the fucking and someone would be getting fucked. No difference.

Okay. He took a few deep breaths as he sat at the desk in Chad's spare room and turned on his laptop. He signed into his PornHub account and searched for something to watch. When the search list came up, he shot to his feet and paced around the room for a few minutes to clear his brain. After he'd calmed down, he returned to his seat and quickly skipped over anything BDSM or with more than two guys. He wasn't ready for something hardcore. What he wanted was something normal. Two decent-looking guys who got together and fucked in a normal way.

Damn. When had two guys having sex become normal in his mind? A memory of him and Bobby surfaced. He swallowed against the sudden dryness in his mouth when Bobby's face became Chad's. Fuck! He punched the keys on his laptop to start one of the videos. A guy was dressed like a motorcycle cop: mirror shades, tight pants shoved into knee-high boots, a leather jacket, and a gun holster at his waist next to a fake-looking badge.

A second guy, young and fashionably dressed, sat in a black Porsche. He smiled nervously up at the cop. "What's the problem, officer?"

"Right taillight's out." The cop's voice was strong, filled with authority.

The younger man's eyes flashed and his cheeks flushed. "I'll get it fixed."

"Still, I have to give you a ticket," the cop said, before lowering his sunglasses on his nose. "Unless you have some other way to make up for wasting my time?"

The camera panned out, showing the dark, secluded alley. Hollywood scoffed at the silliness of the setup. That didn't keep him from leaning forward to catch the younger man's response.

"I'm told I have a smart mouth."

The cop nodded and opened the car door. "We can start with that."

Hollywood fisted his hands and grimaced when his nails left red crescents on his palms. His heart sped up in anticipation of what was coming. He'd seen guys getting blow jobs in porn before. There was nothing wrong with enjoying it.

The driver got out of the car and immediately dropped to his knees. He unzipped the cop's pants and took out his long, thick dick.

Hollywood could see it and the younger man's face reflected in the cop's shades as the driver took the exposed cock into his mouth. The cop's hands went to the driver's hair, gripping it in curled fingers. The younger man's tongue swirled around the purple mushroom head, licking up the pre-cum, his eyes glazing over at the taste. Both men moaned in pleasure.

Hollywood's cock stirred a little, no more than was expected, as he imagined a mouth closing over it. The heat, the wetness, the tightness. God, he loved a good tease.

Before long, the cop pulled on the guy's hair, forcing him to stand. They exchanged a long look, then the cop sneered and shoved the younger man face-first against the wall. "I gotta frisk you. You look like you're carrying."

Hollywood would have laughed at the corny line if he'd had any saliva left in his mouth. But the cop's rough actions, the way he pushed the other man against the bricks and spread his legs with sharp kicks, awakened something in him. He was suddenly aware of his ragged breathing and how aroused he was by the aggressive display.

The cop's hands went to the younger man's shirt, ripping it off him. His fingers touched every inch of tan skin as the guy pressed his ass into the cop's groin. The cop licked the side of the guy's neck, smirking when he moaned. He stepped back. "I'm gonna have to do a strip search."

"Yes, officer," the other guy said, wiggling his ass.

The cop quickly undid the guy's pants, revealing two firm, rounded cheeks. He slapped one hard, leaving an angry red handprint. The driver groaned. The sound, low and needy, made the pressure in Hollywood's gut coil.

"For that, you're going to submit to a cavity search."

"No, sir. No. Please, don't."

The guy protested, but even Hollywood could see he was begging for it. He'd lifted onto his toes and arched his back, making his ass stick out. The cop parted the guy's cheeks, exposing the dusky asshole to the camera. He stuck a finger in his mouth and plunged it into the guy's fluttering hole. The driver's hands clawed at the brick wall as he groaned.

Throughout the whole thing, the officer continued making vaguely cop-like statements, all of which were heavy with sexual innuendo. The power inequality was fascinating.

Soon a second and third finger joined the first, stretching the hole until the skin around it turned white. Hollywood winced. How would the guy handle the cop's big cock?

No slouch himself in the dick department, Hollywood had only had anal sex with a few girls, and then only because they'd claimed to enjoy it, saying they'd had it often. It must have been true because they certainly hadn't complained despite the tight-as-hell fit.

And the young guy? He wasn't complaining either. The camera kept zooming in on him, showing his neck cords sticking out prominently as he gritted his teeth. The cop took his fingers out, then positioned himself behind the slightly taller but thinner, younger man. With one hand he gripped a shoulder, the other guided his cock to the guy's hole.

Hollywood could barely watch as the cop's dick disappeared into the other man's ass. The younger man grunted and closed his eyes as his fingers scrabbled for purchase. The cop pushed all the way in, then stilled. He was fully dressed, while the other man was completely naked. The driver was all lithe muscles and tan skin. After a moment, he blew out and wiggled his hips.

"Tell me what you want," the cop ordered, his mouth at the other man's ear. Hollywood shivered.

"Your big cock. Give it all to me. Fuck me."

"I'm here to serve," the cop said, smirking. Gripping the guy's hips, he began a strong hard rhythm of pounding the guy's ass, then pulling all the way out before driving in again. The younger man's face was plastered against the brick wall as he grunted and pushed back against the cock drilling into him.

It was violent, primal. Two strong men locked in a battle of wills. It was unlike anything Hollywood had ever seen outside of a UFC cage fight. The men's faces were red, their skin covered in sweat, their movements animalistic.

Proud of himself for having watched the scene without having any untoward reaction, Hollywood was about to turn off the video when the cop pulled his dick out of the younger man's body. It was thick and purple, slick and shiny from his spit and pre-cum. Wrapping his hand around it, the cop leaned back and stroked it several times before shooting a long rope of cum onto the back in front of him. When it hit, the younger man screamed as though burned, and thrust his hips forward, painting the wall with his load.

Jesus. Fuck.

Hollywood gaped at the sight of both men coming, the ejaculate shooting from their hard dicks. The connection between the two grew tender as the cop gathered the other man into his arms and licked the cum off his back, before turning him around in his arms and kissing him deeply.

Hollywood's hard as rock cock pushed against his zipper, demanding attention. His temperature soared and his mind shattered. "Oh, God. Oh, God."

As fast as he could, he switched to a video he'd watched many times before. The woman was a hugely breasted brunette. Fast-forwarding through the preliminaries, he started the video at the point where the guy spread her legs wide, exposing her glistening, bare pussy to the camera.

Zipper down, cock out, Hollywood barely managed to pull off a few strokes before he came all over himself.

Panting, he dropped back in the chair and let his head hang over the low seatback. It wasn't the gay video that had turned him on. It had been the timing. He'd needed to come. That was all. It was the woman's breasts and pussy that had thrown him over the edge.

Along with her dark hair and blue eyes.

But as the cum cooled on his fingers, Hollywood had to admit the undeniable: he was totally and completely fucked.

CHAPTER 10

Standing in the dressing room of Bar None on the night of the big event, Chad started to freak. "What do you mean you can't make it?"

Steven, the bassist of Proud, the band scheduled to back up all the entertainment for tonight's fundraiser, let out a groan. "I'm really sick, dude. Been barfing all day."

Even over the phone, Chad could hear the guy's teeth chattering. His professional instincts took over. "Have you seen a doctor?"

"I'll be fine."

"If you've got a fever and you're puking, go to the ER."

"No, I'm—"

"Steven, I'm a paramedic. I know what I'm talking about. Get your ass to the ER and call me. If I don't hear from you in an hour, I'm calling 911." Vomiting and fever could be a sign of the flu or something worse. Either way, he might need to be given fluids to prevent dehydration. Chad wouldn't be comfortable until he heard that a doctor had examined the guy.

"All right. All right. I'm really sorry to leave you hanging."

"You know anyone who can replace you?"

"I've called around, but everyone's booked. It being so close to Christmas and all."

Chad rubbed his temple and looked around for a bottle of Advil. "Don't worry. I'll figure something out. Call me. One hour." He broke the connection and tossed the phone onto the low table in front of him. How could they perform without a bassist? They had about ten acts lined up tonight, and this show meant so much to everyone.

A tap on the door interrupted his thoughts. Shit. He should have left the door open for the other performers. They'd need to start getting ready soon.

"Come in," he called out.

Austin poked his head in, frowning when he caught sight of Chad. "You look like your prized horse just took a dump in your favorite hat."

Despite his pissy mood, Chad cracked a smile. "I don't have a horse."

"You're hung like one."

Chad tossed a throw pillow at his friend's head. "Shut up."

"You gonna tell me what's wrong, or do I gotta pry it outta ya?" The thickening of Austin's Texas accent was a sure sign of his concern. Austin was a great person to brainstorm with, so Chad spilled.

"Steven's sick. I've got two and a half hours to find a replacement bassist or we're screwed."

"None of the guys in the band have a buddy who could—"

Chad shook his head. "It's the holiday season."

"Shit."

"Yeah."

Suddenly Austin's face lit up, then his eyes flicked toward Chad and he frowned.

"What?"

"Nothing. I know a guy, but..."

"But what? I'm fucking desperate, man."

"I don't know if he'll be agreeable to helpin' you out."

Chad shoulders slumped. "He doesn't like gays?"

"Oh, he likes them well enough." He smiled. "In fact, he even plays at Boyzville sometimes."

The musicians at Boyzville were always top-notch. "Then what's the issue?"

Austin remained silent.

"Oh for fuck's sake," Chad said, climbing to his feet. "Why'd you bring him up if you don't want to tell me who he is?"

"This would be good for him."

"Great. Give me his name."

"How prepared are ya to grovel?"

Grovel? "Who the hell is this guy?"

"Harry."

Chad's eyes seemed to want to part from their sockets. He flopped down onto the couch. "Harry? As in blond, brown eyes, short?"

"One and the same."

"Let me see if I've got this right. The only bassist in town who might be available tonight is a guy I fucked in the backroom of Boyzville?"

Austin grinned. "Yes, sir."

"Shit."

Twenty minutes later, after having called the club and convinced the manager to give him Harry's phone number, Chad had texted him and managed to get him to agree to meet at a coffee shop near his place. Chad hadn't said why, just that they needed to talk. He hadn't wanted to ask on the phone. Proper groveling required being face-to-face.

Squaring his shoulders, Chad pushed open the door to the small café. A bell tinkled above his head. He'd never been to this place before, but he immediately liked the cozy atmosphere and the scent of coffee beans and baked goods.

Toward the back, he spotted Harry sitting alone at a small table. The guy's eyes were wary, his jaw set. Chad weaved his way through the tables and stopped behind the empty seat facing Harry. "Thank you for agreeing to see me."

Harry pursed his lips. "I'm not sure why I did."

Chad understood the guy's anger even if he was a little surprised by it. Hooking up for a quick fuck was pretty common in the gay community. No one expected anything from it other than a release, a see ya later, and both men went on their way. Maybe Harry had felt bad about their encounter because Chad had.

Or maybe it's because you used him. Treated him like he was nobody.

Chad indicated the empty seat. "Mind if I sit?"

"Might as well."

Shrugging off his jacket, he placed it on the back of the chair and sat. "Before we get to why I asked you here, I want to apologize for..." He paused and glanced away. This was fucking embarrassing. "For how I acted when—"

Eyes hard, Harry cut him off. "When you fucked me."

"Yes."

Harry sipped his coffee, his slender fingers tightening around the cup.

"What I did was wrong," Chad admitted. "I shouldn't have done that to you or... or anyone else."

Tilting his head, Harry met his gaze. "It *was* pretty shitty."

"I know. It wasn't my intention to do that. I never mean to hurt you. It's just—something changed at some point and..." God. He had no idea how to explain what had happened.

"I became someone else." Harry smiled at him, a sad curve of his lips that let Chad see far more than he'd wanted to. He'd really hurt the kid.

"I feel awful."

"I know you do. That's why I showed up." He exhaled. "Is this guy worth it?"

Chad wanted to pretend that he didn't understand Harry's question, but after what they'd been through together, he couldn't bring himself to lie to the guy again. "He's straight."

"Dude. Straight-straight or straight-slightly bent?"

Chad chuckled. "We're trying to figure that out."

"I hope it works out for you. I fell for my straight best friend in high school. We haven't spoken since." Harry cleared his throat as emotions chased each other in his eyes.

"Ouch. So that was last year?" Chad teased.

"Fuck off. I'm twenty-one."

Chad had thought as much since he'd been selling shots at Boyzville, but it never hurt to confirm.

Harry took another slow sip of his coffee and carefully set the cup back down. "So, what was the other thing you wanted to talk about?"

"Oh right." Chad checked his watch and winced at how much time had passed. "I hear you play bass."

Harry's eyes brightened and his expression became delightfully animated. "Yeah, I play with the band at Boyzville when their regular guy can't." He grinned. "It's actually the main reason I took the job as shot boy."

"Not for all the hot guys looking to hook up?"

"That's just a fringe benefit," Harry said and winked.

Chad toyed with the salt and pepper shakers. He hoped his offer wouldn't make Harry think the apology had been a ploy to get him to cooperate. He'd meant it. "I'm one of the organizers of the LGBTQ fundraiser that's happening tonight at Due None. Our bassist called in sick and Austin, the friend who was with me that night"—he grimaced at the reminder—"he said he'd seen you play. I was hoping maybe you'd want to fill in? You'd be paid, of course."

"I won't take your money." Harry's stony expression made Chad feel twelve inches tall.

"Whatever you're thinking, please stop. This isn't a payoff. I did what I did, and I'm sorry. But tonight, you playing at this fundraiser? It has nothing to do with that."

Harry laughed. "What? You want to be *friends?*"

Chad was surprised to realize that yes, he did actually. "If you'll let me."

Harry squinted. "You're serious about tonight?"

"Very."

"When does it start?"

Chad looked at his watch again. "Just shy of one hour."

"One hour?" Harry stood up and frantically pulled on his jacket. "Oh my God. I have to go home, get my bass, change." He ran for the door.

"Wait," Chad called after him. "How will you get there?"

"I'll take a cab. Text me the address." Harry waved and disappeared through the door.

In the vortex left by his departure, Chad picked up Harry's coffee cup, which was still half-full, and sipped it cautiously. "Mmm." It was some mixture of coffee, caramel, and whipped cream heavenliness.

As he sat finishing off the coffee, trying to center himself before the craziness of the evening started, Chad attempted to sort out his feelings about Harry and what he'd done to the guy. Since that night, he'd tried to forget about it, but now, after having asked for forgiveness, he felt a million pounds lighter. He'd let his unrequited feelings for Hollywood turn him into someone he wasn't, someone who used other people with little regard for how his actions affected them.

He made a vow to himself, then and there: whatever did or didn't happen with Hollywood, he'd never let himself sink so low again.

80 🚋 ଓ

Hollywood stepped into the bar where Chad was going to perform and chafed his hands. The temperature had dropped, leaving Seattle shrouded in a cold, drizzly fog. But inside, things were warm and welcoming. Music played in the background as people milled around alone or in groups. Most of the tables were already taken. No problem. He'd grab a seat at the bar and unwind until Chad came on. He frowned, realizing Chad hadn't told him when he'd be performing, just to show up at seven. Removing his jacket, he slid onto a bar stool and ordered a Grey Goose on the rocks. He took a sip, then turned around to survey the room. Now that his eyes had adjusted to the dim light, he noticed the large banner above the stage: "Welcome to the Fifth Annual Seattle LGBTQ Fundraiser."

Huh. Chad hadn't asked him to buy a ticket or told him anything about a fundraiser. He'd only said to give his name at the door. Had the guy been worried Hollywood would refuse his invitation if he knew it was an LGBTQ fundraiser? He wouldn't have.

Hearing Chad sing was worth stepping out of his comfort zone.

Someone bumped his shoulder. Hollywood turned only to come face-to-face with an incredibly tall woman. "Hello there, handsome," she said with a wink.

The deep voice emerging from those expertly made-up lips startled Hollywood enough that his drink sloshed over the rim of his glass.

The woman—drag queen?—laughed uproariously at the shock that must have been on Hollywood's face. "Sugar, you're in for quite a night."

The bartender wiped the counter with a rag and shook his head. "Don't scare off the allies, Tom."

Tom? Hollywood looked back at the drag queen. She was perfectly put together, from her five-inch heels to her D-cup tits.

"You're a man?"

"All eight thick inches, sugar."

A hand slid onto his shoulder from the other side. This one small and clearly female. Or so he hoped. "Need a rescue, Hollywood?"

The sound of Tori's voice was like a balm to his brain. "Hey, gorgeous. Chad didn't tell me you'd be here." He gave her a hug and a kiss.

"Ooh! I'd like some of that too," Tom cooed. "Come on, sugar. Give Uncle Tom a kiss."

Adrenaline shot through Hollywood's system, and he tightened his grip on Tori's waist, pulling her closer as though he needed to reaffirm his sexuality. What the fuck was wrong with him? He had nothing to prove to anyone.

Tori giggled. "You're barking up the wrong tree, Tom."

"You sure about that, babycakes?"

She tugged on Hollywood's hand, pulling him to his feet, and said, "Oh, I'm sure. Come on, Hollywood. We've got a table near the stage."

"We?"

"The whole family's here. We try to support Chad any way we can. When he first came out, my mom and I joined PFLAG. It was very enlightening. So many LGBTQ kids are rejected by their families. We weren't going to let that happen to Chad."

Hollywood's throat closed as he remembered his own father's words. The man had rejected him for something he'd done when he was only ten. His father had taken an innocent exploration of sexuality and turned it into something vile and degenerate. Something that had fucked Hollywood up so badly, he'd blocked out the incident for over twenty-five years. "Chad's lucky to have you, your whole family."

"Oh no. We're the lucky ones. My twin is something really special. Wait until you see him perform!"

Tori's enthusiasm shone on her face, as did her unconditional love and acceptance. Hollywood couldn't even imagine what it must be like to have that.

When they arrived at the table, Drew and William greeted him with man-hugs and claps on the back. Dani kissed his cheek. "It's nice to see you, LT."

"How are things going at the training center?" Dani's suspension was over, but she hadn't yet returned to the rescue team. Instead, his father and his cronies had insisted that she join an ongoing in-house recruit-training program and finish with that class. At least she'd only have to do half of the grueling fifteen-week program.

She rolled her eyes. "I could teach those classes. In fact—"

"You have," he finished for her, making her laugh.

Jamie came up to them and gave him a fist bump. "Didn't expect to see you here."

"Funny that." Hollywood gave him a pointed look before turning to hug Erica.

She lightly touched the bruise on his jaw. "That looks like it hurts."

Hollywood glared at Jamie. Had he told Erica what Hollywood had shared with him in confidence? When Jamie's lips thinned and he gave an almost imperceptible shake of his head, Hollywood faked a smile and shrugged. "Hazards of the job. You know how it is." Then he smiled for real and indicated Erica's cute little baby bump. "So how far along are you now?"

"Almost fourteen weeks." Her face was radiant as she rubbed a hand over her abdomen. "The doctor says most of the risk is past now." Jamie put his arm around her and they exchanged a tender look.

"I'm really happy to hear that."

Caroline and Bill approached. He shook hands with Bill, then Caroline pulled him down for a kiss on the cheek. "So good to see you again, Hollywood. We missed you at Thanksgiving."

"Some of us have to work." He shot Jamie a teasing look and winked at Caroline.

Jamie crossed his arms. "Ha-ha. Very funny, as—"

Whatever he'd meant to say was cut off when Erica elbowed him in the ribs. "Jamie!"

Hollywood's heart warmed at the joy on the faces of these men and women he'd grown to consider family over the course of the past ten years. The only family he'd known since his mother's death.

Sheesh. Take him to a gay bar and he immediately turned maudlin.

Tori hooked her arm in his and led him to an empty seat between Austin and herself. Jamie and Erica were to Austin's left while Dani and William were to Tori's right. Her parents and Drew completed the circle.

Sucking back his dislike for the guy next to him, Hollywood held out his hand. "Austin."

"Lieutenant." Austin returned Hollywood's death grip. The guy's grin was arrogant, like he knew something Hollywood didn't. Whatever.

The lights dimmed and the music was turned off. A spotlight appeared, illuminating the man, Tom, he'd met at the bar. Hollywood couldn't get over how much the guy really looked like a woman. Had it not been for the voice, he'd never have guessed.

Tom gave a rundown of the events to come, and Hollywood was pleased to hear that Chad would be performing in the first set. If it got to be too much, Hollywood could leave during the break.

The waitress, a curvy blonde who flirted with all the men at the table, took their drink orders. Hollywood asked for a double vodka. He was going to need the reinforcements to make it through ninety minutes sitting next to the dark-haired cowboy.

"Scared yet?" Austin asked.

"Of what?"

Austin waved his hand around the room. "I'm sure this isn't your usual crowd. I doubt you'll find someone to take home with you. Unless you don't mind bisexual women."

Hollywood smiled. He'd had a few threesomes like that. "What's to mind?"

"What about a bisexual man?"

"Never been with one of those."

"You sure?"

Hollywood felt his dander going up. "What are you getting at, Austin?"

How much had Chad told his friend? Hollywood would kick Chad's ass if he'd told Austin about their deal. That was no one's business but theirs. He downed the rest of his drink, then caught the waitress's eye, signaling for a refill.

Austin took slow sips from what looked like a glass of whiskey. "I just meant that some guys swing both ways. There's nothin' wrong with that. You've probably been around guys like that and wouldn't know it unless they told you."

"Are you bi?" Hollywood had to ask. The guy didn't look gay at all.

He shrugged. "I've been with women, but I prefer men. Less drama."

"Less drama? Are you insane? From what I've seen, it's a lot easier to be straight than gay."

Austin stared at the two male dancers on stage. "That's true. Bein' openly gay isn't always easy, although it is gettin' better. I meant, you don't have to deal with the same issues you do with women: the courtin', the tickin' baby clock, the unexpected pregnancies, the jealousies, the monogamy—"

"Gay men aren't monogamous?" Hollywood cut in.

"A lot of 'em are, when they're in a committed relationship. Some have open relationships or invite thirds. But until it reaches the committed stage, there's no expectation of monogamy. Guys like sex. We're all guys, so we understand that sex doesn't have to mean a thing."

"Sounds nice."

Austin arched a brow. "Does it?"

The waitress arrived with his refill, and Hollywood downed half of it. Good thing she'd brought a double. "Thanks, sweetheart," he said, eyeing her ass as she walked away.

Onstage, a curtain lifted, revealing a band, consisting of a drummer, a keyboardist, a guitarist, and a bassist. They started to play, and two pretty women walked onto the stage, holding hands. They sang a cover of Mary Lambert's "She Keeps Me Warm." At the end, they gave each other a light kiss on the lips and walked off, waving to the applauding crowd. Again, Hollywood had to admit, he'd never have guessed the women were lesbians had he seen them apart. Neither fit the butch stereotype.

The next act was a burly man, who proceeded to tell, in a very comedic way, the story of his coming out as a trans man. The humor was bittersweet though. He joked about his ongoing struggles to be accepted as a man, including within the LGBTQ community, especially with gay men.

Hollywood leaned over to Tori, who had tears in her eyes. "What does 'cis' mean?" Given that she was working on a PhD in Psychology, he figured she was the best person to ask.

"It's a term that signifies someone was assigned a particular gender at birth and continues to identify by that same gender. For example, I'm a cis woman, you're a cis man. Gary"—she indicated the man on stage— "is a trans man. At birth he was assigned the female gender, but now identifies as a male."

"Huh. This is all new to me."

"Wait until we chat about intersex," she said, giving him a crooked smile that reminded him so much of her twin.

"Do I even want to ask?"

She patted his hand. "Not tonight."

Nodding, he turned back to the stage. The trans man finished his routine. The applause was loud, but Hollywood could see that for a large number of men their applause was nothing more than polite. Seemed that politics and infighting raged even within what could have been—should have been—a very tight-knit community.

The curtain rose again, exposing the band as four drag queens raced onstage. He was calling them this because they were so obviously men. As it turned out, it was a comedic routine. The group covered a medley of Beyoncé's "Put a Ring on It" and "If I Were a Boy."

As they were leaving the stage, Austin leaned into him. "Chad's up next."

"Uh... thanks." While Tom introduced Chad, detailing Chad's involvement with the fundraiser and the LGBTQ center, Hollywood signaled the waitress for another drink for him and a wine for Tori.

When Chad stepped onto the stage, the audience went wild. He was clearly a crowd-favorite. It was then that it hit Hollywood how little he really knew his roommate. He'd known Chad since the guy was in elementary school, but although Jamie had never hidden the fact that his little brother was gay, he never talked about it much either. It just was. He glanced at Jamie. The guy seemed relaxed. Completely at ease, completely unfazed by everything going on around them. So maybe Jamie's silence on the topic had been less about any discomfort he might have felt and more about his fear of Hollywood's reaction? Jamie had never invited him to a fundraiser or even asked him to donate. Were they not as good friends as Hollywood had thought? Man, that hurt.

Chad introduced the band members, giving a special shout-out to the blond bassist. He one-arm hugged the guy and thanked him for helping them out on short notice.

Hollywood frowned at the easy affection between the two men, who clearly knew each other. The guy, Harry, was barely legal, slender, and short. A twink. His cheeks heated at the memory of the young guy in the porn video he'd watched, and he quickly shoved those thoughts into that box in his mind that hid everything he refused to think about. Chad had told him he'd dated several twinks. So that must be his type. Hollywood looked wistfully down at his own bulk, then back to the blond onstage. Harry was certainly cute with his James Dean styled hair and full red lips.

Christ. His heart sped up at the direction his thoughts were taking. Why was he even noticing the kid's lips?

The music started, and Chad began to sing a slow version of "Mad World." He looked stunning in white jeans, combat boots, a blue T-shirt that matched his eyes, and an open white button-up that offered a glimpse of his leather choker and several silver necklaces of varying lengths. He wore that sexy blue nail polish and a few rings that Hollywood was too far away to see properly. His voice was haunting and powerful, and when he finished singing, the crowd went wild, demanding another song.

Tori whispered in his ear, "Thank you for the wine."

Hollywood hadn't even noticed the waitress deliver the drinks. He'd been too caught up in Chad's performance. "My pleasure," he said, shooting her a quick smile.

Chad conferred a moment with the band, then disappeared as a low-driving beat started. Harry took center stage, laying down the opening notes to The Who's "My Generation."

When Chad rejoined the band, he'd transformed into a veritable rock star. Jesus, the guy was sexy, with his shirt dipping low enough in front to show off his muscular chest. As he leaned forward, Hollywood caught a glimpse of dark chest hair and almost swallowed his tongue.

As he sang, Chad's perfect teeth shone in the lights and the thick eyeliner made his eyes look huge and bright. Hollywood's pulse pounded in his ears as he took in every sway, every shake of Chad's shoulders, every swing of his hips, the way he gripped the mic stand, the way he sang. Hollywood had never seen a man dance so smoothly, like a wave was going through his body.

Blood surged south and Hollywood shifted uncomfortably in his seat. Christ. His gaze darted over to Jamie. Had Jamie caught him staring?

Fuck he hoped not. Hollywood grabbed the vodka and took a healthy swig.

Austin bumped his shoulder. "Ever seen Chad perform before?"

Shaking his head, Hollywood took another sip. "Until a few weeks ago, I didn't even know he could sing."

"A lot of people say he should have tried to make a career out of it, but Chad loves being a firefighter and a paramedic too much."

"He could have made it," Hollywood insisted. "He's really good."

Austin nodded toward the stage. "Maybe he'll perform more, now that he's got Harry."

Hollywood swung his head toward Austin, the room spinning only a little. "What do you mean—*got* Harry?"

Had Chad found a boyfriend? He'd told Hollywood he was single. Hollywood's gut churned. Remembering what Austin had said about the openness of gay relationships, he asked, "Have they uh—" He stopped right there, unable to think the words, much less give voice to them.

"Been together?"

When Hollywood assented, Austin answered, "What do you think?"

Fuck. "Is it serious?"

"I don't know." Austin returned his gaze to the stage, where Chad and Harry were now dancing back to back, while Chad sang and Harry played. Their faces were bright with excitement. Chad gave Harry a sassy bump with his great ass before moving away. Harry followed him with a wistful look on his face. Hollywood was pretty sure it matched the one on his own.

Tori turned to him, pride for her brother clear in her expression. "I could watch him perform all night."

Me too. Hollywood finished off his drink. This kind of reasoning wasn't getting him anywhere. He had to stop all these fanciful ideas of kissing Chad. Chad was gay. Christ, he even had a boyfriend. And, more importantly, Hollywood was straight.

Keep telling yourself that, Wright.

Chad finished the song and thanked the audience and the band for a great time, letting them know he'd be back in the second set with another song.

Hollywood and the whole Caldwell clan stood, clapping and whistling. Chad glanced their way. His cheeks turned bright red, which only made everyone shout more.

Laughing and talking amongst themselves, they sat back down. They were all so proud and accepting of the youngest Caldwell boy. Chad didn't even realize what he had.

Hollywood bent over to whisper in Tori's ear. "Come to the bar with me? I need to stretch my legs."

She smiled up at him, then let Dani know where she was going. As Hollywood took her elbow, conversations stopped, and Hollywood could feel their eyes on his back, whether approving or disapproving, he wasn't sure. Nor did he care.

Tori was the Caldwells' little sister and they protected her like a princess. Hell, he'd been on enough date-spying expeditions with Jamie to know that. Even though he was a terrible catch for a twenty-five-year-old, it didn't matter. He didn't want to marry the girl. Didn't even want to fuck her. He cared too much about his balls for that. No, he just wanted to talk to her. Because it had to be *her* face he kept seeing in his mind. Her dark hair and big blue eyes he saw in his dreams. Her mouth he was kissing in his fantasies. Hers. *Not* Chad's.

So to cure this strange malady, he would talk to her for a while, see that she was too young for him. Too good and pure. Then he'd ask the cute waitress if she wanted to take him home.

℘ 🚃 ℆

Chad was flying high on endorphins and adrenaline. That set had been a blast. He clapped Harry on the back. "You were fucking awesome, man."

The other guys in the band joined in the congratulations. It was well-deserved. Not many bassists could integrate into a group with zero prep time and play so incredibly. "We may have to kick Steven out of the band and take you on instead," Randall, the leader, joked. But there was a flash of something in his eyes that said maybe it wasn't a joke after all.

Well, Chad would leave it to them to figure it out. "Come on. I want to introduce you to my family." Taking Harry's hand, he dragged him through the door leading out to the main floor.

When they neared the table, Chad's mom jumped out of her seat to hug him. "You were so wonderful, honey."

She kept kissing his cheeks and holding him close. He laughed. "Mom, I'm all sweaty."

"I don't care," she said, kissing him some more. Finally she let him go, and he introduced Harry.

"Mom, Dad, this is Harry Cooper." He went around the table, introducing Jamie and Erica, Drew, Dani, William, and Austin. Pride radiated off his family like heat off asphalt as they all took turns hugging and congratulating him. His eyes misted. He was so fucking lucky to have such a great family.

Harry stood shyly to the side. Not wanting his new friend to feel left out, Chad made to go to him, but his mother beat him to it. She took Harry's hand and sat him beside her. "I'm glad to meet you, Harry. You're a wonderful bassist. Is this your first time at the fundraiser?" And with that, they launched into a conversation. Chad could see Harry relaxing, and he loved his mom all the more for taking the kid under her wing. From what little he knew of the guy, he'd had it rough, and a little motherly attention would do him good.

He pointed to the empty seats beside Austin. "Where'd Hollywood and Tori go? I saw them sitting here earlier."

Austin rubbed his jaw, looking guilty.

Chad punched his arm. "What did you do?"

"May have told him you'd slept with Junior over there."

"Fuck. Why'd you have to go tell him that?"

"Reckoned if I made him jealous, he'd be bothered, and think about why he was bothered."

Chad sighed. His friend's twisted plan had some sort of logic to it. "I take it your little scheme backfired?"

"Yep." Austin hung his head. "He and your sister went that way." He indicated behind them to a crowded bar area with a hallway that led to the restrooms.

"I should probably go and thank them for coming."

As he got up to leave, Austin grabbed his arm. "Don't let this guy break your heart."

Chad acknowledged the warning with a dip of his head. He couldn't respond because the truth was, it was already too late.

Eyes peeled, he wandered into the back bar area, looking for the familiar broad shoulders and shock of blond hair. He scanned the tables, the barstools. Nothing. The guy hadn't left though, because his jacket was still hanging off the back of his chair. Chad didn't see Tori either. Okay, well, whatever. He'd go take a leak, then chat with his family for a few minutes before heading backstage. The second set would be starting in twenty minutes.

After shooting one last glance around the bar area, he headed for the restrooms. As he turned the corner leading into the passageway, he heard a deep voice, and spotted the broad shoulders and blond hair he'd been searching for. Hollywood had a woman pressed up against the wall, her face blocked by his big body.

"You enjoying the show, sweetheart?" Hollywood asked, and Chad's blood roiled at the term of endearment that probably meant Hollywood didn't know this conquest's name either.

The woman giggled, slipping her hands around Hollywood's waist. She leaned in close and whispered a response too low for Chad to hear. A pale hand with nails painted a delicate pink trailed up Hollywood's arm, his neck, and ended in his hair.

Hollywood pressed his thigh between the woman's legs. She moaned, pushing her hips against his pelvis, riding his big quad.

88

Jesus. Chad couldn't do this. He couldn't watch Hollywood with the woman, with anyone else. Not again.

The woman gripped Hollywood's head, dragging his mouth closer to hers. Chad clenched his fists, using the anger, the disappointment, to get his feet moving, to at least turn the fuck away.

"No. No. I can't—" Hollywood's slurred words stopped him dead in his tracks.

Chad turned back around. Hollywood was shaking his head. "No... your brother... I... we..."

An agonized look on his face, Hollywood jerked out of the woman's hold, and threw himself against the opposite wall. "Fuck."

"What does Jamie have to do with this?"

Chad's gaze flew back to the woman. It was Tori. Oh God. She hadn't seen him yet. Neither of them had, caught up in their own drama.

Tori tapped her chest. "I'm a twenty-five-year-old woman. I can kiss whoever the hell I want without my brother's permission."

Hollywood continued to slouch against the wall. His eyes closed, he said, "I'm sorry. I shouldn't have done this. I shouldn't have kissed you."

"You're damn right," she spat, glaring at him. "I can't believe even big bad Hollywood is afraid of Jamie."

When Hollywood opened his eyes, they were red-rimmed and slightly lost, but the regret that filled them was clear. Abruptly, Hollywood's head jerked in Chad's direction.

Goddamn. Chad really didn't want to deal with this tonight. But life was rarely about what you wanted. He stepped out of the shadows.

Hollywood's breath hitched visibly and his complexion paled. "I didn't mean... Shit." He shook his head and dropped his chin, the picture of dejection.

Chad turned away and gave his sister a pointed look. "Tori. Go back to the table."

She rolled her eyes. "You're giving me orders too?"

"Now," he said more forcefully. He had to get her out of there before he confronted Hollywood. Her head swiveled between Chad and Hollywood. Tori was smart and really good at reading people. God, he hoped she couldn't read this.

"What's going on here?" she asked, dashing his hopes.

"He hit on you," Chad said. "Crossed the line."

"What line would that be, Chad?" When he didn't respond, she moved directly in front of him and whispered, "The line where he kisses me instead of you?" Her hand cupped his cheek.

Chad swallowed, unable to voice all the dreams and fears clogging his throat.

She stroked his face. "You should have told me." Her eyes flicked

89

away and she gave him a brittle smile. "There was a time, not so long ago, when we used to tell each other everything. Now I barely know who you are."

Chad pulled his sister into a hug, burying his face in her hair. "This is all on me. I'll do better. We'll have lunch next week, okay?"

"Sure," she said, pulling away, her expression clearly saying she didn't believe him.

"I love you, Tori."

"I love you too." Throwing Hollywood a glare, she turned and reentered the bar area.

Chad sucked in a deep breath, feeling shittier than he had in a long time. He was so fucked up about his feelings for Hollywood that he'd pushed his whole family away. He crossed his arms and paced the hall as he tried to decide what to do. People kept passing them on their way to the restrooms and giving them strange looks. What they had to say to each other shouldn't have an audience. He met Hollywood's stare. "Follow me."

"Where to?"

"We need to talk." Chad looked around. "But not here."

Hollywood nodded and followed as Chad slipped through the back door. It was chilly out, but Chad had enough adrenaline flowing through his veins to keep him warm for a while. As they exited the building, Hollywood tripped on the stairs. Chad barely managed to catch him before he face-planted on the asphalt. Jesus, the guy was heavy. "You're drunk? Seriously? My entire family is here, and you get drunk and hit on my sister. Your *best* friend's sister. You're some piece of work, man."

A ripple went through Hollywood's body. He straightened his spine and puffed out his chest. It would have been a magnificent sight, under other circumstances. "So I had a little too much to drink. Big fucking deal. It's all your fault anyway."

"What?" Chad sputtered. "How is your sucking face with my sister my fault?" The ludicrousness of the statement was mind-numbing.

Hands on his head, Hollywood paced back and forth between Chad and the neighboring building like a caged lion. "I'm confused. It's your fault. You and your tight ass. Your tattoos. And don't get me started on your little twink boyfriend."

"My boyfriend?" There was no way Chad could follow Hollywood's leaps of logic.

"Fucking cowboy told me about it. You slept with Blondie. It was that same night with Candy, wasn't it?"

Chad clenched his jaw. "Sandy."

"Who the fuck cares?" Hollywood shouted.

"Why are you so upset?" Chad asked. "You're straight."

"I don't know what the fuck I am. You've got me watching gay porn. Fantasizing about—" Hollywood gnashed his teeth together and rubbed his face with both hands. The sound of his stubble scraping against his palms had Chad's heart rate shooting up. Even when he was a mess, Hollywood was hot.

"What do you fantasize about?" Chad couldn't help asking any more than he could help the rasp in his voice.

Hollywood stopped his pacing, hesitated, then advanced on Chad. Each step slow and deliberate. Chad sucked a breath into suddenly deflated lungs. Oh God. He was so fucking turned on. And what kind of slut did that make him? He didn't know if Hollywood was going to kiss him or beat the shit out of him. All he knew was that he needed to find out.

With rough movements, Hollywood grasped the sides of Chad's head. "I can't think of anything except kissing you. Your lips, are they soft or hard? How would your stubble feel against my skin? What do you taste like? It's driving me crazy." He stared into Chad's eyes. "*You* are driving me crazy."

Chad couldn't believe this was happening, tonight of all nights. He wanted to kiss Hollywood, and so much more. But... "We—we can't."

"Why not?" Hollywood got closer so their chests were touching. Chad inhaled the scent of Hollywood's skin, his soap, that delicious undernote that was his alone, and he shivered. If Hollywood pressed into him anymore, he'd know exactly how much Chad wanted him.

"You've had too much to drink. I can't be an experiment." His voice broke. He cleared his throat. "I can't be someone you just brush off as a drunken mistake."

"I'd never do that to you." Hollywood slid his fingers into Chad's hair, the gentle caress almost bringing him to his knees, a position he'd have been happy to assume were the circumstances right.

"You say that now, but what about tomorrow?"

Hollywood's lips curled into a pout that would have had Chad laughing if it hadn't been so sexy. "You promised. You said three days. Three days is now."

Every cell in his body craved more of Hollywood. Still, he shook his head. "No." They were both stronger than this.

"You can't make me wait anymore." Hollywood pressed their foreheads together and leaned his weight into Chad. His erection dug into Chad's belly.

"Oh God." Chad moaned and his hands went to Hollywood's shirt, pulling him in. "I don't want to wait either."

So much for being strong.

Hollywood's mouth crashed down on Chad's before the last syllable had even been pronounced. His tongue probed at Chad's lips, seeking entrance, which Chad denied until Hollywood bit his bottom lip hard. When Chad gasped in shock, Hollywood plunged inside. He held Chad's cheeks so tightly that Chad couldn't even turn his head. He was pressed against the wall, sandwiched between it and Hollywood's very large body. And he loved it. Except that—

This isn't right.

Hollywood was drunk, and this was going much too fast. Much too fast for a confused straight guy.

Un-twisting his fingers from Hollywood's shirt, Chad tried to push the other man back. Hollywood didn't budge. Not one inch. Jesus.

He tried again. When that didn't work, he attempted to wrest his mouth away as he jammed his palms against Hollywood's shoulders. Anything to get the guy's attention.

Releasing his lips, Hollywood gently twined his fingers through Chad's and pushed them against the wall above his head. Chad was used to being the bigger, more dominant, guy when he hooked up. This was way out of his comfort zone. He didn't know how he felt about it, only that it was exciting as fuck. Is this how other guys felt when they were with him? He'd never hurt them though. Would Hollywood? Would he get mad and claim that Chad had tried to infect him with his gayness and then beat him senseless?

Hollywood nuzzled his neck, dropping a few small kisses on Chad's sensitive skin before lifting his head, a dopey smile on his reddened lips. "What's wrong? Why'd you stop?"

Relieved to see Hollywood return to his normal, sweet self, Chad said, "We can't do this here."

"Let's go home then."

Home. The man was killing him. Right here, right now, Chad had everything he thought he'd wanted: Hollywood in his arms, willingly kissing him, clearly interested in more, and calling the place they lived in—together—home. There was only one problem: Hollywood wasn't sober.

It was easy enough for a guy as confused as Hollywood to claim he'd gotten caught up in the moment without adding alcohol to the mix. Chad tugged on his hands, easily slipping them out of Hollywood's grasp. He raised his head and gave Hollywood a light kiss and a sad smile.

"Get a cab. Go home and sleep it off. We'll talk tomorrow."

Hollywood's dazed expression sharpened and his smile disappeared. Chad immediately missed it.

"You want me to leave?"

"Yeah."

Hollywood reached down and palmed himself through his jeans.

"Don't you want this? I can do what I saw in that porn video. I can pound your ass and make you scream."

Dropping his head against the wall, Chad briefly closed his eyes. This was torture. He couldn't let Hollywood think he wasn't interested, because he certainly was. If the guy was even starting to admit to having feelings for Chad, for another man, the last thing he needed was to feel rejected.

"Hollywood, I want this—you—more than you can know. But the next time we touch, the next time we kiss, it will be when you're one-hundred-percent sober. I want you to be completely aware and on board with whatever we decide to do. This is confusing enough for you. I get that."

Hollywood lowered his face to Chad's neck and inhaled deeply. "You smell so good."

Chad sighed. "So do you."

"You promise?"

"Promise what?" With Hollywood suckling his neck, he'd lost track of the conversation. His knees were trembling and he could hardly think.

"To kiss me again tomorrow."

Chad's heart soared. It was dangerous to let himself dream, let himself hope, but he didn't care. He wanted Hollywood, and he'd take him on whatever terms the guy demanded. "As long as you're sober."

"Oh I will be."

"I'm counting on it." And he was. God help him, but he was.

93

CHAPTER 11

Hollywood opened his bleary eyes. A ray of sun speared his brain dead center. Why was Seattle sunny only when he was hung over? The scent of brewing coffee tickled his nose and made his stomach growl. He didn't feel up to food, but coffee would be nirvana. Using the wall for support, he shuffled out of his bedroom and down the hall to the kitchen. Chad leaned on the breakfast bar and held out a steaming mug, a mocking grin on his way-too-chipper face. How did the guy do it? He'd been out much later than Hollywood had, yet he looked like he'd just gotten twelve hours of beauty sleep.

That's because he's more than a decade younger than you, old man.

Hollywood took the proffered cup, muttering, "Thanks," as he rounded the breakfast bar and slid on to a stool. Moments later, Chad joined him with his own coffee and a plate piled high with toast, bacon, and eggs over easy. Looking at the runny yolk made Hollywood gag. Silence reigned as Chad ate and Hollywood sipped the hot coffee, which Chad had prepared exactly as he liked it.

Chad stopped his happy munching long enough to offer Hollywood a piece of toast. It might settle his stomach, which wasn't helped by his vague memories of the previous night. He didn't remember everything, but enough to know he'd acted like an ass, and not only with Chad. He owed Tori a huge apology. And if she told Jamie that he'd hit on her? *Shit.* Hollywood shook his head and groaned miserably. A bottle of water landed on the counter in front of him. He looked up as Chad was regaining his seat, and nodded his thanks.

"So," Chad said. "Is this drinking thing usual for you?"

Hollywood cracked open the bottle and guzzled half of it as he formulated his answer. He'd gotten drunk more than once since he'd been staying at Chad's. It looked bad. "I'm not an alcoholic."

"If you say so."

Hollywood couldn't look at Chad and fiddled with the label on the water bottle instead. "I know I drink too much."

"Why do it then? You obviously feel like crap afterward," Chad pointed out, ever-so-helpfully.

Hollywood sneaked a glance at his breakfast companion, at his attempted neutral expression, which was completely ruined by the concern in his clear blue eyes. Hollywood leaned his elbows on the granite and scrubbed his head. "We have to do this now?"

"Yes," came Chad's hard answer.

"Fine." Hollywood sighed and sat back. "It helps me forget."

"Forget what?"

"Christ, you're a real bulldog when you want to be."

Chad laid his hand on Hollywood's and squeezed. "I'm trying to be your friend. That's what we are, right?"

How could he tell Chad that drinking helped him forget how lonely he was? God, he was a pathetic loser. He could blame the stress of his high-risk job, of being a lieutenant in one of the busiest fire stations in the city. But that would be a lie, and Chad deserved better. "It helps me get through the days when I'm not at work," he said, finally.

"I get that. But what's so bad that you need to forget? Is it an art? The situation with your dad?"

Hollywood shrugged. He couldn't put into words what he didn't understand. Everyone saw him as successful, handsome, a ladies' man. And all of that was true. But other than his work, everything about his life was meaningless. Here he was, thirty-six years old, and already he was having a fucking midlife crisis. Why did he always feel so damn empty? There was a hole in the middle of his chest that no one since Isabel had been able to fill. Dissatisfaction with his love life was becoming an overwhelming sense of dissatisfaction with his life as a whole.

Chad ate a forkful of eggs and toast, not looking at Hollywood. He seemed to be thinking really hard about something. Then, as though he'd made a decision, he cleared his throat and set down his silverware. "I have some friends who are in the closet to their families or their colleagues. One thing most of them have in common is that they drink too much. They're scared and sad. They're tired of hiding who they are. Who they love."

"I don't have that problem."

"You sure?"

Hollywood stared at his water bottle, spinning it in his hands. What Chad was saying had nothing to do with Hollywood. He wasn't hiding anything.

Then why had you forgotten about Bobby?

"How much do you remember...?" Chad shifted uncomfortably on his stool, then started again. "How much do you remember about last night?"

"Enough." *God, too much.* The way he'd shoved Chad up against the wall, the way he'd rubbed their groins together—

He closed his eyes and dug his palms into the sockets.

"Do you remember kissing me?" Chad asked softly.

Hollywood's knees bounced under the pressure of Chad's questions, questions that forced him to relive every thrilling, intoxicating, hard-on-inducing moment of that kiss. Eyes still closed, he nodded. He remembered. Every excruciatingly exciting detail.

"Did you enjoy it?"

Christ. "Enjoy" didn't even come close to describing his feelings. He'd loved it, hated it. The kiss had terrified him. At the same time, it had sizzled through his bloodstream, lighting him up like a Fourth of July bonfire. If a simple kiss from Chad had made him feel all that, what would it feel like to do more than kiss? Would an intimate touch cause him to self-combust? Would having sex with the guy drive him mad? Turn him into a Chad-addict? He was losing his fucking mind just thinking about it.

Abruptly he pushed his stool back and got up. "I can't do this right now. Thanks for the coffee." And as though the fires of hell were licking at his ankles, he practically ran to the bathroom. With rigid movements, he turned the water on and set it as cold as possible before jumping under the spray. He couldn't have a conversation about how incredible kissing Chad had been when he felt like the sludge under his bunker boots.

ↄ🎺ↂ

His heart breaking, Chad watched Hollywood trip over himself as he ran away from the discussion they'd been having.

You pushed too hard.

Weighed down like he was wearing full turnout gear, he forced himself to clean up the kitchen before leaving Hollywood in peace. Deciding to go for a walk down by the pier, he grabbed his wallet, jacket, keys, and phone, then headed out.

The day was warm, the sky clear and blue. With Mount Rainier unobstructed by clouds on the other side of the bay, the scene looked like a postcard. He really loved Seattle and loved being a firefighter and paramedic here. The mostly left-leaning politics also made his life as a gay man easier, though the gay-bashers still came out to play sometimes, as evidenced by the attack on his car and the beating last summer. He could understand why some people were afraid to come out. Hopefully, the

LGBTQ center helped with that. Being gay was doubly hard when you didn't have the support of family and friends. Speaking of friends, he should check up on Harry.

Pulling out his phone, he dialed the guy's number and had a brief moment of wondering if it was too early to call before Harry answered.

"Hey, Chad. Thank you. Thank you. Thank you!"

"You're welcome," Chad said, laughing at the guy's cheerful exuberance so early in the day. It was the complete opposite of Hollywood's dejected Eeyore tone. "What did I do?"

"What did you do? Everything! Dude, I had so much fun playing with the band last night. The guys were really cool and said I could fill in for Steven anytime."

Chad crouched down to pick up a rock. It was smooth and flat. Shifting the phone to his left hand, he leaned sideways and tossed the stone into the harbor, satisfied when it skipped four times before sinking below the surface. "I'm glad it worked out."

"No kidding." Harry chuckled. "You're off the hook now."

Chad tensed. "Off the hook?"

"Yeah, you know. For fucking me while you were thinking of someone else."

Chad dropped onto a nearby bench. "Yeah, about that. I'm really sorry."

"You already told me. Plus what it's worth, your guy's super hot."

"My guy?"

"Yeah, the tall blond who was sitting next to your sister. He's the one, right?"

"He's not my guy. In fact, he snuck off with Tori while we were chatting with my mom."

"Loved her!"

Chad smiled. "She loved you too." His mother had always excelled at taking vulnerable kids under her wing. She'd done it often enough with those of his friends who'd had difficult coming-out experiences. They'd always known they had a safe place to stay with the Caldwells.

"Speaking of people who imagine someone else..." Harry's voice trailed off.

"Yeah?" Chad stared out at the quiet water, having no clue what Harry was hinting at.

"Do you have any idea how much you and your sister look alike?"

Barely resisting the urge to flex his guns, Chad scoffed. He didn't look like a woman.

"Sure, she's not as tall as you, or as built, but your hair color and eyes are identical, and you have very similar skin tone, and facial features, minus the stubble, of course."

"Of course," Chad echoed wryly. "What are you trying to say? That I should do drag?"

Harry's easy laughter rolled over Chad. "You'd be fucking gorgeous, like your sister. But no, that's not what I'm trying to say. I mean... Maybe..."

"Come on, spit it out."

There was a loud exhale over the line, then Harry said, "What if Hollywood hit on your sister because she looks like you?"

Chad was glad to already be sitting down. His heart sped up and he pressed a hand to his chest. Could it be?

He thought back to their conversation in the alley behind the club, to Hollywood's angry admission. *I can't think of anything except kissing you.* And when he'd said "your brother" to Tori, maybe he'd meant Chad, not Jamie, as he and Tori had assumed.

God, that kiss. Chad had spent his first hour in bed wanking off to the memory. No kiss had ever shaken him so completely. It was like Hollywood had reached deep inside Chad and finally taken possession of the heart that already belonged to him.

Harry's soft voice came over the line, interrupting Chad's thoughts. "When Hollywood came back to the table, he looked flushed and uh... shell-shocked. Did anything happen between you two?"

Trying to sound as unaffected as possible, Chad said in a teasing voice, "Maybe."

"One thing's for sure, he doesn't like *me* much."

"Why do you say that?" The two men had barely gotten a glance at each other before Hollywood had hightailed it out of there with Tori.

"He scowled every time you looked at me, and then when you put your arm on my shoulder and introduced me to the audience, I thought I'd be incinerated by the fire shooting from his eyes." The earlier exuberance had faded from Harry's voice. Chad missed it.

"Good thing there were a bunch of firefighters around then," Chad joked.

"There were? Oh my God."

"Yeah, me, two of my brothers, Hollywood, and my other brother's fiancée, Dani."

"Wow. That's impressive. I can't believe you're a firefighter. That's so hot. Now I'm even more bummed that things didn't work out between us," Harry teased.

Chad laughed. "I'll introduce you to a few gay men I know in the service. Maybe you'll get lucky."

"I'm all tingly just thinking about it." Harry hesitated. "Do you uh... Does Hollywood know we fucked?"

"Yep. Austin told him."

"Shit! Should I be worried?"

"Fuck no. It's none of his business who I have sex with."

"You sure *he* understands that?"

"He was making out with some chick on my living room couch when I got home that night, so he's got no leg to stand on." Chad shivered at the memory of Hollywood getting a hand job from Sandy, the expression on his face when he'd come.

"So what's the deal with him?" Harry asked. "Is he straight? Bi?"

"I don't know." And Chad honestly didn't. "Right now, I'd say maybe he's bi-curious."

Harry made a sound like he was shuddering. "Dude, be careful. I've got nothing against bisexuals: the more the merrier, right? But gays who are still in the closet? They're dangerous. Especially one who's thought of himself as straight for so long. The guy's what, ten years older than you?"

"Eleven."

"Huh."

"What?"

"He could be my dad."

"Fuck you. He's not that old."

"No? My dad's thirty-nine. My folks had me when they were eighteen."

"Hey, listen." Chad wiped his mouth with the back of his hand. He didn't like where this conversation was going. "I'm glad things worked out last night. I'll call you in a few days when I'm off-shift. We'll go for coffee."

"Sure. Sounds good. I hope I didn't say anything to piss you off. Sometimes my mouth moves faster than my brain."

Chad chuckled. "It's fine. Talking helped."

Finishing the call, Chad pushed off the bench and started to walk again. Age wasn't something he thought about often, especially not the age difference between him and Hollywood. Hell, the guy wasn't even three years older than Jamie, and he'd certainly never thought of Jamie as old. He kicked a branch into a small incoming wave and watched it bob on the water. Did Jamie think of Chad as a kid, or as a man? What about Hollywood? Did he think of Chad as a man in his own right or just as Jamie's little brother? God, that would suck balls.

Could that be part of Hollywood's issues? Not only that he was attracted to Chad—a man—but also that Chad was so much younger?

If so, Chad would set him straight, so to speak. Not only did he think Hollywood was fuckable and super sexy, he preferred men older than himself. Young guys like Harry were fun to pal around with, fun to hook up with, but when it came to relationships, Chad wanted a man who already knew who he was.

Okay, maybe he shouldn't put it in quite those words. Hollywood clearly had no idea who he really was or what he really wanted. But

Chad hoped to help him find out.

॰ 🎞 ॰

When the sun began to set over the harbor, Chad turned to head back home. All afternoon, he'd walked the beach, his mind on the sexy, confused, demi-god he'd left behind in his condo.

If Hollywood was home, and he was sober, Chad would lay all his cards on the table and have it out with the man. He'd had feelings for Hollywood for too long, and right now he felt like he was playing with fire. His relationship with Hollywood could turn into a beautiful flame, or it could explode and fry his fucking face off.

Straight men were bad for your health, and this was why.

Opening the front door, he heard what sounded like a high-speed car chase. Hollywood was sitting on the couch, hugging a heavy throw pillow to his chest. He stared blankly at the television screen, where a jaded detective smoked a fat cigar while his younger, more-fit colleagues chased after the bad guys. Hollywood didn't even blink when Chad stepped in front of the set, blocking his view.

Moving out of the way, Chad grabbed a bottle of water from the fridge and crossed the living room to sit on the couch next to Hollywood. Still no reaction. He picked up the remote and turned off the television.

Hollywood finally blinked. He turned his head and gave Chad a weak smile. "You're back."

"Yeah. You okay? You seem a little"—he shrugged—"I don't know. Off?"

Hollywood's countenance darkened. "I haven't had so much as a beer, if that's what you're implying."

Chad held his hands up. "No, no. Not at all."

Silence hung thick between them, like a toxic smog. When Hollywood looked away, Chad dropped his hands. Shit. This wasn't going to be easy. How did one broach the subject? *Hey, man. I think you like guys.* Yeah.

Several tense minutes later, Hollywood's voice split the air like a sonic boom. "Where were you?"

"I went down to the pier. Spent the day walking and... thinking."

"About what?"

Hollywood continued to stare straight ahead. Chad wanted to grab his face and force the man to look at him. But, he knew from experience, and from Tori, that talking about serious stuff face-to-face was tough for a lot of guys. "I was thinking about you..." He hesitated for a moment, just long enough to give himself a figurative kick in the ass. "About us."

Hollywood licked his lips and swallowed as though his throat had suddenly gone dry. Chad handed him the bottle of water. After taking a gulp, Hollywood wiped his mouth with the back of his hand. "Thanks." He arched a brow. "There's an us?"

It took everything in Chad, more courage than he'd ever needed to race into a burning building or slide under a two-ton forklift to help a trapped victim, but he forced out the truth. "I'd like there to be."

Hollywood's hands tightened around the bottle as he hugged the throw pillow closer with his elbows. "I—I don't know what I'm doing, Chad. I don't know what I want."

"I get that." Chad tugged on his shirt to straighten it. Anything to keep himself from thinking about how terribly wrong this conversation could go. "It's difficult to get a handle on your sexuality when you're bombarded by a lot of unexpected emotions."

Hollywood snorted. "You've always known who you are, who you... want."

"True. But I never expected to have feelings for a straight man. Feelings that won't go away no matter how hard I try."

Hollywood turned his head, holding Chad's gaze. "You have feelings for me?"

Did Chad imagine the slight kick at the corner of Hollywood's mouth? It couldn't have been there for more than a second. Chad licked his dry lips, a glimmer of hope taking root when Hollywood's eyes tracked the movement of his tongue.

"I do," Chad finally said, his voice low and rough. Vulnerable. "How do you feel about me?"

Hollywood set aside the bottle and the cushion he'd been holding. Slowly he turned his body, slinging his arm over the back of the couch. "All I know is that I want to kiss you more than I want to breathe."

"Okay."

"Okay?"

"Do it. Kiss me before I die."

Hollywood leaned in, his eyes locked on Chad's. He tentatively stroked Chad's cheek, the touch light and tender as his fingers tracked over Chad's jaw, to his lips.

"So soft," he whispered.

Chad moaned, the anticipation delicious torture. Every nerve ending in his face was primed for Hollywood's touch. "Please," he begged.

Hollywood gave him a small, quick grin before sliding his hand to the back of Chad's head. Chad's heart kicked into high gear. Their lips pressed together in a gentle, fleeting kiss. He heard a small sound of protest and blushed when he realized it had come from him. God, he wanted so much more.

Hollywood chuckled against his mouth as he came back for another taste. His teeth latched onto Chad's lower lip and tugged. Chad's cock

101

stirred, filling his jeans. Hollywood bit harder, and Chad groaned. The sound seemed to excite Hollywood. His tongue lapped at Chad's lips, pushing into the seam. Chad willingly opened up, sucking in the other man's tongue, enjoying the faint hint of chocolate. So Hollywood had a sweet tooth. Chad would have to remember that.

Before he could think more about it, Hollywood dug his fingers into Chad's hair, angling his head to deepen the kiss. Chad felt devoured as Hollywood used his tongue to stroke every inch of Chad's mouth, the touch soft yet rough, soothing yet exciting.

His head spun and he panted for breath when they broke apart, staring into each other's eyes.

"So," Chad started, then stopped, unable to say more. A marathoner's heart couldn't have pumped faster.

Hollywood loosened his grip on Chad's hair and let the strands glide through his fingers. He looked a little stunned, his face a little pale, but he didn't move away. Chad took that as a good sign.

"So," Hollywood drawled.

"On a scale of one to ten?" Chad said.

"Hmmm... an eight."

"An eight?" Chad knew he sounded indignant. Still. An *eight*? He'd have given it a nine and a half, if not a ten.

Hollywood smirked. "I'd have scored it higher except..."—his eyes twinkled—"we still have our clothes on."

Chad grabbed a throw pillow off the couch and smacked it on Hollywood's head. "You ass."

Laughing, Hollywood grabbed the pillow he'd previously been holding and landed a side hit on Chad's shoulder, tipping him off balance so he fell against the couch back.

"Oh no, you didn't."

Hollywood jumped away and took position behind the coffee table. Holding the back of the couch, Chad stood. Damn, the man was tall. Even with the extra height of the couch, Chad was barely a few inches taller than Hollywood. Their gazes met over matching grins. Chad was confident though. He'd had years of pillow fights with his brothers. There was no way Hollywood could win this.

Raising his pillow, Chad shouted, "You're on!"

80 🚋 ଔ

Hollywood couldn't believe how he'd gone from kissing Chad—a man—to having an all-out pillow fight in no time flat. One thing was sure: he had enough martial arts training to best Chad. No way was he going to end up anywhere but on top. Clutching the corners of the heavy throw pillow, he began swinging it from side to side as he advanced on

Chad. "You're going to regret this, kid."

"Give it your best shot, old man."

"Old man? Fuck you, Caldwell." And then he was on the attack. Bang, bang, one side, the other side. Bang. Bang. Chad grunted and jumped over the couch, getting in several good hits along the way.

They met in the empty space between the dining area and the living area. Pillows collided with heads and backs, arms and legs. Laughing, they ducked hits and groaned dramatically when contact was made. Hollywood couldn't remember the last time he'd laughed so much. His throat was raw from all the manly shouting.

Chad twisted, trying to get away from the barrage of hits Hollywood was raining down on him. It was like Rocky Balboa against Mr. T. As Hollywood came in for the final, decisive smash, Chad ducked his head and grabbed onto Hollywood's waist. They tumbled to the floor in a heap of tangled limbs and pillows.

Chad's shoulders shook as he continued to laugh. His warm breath heated the bare skin on Hollywood's stomach where his shirt had risen in the scuffle. Hollywood's laughter faded as his gut clenched. His pulse, already racing from the pillow fight, now thundered in his ears for an entirely different reason.

His cock began to fill, to throb.

Chad looked up then, his partly [illegible] a victorious grin, his white teeth flashing, his blue eyes shining. So sexy, so fucking beautiful.

You know what you want.

Yeah, he did. But would he still want Chad tomorrow? Hurting Chad wasn't on his to-do list.

Chad's hand slid up Hollywood's thigh. Hollywood gasped—literally gasped—at the sparks that followed the trajectory. The closer the hand got to his groin, the stronger the sparks, until Hollywood was writhing beneath Chad's weight.

Was it wrong to let Chad touch him like this when he still wasn't sure? Maybe he should stop him. Hollywood willed his hands to move, to push Chad off. To tell him he wasn't gay.

You like it too much though, don't you?

Chad's hand closed over Hollywood's length through his sweatpants. Those long fingers gripped him firmly, just this side of pain. Hollywood moaned and involuntarily bucked his hips. Chad smiled and slipped his hand under the waistband. At the first contact of skin on skin, Hollywood admitted defeat. There was nothing in heaven or hell that could get him to push Chad away now. In fact, he prayed for more.

Hollywood closed his eyes, his hands clenched at his sides. He wanted Chad's mouth on his cock. Oh God. He wanted a *man's* mouth on his cock.

When he felt the tug of Chad lowering his sweatpants, Hollywood tilted his hips, and then the sweats were gone. At the first lick of Chad's tongue on his bare foot, Hollywood's eyes snapped open. He lifted his head to see what was going on down there. Chad was fully dressed, kneeling between Hollywood's legs as he eagerly sucked on Hollywood's little toe. With a devilish glint in his eye, he bit a path up Hollywood's ankle, his calf, stopping behind his knee for a few wet nibbles and licks.

Hollywood dug his fingers into the carpet to keep from squirming. His cock was fully hard and leaking pre-cum on his abs. Had he ever been so turned on? Last night had come close, but this, having Chad touch him, was so much better.

Chad reached the crease between Hollywood's groin and his thigh. Hollywood sucked in air and held his breath, waiting to see what Chad would do next. Hoping he would—

A shout of pleasure burst from his chest as Chad's hot, tight mouth closed over the head of Hollywood's cock. His beautiful lips stretched wide... Jesus. It was everything he wanted and everything he didn't.

Chad released the crown and playfully dipped the tip of his tongue in Hollywood's slit. Hollywood's eyes rolled back, his moans echoing Chad's. He loved how into this Chad was. Women pretended to be, but few really were. Chad's reactions were the real deal. Hollywood knew because the guy's massive erection was pressed against his thigh.

Shifting to stick a throw pillow below his head, Hollywood settled in to watch the show. Chad's heated gaze met his. He blinked, then went down on Hollywood's eight inches until his lips touched Hollywood's pubes. For a moment, Hollywood's vision blurred. It was too much. He panted, fighting for control. He didn't want this to be over already. Fuck, he wanted this to go on forever.

Chad swallowed and the muscles of his throat gripped Hollywood so firmly, he saw stars. "Oh God," he groaned, thrusting his hips, even though he knew he was in as deep as he could go. How could the guy even breathe with Hollywood's dick jammed so far down his throat? "I'm gonna—"

The pressure eased as Chad pulled back to place tiny, prickly bites along Hollywood's shaft. He shifted lower and took one of Hollywood's balls into his mouth. "Shit!"

Chad reached for Hollywood's cock, squeezing hard at the base to stave off the orgasm that was building to a crescendo. He was almost at the point of no return. He should stop Chad now. No harm, no foul. Except for a nasty case of blue balls.

He could, but he didn't want to. Right or wrong, he wanted Chad to bring him off.

Contracting his abs, he raised his upper body off the carpet until he could reach Chad's head. His fingers dug into the guy's thick, soft hair, massaging into his scalp. Chad let go of his balls with a comical pop. He took one look at Hollywood's face before scooting up to swallow his cock. And swallow he did, right to the root.

Unable to hold the position, Hollywood dropped to the floor. He wanted to thrust, but Chad's strong hands on his abs held him down. All Hollywood could do was lie back and take it. Take the powerful suction, the slow then fast, up then down glide, until, back arching off the floor, he shouted. The release shot from the nape of his neck, to the base of his spine, and out the head of his cock.

Chad's lips and throat worked to swallow him down, swallow his cum. Hollywood shook, went blind, every muscle a participant in the whole-body experience.

When it was over, he lay there in euphoric bliss. He had just enough energy to lift his head and see Chad lazily licking clean his softening cock. Chad caught his gaze and smiled a little uncertainly. He crawled up Hollywood's body and lay beside him, not touching except for the hand sifting through the hair on Hollywood's chest.

"So," Chad said, staring at his hand. Hollywood could hear Chad's worry, his concern. He'd heard that tone often enough after furtive late-night blow jobs with bar hookups. The tone that said his partner wondered if Hollywood, having gotten his, would hike up his pants, say thank you, and leave. It was something he'd done too often to count. Something he could do again.

Not this time.

No, not this time. With a finger under Chad's chin, Hollywood urged him to turn his head. When Chad finally looked at him, Hollywood smiled. "I'm fine."

Chad blew out and dropped his head on Hollywood's shoulder. Hollywood shifted a bit so his arm was around Chad's back, holding him to his side. Chad was warm, his body alive and vibrant next to him. After a few minutes, Chad stirred. "On a scale of one to ten?"

"Hmmm... I'd say, nine."

"Nine? I'll have you know that was a class-A blow job."

"True. You're one hell of a cocksucker."

Chad grinned. "Then what's the problem?"

Hollywood arched a meaningful brow. "Only one of us is naked."

CHAPTER 12

Chad lifted his head off Hollywood's muscled shoulder and stared down at the man laid out beside him, naked except for the T-shirt rucked up to his pits. It was all there, everything he wanted, like some X-rated all-you-can-eat buffet. Having had his first taste of Hollywood's cock, the remnants of the guy's orgasm still on his tongue, Chad was hard as a rock and more than ready to respond to Hollywood's challenge.

But did Hollywood fully understand what would happen between them if Chad were to take him up on his offer? His green gaze was full of mischief and arrogance, his body language as cocksure as any time Chad had seen him putting the moves on a woman. Chad arched a brow to match Hollywood's. "You seem pretty confident that I'm a sure thing."

Hollywood's mocking laughter shook his frame, the humor in his expression growing more pronounced. His focus drifted lower, to the bulge in Chad's jeans, making his cock jerk in response to the attention. "Aren't you?"

Chad pushed up on his arm so he was sitting on his hips. The zipper of his jeans bit into his swollen dick, but it didn't matter. His willpower was fading fast, and he needed the boost that the more upright position would give him. "I told you before, I'm not going to be your experiment, your walk on the wild side. If we go further—"

Hollywood grinned.

"If we fuck right now, when you're feeling all horny and post-orgasmic, it'll be too easy for you to say I took advantage of your vulnerable state."

Hollywood's grin faded. Shoving his shirt down, he sat up and wiggled into his sweatpants. When he turned back to Chad, his face was blank. "You're right. I shouldn't have let you do... that."

Chad grabbed his arm to prevent him from moving away. "Don't do this."

Hollywood's muscles flexed, but he didn't resist, didn't shrink from Chad's touch. At least that was something. Maybe Chad could somehow salvage the evening. "Don't distance yourself from me. I can see you erecting walls as we speak."

Hollywood sniggered. "Nice word choice."

Chad shoved Hollywood's arm. "You're such a kid sometimes."

"Hardly. Compared to you, I'm an old man." He pulled his knees up to his chest, hugging them. "I can't even remember what it was like being as young as you are. No worries, no responsibilities, a different chick to fuck whenever I got the urge."

"Doesn't sound like much has changed."

"Ha! Then, I was a guy exploring my options, sowing my wild oats. And now..." He paused, took a breath, and shook his head. "Well, now I'm a pathetic loser who forgot to grow up."

"Bullshit." Chad wanted so badly to hug the guy, but he didn't think Hollywood would be very receptive. Still, he risked scooting closer, not touching, but near enough to feel the heat of Hollywood's body. "You're gorgeous, healthy, you've got a great job—"

"I drink too much, work terrible hours—"

"You're loyal and dedicated. A valiant public servant. Anyone would be lucky to have you."

"I'd make a terrible husband and an even worse father."

Chad couldn't stand the look on Hollywood's face. A few minutes ago, it had been bright and eager, his mouth open in an ecstatic shout. Now, he looked sad and dejected. Broken. Throwing caution out the window, he put an arm around Hollywood's back and laid his head once again on the broad shoulder. "None of that is true, except that you drink too much. Women chase after you everywhere you go." Why was he talking about women? Shit. He didn't need to remind the guy that what they'd just done was out of the ordinary for him.

Hollywood stretched his legs out, spreading them wide and leaned back on his arms. "They only want me for a quick fuck. The ones who stick around longer do it for my steady pay and benefits. The fact that I'm statistically very likely to die decades before them doesn't hurt."

"Again, I call bullshit. Why are you so stuck on age? You're barely older than Jamie and William."

Hollywood laughed, his eyes darkening. "I'm nothing like your brothers. Jamie's been married for five years and William was married to his job way before Dani got a hold of him."

"True, but neither of them have let age get in the way of finding out who they are and what they like."

Almost before he finished speaking, Chad got an elbow to the ribs and an irritated glower.

"I'm here, aren't I? I kissed you, didn't I? I let you suck my dick, for fuck's sake. I think that qualifies as *finding out who I am and what I like*."

The fury on Hollywood's face surprised Chad. He dropped his arm and shifted in case he needed to protect himself. "Are you that pissed at me?"

"Are you that afraid of me?" Hollywood countered.

Chad held his ground. "You first."

"Fuck. No, I'm not pissed at you."

"What, then? Something's got your panties in a wad."

Hollywood's brow furrowed even more. "I am not wearing, nor will I ever wear, panties."

"Now that's a shame, handsome." Chad tilted his head and winked. "A nice satin pair with black lace trim would look amazing on you."

Hollywood snarled, taking him by the shoulders. As soon as his hands made contact, Chad froze.

"Don't do that," Hollywood growled.

"D-do what?" Shit. Had he actually stuttered?

Curling his lip in disgust, Hollywood let Chad go and got off the floor. He clutched the back of his neck with both hands. "You *are* afraid of me. Whenever you get nervous, you do that thing where you raise your register and go all limp-wristed."

"I do?" Chad tried to recall the times he'd done the queeny retort recently, to see if there was any truth to Hollywood's observation. At first, he'd started doing it as a joke to irritate homophobes. But lately... Yeah, Hollywood might be right.

"Yeah, you pull this ridiculous 'I'm *such* a homo' bullshit. It's not how you normally are."

"So my defense mechanism is to act ultra-gay, and yours is to what? Use people?"

"Hey, I didn't ask for that blow job."

"I wasn't referring to that, but it's interesting that you brought it up." Chad rose and headed for his room. That had hurt.

Really fucking hurt.

It was exactly what he'd been afraid of, and Hollywood had confirmed it. Christ, he was a fool.

The only problem with his getaway plan was that Hollywood and his beautiful broad shoulders were blocking the path to the hall, and when he tried to slip past, Hollywood caught him around the biceps. "It's not like that."

Chad shrugged to dislodge Hollywood's grip. He had to put an end to this fantasy. Going after a straight man could only end in misery for both of them. It might kill him, but to preserve what little self-esteem he had left, Chad had to give up on Hollywood. "Is your apartment ready yet?"

Hollywood nodded slowly.

"Then I think you should go."

ᘓ 🎥 ᘓ

Hollywood shouldered open the door to his apartment after finishing up a twenty-four-hour shift, carrying a duffle bag full of his clothes and other necessities he'd brought with him to Chad's. After Chad had kicked him out of the condo, Hollywood had booked a cheap hotel room in the SoDo district instead of coming back to the apartment before the carpet had been laid. Fewer explanations to be made that way.

Tired and hungry, he dropped his luggage by the door, took off his running shoes and socks, and sank his feet into the plush caramel-colored pile. He groaned. It was like walking on a little bit of heaven. He padded over to the kitchen to admire the new black cabinetry and granite countertops. The walls, painted modern gray, made the place look like an ad in one of those fancy renovation magazines.

Grabbing a bottle of water from the fridge, he finished touring the rest of the apartment. It looked fantastic. He'd have to make plans to upgrade the other units in the building as well. The job would have to be spread out over several years, but it needed to be done. In the end, the higher rents and property value would make it worthwhile. Maybe when he had some extra cash, he'd have hardwood put in, starting with the living room.

Chad's place had hardwood floors.

Really nice ones.

He sank onto the couch, which the water-damage restoration crew had managed to save, and stretched out, thinking of Chad. Thinking of that night. Every detail, every look, every word spoken was etched in his brain. And the pain on Chad's face, he'd remember that until the day he died.

Maybe it was best that their—God, what was the word for what they'd had? It hadn't been a relationship, nor had it been a one-night stand. Was Chad right? Had he just been curious, wanting to experiment, and using Chad to do it?

Too restless to sleep, he got to his feet and finished the water, then moved to the patio door. Leaning on the frame, he stared at the street below. Traffic was still heavy, despite it being nine in the morning. People hurried along the sidewalks, anxious to reach their destinations. Two men exited a café. One wrapped a scarf around the other, then used the two ends to pull him in for a leisurely kiss. They exchanged dopey smiles, clearly in love.

Hollywood couldn't remember feeling like that about anyone except Isabel. How sad was that? In thirty-six years of life, he'd been in love exactly once. He'd long since accepted that for him love had been a one-shot deal. There were no do-overs, no second chances, no new starts. He'd had one opportunity, and he'd lost it.

Since Isabel's death, Hollywood's life had been an endless string of women who meant nothing to him, and how much longer would that last? Pretty soon, his hair would go gray, then it would start to thin. The excessive drinking would give him a paunch and a bulbous nose. When he was puffy faced and bald, would hot women still chase him? Hell no. Not unless his job became a lot more lucrative. Long ago, he'd understood that the less attractive you became, the more money you needed to make.

And no one ever became a millionaire working for the fire service.

Nope. At the rate he was going, he would die a lonely old man, provided he lived that long.

Fuck. Could he possibly get lonelier than he already was? He was social with the guys at work, but really, his only close friend was Jamie.

You were friends with Chad too.

The thought punched into his gut. He'd royally fucked that up. How did you make up for acting like a world-class dick?

You start with an apology.

He smacked his fist against the glass. What could he say? *Sorry I used you to see if I was gay?* Yeah, that would go over real nice.

You liked the experimenting though, didn't you?

His cock sprang to attention at the memory of slamming Chad up against the wall outside the club, of kissing his firm lips, of touching his scratchy stubble. The scent of his cologne. He recalled kissing Chad on his couch, the tender, fleeting caress of their tongues intertwining. Having that long hard body lying on top of him when Chad had tackled him to the ground. Chad's throat milking his cock.

"Oh fuck." His knees buckled and he let himself drop to the floor. A strange despair filled him. But what was the source? That he'd lost Chad before he'd ever really had him, or that he wanted the man at all?

He was so fucking confused.

Worst of all, he had no one to talk to. There was no way he could discuss this with Jamie, and not only because he was Chad's brother. Hollywood wasn't ready to come out to his best friend yet.

Christ, now he was thinking about coming out.

He *had* to talk to someone. Get another opinion. Maybe it was normal to get a hard-on from watching another man stretching and dancing around to "Uptown Funk." Maybe it was normal to be jealous of a new friend's ex.

Yeah, normal for a gay man.

Well, now he'd never know for sure, because the man he liked, the man he was becoming friends with, the man who'd given him the best goddamn blow job he'd ever had, didn't want anything more to do with him.

℘ 🚆 ෨

Hunger woke Hollywood up. Too tired to tackle his confusing thoughts about Chad, he'd passed out on his couch. Now the rumbling of his stomach alerted him to a very important fact: he hadn't eaten since last night. He pushed to his feet and stretched, each bone in his spine cracking as it slipped into place.

I'm too fucking old to sleep on the couch.

His stomach growled again, which reminded him of food, which reminded him of the great spaghetti at Vicenzo's, which reminded him of Tori. Shit. He hadn't spoken to her since the fundraiser, since that kiss. He didn't remember everything that had happened, but he did remember that. And the look on her face when she'd put two and two together. Damn.

She deserved an apology.

An hour later, he'd showered, shaved, dressed and was now pushing open the door to Vicenzo's. If Tori wasn't working, he'd grab some lunch, then figure out where he could find her. When he spotted her from behind, his gut tightened. Would she tell him off? Kick him out of the restaurant? Nah, she was too classy for that.

A moment later, she turned and caught sight of him. Her smooth brow creased and she pursed her lips as though she were biting the corner of her mouth. Nervous? Angry? He wasn't sure how to handle either option. After serving the man and woman at the table their plates, she wiped her hands on her apron and came over to him.

"A table for one?" she asked, as if he were a stranger. No *Hello*, no *How are you, Hollywood.*

He swallowed and shoved his hands into his jacket pockets. "Yep. Just one."

"This way, please." She turned and headed for a table in the back where he'd have a view of the bay. At least she hadn't relegated him to the table next to the swinging kitchen door.

Once he'd sat down, she handed him a menu and rattled off the day's specials. "So what can I get you?" she concluded.

"Surprise me." He'd been so busy staring at her face, trying to read her, that he'd barely heard a word.

Her brows rose and she struck a pose with her hip out that reminded him of Chad. "Oh, I don't think I could surprise you more than you've

111

already surprised me." Even her sassy tone reminded him of Chad.

Hollywood set his menu down. "Tori, can we talk?"

"I'm at work. I've got customers."

He followed her gesture as she indicated the room. Besides himself and the couple at the table she'd just served, the section was empty. The lunch rush was clearly over. But he wasn't going to argue the point with her. Better to try a different tack. "When's your break?"

She glanced at her watch and shifted. He knew she wanted to lie to him. He also knew she wouldn't. Had to love those Caldwell values. With a huff, she rolled her eyes. "In fifteen minutes, but you knew that already, didn't you?"

He laughed. "Nah. I guessed."

"Fine." She left and returned a minute later with a bowl of minestrone and a loaf of warm homemade bread, setting it in front of him.

Breathing in the scents, he smiled. "God, I love the food here."

"You should stop by more often then."

That caught him by surprise. "You wouldn't mind?"

She closed her eyes for a moment, then gave him a cheerless smile. "I don't hate you, Hollywood."

"That's a relief." And it truly was. He'd known Tori since she was eleven and had always enjoyed their lively conversations and her insights into human nature. Beautiful and intelligent, she was a woman men would die to have. But he'd never thought of her that way. She'd always been Jamie's little sister, the one they all protected, himself included.

Until he'd gotten drunk and tried to seduce her.

As though sensing his change in mood, she squeezed his shoulder. "Eat your soup. Chef Ivy made it extra delicious today."

Eleven years his junior and between the two of them, she was the more mature. Hands down. Following her advice, he ripped off a piece of the loaf and slathered it with a thick layer of butter. If he was going to splurge, he was going to go all out. The spicy aromas of pancetta, rosemary, and garlic rose from his bowl and he scooped up a healthy spoonful, filled with vegetables. As soon as he placed it on his tongue, flavors exploded in his mouth. He bit back a groan as he followed the soup with a bite of warm bread. Christ, if he came here more often, he'd have to add a mile to his daily run.

As soon as he finished his bowl, Tori showed up, bearing a plate heaped high with spaghetti Bolognese. After refilling his water glass, she asked, "Need anything else?"

"Just you."

"All right, all right," she growled playfully. "I'll be back in a couple minutes."

While she handled the other couple's bill, he dug into the spaghetti.

This time, he couldn't hold back the moan. This was damn fine pasta. He'd heard that Chef Ivy made it herself from an old family recipe, and based on the taste, he didn't doubt it for a second.

When Tori returned with a tray, which she set on the table beside his, he'd almost finished his plate. "I see you're enjoying your surprise," she said, sitting across from him.

"My compliments to the chef," he said, adding, "and to you for the selection. It was exactly what I needed."

Her smile dimmed. "You wanted to talk?"

"I owe you an apology." He finished the last bite of spaghetti, then pushed his plate aside. She quickly got up and swapped it with a dessert plate containing a cannolo, lightly sprinkled with sugar. Before he could blink, she'd also served him a cup of steaming espresso. "Have I died and gone to heaven?"

Her tinkling laugh eased his nerves. And when she sat with her own espresso and dessert, he relaxed even further. Tori was studying to be a psychologist, was almost done with her PhD. If anyone could help him, she could. But first, he needed to apologize.

"Um... about the other night." He rubbed at his hair, glancing at her, then away. A seagull landed on the railing outside, but he wasn't really seeing it. He was remembering pulling Tori into that hallway, the feeling of her in his arms, the stupid things he'd said. The way he'd pushed his thigh between her legs. Heat rose to his cheeks. *Stop staring at the dumb bird and man up.* Somehow he forced himself to look at her. "I'm really sorry. I never should have..." Each word was such a struggle, with her staring at him like that.

She curled her hands around her espresso cup, her gaze never wavering. "I can't deny that I'm hurt by what you did. For a minute, I actually thought—" Cutting herself off, she waved her hand. "It doesn't matter what I thought. The point is, I didn't know that you and Chad... I should have known. He's my damn twin, but I didn't."

Hollywood took a moment before responding, studied her pinched brow, her thinned lips, the way her hands had tightened on the cup she held. This was about more than him hitting on her at the club. Taking a deep breath, he reached for her hand. Almost reluctantly, she released her cup and placed her fingers in his palm. "Tori, what's going on?"

"Uh-uh, this is about you."

Had he been deflecting? Probably, but so was she. "I'll share if you agree to do the same."

For a moment, she simply stared at him, blinking slowly. Then she nodded. "Fine."

"So, uh, lately, I've been having some dreams. Someone with dark hair, blue eyes... I thought it had to be you." She snorted and he quickly

113

added, "I swear, I only wanted to talk to you that night. I never planned for it to go further than that." He ran his thumb across the back of her hand. "I'd had way too much to drink and things got muddled in my brain. It's not an excuse, but it's a reason."

She let go of his hand and sat back in her chair. Her eyes focused downward as she toyed with the edge of the tablecloth, her cheeks flushed. Bright-eyed, confident Tori had fled, and something clutched at his heart. Christ, he'd really hurt her, and he was majorly fucking up this apology. "Listen, everything that happened, it was all my fault. I take full responsibility."

"No." She shook her head and finally looked up. "I'm an adult. I have to take responsibility for my part too. I knew you'd had too much to drink. And hell, I know you see me as a little sister. But sometimes, it gets to be too much, you know?"

No, he didn't know. "What gets to be too much, sweetie?"

Her laughter was tinged with bitterness. "All this brotherly love stuff. Jamie's paired off, and now so is William. Chad seemed pretty cozy with Harry. And I guess I got a little…" She blew out a breath that sent a few strands of her hair flying.

It was such a cute gesture, one he'd seen her do so many times over the years that it made him smile. "Jealous?" he supplied.

"Yes." Her chin dropped.

Reaching across the table, he lifted it up with a gentle finger. "Hey, don't hide from me. We can talk about anything, right?" Despite her tremulous smile and the sheen of tears in her eyes, he knew his question had pleased her. "I get jealous too. Hell, I'm thirty-six, an old man, and I'm still alone. You're a spring chicken by comparison."

"It's lonely sometimes though."

"I know. Is that why you—"

"Hit on you?" she finished for him.

He laughed. "I was going to say, let me hit on you, but okay. Let's say it was mutual."

"I don't know. I just wanted *something* to happen. And besides, you're pretty hot."

"For an old guy."

"For an any-age guy." The teasing glint in her eyes faded. "Unfortunately for you, now that I know Chad has feelings for you, you're off-limits."

He leaned his elbows on the table and rubbed his eyes. Until a month ago, his life had been one big party, one big fuck fest. Now every day was like wading through an *American Ninja Warrior* course, and he had to wonder if he'd make it to the end with all his limbs.

"How do you feel about that?" she prodded.

Ah, so this was her psychologist voice, a little softer, a little more soothing. He'd play along. For now. "About Chad, or about his feelings for me?"

"Either. Both."

To delay answering her question, he cut off a healthy piece of cannolo and stuffed it in his mouth. Fuck, that was good. He chewed slowly as he decided how to respond. Hell, he wasn't even sure how he felt. "Confused."

She sipped her espresso. "What parts confuse you?"

"I get why he likes me." He gave her a big shit-eating grin that made her chuckle. "Okay, seriously, the guy is eleven years younger than me." She arched a brow and he hurried to tack on, "And I'm straight."

"I see." She didn't even try to hide her amusement. "Based on the women, and I use the term loosely, that I've seen you with, I didn't think age was really a factor for you."

"Not with women that I only wanted to f—" He clamped his mouth shut before the rest of the word made it out. He pressed his palm against his forehead. Now she'd think he'd wanted to fuck her like some nameless girl in a bar.

"So age matters now because Chad is something more to you?"

He jerked his head up. "What?"

"Chad isn't someone you just want to fuck?"

"Of course not!"

"Because he's a man, or because he means more than that to you?"

Jesus Christ. She was making his head spin. "I don't know."

"Well, think about it. Do you want to fuck Chad?"

"Yes. No." Fuck. "I mean..." Fuck. He buried his face in his hands again. "Why are you pushing me like this?" he asked, sounding pathetic even to his own ears.

Wordlessly, she stood and dragged a chair over from the neighboring table so that she could sit beside him. Then she put a slim arm around his back. "Because I know that coming to terms with one's sexuality is difficult, especially at your age."

"I'm straight."

"Are you sure?"

He ducked his head. "No."

"Hey, it's okay." She rubbed her hand in soothing circles on his back. "Tell me how Chad makes you feel."

Turning his head, he was the one who arched a brow this time. "Tori, he's your brother."

"So keep it PG-13."

Her grin was too fucking knowing. "Okay, but go back to your seat." He couldn't talk about how Chad turned him on with his sister sitting so close to him. After she'd complied and started to dig into her own

115

cannolo, he decided to give this a shot. Now that he'd gotten this far, maybe she could help him sort out his feelings.

"I find myself reacting to Chad in a way I haven't reacted to a guy since I was a kid."

"You had feelings for a boy when you were young?"

Swallowing hard, he nodded.

"That's not uncommon. Many pubescent and pre-pubescent children experience curiosity or even desire for others of their own gender. Were you attracted to girls too?"

"Still am." He glanced up sharply, feeling the blood drain from his head. "Women... I mean women, not girls."

She laughed. "I knew what you meant."

"Then you see why I'm confused. Besides that one boy, I've always been attracted to women. Then Chad comes along and..." He looked out the window. "Chad comes along and turns my world upside down."

"Tell me something, Hollywood." She waited until he looked at her. "Does Chad attract you only sexually, or is there another component to it?"

"What do you mean?"

"Do you like him? Do you enjoy spending time with him?"

"Like a buddy, you mean?"

She scrunched her face. "Not exactly, but okay."

Where was she going with this? Chad was a great guy. Of course he enjoyed hanging out with him. Just like he enjoyed hanging out with Jamie.

Really, Hollywood?

Focusing on cutting up his cannolo to avoid meeting Tori's probing gaze, he tried to put his thoughts into words. More importantly, he tried to be honest with himself. "He's a fun guy. We got along pretty well when I was at his place. So, in that way, he's like a buddy. But..." He paused and took several deep breaths. "But, well... the things I want to do with him aren't things I've *ever* wanted to do with Jamie."

"And that makes you uncomfortable."

"Damn right. Instead of simply enjoying myself, I spend all my time wondering why I want to do those things. Am I gay, or is this just curiosity? It's driving me crazy."

"Have you and Chad progressed beyond the thinking stage?"

Heat raced up Hollywood's neck and burned his face. "Christ."

"A simple yes or no will do."

"Yes. All right? Yes."

"And how did that make you feel?"

Fucking fantastic. He'd felt like he was flying. The aftermath hadn't been so good though.

"Hey, what's wrong?" she asked, gripping his forearm.

"It doesn't matter how I felt because Chad and I had a fight. He kicked me out of his place."

Setting her fork down, she leaned back and crossed her legs, eyeing him curiously. "That doesn't sound like Chad."

"Maybe not, but it's what happened."

"Start at the beginning." When he snorted, she hurried to add, "I meant of the argument."

He cleared his throat. "Okay, so we were having a good time. Then we got on the subject of age and how I wasn't a good catch for anyone. Chad got pissed and he kicked me out."

She tapped her lips with a blue nail that looked like the exact shade of nail polish Chad had been wearing when he'd performed at Bar None. Christ, everything he saw reminded him of the man. "Interesting. So you engaged in some sexual activity with Chad, then you insisted that you were bad for him. I assume he didn't agree."

"No."

"But you really believe this to be true."

"I'm not good for anyone, male or female."

"You told me you felt friendship toward Chad. Is that correct?"

Shit. Was she a psychologist or a damn lawyer? "Yes," he said, grinding his teeth.

"Based on your discussion of age, did it sound like Chad wants a relationship with you?"

Hollywood closed his eyes and thought back to the conversation, to all their conversations. Chad had become his friend. Chad had been reluctant to kiss him or do anything else for that matter. It was Hollywood who'd pushed until Chad had given in. "He accused me of using him."

"And did you?"

He looked up. His eyes burned. "I can see how Chad might think so."

"What do you think he thinks?"

"That he's an experiment. A gay experiment. But he's not. I really like him. I'm just afraid to hurt him. Fuck." He shook his head. "I don't know if I'm gay. How can I even begin to think about a relationship with him until I know for sure?"

With gentle strokes, she patted his arm. "By your own admission, you like Chad. You enjoy hanging out with him. This is what dating is." She smiled.

"Dating?" His eyes bugged out. "I can't date him. Did you miss what I said earlier? I can't date him until I know for sure."

"Answer me this: Did you engage in physical intimacy with him, with someone you consider a friend, because all you wanted was a fuck?"

"Of course not."

"Then why did you?"

Because he did want more than a fuck. He wanted Chad. Leaning his elbows on the table, he gripped his head. "You're good."

"I know. You still have to answer my question out loud."

"It's not about sex. It's about him. I want to see where this will go."

"You want a relationship with him."

Fuck. "Yes," he spit out.

At her soft chuckling, he raised his head and glowered at her. "You enjoyed that, didn't you?"

"More than you can know." Her grin lit up the room.

"But what if I'm not really gay? What if it's just him?"

"From what you've told me already, I think it's not just him. But maybe your feelings for him are strong enough that you couldn't repress them like you've done with others."

"My attraction to women is real."

"I know it is." She winked, and he flushed, reminded of exactly *how* she knew. "You're most likely bisexual. Some bisexual men and women are attracted to both genders equally, some are attracted to both, but not necessarily equally. Some enjoy sex with one gender while preferring relationships with the other. There are as many variations as there are people. There's no right and no wrong here, Hollywood. There's only love and attraction."

Maybe it was finally admitting his feelings for Chad, or maybe it was how she'd described bisexuality, but whatever the reason, Hollywood felt like a heavy burden had been lifted from his shoulders. Was this who he was?

Sure felt like it. And that meant this wasn't just an experiment.

"You're going to make a fantastic psychologist one day." Taking Tori's hand, he rose and walked around to her side of the table, then kissed her knuckles. He hadn't forgotten her distress about Chad when he'd first arrived though. "I'm available if you want to talk about what's going on with you."

She threw her arms around his waist and hugged him close. "Let Chad know I miss him."

Tori obviously had great faith in either Hollywood's ability to beg forgiveness or in Chad's ability to grant it. More faith than Hollywood had, that was for sure. He'd do his best to convince Chad to see him again. To give him a chance to explain himself. To grovel if he had to. Maybe they wouldn't continue the physical aspect of their relationship, but he really wanted to continue their friendship. It meant a lot to him. *Chad* meant a lot to him.

"I promise. If he gives me a chance, I'll let him know."

For the first time in a long time, Hollywood had a goal, a purpose, a direction. And all roads led to Chad.

ℬ 🚋 ℭ

Having just dropped off a patient in the emergency room at Harborview Medical Center, Chad and Liam took the short hallway that led to their own station, conveniently located inside the hospital. It was an unusual setup, but it worked well for them, as they had one foot in each world.

The fire station at Harborview housed two of the seven Medic One units, as well as M34, the unit reserved for the on-duty Medical Services Officer, their paramedic lieutenant. The other Medic One units were housed out of fire stations around the city.

The four HMC on-duty paramedics and the on-duty paramedic lieutenant lived on the floor above their vehicles. Like any other station, it had a beanery—the historical SFD nickname for the kitchen—a day room, bathrooms, and the lieutenant's office, as well bunkrooms where they could rest during a rare slow shift. Deeper in the hospital, the Battalion 3 Chief and administrative staff also had offices.

The scent of slowly charring coffee drew Chad to the beanery. He sighed at the familiar sight of half-eaten meals left behind on the large table by the other Medic One crew, who'd clearly had their meal interrupted by a call. Emptying the old coffee in the sink, he set about cleaning the pot and making some fresh brew. The other platoon members would appreciate it when they came in later. Even those that weren't housed at HMC often stopped by to drop off paperwork.

Liam rooted in the refrigerator, getting out his thermal lunch box. Chad watched his face brighten when he pulled out a plastic bag with bran muffins inside. "That woman," he said with obvious pride. "And look, she gave me two."

Chad smirked. "You know the second one's for me." Anna always packed a snack for him as well.

"Yeah, yeah." Liam set the muffins on the table and put his lunch bag away. "How are things with your… roommate? Any progress?"

"He went back home." The rock in Chad's stomach got a little heavier. Had he done the right thing kicking Hollywood out, or had he overreacted? Probably six of one, half a dozen of the other. He'd been so riled up after days of playing cat and mouse that when he'd finally gotten his mouth on the guy, his brain had short-circuited. He'd wanted to have sex, would even have bottomed for Hollywood, but more than that, he'd wanted some kind of acknowledgment that Hollywood had understood the significance of what they'd been doing.

"You okay?" Liam asked, scanning his face.

Chad rubbed a hand over the tightening in his chest. "I will be."

119

This thing, this infatuation, he had for the lieutenant had been going on too long, and Chad's feelings were too strong for him to be just another item crossed off Hollywood's to-do list.

Try gay sex. Check.

Chad was ready for a relationship. A real one, between two committed adults. Problem was, he wanted that relationship to be with Hollywood, and if he couldn't at least get some honesty from the man, he'd rather be alone.

Fucking straight guys.

He should have nipped this thing in the bud when he'd felt a resurgence of that all-too-familiar tingle in his belly last summer. It had happened when he'd seen Hollywood in his bunker gear the day of the big earthquake. The guy had given Chad a dark look that had hardened his cock in an instant, despite all the chaos around them. Even though he'd tried to reason it away, the crush that had started when he'd been eleven had mushroomed from glowing coals to a roaring blaze that consumed him a little more each time he saw the big blond.

Their fight had been the perfect catalyst for Chad to pull his head out of his ass. Hollywood had revealed his true self, and none of it was good for Chad's well-being.

It was definitely better this way.

When the coffee was ready, he filled two travel mugs. As he was screwing on the covers, his and Liam's pagers went off. A possible heart attack a dozen blocks away.

In perfect accord, Chad grabbed the mugs, Liam scooped up the bag of muffins, and they raced to their unit.

Liam unlocked the doors of Medic 11 and they climbed into their usual spots, Liam behind the wheel and Chad in the passenger seat. As Liam pulled out of the ambulance bay, Chad checked the Computer Aided Dispatch View reports on the MDC, the Mobile Data Computer, to confirm the address and read it off to Liam.

Twenty minutes later, they were walking out of the downtown apartment building. It had been a false alarm. Recurring anxiety, not a heart attack. After verifying the patient's ECG and confirming her medical history, they'd advised her to talk about the incident with her family doctor, then they'd left.

Back inside Medic 11, Chad buckled his seat belt and reached for his coffee. Still hot. Grateful for the magic of thermos mugs, Chad took a long sip. When he realized that the ambulance still hadn't moved, he turned to Liam with a frown.

Liam arched a brow. "Want to talk about it?"

Without asking, Chad knew Liam was referring to Hollywood. "Nope. I'm good."

"If he said anything to upset you, I'll kick his ass, lieutenant or no."

Chad chuckled at the image of Liam, all five foot nine of him, going up against Hollywood's six feet four. The guy would be crushed like a spider under a shoe. He squeezed Liam's shoulder, feeling the tiniest bit better. He had some great friends, and Liam was one of the best. "You and Anna have holiday plans?"

Liam started up Medic 11 and pulled into traffic. "We're heading out to see her parents in Oregon for a few days. That's about it. You?"

"The usual get-togethers with the family."

"I'm sure you'll have a better time than I will," Liam joked. "At least your folks let you drink in the house. I have to put up with all that family chaos stone-cold sober."

Anna had grown up with an alcoholic father who, although he'd never physically abused his family, had definitely neglected them. According to what Liam had shared with him, the man had often gone on binges, drinking away the family's rent money. It had taken his wife leaving with the kids for the guy to find God and AA. Anna's mother had to be one hell of a strong woman to deal with all of that and keep loving her alcoholic husband.

While Chad's parents hadn't had the same problems, they'd had years of financial insecurity, and God knew how money problems could tear a family apart. Then there were Jamie and Erica. They'd been on the brink of divorce, but they'd hung on and pulled through, and now they were happier than Chad had ever seen them.

Did he have what it took to make a relationship work for a year, a decade, a lifetime?

Up to now, he'd thought he did. But sending his friend—potential lover?—packing at the first sign of trouble had told him differently. What was the alternative though? Let the guy walk all over him? Fuck no. He'd never been the type, and he had no plans to change now.

As they drove in silence, listening to the calls that came across the radio, Chad's phone buzzed, signaling an incoming text message. Juggling the coffee and the muffin on his lap, he fished his cell out of the back pocket of his pants. It was Hollywood.

H: I'm an ass.

No argument there.

Liam indicated the phone with his head. "Anything important?"

"Nope." He shoved the phone back in his pocket, then took another bite of his muffin and washed it down with the crappy station coffee. "We should've gone to Starbucks," he grumbled. "Their shit is so much better."

Liam shook his head. "Too expensive. I'm saving up for the baby's nursery."

"Please tell me Anna will be picking out the furniture and accessories."

"Don't worry, gay boy." Liam raised an eyebrow. "She's already told me that my job is to be the brawn and nothing more."

"Come on, tell the truth. What did you suggest? Brown and mauve? Fuchsia and yellow?"

"Fuchsia?" Liam snorted. "What the hell is that?"

Chad laughed. "Red, white, and blue?"

Liam's lips thinned, and Chad knew he'd hit a home run. His grin widened. "That's it, isn't it? Oh my God. I'd have paid anything to see her face."

"Nothing wrong with patriotic colors."

"True, and those are good, stimulating colors," Chad agreed. He knew there was more to it. Laughter threatened to choke him as he waited for Liam to spill like he always did.

After a few minutes, Liam scrunched up his face. "It might have been the suggestion to paint a mural of the battle of Yorktown that did it."

Chad tossed his head back and laughed.

"It isn't funny," Liam groused, shooting daggers at Chad. "Yorktown was a key victory."

That only served to set him off again. Chad thumbed away the wetness under his eyes as he clutched his stomach with his free hand. "Thank you, buddy. I really needed that."

"If you laughed at Hollywood that way, it's no wonder the guy hightailed it back to his place."

That wiped the smile off Chad's face. He hung his head. "He didn't run. I told him to leave."

"Why? I thought you liked him."

"I do."

"But Hollywood doesn't like you *that* way? He's straight after all?"

"I don't know." His good humor gone, Chad fiddled with the liner on his muffin, before breaking off a piece and eating it. "He seemed to enjoy it enough."

Liam's mouth twisted and he bit down on the corner as he focused on driving, or maybe he was focused on figuring out what the hell Chad was saying. He didn't understand his own actions either.

"So why'd you give him the boot?"

Chad shrugged. "I guess I felt like he wasn't even seeing me, like I could have been anyone as long as he got off."

"Hmmm."

Liam was quiet for so long that Chad got impatient. He really needed another perspective on what had happened. "That's all you got?"

"No. I'm just not sure you want to hear what I've got to say."

Chad threw his hands up, almost dropping his coffee. Slugging the rest of it down, he set the empty travel mug on the mat at his feet and tossed the liner into the garbage bag that hung off a knob on the center console.

"You're being a little bitch."

Chad's eyes widened so much, he felt the stretch between his eyebrows. "What? *I'm* being a—" he sputtered, before folding his arms across his chest and slumping back in his seat, muttering under his breath.

"You done?" Liam asked, his tone oh-so-fucking patient.

"Yes," Chad spat.

"Put yourself in the lieutenant's shoes. You've been straight"—he shot Chad a glance—"or mostly straight, all your life, then this hot guy comes along who makes you rethink everything. You make the decision to try out these new feelings with this guy who's been pursuing you for weeks. It feels good. You're confused, but you cover it up with a little false bravado. Maybe you get a little too handsy, a little too confident. Maybe you're a little too blown away by everything that's happening to think clearly, to say the right things. Maybe you go with your gut, and fall into old patterns because you don't know how else to handle the fact that you might be someone you didn't think you were."

Chad sat stunned. Every word hit home, explaining to a T what he now had no doubt Hollywood had been telling. That night hadn't been about him. It had been about Hollywood having enough courage to push his limits with Chad. The guy had to try being with another man before he could know if he liked it, and Chad was the lucky fucker Hollywood had chosen to go with him on this adventure.

And, in return, Chad had told him to fuck off. "I really am a bitch."

"Not all the time, but this time? Yeah."

Chad rolled his lip between his teeth and clasped his hands on his lap. "You don't have to answer, but I've got to ask. How do you know all this?" There had to be a story behind his buddy's words. No one could be that empathetic to a situation they'd never been in.

Liam's hands clenched around the steering wheel, his face a neutral mask. "College. My roommate and I got high one night with a couple girls in our dorm room. Before we knew it, we were having a four-way orgy. I'd never even looked at a guy before that night. I don't know if it was him, or the fact that the girls were with us, but I wanted to touch him, to run my fingers through the curls on his head. We were fucking the girls, side by side. Our gazes met and then we were kissing. It was such a rush. The girls loved it and started kissing too."

He paused, his eyes slightly glazed as he recalled that night so many years before. "I didn't fuck him, but I would have. So I understand exactly what your lieutenant was going through. That much testosterone and lust are hard to resist."

Chad swallowed, looking at his partner in a whole new way. "Have you ever... uh...?"

"Fucked a guy? No."

"I was going to say, have you ever been attracted to another guy since then?"

"Same answer, no. I haven't ever gotten high again either." He smirked.

"Wow."

"I'm pretty secure with my sexuality. I love Anna, and the sex is better than I've ever had. I know I'm not a closet case, but..." He shrugged. "Maybe sometimes it's just a question of the right person happening along."

"What became of your roommate?"

"He got married last month to a guy named John."

"You dog." Chad chuckled. "You turned the guy gay."

Liam raised his hand for a fist bump. "Yeah. I'm *that* good."

"Does Anna know?"

"I'd never keep something like this from her."

"She's okay with it?"

Liam laughed. "She says if I ever get the urge to explore that side of myself again, we could get a third."

"Jesus, man. Never let this woman go. Do whatever you have to do to keep her happy."

"Every day, my friend. Every day."

Chad's phone buzzed again. He pulled it out of his pocket. His gut clenched. Another text from Hollywood.

H: I'm sorry

Gripping the phone tightly, Chad leaned on the armrest and stared out the window. He was sorry too, but he couldn't handle it if Hollywood was playing with him. His heart was already too involved. What he wanted could be within his grasp, but to reach it, he'd have to take a risk. Assuming Hollywood was being frank with his interest, was he worth getting hurt?

His phone buzzed again.

H: I miss your fancy coffee machine.

Chad's lips curved into a smile. He pressed the hand holding the phone against his mouth.

"That him?" Liam asked.

"Yeah. He misses my appliances."

Liam shook his head. "I'm not touching that one."

Chad typed in a quick response.

C: They sell Keurigs at Costco

H: It won't be the same :(

As Chad tried to read between the lines of Hollywood's messages, Liam asked, "You going to give him a chance to explain?"

"I'm thinking about it."

"Given the smile on your face, I'd say you've already thought about it."

"Get your mind out of the gutter, foursome boy."

Another text came in.

H: We good?

C: We should talk

Hollywood's response came before Chad had a chance to tell Liam what he was planning.

H: My place? Tonight?

C: Tomorrow. I'm working today

H: Come at six. I'll cook

I'll cook. Chad couldn't resist teasing Hollywood a little.

C: I'd better alert the boys at Station 37

H: STFU

C: c u tomorrow

H: ok

After pulling into the ambulance bay at HMC, where they'd wait for their next call, Liam turned to face Chad. "Well?"

This time Chad held his fist up for a bump. "I've got a date with a smoking hot firefighter."

"Woohoo!" Liam tapped his fist against Chad's.

"He's cooking me dinner."

"Uh-oh. In that case, you'd better bring this." An evil grin on his face, Liam reached under his seat and handed Chad an emergency first aid kit.

CHAPTER 13

The following evening, Chad stepped off the elevator on Hollywood's floor, nervous as hell. This whole Hollywood cooking dinner thing felt suspiciously like a date. But was it? He hadn't felt so unsure of himself since his first date with Greg Bertrand after they'd come out to their families.

Only Hollywood wasn't out.

Horse. Cart. Slow down, Caldwell.

How could Hollywood be out at this point? The poor guy didn't know anything more than that he'd enjoyed kissing a guy and getting a blow job. If that was all it took to be considered gay, a lot more men would be waving the rainbow flag.

Across from the elevator stood a full-length mirror. The wind had done a number on Chad's hair, so he took a moment to fix it. He'd chosen to wear something understated: tight black trousers, a white button-down shirt, a loosely done up black silk tie, and his gray topcoat. His black leather boots and gloves completed the outfit. He looked good, so why was he so damn nervous?

They were just two guys getting together to hang out, right?

Juggling the box of French pastries he'd bought from a little bakery on his street, Chad rolled his shoulders and forced himself to ignore the fact that this evening could go one of two ways: horribly wrong, or incredibly right.

At Hollywood's door, he lifted his hand and landed three quick raps on the solid wood. The door opened immediately, as though Hollywood had been standing right beside it, awaiting Chad's arrival. Trying not to be warmed by that thought, Chad took a leisurely look at his dinner partner. Hollywood's blond spikes glistened with drops of moisture as he stood in the doorway reciprocating Chad's survey with an uncertain smile.

Barefoot, wearing only snug, worn jeans and a close-fitting black T-shirt, Hollywood was like a hit of a powerful drug. A drug that had Chad imagining all kinds of directions their evening together could take. Heart hammering in his chest, Chad angled his head and, hoping his voice didn't go all queeny on him, asked, "Aren't you going to invite me in?"

"I wasn't certain you'd show." Hollywood's gaze hadn't wavered from its perusal of Chad, and Chad's cock was starting to take notice.

He pushed the bakery box into Hollywood's hands. "What? And miss the chance to see you at work?"

"I won't be putting out any fires tonight."

"You sure?" Chad teased.

Hollywood's lips twisted into a sinful smile that almost knocked Chad on his ass, and his casually added, "Not that kind of fire, anyway," finished Chad off.

Hollywood stepped back to let Chad enter. Totally thrown off balance, Chad forced his eyes away from the man as he walked into the newly renovated apartment. "Wow. The place looks great." The only other time he'd seen it, Hollywood's apartment had been a sad, sodden mess. Now it looked like something in a showroom.

"Thanks." Hollywood slipped past him on the way to the kitchen, where he set the pink box on the counter and opened the fridge, leaning down to inspect its contents. The soft denim of Hollywood's jeans cupped his perfect ass in a way that made Chad salivate.

"Want a drink? I've got water, pop, tea, and coffee. Oh, and orange juice," Hollywood asked, looking over his shoulder.

No mention of anything alcoholic. Chad's brow arched, despite his best efforts to keep it down. It wasn't any of his business. Unless, of course, Hollywood was insulted by their earlier discussion on the subject of drinking.

Obviously noticing Chad's expression, Hollywood closed the fridge and came to stand in front of him, their chests only a few inches apart. So close, in fact, that Hollywood's minty breath fanned Chad's cheek when he said, "I'm not letting anything cloud my mind or my judgment tonight."

The glint in the man's eye was brutal and honest. Was he aware of the heat in his gaze as it dropped to Chad's mouth?

Chad swallowed and shoved his hands in his pockets to keep from grabbing the guy and pulling him into a kiss neither would ever forget. "So, no liquid courage?" he finally managed.

"I don't need any."

"No?"

Hollywood's focus rose to Chad's eyes, and held. "I know what I want now."

Unable to believe, hell, unable to think, under the force of that seductive green assault, Chad's blood roared southward. He licked his lips. "And what's that?"

The fire in Hollywood's eyes flared, turning Chad's blood into lava as he waited, feet on the edge of a cliff, for Hollywood's response.

"You."

Chad swayed. "Oh boy."

Stepping back, Hollywood chuckled, clearly aware of his effect on Chad. "Get that look off your face. I'm keeping my hands to myself tonight."

"All night?" The words barely out of his mouth, Chad winced at the disappointment in his voice. But, Jesus, he *was* disappointed. For months now—no, if he were being honest, it had been years—he'd been dreaming of what it would be like to hold Hollywood, to kiss and touch him, to sink his cock between those muscled ass cheeks. Not that he expected to do all that tonight, or anytime soon, but *something*. Christ, he needed something.

Hollywood gently tapped his cheek and snorted. "At least until after dessert, Loverboy."

Loverboy. Chad felt as though he'd entered some kind of twilight zone or an alternate universe where a determined, confident Hollywood said all the things Chad desperately wanted to hear. "Is that what I am to you?"

Hollywood brushed two fingers along the edge of Chad's hairline and wiped away the beads of sweat popping out as Chad's heart hammered faster and faster. "It's what I'd like you to be." He moved closer and, slipping his hands under Chad's topcoat, pushed it off his shoulders.

Chad shuddered as the coat slid down his arms and dropped onto the carpeted floor with a muted thud. Taking a deep, calming breath, Chad leaned in so his chest was almost touching Hollywood's. "Where is all this self-assurance coming from?"

He hoped like hell this new version of Hollywood stuck around, because this man was hot-as-fuck. Not only did Hollywood not take the expected step back, he took one forward, pressing their chests fully against each other. "I've done a lot of thinking in the past couple of days."

"Oh, yeah? And?"

Hollywood grabbed Chad's ass and ground against him. "And I've missed you."

Feeling Hollywood's hard-on against his own, Chad's head reeled. He'd missed Hollywood too. So fucking much. And here they were, hard cocks rubbing together.

Dreams did come true.

He shot Hollywood his sultriest grin. "You sure you don't just miss my Keurig?"

Hollywood responded with a warm, wet lick up the side of Chad's neck. "That too."

ℒ 🚃 ℛ

Hollywood nuzzled Chad's throat, filling his nose with the man's cologne. He could bathe in the stuff, it smelled so damn good. Even more fun would be to get the scent on himself by rubbing all over Chad—

Closing his eyes, he let himself breathe Chad in one more time. Simply being near him made his head spin. If he had any chance in hell of keeping his hands off the guy until after dessert, he needed to take a big fucking step back.

He cleared his throat, for all the good it did. He still sounded as turned on as he was. "So, that drink?"

"I'll have... uh... a Coke, if you've got it."

Hollywood smiled. *That voice.* Thick, gravelly. Filled with want. It was what Chad would sound like in bed, hot and bothered. Ready to come. He hoped he'd get the chance to confirm it tonight. Chad tilted his head to the left, his expression questioning. Oh yeah. Whatever happened or didn't happen tonight, he really wanted to see and hear Chad come. He wanted it even more than his own release. And wasn't that shocking as hell? Most of the time, he wasn't an insensitive or uncaring lover, but he'd never been or wanted to be a selfless one. Until now. Until Chad.

With that thought playing pinball in his brain, he waved Chad over to the small table in the breakfast nook. He'd set it earlier with his best dishes and a linen tablecloth he'd bought on a whim. Fuck yeah, he was trying to impress the guy. Chad might be younger, but he had it together. His condo was perfectly decorated for a man, and even in the short time he'd lived there, Hollywood had seen that when Chad did something, he did it with flair and determination. The man didn't take half-measures, and where Chad was concerned, Hollywood wouldn't either.

Taking the lasagna out of the oven, he set it on the counter to cool while he heated up the garlic bread. It was one of his mother's recipes. Her cookbook was really the only thing he had of her, other than a few badly creased photos. Still, it was something, and each time he made her lasagna, he recalled her beside him, chatting as she showed him how to layer the sauce, noodles, and cheese. It always left him feeling loved and centered. Something he badly needed these days.

He set two cans of Coke on the table, along with two tall glasses filled with ice. Chad tracked his every move in an obvious way that had his gut clenching in anticipation of their after-dinner activities.

"Need help?" Chad asked.

Hollywood set a bowl of salad on the table. "Nah. Everything's under control."

"So there won't be any hot firefighters traipsing through your apartment, then?" Chad's bottom lip pushed out in a full pout.

Unable to resist any longer, Hollywood brushed a fingertip along Chad's plush lip. "You got a thing for the uniform?"

Chad shot him a wink. "Why do you think I went to the fire academy? Bunker gear does it for me every time."

Going around the breakfast bar, Hollywood warmed at the amusement in Chad's voice, mixed in, he was sure, with a healthy dose of honesty. "I'll have to remember that next time you're pissed at me."

"You think there'll be a next time?" Chad asked as Hollywood made up two plates with large pieces of the lasagna.

"I hope there is."

Standing with Chad's plate in his hand, he gauged the guy's reaction to his statement. Arms crossed, expression serious, Chad seemed lost in thought. "You okay?" Hollywood asked, depositing the plate in front of him. Chad blinked, but didn't otherwise move.

Sighing, Hollywood grabbed his own plate and the bread, then took his seat across from him. The time he'd been dreading—even though it was the main reason he'd invited Chad over—had come. "Talk to me."

His expression falsely casual, Chad sat up and served the salad into two bowls. "I'm just curious why you think you'll piss me off again."

Oddly relieved by the direction of Chad's thoughts, Hollywood cut into his lasagna, letting out the mouth-watering aroma of melted mozzarella, tomatoes, basil, and meat. He looked across the table at the man he was happy to break bread with and decided to admit the truth. "I *am* really sorry about how I reacted the other night. I wasn't using you to get off."

Chad swallowed his bite and nodded encouragingly.

"I hope you'll be patient with me. This is all new, and the way I see it, I have two choices: walk on eggshells and keep my thoughts to myself, or be spontaneous and let you in. The first is safer—"

"Boring."

"The second is—"

"Dangerous."

Hollywood picked up a slice of bread and brought it to his mouth. "You see my dilemma? Either way I'm going to fuck up, and you're going to get mad." Before he could dig himself in deeper, he shoved the bread into his mouth.

Taking his sweet motherfucking time, Chad cracked open his can of Coke and poured it, sizzling and popping, over the cubes of ice. Then, lifting the glass to his perfect, parted lips, he drank. His throat working, his Adam's apple bobbed with each swallow. Finally, after what simultaneously seemed either a really long or really short time, Chad set his glass down. Hollywood's mouth quirked at the satisfied look in Chad's eyes. *This is going to be good.*

"Since we've established that I'm bound to get upset again, let's go with door number two. Just imagining the shit that might come out of your mouth is turning me on."

"Yeah?" Hollywood asked, knowing he sounded breathless and not giving a fuck.

"Yeah. And you know what else is even more exciting?" When Hollywood shook his head mutely, Chad continued. "Imagining how we'll make up."

Red as a damn fire truck, that's the color Hollywood knew his face had to be as he sat there picturing himself and Chad doing the things he'd seen on that gay porn video. God, he wanted that. "Sounds like you're on board with seeing where this thing between us goes."

"Absolutely."

"There's something else I'd like, too," Hollywood said, his mouth suddenly as dry as the Sahara. His gaze had locked onto Chad's lips and wouldn't budge.

"What's that?"

Hollywood took a deep breath, squared his shoulders, and pushed out the words he'd wanted to say since the previous afternoon when they'd texted. Words he should have said that night at Chad's place. "I'd like to do to you what you did to me."

"You want to give me a blow job?" Chad's voice sounded strangled.

"Like my life depends on it."

And maybe it did. Maybe doing this would make him gay. Maybe it wouldn't. At least he'd know.

"You sure?" Chad asked, sounding anything but sure himself.

Hollywood angled his head, unable to understand why Chad wasn't jumping at his offer. "Ouch. I didn't expect to get turned down."

Chad's brows winged up as he pushed his chair back. "Are you fucking kidding me?" Standing up, he palmed his crotch, rubbing his hand against it "I'm hard as a goddamn backboard at the thought of your mouth stretched around my cock. Now get your ass over here."

℠ 🎥 ℞

In the ringing silence, Chad stood by his chair waiting to see what Hollywood's next move would be. Either he'd be offended or—

Eyes never leaving Chad's face, Hollywood pushed to his feet and stepped around the table with a sexy loose-hipped swagger that said exactly how much the guy was affected by their talk. But Chad wanted so much more than talk. Did Hollywood?

Despite it being the last thing he wanted to say, since it might make Hollywood reconsider, Chad had to. He didn't want Hollywood to do this because he felt guilty or obligated. He wanted him to do it because it felt right.

"You don't have to do this." He infused the words with as much calm as he could manage under the circumstances.

Hollywood took a final step. He was close enough now that Chad could feel the heat emanating from the guy. Hollywood's lips curved into a self-deprecating smile that tugged at Chad's inflamed heart-strings. "I know."

Hollywood's long fingers reached out to undo the button on Chad's trousers. The hiss of the zipper being lowered was as loud as the roar of a chainsaw. He shoved the pants down Chad's legs and, leaving them to pool at his ankles, Hollywood hooked his fingers in the low waistband of his very tight trunks. "I want to see all of you."

He sank to his knees, then yanked Chad's underwear down his legs to join his pants. Chad moaned as his cock sprang free from its confines, and because he was so focused on Hollywood, he saw more than heard the guy gasp.

Christ, here it comes.

Chad steeled himself against the revulsion that was sure to follow if Hollywood was as straight as he claimed to be. Seeing another aroused man up close and personal was a lot different than seeing one on a computer screen. But Hollywood's face didn't scrunch up in disgust, nor did he shy away, or back up. In fact, he leaned closer, and Chad could have sworn the guy—inhaled? *Oh God.* Hollywood's chest expanded as he breathed in through his nose. His nostrils flared and the green of his eyes darkened, almost disappearing.

His knees threatening to buckle, Chad gripped the back of his chair and attempted to withstand the impact of Hollywood's attention—all six feet four of solid muscle—focused on his cock. Hobbled as he was, if he didn't get a handle on the situation, and quickly, he'd end up on his ass and embarrassed as hell.

Hollywood eyed him curiously, tilting his head to the left, then the right, as though Chad's cock were the most fascinating thing in the universe. The guy's slow perusal was destroying his resolve to let Hollywood lead, one excruciating second at a time. Chad was afraid to speak, to ruin the moment, to do something to remind Hollywood that he wasn't into men.

When Hollywood finally finished his inspection, he lifted his head, cheeks flushed, eyes filled with burning heat—and excitement. And something else. Awe? Chad hoped like fuck it was. There had been compliments...

"Christ, you're hung," Hollywood said, on a chuckle.

Groaning at the rush of lust hitting him low in his belly, Chad wrapped his fingers around his aching cock and allowed himself a few languorous pulls to take the edge off. "You're killing me, man."

A sudden look of uncertainty flashed across Hollywood's eyes, filling Chad with anxiety. He let go of his shaft and went to pull up his trunks. Hollywood stopped him with a hand on his arm and a question. "Can I touch you?"

Laughter, damn near hysteria, bubbled up in Chad's chest at the ridiculousness of it all. They were both so tense, so nervous. So worried about doing the wrong thing. And Chad had the added concern of his feet being all but tied together. Slowly he placed his palm on Hollywood's cheek, and almost swooned when the guy turned into it. Chad smiled, heart thoroughly warmed. "I'd love that. But let's take this to the living room, okay?" He indicated his ankles with a wry grin. "My position is somewhat precarious."

Hollywood laughed, loud and relieved. His eyes twinkled. "Yeah, and mine is a little back-alley-blow-job."

Chad had to agree. Having Hollywood on his knees, eager to swallow his cock while Chad stood before him, was pushing all his buttons, but the obvious power imbalance wasn't exactly ideal for first timers. Using Hollywood's shoulder for balance, Chad pulled off his boots, then shucked off his pants and underwear, incredibly and uncomfortably aware of his naked bottom-half. At least his shirttails covered him. Mostly. He took Hollywood's hand to help him up, then led him to the couch, surprised that Hollywood didn't pull his hand away.

"So uh... how should we do this?" Hollywood's eyes flipped between Chad and the couch.

"This is your show," Chad said, adding a reassuring smile.

Hollywood ran a hand behind his head and sighed. "I know how I like to get it, but—"

Chad put a finger to his mouth, stopping him. All guys liked to thrust into a waiting mouth, but the experience on the receiving end could be a little overwhelming. For this to work, Hollywood needed to be the one in control. "How about the couch, or the floor?"

Hollywood seemed to consider his options for a moment, then pointed to the couch. "Lie down."

Feeling like a character in an alien abduction movie, Chad did as instructed. He'd never been a big fan of passivity during sex, but tonight it was what Hollywood needed from him. And in a secret, deeply buried part of him, Chad had to admit he was the teensiest bit turned on by it.

With one hand behind his head, he used the other to stroke the erection that had slightly waned as they'd figured out the whats and wheres of the main event.

Hollywood knelt beside the couch, looking uncertain. Chad smiled. They'd lost the momentum and any impulsivity was shot out the window, but he could still bring back the romance. He crooked a finger at Hollywood. "Come here."

Although he arched a mocking brow, Hollywood shuffled along the couch until his head was close to Chad's. So close that all Chad had to do was hook a hand behind the guy's head to pull him down. Hollywood's smile, right before their lips connected, made his toes curl. Chad flicked his tongue over Hollywood's lips, finding the faint taste of the lasagna they'd eaten.

A hand not his own touched his cock, tentatively at first, stroking up from the base to the crown. A long finger traced the bulging vein on the underside. Chad arched into the sensations and moaned. Taking advantage of his parted lips, Hollywood's tongue plunged inside, marking its ownership of Chad's mouth. Like sparring partners, their tongues danced around each other, darting forward for a quick touch before retreating, only to do so again.

Chad's head spun at the dual assault on his senses, and embarrassing sounds of pleasure escaped him. He wasn't even remotely able to stay cool and controlled. What was happening here was the culmination of years of fantasies. Hollywood had been a candidate, just finishing up at the fire academy when Jamie had first brought him home for dinner. One blinding smile from the guy, with his broad shoulders and tall muscular body, was all it had taken for Chad to fall.

It had been a crush—then—a passing fancy like one of many Chad had had before and since, but over time it had grown into something much more real. Something strong. Something Chad refused to put a name to until he was certain he could expose it to Hollywood without fear of having his dreams destroyed.

Tonight isn't that night.

That didn't mean he couldn't enjoy himself. Enjoy having Hollywood's hands and lips on him. Christ, he was already more than halfway to coming and Hollywood's mouth hadn't even gone near his cock yet.

Hollywood ended the kiss and pulled back.

Oh God, don't stop. Suck me, fuck me. Something, anything!

A boyish grin spread across Hollywood's handsome face. "Patience, young Skywalker. Patience."

Chad rolled his eyes. "Oh my God. Are you seriously quoting *Star Wars* to me? Now?" Something occurred to him and his face started to burn. Either Hollywood was a mind reader or—"Please, tell me I didn't say that out loud."

"You always such a chatty Cathy during sex?" Hollywood raised his brow, and Chad knew.

"Fuck."

"You offering?"

Chad gulped. "Not tonight."

"Didn't think so." Hollywood angled his head toward the other end of the couch. "Back to the program?"

"Yes, please."

Hollywood's wicked laugh sent all the remaining blood in Chad's body to his groin. His brain stopped working. He couldn't think, couldn't talk—*thank you, Jesus*—as Hollywood crawled down the couch and slowly guided Chad's cock toward his open and waiting mouth.

CHAPTER 14

Hollywood refused to let his fingers tremble as they gripped Chad's hard cock. A pulse beat in the thick vein under Hollywood's fingertip, accelerating the closer his lips came to the engorged head. Hollywood didn't have a lot of experience as far as dicks went, especially erect ones, but even he could tell that Chad's was something special, a goddamn masterpiece. Wow. He couldn't believe he was here, on his knees, admiring another man's cock as though it were the fucking Leaning Tower of Pisa.

But he was.

And it was exactly where he wanted to be. Inhaling deeply, he took in the musky odor of Chad's arousal, beading from his slit like a tear, the clean citrusy scent of his soap, and the darkly spicy fragrance of his skin. The combination was headier than any five-hundred-dollar-an-ounce perfume he'd ever smelled.

Stop stalling.

It was here—the moment of truth. The time to get his first taste of man. Would he love it or hate it? And how would he feel if the answer were the former rather than the latter?

Christ. One way or another, he couldn't hurt Chad again. They were starting to be friends, and that was important to him. Closing his eyes, because seeing what he was taking into his mouth might be a bit more than he could handle right now, he stuck out his tongue and took a blind swipe. Salty, a little tangy and bitter, but not unpleasant. He'd already tasted himself on women's mouths when he'd kissed them. Chad tasted similar, but not the same. Much like his skin, his pre-cum was a touch spicy.

Hollywood put his free hand on Chad's thigh as he leaned over more fully. That's when he noticed how rigidly Chad held himself, and the trembling in his muscles. Immediately, he understood: Chad was struggling not to move. A sense of safety, of comfort, of knowing he was trying this with the right person, swept over him, and ramped up his desire to return the pleasure, to make Chad happy.

With renewed determination, he licked around the crown of Chad's cock, stroking the sensitive underside, and prodded that little spot he knew felt so damn good. Once Chad was wet, Hollywood opened wide, and slipped his lips around the bulbous head. Christ, the guy was big. Loosening his jaw, he opened wider still, and took all of Chad in his mouth. Well, the head anyway. Despite his best efforts to stay calm, Hollywood's heart raced. How the hell had Chad swallowed him to the root? He didn't have Chad's girth, but his cock was a little longer. It hadn't fazed the guy though. He hadn't even gagged. Shit. How was he going to do this? His mouth was already full to bursting.

Beneath him, Chad's body shook. Concerned, Hollywood shifted his gaze up to Chad's face and stalled there. The guy was turned on. No doubt about that. But the fucker was also grinning. Popping off Chad, he growled. "You better not be laughing at me."

Chad groaned, eyes rolling back in his head. It wasn't Hollywood's fault if his hand had tightened on Chad's shaft. Honest.

"No, no," Chad said. Not laughing, just..." He paused and panted. "Remembering."

Hollywood let up the pressure and narrowed his eyes. "Remembering what?"

Chad arched his back and pushed himself into Hollywood's fist, which was still holding him firmly. Pre-cum leaked from his slit, making the shaft slick and shiny. The guy was beautiful this way. Laid out in front of him. Wanting.

The only thing that could make it more perfect would be if Chad were naked, but one thing at a time. "What were you remembering?" he prompted.

"How daunting it can be at first. Just... ah... concentrate on the head."

Okay, good advice. This time when he took Chad in his mouth, Hollywood kept his gaze on Chad's face, enjoying each gasp, each moan, each clenched muscle in his neck as he strained not to move. God. Was he really getting turned on by this? Hollywood's cock flexed against the zipper of his jeans. Yeah, he was. With his free hand, he reached down and readjusted himself so he was slightly more comfortable.

Using his fist, he pumped the part of Chad's erection that he couldn't cover with his mouth. Pretty soon, he had a nice rhythm going. He hollowed his cheeks, rising up as far as he could without completely

137

releasing the hot meat in his mouth, then he plunged as low as he could go. The third time he did this, Chad's hips gave a small buck, pushing deeper and hitting the back of Hollywood's throat, making him gag. His eyes watered and he began to pull back.

"Breathe through it." Chad put a hand on his shoulder. "Breathe through your nose."

The guttural quality of Chad's tone was a sure sign that the guy was close to coming, and Hollywood wanted to bring him there.

Really?

Raising his eyes, he focused again on Chad's face, the color on his cheeks, the whiteness of his lips stretched out in delicious pain. The sights and sounds went straight to his cock.

Oh yeah. Fucking right, he wanted to make Chad come.

Following Chad's advice, Hollywood forced air to flow through his nose as he slowly descended, taking more and more of that hard cock into his mouth. When the heat hit his throat, he breathed rapidly and concentrated on relaxing his muscles, before lowering a little more. He repeated this twice until Chad's crown was as deep as he could handle it. Remembering how it had felt when Chad swallowed around his own shaft, he did the same. His muscles tightened, eliciting a shout from the guy. Hands clutched his head, fingers dug into his scalp, trying to pull him off.

"I'm gonna—"

There was no way Hollywood was backing off now. Ignoring the bite of pain—actually it was driving him crazy and making him even harder—Hollywood rose on his knees and took in the rest of Chad's cock. With his nose in Chad's well-groomed crotch, the man's cock firmly lodged in his throat, Hollywood started to see stars.

Chad's hands gripped Hollywood's head, and he pumped his hips two times, short, sharp thrusts, then shouted his release. Hot cum poured down Hollywood's throat with each thrust and spasm. The taste, the tightness, the lack of air—the combination of new experiences pushed Hollywood over the edge. Lifting off Chad's softening cock, he rested his head on Chad's thigh, closed his eyes, and let himself go.

Holy fuck. He'd come in his pants like a seventh grader.

With a dick in your mouth.

Yeah, with a dick in his mouth. Un-fucking-believable.

Strong fingers gently played with his hair. Hollywood turned his head to see Chad, who looked blissed out and sexed out and so freaking beautiful it hurt Hollywood's heart. The corner of Chad's lips quirked into a small smile, but underneath it, Hollywood could tell the guy was nervous. Waiting for Hollywood's reaction.

"How do you feel?" Chad asked, giving voice to his obvious concern.

Hollywood mentally scanned his body. His throat was raw, his jaw sore, he'd unloaded in his pants, and Chad's taste was still on his tongue.

He grinned up at the man who'd grabbed him by the balls and turned his world over on its ass. How did he feel? "So very gay."

§∂ 🎥 ᗋ

Chad stared at Hollywood for about fifteen seconds, shocked stupid, before he threw his head back and laughed, letting loose the tension that had built up in his chest as he'd awaited Hollywood's verdict.

"Yeah, I get that."

After all, there was nothing more gay than sucking another guy off and coming while you were doing it, without even the benefit of a hand to help you along. He'd noticed, and it had made him feel really fucking hopeful.

Sitting up, he cupped Hollywood's heated cheeks and brought him in for a kiss. Hollywood gasped and Chad's tongue dipped into his mouth just long enough for him to taste himself there. Such a damn turn-on. "Thank you," he whispered against the other man's mouth.

Hollywood moaned and caught Chad's bottom lip with his teeth, nipping gently before releasing it and pressing their foreheads together.

"What now?" Hollywood asked, breathless, and clearly ready to go again.

But instinctively, Chad knew continuing the explorations right now would be a wrong move. Just as it would have been that night at his house. Hollywood was in a state of euphoria, his body driven by a primordial need to seek out more pleasure. He needed to give his mind time to catch up, to process what had happened and analyze how he felt about it.

Chad was determined to give him that time. "Dessert?"

"And here I thought *you* were dessert." Hollywood smirked.

Chad kissed him again and shifted to get off the couch. When his naked ass pulled on the leather, making a squelching sound, he pinned Hollywood with a glare.

Hollywood backed off, hands in the air. "I didn't say a thing."

"I can see the wheels turning from here."

"Just didn't think we were already at the I'm-comfortable-farting-in-front-of-you stage." As soon as the words were out of his mouth, Hollywood jumped to his feet and took several giant steps back. But not fast enough.

Chad raced after him, gripping his T-shirt. "I did not fart, and you know it."

A sly smile slid across Hollywood's gorgeous face, lighting up his green eyes. "Maybe," he teased. His eyes dropped down to Chad's bare ass. "Want me to check?"

"Fuck off," Chad said, smacking his arm, and turned to fetch his trunks. Once he was dressed again and on even footing with his host, he felt better. At least that's what he thought until Hollywood came up behind him, slid his arms around Chad's waist, and pulled him against his chest. He nuzzled Chad's neck. The small puffs of air on each exhale sent shivers racing up and down Chad's spine. God, he could so get used to this.

The thought terrified him.

He and Hollywood were nowhere near to being on even footing. Chad had been gay, openly and proudly, for years. He'd been in relationships with other men. Hollywood, on the other hand, had no frame of reference, except for a few fleeting experiences as a kid. And as good as it felt to sink into Hollywood's embrace, to feel the heat of his chest and arms around him, he had to stop himself from imagining more, from imagining a future together, because if there was to be even a remote chance of that happening, they had to go slow. And he had to keep his hopes and expectations to himself. He had to give Hollywood time to sort out who he was and what he wanted, and most importantly, if Chad figured into any of that.

Hollywood's tongue licked up the side of his neck, then he turned Chad in his arms. "Are we okay?"

Chad blinked away his too-serious thoughts and his too-real fears, then forced a confident, sassy smile to his lips as he pressed their groins together. "We're more than okay."

80 🎥 ଓ

Later that night, after they'd finished off the box of French pastries and a pot of herbal tea Hollywood had bought for Chad, they lay sprawled out on the couch, watching a very manly Bruce Willis blow up half of Moscow. Somehow, they'd ended up lying back to front with Chad happily in the position of little spoon, his head resting on one of Hollywood's arms while Hollywood's other arm was casually thrown over Chad's waist. He could feel the semi the guy had been sporting all evening press against his ass, and it was driving him fucking insane.

It was impossible to concentrate on the action taking place on the screen when all he could think about was getting a little action of his own. His breath hitched when Hollywood's arm moved up and tightened on his chest, pulling Chad back so he was in little doubt that Hollywood's semi had bloomed into a full-blown hard-on.

Cradled in Hollywood's arms and plastered against his body, Chad was in nirvana. The only thing that could make it better was if Chad's cock were in Hollywood's—

Cool lips and searing breath touched his neck. Sharp teeth nibbled a path up to his earlobe, then bit down. Chad moaned and writhed in Hollywood's strong arms, pushing his ass back against the hard length teasing him.

"Feels good?" Hollywood whispered next to his ear.

"Good doesn't begin to describe it."

Hollywood shifted behind him and the pressure on Chad's butt increased. When he spoke again, Hollywood's voice was filled with gravel. "Transcendent."

Transcendent? Laughing, Chad twisted his head back so he could see Hollywood's face, which was now scrunched into a frown.

"What?" Hollywood said. "I went to college."

At that, Chad turned around completely so they were both lying on their sides face-to-face. It was a tight fit, but in his opinion, that was half the fun. He traced the shell of Hollywood's perfectly small, perfectly shaped ear. "What did you study?"

"Business administration. I got a bachelor's degree, then applied for the fire academy. My dad thought it would help me move up faster. Guess he was wrong."

Chad pushed up on his elbow. "What are you talking about? You're a lieutenant in the most trained unit in the SFD."

Hollywood scoffed and let his head fall back against the couch. "I'm older than Jamie. We have the same job, and he only went to college for a year. It hasn't helped. It was just one more way for my father to lord it over me."

That statement brought back everything Chad knew about Hollywood's dad, including the fading bruise he'd left on Hollywood's cheek that night Hollywood had come home so fucked up. He cupped Hollywood's face and kissed him lightly, a butterfly touch of their lips. "I'm sorry," he whispered.

"For what?" Hollywood's hand went to Chad's ass, and Chad lost all ability to communicate when that big paw squeezed a cheek and dragged him closer. "I'm pretty damn happy with everything you've done tonight."

He sounded oblivious, but under all the teasing, Chad heard the note of hurt in Hollywood's voice. He was beginning to get an inkling of what Hollywood's life had been like under the chief's iron rule. A man who would strike his adult son, one as big and formidable as Hollywood, wasn't likely to have held back when that son had been just a boy. Especially one without a mother to protect him. He hoped that one day Hollywood would come to trust him enough to share. For now, he'd try to be there for the guy.

Waggling his brows, Chad bumped their groins together. "I'm pretty happy too." What had started out as a little joke turned on him when Hollywood pushed back. Their cocks connected and Chad felt the jolt down to his toes.

"Jesus Christ," Hollywood said, shock on his face. "Do that again."

Biting back a grin, Chad thrust his hips forward, but this time, he added a little upward motion. The friction was divine, and Chad forced himself to keep his eyes open so he could watch Hollywood's reaction. The guy's lids closed like shutters as his eyes rolled back. When he opened his eyes again, they were slightly unfocused, his breathing erratic. Chad couldn't help chuckling. "You like?"

"I bet this would feel even better without clothes."

Chad winked. "You have no idea."

"But I'm going to find out, aren't I?" It sounded more like an invitation than a question, and Chad decided to take it that way.

Sitting up, he took Hollywood's hand and tugged him into an upright position before throwing one leg over Hollywood's lap and straddling him. It was a little awkward given their sizes, but wiggling a little closer so their groins bumped, Chad made it work. He wrapped his arms around Hollywood's neck and smiled down at the man who surprised him at every turn. "If you don't like it and you want to stop, say so."

Hollywood's mouth interrupted his well-intentioned words of caution. Chad parted his lips, and Hollywood entered. And plundered. His hands tugged Chad's shirt out of his pants and slid under the soft cotton. The touch lit Chad up like a Christmas tree, and moaning, he rocked his hips forward, driven by the need to feel Hollywood's erection against his own.

Hollywood wrenched his mouth away, his hands bunching the shirt up. "Off," he ground out.

Laughing silently because there wasn't an ounce of air in his lungs, Chad removed his tie and unbuttoned his shirt as quickly as he could with trembling fingers. Impatience clearly written on his face, Hollywood shoved the shirt down Chad's arms, all activity stopping once Chad's chest was bare.

Worried, Chad froze, observing Hollywood. What was he staring at? It wasn't as though Hollywood had never seen him shirtless before. And really, after having sucked his cock, what could be so disturbing about his naked chest?

"What's wrong?" he asked, his voice barely louder than a whisper.

But Chad's worry was misplaced. The sudden heat blazing in Hollywood's eyes ratcheted up his arousal and blood rushed in his ears. Hollywood's fingers fanned out on his shoulders, then came down to his pectorals. The touch, as soft as a kiss, gave him goose bumps. Chad's nipples hardened into tiny nubs that drew Hollywood's attention. When he lunged forward and drew one between his teeth, Chad's heart skipped a beat. Moaning, he held onto Hollywood's shoulders with both hands and pushed his chest forward into Hollywood's hot mouth. Strong hands gripped his ass and yanked him even closer. Not a hair's width separated their groins. Hollywood slowly bit down on Chad's nipple, until Chad grunted and punched his hips forward.

They didn't even have their clothes off yet, and already, as far as Chad was concerned, this was the best frot experience he'd ever had. The teeth clamped onto his nub released and Chad breathed out a sigh of relief and frustration. He pulled Hollywood's head up, ready to kiss the man senseless, when he was met with Hollywood's hard expression: jaw like granite, eyes piercing. Chad's pulse spiked and a cold sensation washed over him. *Fuck, here it comes.*

ℴ ♠ ℥

"Get up," Hollywood ordered, pushing Chad off him and quickly getting to his feet.

Chad stepped back, looking like a disgruntled porn star. That was okay. He wouldn't be upset for long. Not with what Hollywood hoped was about to happen. The energy that had surged around them was like nothing he'd ever felt before.

Every touch, every sensation, was heightened, and he couldn't wait to see Chad naked. All of him at the same time. He wanted to trace the man's sexy-as-fuck tattoos. Run his tongue over them, and feel Chad's cock against his own. Hollywood enjoyed sex as much as anyone, but he wasn't particularly adventurous. He knew what he was good at and tended to stick with his favorite moves and positions, because they were a guaranteed way to get both himself and his partner off.

Except that with Chad everything was different.

He had no favorite positions, no plan B. The only thing he knew was that he needed to feel Chad's skin against his own. The amount of effort he was expending not to come at the sight of Chad's smooth golden skin and badass tattoos was making him grit his teeth. The pounding in his cock matched the roar in his ears.

"You want me to leave?"

The sound of Chad's voice, the tone of his question, and the meaning of his words caught Hollywood off-guard. He tore his eyes away from that amazing chest and fell into the storm that was Chad's gaze.

"Leave?" he choked out. "Fuck no. What gave you that idea?"

"Oh, I don't know," Chad spat, cocking his hip and snapping his fingers. "Could it be the fact that you shoved me off your lap and couldn't get away fast enough?"

Hollywood sighed and rubbed a hand on the back of his head. He had to fix this before Chad went into full queen mode. He stepped closer, relieved that the guy didn't back away. "I was in a hurry to get you naked."

Chad's breath stuttered and he pushed on Hollywood's chest. "What?"

"I want to see you, to feel you. All of you. Without your clothes on."

"You do?"

He nodded. "So, can we keep going?"

Chad's hands tunneled under Hollywood's T-shirt and shoved it up. Laughing, Hollywood raised his arms and stole a kiss as soon as the shirt cleared his head. But Chad was apparently in no mood to linger on the striptease. His hands went for Hollywood's jeans, unbuttoning and unzipping them in the blink of an eye.

He's had practice.

Hollywood pushed away the unwanted thought. Whatever, whoever, the guy had done in his past, including the cute bassist, it was none of Hollywood's business. What mattered was that Chad was here with him now. And Hollywood was damn glad for that.

He fumbled with Chad's trouser button until Chad swatted his hands away. "Strip," Chad ordered as he went to work taking off his own trousers and underwear.

Hollywood hurried to kick off his jeans, but in the end Chad was faster. A tremor wracked Hollywood's body when Chad—tall, built, and cut like a model—crouched in front of him and peeled off his boxer briefs. "I really love these."

Chad cupped his ass and took his weeping cock into his mouth. All the way.

Hollywood's knees buckled, and he'd have fallen if not for the strength of Chad's arms supporting him. The fact that they were so similarly built should have put Hollywood off completely. He'd always loved small, compact women. The huge difference in size had made him feel strong, powerful even. By that logic, being with Chad, who was almost as tall and built as he was, should have turned him off.

Except that it didn't.

Hollywood loved that he could stare Chad in the eye without having to bend his knees. He could kiss the man without hunching over. And when he held Chad against him, his whole body felt the contact.

Gently, he tugged Chad off his cock and urged him to stand. "Get up here."

Chad's eyes widened, but he did as he was asked. Hollywood slid a hand in his short hair and urged him into a passionate kiss, one he hoped expressed everything he was feeling right then. "You'll show me how to do this?"

Taking his hand, Chad smiled and led him to the couch. "Lie down."

Once Hollywood was stretched out, Chad placed a hand on either side of Hollywood's head, then climbed on top of him, using his arms to hold himself up. But Hollywood craved the contact. Wrapping his arms around Chad, he exerted pressure until Chad relented and settled all his considerable weight on him. It was as he'd imagined. All that hot skin molded to his own. Hollywood thought for a moment his brain would explode from all the pleasure. Every one of his nerves was attuned to Chad's touch, to his delicious scent, and he couldn't believe how good it felt to have a man in his arms.

"I've been missing out," he said. It might have sounded like a joke, but he was dead serious.

Chad snorted and buried his face in Hollywood's neck. "Wait. You haven't seen nothing yet."

"I'm not sure I'll live through the experience."

"Don't worry, sir," Chad said, his voice more serious than Hollywood had heard it all night. "I'm a paramedic."

Hollywood cracked up, and against his chest he felt the reverberations of the rumbles in Chad's own chest. He couldn't remember ever being so close to another human being that he literally *felt* that person's laughter. Lifting his head, he nipped at Chad's lips until he opened and let him in. Chad returned the kiss, sucking on Hollywood's tongue as his hips began to move. He aligned their cocks and thrust in an up-and-down motion. Hollywood felt the caress of Chad's cock from root to crown. It didn't feel like a hand, or a mouth, or even a leg.

This was something else.

Something completely different.

Something really fucking good.

The friction increased until every ounce of Hollywood's focus was centered on his spiraling arousal. His hands gripped the other man's ass, pushing up as Chad shoved his hips down. The added pressure had them both groaning.

Chad broke the kiss and rose up on his arms. His face above Hollywood's was creased in concentration, his cheeks darker than usual, his eyes narrowed, the blue almost gone. His biceps bulged as he moved his hips.

Down below, Chad's cock slipped into the notch between Hollywood's dick and his quad. His own cock wedged itself in the same place in Chad's crotch. Chad shot him a filthy smirk, then began to undulate above him, the motion smooth and silky like an eel underwater, reminding Hollywood of the way Chad had danced on stage.

As he stared into Chad's eyes, all felt right in his world. He didn't care about what his father had said, didn't care that his life was a failure, that he basically had no friends. All he cared about was the man in his arms. He slid one hand up Chad's back along the groove of his spine, until he gripped his neck. "So good," he said on a grunt, as Chad increased the pace.

"Yeah?"

"Yeah."

"It's about to get even better," Chad said. "Roll your hips."

It took a few starts and stops, but soon Hollywood was doing his own version of the eel dance in perfect counterpoint to Chad's. Pre-cum had slicked their cocks enough that they slid easily in their notches, and with each stroke, each thrust, Chad's cock rubbed against his own. Solid steel, silky skin. It was a sensual, sexy-as-fuck dance, one he'd have been happy to continue all night. But Chad had other ideas.

"Spread your legs," he ordered.

Without a word, Hollywood complied, and grunted loudly when Chad repositioned himself so his weight was firmly pinning their groins together. Hollywood raised his head to watch Chad, firmly nestled in the cradle of his thighs.

"I'm close." Hollywood's hands clutched Chad's arms. Their gazes met and the lust-filled look in Chad's denim eyes threw Hollywood over the edge. The tingling that had started at the base of his spine transformed into a fireball that shot out of his nuts. Punching his hips, Hollywood shouted, swore, and came all over their stomachs in an orgasm more powerful, more overwhelming, than anything he'd ever experienced. He fought to keep the darkness at bay. Fought to keep his eyes open so he could watch Chad reach his own release.

Chad burrowed his knees under Hollywood's thighs and used his hands on Hollywood's hips to slam their groins together two, three, more times until he closed his eyes and groaned as he erupted in thick ropes. Because of the angle, all of it landed on Hollywood. The warmth seemed to mark him in a strange way as their cum mixed and combined.

He watched in fascination as Chad dragged a finger through the sticky mess and brought it to his lips. The visual did something to him, touched some primitive part of his brain, a part that he'd never before been aware of. A part that wanted Chad.

Pulling Chad down, Hollywood kissed him deeply, desperate to taste both of them on his lover's tongue.

He closed his eyes, loving every second of having Chad in his arms, their taste in his mouth. He wanted this again. He wanted more. He wanted Chad. He wanted a man.

Oh God. His dad *was* right.

CHAPTER 15

Nothing.

Chad stared at the blank screen of the cell phone while he waited for Liam to join him at the table he'd snagged near the door of the restaurant. They were allowed to stop to grab food after a call, but they had to be ready to leave at a moment's notice. Thus the reason they never went to places with wait staff. Involuntarily, his gaze strayed to his phone again, hoping and praying for a response to the "You okay?" text he'd sent Hollywood on his way to work that morning.

After getting off in a spectacular way on Hollywood's couch last night, Chad had figured they both needed some sleep since they were both on shift the next day, and they sure as hell wouldn't have gotten any if he'd stayed the night.

That's not the real reason.

Fuck. No, it wasn't. The shocked, barely-able-to-follow-a-conversation look on Hollywood's face after he'd scrambled to put his clothes back on had spoken volumes. Chad had chosen to believe all the guy needed was a little alone time to figure things out, to see how he felt about what had gone down—or should he say who?

Had it been a mistake to leave?

Maybe Hollywood had needed him to stay and talk it through. Shit, the guy was probably drowning in all sorts of what-the-fuck-did-I-do right about now. And Chad hadn't even stayed around to throw him a life preserver.

"Hey, why so glum?" Liam asked, nudging him with his shoulder before he took his seat. "At least you don't have to eat this crap." He scowled at the salad on his tray. Since getting pregnant, Anna had decided that if she had to eat healthy, her husband did too. To his credit,

147

Liam had been keeping his end of the bargain, no matter how much Chad tried to tempt him.

He must have been silent too long because Liam kicked his foot under the table. "Talk."

Figuring it would be easier to distract Liam from the truth if he gave him something to chew on, Chad shrugged. "I'm a little tired, that's all."

"If those red marks on your neck are the reason, then all I can say is fucking A!" He held his hand up for a high five.

"No high five," Chad said, allowing himself a small smile at his friend's antics.

"Things didn't go well with Hollywood?"

"Shh!" Chad hissed, looking around to see if anyone had heard. "You're going to out him before he even knows what he wants."

Liam put up his hands. "Okay, okay. Sorry." He grimaced through a bite of salad then pointed to Chad's phone with his fork, conveniently ignoring the droplets of dressing that sprayed the screen and the table. "So you're getting radio silence and you weren't expecting to." His expression softened. "This one is serious?"

"I'd like him to be." Chad remembered the way he and Hollywood had been so in sync the previous evening. How the big blond's eyes had darkened seconds before he'd arched his back and shouted his release. Yeah. He'd love to see that again. Maybe for a really long time. But he'd never see it again if Hollywood didn't call him back. "I don't know if that's what he wants though."

"Sucks," Liam commiserated, although it wasn't clear if he meant Chad's problem or the salad.

Nodding anyway, Chad bit into his sandwich, and unable to stomach the sensation of the bread turning to dust in his mouth, pushed his plate away and focused on his cup of tea. At least that still tasted good.

Liam eyed Chad's plate and the sandwich that was missing only a bite. "You gonna starve yourself to death if he doesn't call?"

"Maybe." Chad wiped his mouth and tossed the napkin on top of his dinner. "Isn't that what people do when the person they've been crushing on for years doesn't return their affection?" Christ, he sounded like some teenager writing dire poems about unrequited love.

Love. That word stopped him cold. Was he in love with Hollywood? He didn't know, but what was sure was that he *could* love the guy. The hours they'd spent together since the fire had proved that. And last night had cemented it. He was in for so much pain if Hollywood chose this as the last stop on his gay adventure.

There was the rumble of an engine idling in the parking lot, then the door opened and in tromped Hollywood and his entire platoon. They looked tired, hungry, and very dirty. Hollywood was amazing in his bunker pants and boots, the large suspenders strapping him into a navy blue SFD sweatshirt. The soot on his cheek and the ashes in his hair made him look like a conquering hero. Chad couldn't breathe as his cock went from zero to sixty in two-point-five seconds. The guy had never been hotter, and Chad desperately wanted to get his hands on him. Every glorious inch.

As Hollywood approached his table, Chad started to smile. But that smile evaporated when Hollywood walked right past him like he hadn't seen him sitting there, ten feet from the fucking door. Humiliation washed over him as he watched Hollywood's retreating back make its way to the order counter. *Jesus Christ.* Just because the guy was upset didn't mean he could treat him like he didn't exist.

"Hey, Chad. Liam. How's it going, guys? Easy shift?" The members of Hollywood's platoon crowded around Chad and Liam's table, clapping them on the back as they exchanged greetings.

Liam tilted his head in Hollywood's direction. "Tough call?"

Mario, Platoon D's driver, glanced at his boss, then shook his head. "Nah. The LT's had something up his butt all day."

Chad choked, and had to cover it with a cough and a sip of his tea. Maybe the LT would be in a better mood if he really did have something up his ass. Something like Chad's dick.

Swallowing down the bitterness in his throat, Chad did his best to ignore his partner's concerned expression. Fuck. He was barely holding it together, and if Liam knew how hurt Chad was, he'd do something stupid. Chad smiled brightly at his colleagues and, in an attempt to deflect the conversation away from the grumpy lieutenant, he cracked a few raunchy jokes at his own expense that soon had the guys laughing.

"Hope the rest of your shift goes better," Chad said as they moved to get in line behind Hollywood.

Wendy stayed back. They'd worked together at Station 25 before she'd joined the TRT and he'd become a paramedic. She propped her hip on Chad's chair and stroked his back. "Hey, handsome."

"Hey, beautiful."

She smiled down at him. A finger trailed along his jaw. "You sure I can't get you to switch teams?" When he grinned and shook his head, her lip jutted out in a pout. "Such a shame. We'd make truly beautiful babies together."

Chad put his arm around her waist, squeezing her tight. "If I ever do, you'll be the first woman I call."

She laughed and bent down to kiss his cheek. "And the last, baby. And the last." She winked at Liam, who seemed highly amused by their exchange, before stepping away to join her platoon.

Chad's gaze followed her until it landed on a pair of angry green eyes.

The intensity in them, the heat and aggression, drilled into Chad, confusing the shit out of him. What was Hollywood's problem? So, he didn't want to talk to Chad. Did that mean no one else could either?

Or… nah. He pushed the idea out of his head. That couldn't be right. Could it?

Hollywood was still glaring at him, a muscle ticking in his cheek. How Chad wanted to lick that muscle. Instead, he raised a challenging brow. Hollywood's lips curled into a sneer that took in Chad, his platoon, and, apparently, the whole world.

Liam's chair screeched against the tile floor as he shoved to his feet. "You done here?" His face was red and his fingers clenched the edges of his tray so hard they were white.

Oh shit. They needed to get out of the restaurant before his partner did something they'd all regret. Chad shot a hasty glance in Hollywood's direction and nodded. "Yeah, I'm done."

For now.

ജ 🚆 ര

The next evening, scared out of his mind, Hollywood waited in the dark pub for Jamie to arrive. He needed to talk to someone. Needed to talk to his best friend. He'd picked this place because he was reasonably sure no one knew him here. So, if Jamie ended up punching him out, well… at least no one at work would know.

Swallowing the rest of his vodka, he signaled for the waiter to bring another. When he turned back, Jamie was sliding into the booth across from him.

Jamie picked up the Redhook Hollywood had ordered for him earlier, then pointed to Hollywood's empty glass. "Looks like you started without me."

"Sorry." He'd needed something to loosen his tongue if he was going to admit to Jamie what was going on. Not that he was planning to bring Chad into the discussion. The waiter, a handsome man in his early twenties, replaced his empty glass with a fresh one, then smiled at them both before moving on to help his other customers. Hollywood watched him for a moment, the slim waist, tight ass. Nope, it wasn't doing anything for him. Only one man did.

Hollywood flattened his hand on the tabletop, forcing himself to relax. "Thank you for coming."

Jamie slid his bottle across the scarred wood, passing it from hand to hand as he observed Hollywood. He cocked his head, eyes filled with concern. "You sounded a little off on the phone. Something wrong?"

Okay. It was now or never. Jamie had provided the perfect segue. "Remember that conversation we had at the station about a week ago?"

Jamie stopped playing with his bottle and frowned. "The one where I told you about Rickie and me?"

"Being into BDSM. Yeah."

"Is that going to be a problem?"

The aggressive tone in Jamie's voice had Hollywood's head jerking up. "What? No, of course not. I don't care how you guys get off. I just care that you're happy."

"We are."

Hollywood smiled and all the tension seemed to leave Jamie's body. Hollywood hoped that Jamie would be as accepting of what he was about to tell him. His stomach in knots, not aided by the booze, Hollywood pushed himself to talk. "So... uh... lately, I've been remembering stuff."

His eyes kept darting away from Jamie, and his hands gripped his glass like it was a safety line. God, he exhaled sharply. How had Chad done this when he'd been only sixteen? Jamie was one intimidating fucker, even when he wasn't trying.

"Remembering stuff?" Jamie leaned forward, capturing Hollywood's attention. His gaze sharpened. They'd been friends long enough for Jamie to know more about Hollywood's childhood than Hollywood liked him knowing. "About what?"

"About being young and curious."

Jamie's lip quirked. "You mentioned playing doctor."

"It was a bit more than that." He took another sip of vodka, then set the glass down on the table. The loud *thunk* made him jump. He clutched the back of his neck. "I... shit." Why was this so fucking hard?

Come on. Tell him.

"There was this kid. Bobby. After my mom died, we became good friends. He'd come over after school and we'd play. Anyway, one day we got a little experimental and my dad caught us."

"Caught you smoking? Drinking? We've all done that."

He lowered his gaze, unable to look Jamie in the eye while he spilled his guts. "Caught us giving each other hand jobs."

"Oh fuck."

At his friend's muttered curse, Hollywood added, "We were in a sixty-nine. Naked. If my dad hadn't walked in right then, I was about to... shit." He took a deep breath and spit out the rest. "I was about to blow him."

He palmed his vodka and downed it. While Jamie did the same with his beer, Hollywood signaled the waiter for another round.

"How old were you?"

"Ten."

"And you just now remembered all this?"

Hollywood laughed, the sound raw and bitter. "Yeah. Good old Dad decided to remind me of it a week ago."

"That when he punched you?"

"Asshole called me a fag, and the Bobby incident was his proof that I'd always been one."

Jamie rubbed two fingers along his jaw, his eyes briefly going to the television screen where a basketball game was in progress. "What did you do?"

"I told him hell no." He hesitated and pinched the bridge of his nose. Christ, all this fucking tension was giving him a headache. "But now, I don't know. I mean, maybe it wasn't simple curiosity."

The waiter chose that opportune time to deliver their drinks. As he cleared away the empties, he asked, "Anything else? The wings smell great tonight."

"Maybe later," Jamie said, since all Hollywood could do was open and close his mouth soundlessly like a goddamn fish out of water.

With the music playing softly in the background and the muted sounds of conversation in the booths around them, they took sips of their drinks. Jamie's eyes never left his and Hollywood didn't have the nerve to look away. After what seemed like forever, Jamie leaned his elbows on the table and asked quietly, "Have there been other guys?"

Hollywood nodded.

"Recently?"

He nodded again. Then his eyes went round at what he'd implied. "Not sex. I've never... you know." Heat crept up his neck and face, knowing what Jamie had to be thinking. Imagining. He crossed his arms and covered his eyes with the top hand. As if this weren't embarrassing enough, images from the video he'd watched flashed behind his lids. Slow motion, blinking in and out like a strobe light. But in each image, the two actors were replaced with him and Chad. He blew out and willed his body to cooperate. He couldn't talk about all this with a hard-on.

Jamie cleared his throat. "Hell. I really thought you were straight."

"So did I."

"But?"

He took a quick gulp of his drink, and spun the glass in his hands as he tried to make sense of what he'd been feeling. "This... guy I met, he makes me feel things I've never felt before." His eyes lifted to Jamie's. "I'm so fucking confused, man. How can I not be straight? I love pussy. I loved Isabel."

Maybe he was a freak. He sure felt like one.

Jamie raised a knee onto the seat and stretched his arm along the edge of the booth. His eyes narrowed, no doubt trying to unravel the puzzle that was Hollywood's sexuality. "So there've been no guys other than this Bobby kid and this guy you fooled around with recently. Not even in college?"

Hollywood thought back to those years. If he'd only just now remembered Bobby, maybe there were others he'd forgotten about. His ass clenched at the idea. God knows what he'd done during his numerous drunken binges. He kept his head down, but glanced up at his friend. "I honestly don't know. I used to drink a lot back then."

Jamie gave him an all-too-knowing look to which Hollywood added, "Yeah, yeah. Fuck off. I'm trying to cut back."

"Are you?"

Jamie's tone was heavy with disbelief. Not surprising seeing as how Hollywood had downed three drinks since Jamie's arrival less than an hour ago. He dragged his hands through his hair, then dropped his arms and flopped back in his seat. "This guy... he says I have to be sober when we... so I can't blame anything on the booze."

"Sounds like a smart man."

"He is," Hollywood agreed, just then appreciating how much. If he'd been drinking last night when he'd given Chad a blow job—oh God!— he'd probably be denying it right now.

After a few minutes of Jamie patiently drinking his beer and watching the game on the TV, Hollywood stated the obvious. "You're remarkably calm about all this."

Jamie dragged his eyes from the screen and pinned Hollywood with a sardonic stare. "Did you think I'd kick your ass and never speak to you again?"

"Something like that."

"It's like you said, I don't care how you get off. Just that you're happy. This guy, does he make you happy?"

"I think he might."

"What do you mean?"

Hollywood fixed his eyes on the clear liquid in his glass so he could say the words that were on his mind. "When I'm in the moment, I'm really okay with everything. But then when I'm on my own, I'm scared shitless. I don't know if I can handle telling everyone. God, you know my dad. He had a fit when he heard I was staying at Chad's."

"*Does* this have anything to do with Chad?" The tone of Jamie's question more than the actual words had Hollywood sitting up straight, fear and the alcohol in his stomach blending into a toxic brew.

"What makes you think that?"

Jamie held up his hand. "Let's see. My brother's gay"—he ticked off his index finger—"you go stay with him"—he ticked off his middle finger—"and now"—he ticked off his ring finger—"you're macking on gay guys."

Fuck. If Jamie figured out that the gay guy he was macking on was his little brother... His chest tightened so sharply he thought he might puke. The men at Station 44, they had a code: you didn't mess with your friend's sisters, mothers, aunts, or female cousins. He had to assume that rule included messing with brothers, fathers, uncles, and male cousins. His stomach lurched. He had to get Jamie's focus away from this particular train wreck. But how to do it without lying? Their friendship was based on mutual trust and respect, and he never wanted to jeopardize that.

"I guess in a way it does have to do with Chad." He licked his bottom lip before continuing. "I met this guy at the fundraiser." It wasn't a complete lie. That was when he'd kissed Chad for the first time. And that was when everything had changed.

"He's a friend of Chad's?"

"They know each other." He shook his glass. Fucking bone dry. Where was that waiter? Jamie caught his wrist, startling the crap out of him. When he looked up, his friend's eyes were warm, sympathetic even. And Hollywood felt like even more of a dog.

"Talk to Chad."

"Chad?" Hollywood squeaked before he could force his voice into a manly drawl.

"Yeah." Jamie watched him curiously. "He's been through this. He can help."

Hollywood had to wonder what was going through his friend's mind and if he was really as accepting as he appeared to be. Would this change things between them?

"I'm hoping this is a passing thing." Hollywood really meant that, even though those times he'd been with Chad had shown him that as good as sex had been before, he'd only been scratching the surface. The feelings Chad had roused in him had the power to blow his mind. To level his fucking world.

"Do you think it is?" Jamie asked, his voice soft.

Hollywood shook his head. It was too powerful. And even now, the craving to hear Chad's voice, to touch his golden skin, to taste his—Yeah. He swallowed hard. "So, do you think I should do this? Get even more involved with this guy?"

"Do you want to?"

He bit his lip as a rush of memories rolled over him. "Yeah."

"But?"

"He's out. And I'm—"

"Not," Jamie finished for him.

"Fuck. How can I come out when I'm not even sure what I am? Gay, bisexual, who the fuck knows?" He pressed the heel of his hand against his aching temple. "And my dad—"

"To hell with him. It's high fucking time you told the chief to fuck off." Jamie's expression was fierce, like a warrior on a rampage, or one protecting his family. "Whatever you are, you need to open that closet door and step out into the sunshine." His voice lowered and his eyes softened. "I bet it's real lonely in there." He gave Hollywood a gentle smile, one that tugged at everything Hollywood was holding back.

Deep inside him, the lock on that fortified box where Hollywood kept hidden all his unwanted feelings, his unwanted memories, turned and the top cracked open. Would opening this Pandora's box kill him, or would it set him free?

CHAPTER 16

Chad stood shivering outside Sweet Cakes, huddled in the doorway to avoid the icy drizzle as he waited for Tori. Hollywood had told him he'd gone to Vicenzo's for lunch and had apologized to Tori for his behavior at Bar None. He'd also passed on Tori's message.

Feeling like a heel for even needing the reminder, he'd called and invited his twin to the dessert shop in the hope that the sugar overload would help his cause. Her words at the fundraiser after he'd ordered her back to their parents' table had ripped his heart: *I barely know you anymore.* Hell, he barely knew himself anymore either.

A taxi pulled up to the curb and he recognized the slim, dark-haired beauty inside. He immediately went over and, taking her hand, helped her out of the cab and across the sidewalk to the overhang where they'd be out of the rain. He pulled her into a tight hug. "Thanks for coming."

"I'd never miss a chance to see my favorite brother." Her eyes softened and she kissed his cheek. "Oh! You're freezing. Let's go inside."

The hostess led them to a quiet spot near the window and placed their menus on the table. "Your waiter will be with you shortly."

Chad thanked her, then helped Tori out of her coat before sitting across from her.

"I was surprised to hear from you," she said, lowering herself onto her chair, eyes firmly on the table. Her lip trembled the tiniest bit, and Chad felt like a dick.

"I told you I'd call. This isn't lunch, but I thought it might be better."

"To sweeten me up?"

"Maybe."

"Sounds like someone thinks he has some apologizing to do."

He took her hand. "I know I do."

She placed her other hand on top of his, and squeezed it gently. "So start. Tell me why we haven't spoken since our birthday party."

Had it already been three weeks since the combined Thanksgiving/birthday party his mom and Erica had thrown for them? "I'm sorry about that. I've been... busy."

She flipped her hair over her shoulder in the way she only did when she was nervous. Or pissed. "So I heard," she said, her tone confirming the latter.

What exactly had she and Hollywood discussed? "I really am sorry."

"Me too. I miss you." She gave him a sad smile and her eyes glistened. "I miss our chats, and our shopping trips. Going dancing, and talking about hot guys. We used to be so close, Chad. How did we go from that to not talking for weeks at a time?"

Each word was a nail in his heart. He'd missed her and their times together too. Hollywood wasn't to blame for this, though. Chad had let his relationship with his twin start to drift before Hollywood had come into the picture. Long before. He offered her a crooked smile. "We grew up?"

"That's crap. I talk to Mom every day. Laura too."

Laura was Tori's long-time best female friend, while Chad was Tori's all-around bestie. Or rather, he had been. At some point, he'd let the fact that she was his sister start to get in the way. He'd gone from hanging out with her to needing to protect her. Fucking Jamie, and all his big brother bullshit. Chad was nine minutes older than Tori. Nine.

The waiter arrived to get their orders, saving Chad from trying to come up with a reply that wouldn't completely piss his sister off. As the waiter left, Chad's gaze took in the tight build and the even tighter ass encased in formfitting black slacks. The guy was cute, shorter than Chad, thinner too, with longish chestnut hair. He was exactly the type Chad would normally have been salivating over, devising ways to get in the guy's pants. But now? Not a twitch, not even a tingle. Nothing. He should have followed his own damn rule: no straight guys.

Tori cleared her throat, drawing his attention back to her. She arched a brow. "So, the fundraiser."

Choosing to ignore what she was hinting at, he smiled. "It went really well. We raised more money than expected for the center."

"That's fantastic," she said, brightly. "Did I tell you, I applied to volunteer there?"

Tori's PhD program in clinical psychology required her to work with various organizations to gain practical experience. "I'm sure Betty will be thrilled to have you. They never have enough volunteer counselors."

"I'm really looking forward to it." Her gaze flicked to something, then she brought it back to him. "About the fundraiser." He held his breath.

This was why they were here, so why was he so nervous?

She smiled. "You were really on fire. In fact, I don't think I've ever seen you perform so well. Any *special* reason?"

Chad's heart thumped loudly in his chest as he eyed his sister, the forced smile on her face, the stiffness of her shoulders. He swallowed and lowered his hands to his thighs to wipe his sweaty palms on his trousers. "The band was really good. Having Harry there seemed to energize them."

"Is he a friend of yours?"

"Sort of. I met him a few weeks ago."

"You two seemed…" She hesitated. "Close."

"Tori," he said, with a note of warning in his voice.

"What? I can't ask my brother about his friends?"

"That's not what you're doing."

She folded her hands on the table and said in a calm voice, "Okay, what am I doing then?"

Annoyance flared in his gut. "You're psychoanalyzing me. Stop it."

Her laughter caught the attention of several customers at nearby tables. Unperturbed, she ignored them, her gaze focused on Chad alone. "No, I'm not. I had that situation figured out in no time."

Chad gulped down some water, even as he felt the heat rise in his neck. "Situation?"

"It was quite obvious that you and Harry had—"

"Tori," he interrupted.

"Fucked," she continued. "And that you felt terrible afterward, because you really wanted to be fucking—"

"Tori!"

"Hollywood."

The man's name reverberated between them like the bang of a judge's hammer. Tori pursed her lips before breaking the thick silence. "Don't try to deny it. I was there. I saw."

He cringed to even ask. "What did you see?"

"The desire. The confusion. The *fear*."

Fuck, yes, he was scared. Shitless, in fact.

"Am I right?" she asked, taking his hand in hers once again. With her mix of determination and empathy, she'd no doubt make a great psychologist.

He wet his lips, and exhaled long and slow, before dragging his gaze from their joined hands. "I can't speak for him."

Her mouth curved. "You don't need to, Chad. It was all right there. The guy was three sheets to the wind with zero ability to hide his emotions."

"That's not always a good thing."

"No. What about you? You like him?"

He nodded, unable—no, unwilling—to hide his feelings any longer. Not from Tori at least. "I have for a long time."

"I thought so." There was an amused glint in her eye. "I remember you following him and Jamie around with big puppy dog eyes until Jamie would lose patience and tell you to bug off."

"You think he knows?"

"Who?"

"Jamie."

"I don't think so. But so what if he does?"

"You know how he is."

She whipped her hair back. "Boy, do I ever."

Her sharp tone piqued his curiosity, but her thinned lips and stiff shoulders made his gut twist. "Hey, what's going on?"

She ground her teeth together, then seemed to explode. "I love all of you, so much, but sometimes I wish I had sisters." She glared at him. "Only sisters."

A chuckle rumbled in his chest, one he had to quickly cover with a cough or risk losing his head. "Why is that?"

"You're all so damned protective. Ordering me around, telling me who I can talk to, who I can date."

"What's wrong with that? You're our little sister and we love you."

"Little sister? I'm twenty-five. Same age as you, by the way. That's what being twins means."

He grinned, knowing exactly how to get her goat. "I'm the oldest."

"By nine damn minutes."

It had been a while since he'd seen Tori so worked up and he had to admit, if only to himself, that he was really enjoying it. Her blue eyes, the same shade as his and their brothers', flashed with indignation. She crossed her arms and huffed. "Let's see how you feel when it's your turn to be on the receiving end."

His face went hot, burning hot, as he stuttered, "On the receiving end?"

"Of their overprotectiveness." She laughed and threw her napkin in his face. "You're such an idiot."

"Why would they be protective of me? I can handle myself." He had been for years.

"What exactly do you think Jamie's reaction will be when he finds out about you and Hollywood?"

"First of all, there is no me and Hollywood." She arched that damn perfectly plucked brow at him, dragging the truth out. "Yet."

"Mmm-hmm." She nodded, arms still crossed.

"Secondly, why would he care? He's Hollywood's best friend, so we know he already likes the guy."

Uncrossing her arms, she rested her elbows on the edge of the table and her chin on her threaded fingers. Christ, he hated when she examined him, like she was trying to pick apart his psyche, layer by layer. "Okay, smart guy," she said. "Tell me, how would you react if, let's say, that scene between me and Hollywood had ended with something more than a kiss? What if we'd started dating?"

Chad's response was immediate and forceful. "Hell, no!" His vision was immediately filled with the image of Hollywood in the back hallway of the bar, crowding Tori against the wall, her hands in his hair, tugging his head down for a kiss. His stomach cramped.

She eyed him curiously. "Why not?"

"He's too experienced for you."

"But not for you?"

"No."

"Anything else?"

"He's too old for you."

That made her laugh. "Need I remind you again that we're the same age?"

He squirmed and couldn't meet her eyes. "It's different with guys."

"Really? Why is that?"

He shrugged, not knowing how to answer, only that it was true.

Tori pressed on. "He's got a good job, good benefits. He'd be a good provider."

Chad scoffed at that. "He's a player, Tori. From what I can tell, he's never had a girlfriend for more than a few weeks. You can't get a guy like that to settle down."

"And that's exactly what Jamie will say to you when he finds out." She smiled, like she'd just won a gold medal at the Olympics.

He sighed, knowing she was right and hating it. "I'm not looking for a husband and kids."

Leaning over, she stroked his jaw, the love in her eyes tightening his throat. "You'd make a great father, Chad. Don't give up on that."

He swallowed hard, desperate to clear the emotions away. *That* was not a conversation he could handle today. "So, are you going to tell Jamie?"

"Nope. He's already turned all my brothers into guard dogs. He won't turn me into one too." She lowered her voice as the waiter approached with their coffee and cake. "Don't let him ruin this for you or scare Hollywood off. You're both adults. Test this out. See where it goes. And be happy. That's what I want for you, Chad. To see you happy."

Taking her hand, he pressed it to his lips. "God, I love you. Don't let me pull away again, okay?"

She squeezed his fingers and blew him a kiss. "Never."

಄ 🚌 ಊ

Once he'd seen Tori safely into a cab, Chad went home... to pace with his sister's advice on a loop in his head: *test this out. See where it goes. Test this out. See where it goes.* His chest felt sore and achy after two days of not talking to Hollywood. The guy was scared. His whole life had been turned on its head. His reality thrown out with the dishwater. Chad got it. He really did, and he wanted to be there for Hollywood even if they were destined to never be more than friends.

But how could he do that when the guy refused to acknowledge his presence?

Staring out the sliding door at the downtown lights twinkling off the dark harbor water, he punched the doorframe, barely feeling the skin on his knuckles split. Somehow, he had to get rid of all the emotions trapped inside him. Maybe he'd call Drew and invite him to spar. Drew was his closest brother, and he hadn't spent any time with him lately other than that hour or two at their parents' when they'd moved boxes together. Was there anyone he hadn't let down lately?

As he started to dial Drew's number, a text came in. Holding his breath, he navigated to his messages. It was from Hollywood. Seeing that name on his screen, along with the snapshot of Hollywood in an SPLT-shirt, filled him with hope, anger, resentment, and happiness. Yes, he was a fucking mess. Yes, his feelings were all over the place. And yes, he desperately wanted to see the guy again. Should he pay Hollywood back by ignoring his message? Let him see how it felt? Maybe, but he was sure as shit going to read it first.

H: I'm an asshole.

A dry chuckle burst from Chad's tense throat. Without a second thought, he typed out a response.

C: And I'm having déjà vu

H: Can we talk?

C: I don't know. You going to ignore me again?

Yeah, that had hurt and he wanted Hollywood to know.

H: Please?

Chad circled his living room, debating the pros and cons. What if Hollywood just wanted to come over to say, "It's done. The experiment's over"? God that would kill him. But better he find out now than later when his heart was completely invested.

Ha! What a joke. He wasn't sure he could be any more invested. Best to get it over with, either way.

C: All right. When and where?

H: Now. I'm outside your door.

161

Chad shook his head. Christ, the guy had balls. Stalking over to the door, Chad flung it open and glared at the tall blond.

Hollywood's eyes lit up, and his lips twitched. "You look like you can't decide what you want more: to kiss me or punch me."

Chad's fist clenched involuntarily, a sure sign that right now he was leaning more toward punching. He stepped to the side so Hollywood could come in. "Talk first, then I'll decide."

Nostrils flaring, just the teensiest bit, Hollywood squeezed past Chad. In the narrow hallway, they were close enough for Hollywood's cologne, something with cedar and sandalwood notes, to hit Chad full-force. Arousal slammed into him, making him hard as stone, despite his lingering annoyance with how Hollywood had treated him. After adjusting himself behind Hollywood's back, he followed the guy into the living room. Hollywood took the couch, while Chad took the armchair, taking care to cross his legs to hide the bulge in his jeans.

For several long minutes, they simply stared at each other. There was heat in Hollywood's eyes, as well as a not-so-healthy dose of anxiety. His left knee bounced up and down until a closed fist banged on it, forcing the bouncing to stop. In all the years Chad had known Hollywood, he'd never seen him like this. The man had always been larger-than-life, full of confidence and arrogance. That Hollywood was letting him see this other side of himself was actually pretty endearing. At the same time, Chad had to wonder what the hell was going on. Hollywood wasn't this distressed simply because he'd ignored Chad at the restaurant.

Hollywood cleared his throat, breaking the stiff silence. "I told Jamie."

"You what?" Holy shit. That was the last fucking thing Chad had expected Hollywood to say.

Hollywood's hand clenched and unclenched on his knee. "Last night, I—I told Jamie."

"Let me get this straight. You told my brother what? That we'd exchanged blow jobs and had one hell of a frot session?"

His eyes searched Hollywood's body for any sign of a fight or physical altercation. He was surprised when he didn't find any.

"No." Hollywood's hands dragged through his short hair. "Fuck no. I told him that I think I'm gay, or bi. Whatever."

"Oh." Chad blinked. "How'd he take it?"

Hollywood's smile made a reappearance. "Surprisingly well."

"Did… uh… did my name come up at all?"

An uncomfortable expression passed over Hollywood's face before he shrugged. It did nothing to reassure Chad. Jamie, like Tori, had always been very perceptive. "He said I should talk to you about it. That maybe you could help me."

"He did, did he?"

"Imagine that." Hollywood grinned. "Your brother actually *wants* me to see you."

Chad snorted. "That's because he doesn't know I was the guy you experimented with."

Hollywood slumped against the couch and closed his eyes. "Yeah, I know."

"He's going to be pissed."

"I know that too." His eyes flicked open. "Does he have to find out?"

This right here was why he avoided straight guys and closeted gays. He leaned his elbows on his knees and watched Hollywood carefully. "Coming out was tough, but I made the decision then that I'd never hide again. I'm proud of who I am, and I won't go back in the closet, even for you."

Leaving Hollywood to think, Chad went to the kitchen and made himself busy getting them a drink. Was he being unreasonable? The guy had barely admitted that he might be gay or bisexual and Chad was already pushing him to come out. Considering who his father was, it probably seemed like a feat more terrifying than jumping out of a plane.

When he returned to the living room, he found Hollywood in exactly the same position he'd been in before. Chad's heart hurt for the guy. When he'd come out, it had been hard, but he'd been reasonably certain he wouldn't end up on the street. He also hadn't had a career on the line. Hollywood did. Not officially, of course. But Hollywood's dad could ruin him if he so chose.

"You look like you could use this," he said quietly, handing Hollywood a glass of Grey Goose.

Hollywood took the glass, their fingers connecting as it transferred from one to the other. Even that small touch made Chad's skin tingle. Before he could move away, Hollywood placed both their glasses on the coffee table and stood, one hand going to the back of Chad's head. "There's something I need more."

A shiver raced up his spine. "Oh yeah?" he breathed. "What's that?"

"You."

80 ☕ 03

Hollywood's arms ached with the effort it took to keep from pulling Chad's mouth to his. He'd acted like a bastard, turning away from Chad after they'd gotten so close. So intimate. More intimate than he'd ever been with anyone else. Chad made him happy, being with Chad made him feel normal. How ironic was that? Barely breathing, he waited for a sign, some indication that Chad wanted what was happening between them.

Chad's gaze darted from Hollywood's eyes to his mouth and throat, then back again in a manic pattern, and his chest—that gorgeous, ripped chest—heaved with every inhale.

"Tell me, Chad. What do *you* need?"

That blue gaze finally settled on his own, hands gripped his shoulders, and Chad said, his voice thick with sensual intent, "I need you. Inside me."

Lust raged through his system in a blinding flash. He wanted that too. So fucking badly. In a desperate grab, Hollywood yanked Chad to his chest and melded their bodies from head to toe. His free hand clutched Chad's firm ass, as his mouth came down on the other man's.

Chad moaned, grinding their hips together. The sound, urgent and primal, overcame any fear, any reservations, Hollywood still might have had about what he was doing.

He wanted Chad.

And tonight, he would have him.

His tongue licking at Chad's full lips, Hollywood walked him backward toward his bedroom. When Chad opened for him, Hollywood slipped in, tasting coffee and something sweet. That's what Chad was for him: bittersweet. He'd finally found someone he connected with, someone he wanted for more than sex, and that someone was a *man*.

Well fuck it. So he was bisexual. Big fucking deal. He was incredibly attracted to a gorgeous, funny, caring person, and it no longer mattered that Chad wasn't a woman. His hand slid over the defined muscles on Chad's back. In fact, he was damn glad that Chad was a man.

Pushing his hands up, he released Chad's mouth only long enough to free him of his shirt, before his lips found Chad's clavicle. He sucked at the thin skin along the bone until he reached that tiny notch at the base of Chad's throat. With his tongue pressed against it, he could feel every beat of Chad's heart, every swallow, every gasp. And when he sucked a little and Chad groaned, the vibrations zinged from his lips to his cock. The intensity of the sensations was so strong, it almost brought him to his knees.

Before he could fully recover, Chad swung them around, and Hollywood's back hit the wall, startling a curse out of him. As he stared into Chad's determined eyes, the aggressive tilt of his chin, the muscles flexing in his arms, a thrill shot up Hollywood's spine and adrenaline flashed through him. This was a side of Chad that really cranked his shaft. A shaft that was now fully engorged and pushing painfully against his zipper. But Chad's dark gaze held him in place. It was as though he were under some sort of spell. No wonder Chad had guys flocking to him.

That thought had him frowning.

Chad grinned, transforming his expression from scary badass to naughty badass. He tore open Hollywood's shirt. Buttons flew left and right, pinging on the hardwood floor. In a move so macho it sucked the air out of Hollywood's lungs, Chad kicked his feet apart and stepped between his legs. When their erections ground together, the room whirled around them and Hollywood felt the earth tilt.

Hollywood groaned at the much-needed pressure and pressed his face into Chad's neck, using the familiar scent of Chad's soap and skin to ground him. He felt high, like everything was happening to someone else. But it wasn't happening to someone else, it was happening to *him*.

Chad shifted and his teeth closed on Hollywood's nipple. His knees shook at the rush of exquisite pleasure that was happening to him *because* he was with Chad. No one else had ever made him feel like this. Being plastered against a wall at another man's mercy was a position he'd never been in before. But one that apparently pushed all his buttons. When Chad's knee pressed against his balls, the pressure was more than welcome, but it left him reeling at just how vulnerable he was.

"What are you thinking?" Chad whispered, and Hollywood shivered at the hot air fanning over the skin made moist by Chad's kisses.

"This is intense."

Chad raised his head and winked, his hand going to Hollywood's groin and rubbing hard. "This is only the beginning."

Hollywood sucked in a sharp breath. "Fuck. I'm not sure I'm gonna live through it."

Laughing, Chad moved away. Instantly missing Chad's long hard body pressed against his, Hollywood grabbed his hand and tried to pull him back. Chad shook his head, and there was a flash of regret in his gaze. "Your first time won't be up against the wall."

Hollywood snorted. "I'm not a virgin."

"Maybe not, but you're going to feel like one."

With that, he turned and dragged Hollywood into his bedroom. Hollywood was only too happy to follow that luscious ass until he realized what he'd soon be doing with it. That in a matter of minutes, his cock would be buried deep inside all that snug heat. Panic tightened his chest and caused his step to falter. "You did that on purpose," he accused when Chad turned back to see what the holdup was.

Chad grinned. "Is it working?"

"Yes, you little fucker."

The smile never leaving his face, Chad pressed a quick kiss to his mouth. "Yeah, I am the fucker, but not tonight."

Hollywood's jaw dropped. Was Chad implying what Hollywood thought he was? "Chad, I—I..." Fucking a guy was one thing. It wasn't so different from fucking a woman. But letting a guy shove his dick up your ass? Well, there was no taking that back.

"Hey, I'm teasing." Chad kissed him again, his hands quickly shoving Hollywood's jeans and boxers down his legs. When Hollywood toed off his shoes and stepped over the pile of clothes naked, Chad made an appreciative sound in the back of his throat and took Hollywood's straining cock in his hand.

Unable to help himself, Hollywood groaned and pumped his hips, fucking himself with Chad's tight fist. "Feels so good."

"That's just the appetizer." Chad released him and moved back a few steps. Hollywood was about to complain, but then Chad started to sing a slow sultry classic and began to move his hips in a cock-teasing dance. When Chad slowly pushed his zipper down, his hips shimmying in time to his singing, Hollywood's hand shot out to grip Chad's tallboy dresser for balance.

Turning, Chad arched his back, which pushed his muscular ass out. Hollywood's breath caught at the sight of all that flesh being revealed one slow inch at a time. Christ, he'd never seen anything sexier in his life. His mouth watered with the desire to bite into Chad's smooth butt cheeks. Allowing his desire to do the thinking, he fell to his knees and raised his hands to caress Chad's ass.

His fingers dug into the flesh, squeezing it for his teeth to clamp down on. Chad groaned, pushing against Hollywood's mouth. The sweet taste of the lightly furred skin exploded on his tongue, and Hollywood began to lap in earnest at the area he'd bitten.

"Oh God," Chad said softly. He kicked off his jeans and bent over, supporting himself with his hands on the bed.

The position opened him up, and Hollywood could see his balls hanging, calling for attention. Shit. He couldn't believe he was actually doing this. Couldn't believe he was so turned on by the sight of another man's tackle. But he was. He really fucking was.

Reaching out, he rolled the fragile orbs in his hand, enjoying Chad's little sounds of pleasure. He gave his own envious balls a firm squeeze to slow down his arousal. He wasn't ready yet to pound Chad's ass. There was still too much to explore before then. Cupping each cheek in one hand, he pulled them apart, eager to see where his cock would be going. His previous experiences with anal sex hadn't been all that, but he sensed this time would be different.

As he spread his hands, Chad's dusky hole appeared. He'd never thought much about assholes before… At least not beyond their primary function. For some reason, tonight at least, Chad's looked beautiful. Maybe it was the lust talking. Had to be. A beautiful asshole? Fuck, he was losing his mind.

Still, he couldn't deny that it called to him.

Before he could think about what he was doing, he dragged his tongue from the base of Chad's balls to the top of his crack.

Chad's hips bucked under his mouth. "Fuuuck."

"Not good?" he asked, wondering if what he'd done had grossed Chad out. It certainly hadn't grossed him out. In fact, the slightly musky taste was oddly addictive.

"Really good. Just surprising."

"Then you won't mind if I do it again." Chad's hips pushing back was his only answer.

Inspired by Chad's obvious enjoyment, Hollywood did the long slow glide of his tongue again. Then focused his attention on the tight ring of muscle. It resisted his attempts to penetrate. Hollywood's eyes narrowed. If he couldn't get his tongue in there, how the hell would his cock fit?

"You sure about this, Caldwell?"

Chad's voice was strained when he answered. "Keep going. It's been a while, that's all."

A while since Chad had had sex? According to Austin, Chad had done the dirty mambo with Harry only a few weeks ago. "Is gay sex some sort of weird breaking-the-hymen thing every time? Because if so, I don't know if I'm on board with that." He'd had a couple virgins in his day and had always found the experience to be more effort than it was worth.

"No, it fucking isn't. Just get on with it, asshole." Chad chuckled, the sound thick and turned on. Hollywood responded with several flicks of his tongue on said body part. Chad moaned low and arched his back. Hollywood pressed his tongue against the little opening and suddenly, he was inside.

"Oh, my God." Chad's pelvis started to move, throwing Hollywood off his rhythm. He gripped the guy's hips, using all his strength to hold him in place as he pumped his tongue in and out of Chad's hole, all the while trying not to think about where exactly his tongue was. All he knew was that, right now, Chad was really digging this.

"Lube," Chad choked out, his hand scrambling for the drawer of his nightstand. Hollywood was closer, so he opened it up and got the lube and a condom, glad to see the guy was prepared.

Of course he is. This isn't his first rodeo.

Shut up, he ordered the voice in his head. This wasn't Hollywood's first rodeo either. Well, with a guy it was, but... Whatever.

"Give me a sec to prepare." Chad tried to grab the lube.

Hollywood's fingers closed around the tube. "Tell me what to do."

"You sure?"

"Yeah." If he was going to do this, he was damn well going to do it like a man.

"Finger-fuck me like you would a woman. But use lube"—Chad shot him a sharp look over his shoulder—"lots of lube."

Hollywood smirked. "Lots of lube. Got it." As instructed, he squeezed some lube onto Chad's pucker, now slick with saliva, and pressed his finger against it. Chad took a deep breath, then, as if by magic, Hollywood was admitted inside. The strength of Chad's muscles squeezing his finger was exquisite and Hollywood almost came as he imagined his cock in the place of his fingers.

Soon.

Slowly, he sank his finger in deeper, until it was in past his second knuckle, then he began to pump it. Chad dropped his head between his outstretched arms and his thighs trembled. Hollywood pushed in a little deeper, and Chad gasped, his entire body going rigid.

"Problem?" Had he hurt Chad?

"Fuck no. Do that again." Despite his words, Chad pulled forward, then back, impaling himself on Hollywood's finger. "Oh God," he cried as his movements became more frantic. Hollywood had no idea what the hell was going on, just that his lover was quite clearly enjoying having his finger in his ass. "Add another one," Chad ordered.

Hollywood pulled his finger out, drizzled some lube on his index and middle fingers, then pressed both of them against the ring that had considerably loosened in the last however long they'd been doing this. When his fingers disappeared, his cock gave a jerk as though asking *what about me?* Never big on delayed gratification, Hollywood gave himself a couple long thrilling pulls before returning to the task at hand. He scissored his fingers, pushing them in, then curling them to rub against a patch deep inside Chad where the texture was different. Instantly, Chad yelped as though zapped by an electric current. Startled, Hollywood stopped. "What happened?"

"Prostate. God's gift to men." Chad's guttural, breathless voice filtered through Hollywood, touching every nerve in his body.

"God's gift, huh?"

"Fucking A." Chad rocked his hips. "One more," he gasped.

Hollywood chuckled at Chad's enthusiastic response. Chad groaned, the sound close to pain, as Hollywood pushed another finger in. "Okay?" The guy was so vulnerable, so trusting, and Hollywood would rather die than hurt him.

"Yeah." Chad's voice sounded like he was being sucked off by a girl with braces—caught somewhere between pleasure and pain. "Keep going. I'm almost ready."

Encouraged, Hollywood pumped his fingers a few times, then Chad pulled forward. "Now."

Hollywood wiped his hands off on the pair of jeans closest to him, slid on the condom and lubed up, adding a generous amount to Chad's hole. Standing up, he aligned his cock to the other man's entrance, grabbed his hips, and slowly pressed in. Chad's well-prepared ring resisted for a second before giving way and allowing Hollywood's cock into the hottest, tightest place it had ever been.

Stars whirled around his head and he lost his breath.

Chad glanced over his shoulder, a grin showing off his perfectly straight white teeth. "Everything okay back there?"

Hollywood struggled to force air into his lungs and unlock his limbs. "Holy fuck." It was all he could manage, overwhelmed as he was by all the newness of the experience. Chad's hips were hard where a woman's were soft, his legs furred where a woman's were smooth. The strength in the body beneath Hollywood's, almost equal to his own, submitting to him, affected him in a way sex with a woman never had. Even the man's smell, and the sheen of sweat slicking his body only served to enhance Hollywood's arousal.

"Yeah I know." Chad inhaled deeply. "Start moving."

That was all the signal Hollywood needed. He let his hands slide up Chad's cut back, then over his broad shoulders where his fingers latched on as he rocked his pelvis. Slowly at first, until he was all the way in. Christ. "I'm inside you. So fucking deep." Balls deep, in fact. It was mind-blowing to be so connected to another man.

Chad was breathing heavily. Was he doing it right? He eased one hand down Chad's chest until he found Chad's cock, blowing out in relief when he found it hard and leaking pre-cum. Curling his palm around the top, he slicked it up, then started to jerk him off. Long strokes that matched the tempo of his thrusts into Chad's body.

Crying out, Chad pushed off the bed and wrapped an arm around Hollywood's neck. He turned his head and took his mouth, at the same time grinding against Hollywood's groin.

It was perfect.

They were joined in every way two humans could be. And as Chad sucked on his tongue, Hollywood pounded into his ass. Chad's hand closed over his and together they stroked up and down his thick cock.

"I'm so close. Don't stop," Chad whispered, his voice pure sex.

Hollywood would die first. He picked up the speed, splaying his hand over Chad's abs to hold their bodies tightly together. A few shallow thrusts later, and Chad groaned, looking straight into Hollywood's eyes as he came in warm spurts all over their hands and his stomach. Hollywood held him through the aftershocks and felt Chad's lips curve into a smile against his own. "So?"

"So." Hollywood grinned as he pushed the guy down onto the bed. "I'm not finished."

CHAPTER 17

Chad let out an oof as he landed on the mattress, laughter and surprise warring for supremacy. Hollywood's wide hand smacked his ass. "Up. On your knees in the middle of the bed."

"Ow! Fucker. So you're giving orders now, huh?"

Hollywood flashed him that sexy grin, the one that said "I'm in control," and Chad loved it.

"I'll give you today, then we'll put the universe back to rights."

Laughter met his pronouncement. "You think so? I'm a lieutenant. Giving orders is what I do."

Chad smiled as he crawled onto his hands and knees. He'd give Hollywood what he thought he wanted today, but soon Chad would give the man what he really needed. What only someone like Chad could give him.

The bed dipped as Hollywood got behind him in a position that was, no doubt, very familiar to him. Soon though, Chad would take him far out of his comfort zone and shatter his world. Chad closed his eyes as hands gripped his hips and a big cock pressed at his hole. Bottoming was always more difficult when he'd already come, but having Hollywood in his ass and the man's tongue in his mouth had sent him flying.

Breathing slowly, he forced himself to relax, to let Hollywood inside. And then he was there. He groaned as the burning transitioned into an exquisite fullness. Something he hadn't felt since his teen years when in his eagerness to get rid of the V, he'd bottomed for Greg, his first big crush. He'd never trusted anyone to take him since then, not even his ex, Quincy. After those first couple of times with Greg though, they'd both decided he was a natural top.

Chad grunted when Hollywood thrust in, seating himself fully. He loved the feel of balls slapping balls, of Hollywood's cock dragging along inside him. His muscles instinctively squeezed it, desperate as he was to keep it there. Hollywood's smooth thrusts soon had him stiff again and more than ready to come.

"Harder."

As soon as the words left Chad's mouth, Hollywood slowed. "I give the orders around here."

Twisting his head and shoulders, Chad glared. "Excuse me?"

Hollywood grinned again, but this time it was with far less confidence. "I... uh... I give the orders."

"Oh yeah?" In a flash, Chad was straddling Hollywood's hips, while the guy lay flat on his back, hands pinned above his head. "I may be bottoming, but don't ever think you're the one in charge."

To punctuate his words, Chad gripped Hollywood's gorgeous cock and impaled himself on it. His hips swung back and forth, in lazy circles, up and down. Hollywood writhed beneath him, throaty moans filling the air. "Oh, God, Chad."

Yeah, now they *both* knew who was running the show. Hollywood's whispered words going straight to his cock, Chad leaned down to capture his lover's mouth in a hard, dominating kiss. "Jerk me," he ordered.

Hollywood's green gaze flew to his red and ready cock. "Again?"

Chad wanted to tease him about being young and having a quick recovery time, but something told him Hollywood would take it the wrong way. Instead he smiled, and said, "Can't let you have all the fun."

As Hollywood's hand closed over him, squeezing exactly right, Chad kissed Hollywood again. He loved the taste of this man's mouth, the sensation of their tongues twining, the rub of his chest hairs, the scrape of his five o'clock shadow. Everything about the blond lieutenant turned him on. Especially that little catch in his breath, the small gasp right before he reached the point of no return.

"Let go," Chad whispered against the other man's parted lips. "I'll be there to catch you."

Hollywood opened his eyes, holding Chad's as his hips pushed up, pumping into Chad like a piston gone wild. Then Chad heard it, the catch, the gasp, the cry that carried his name. He exploded as Hollywood bucked one last time and came inside him.

ഉ 🚂 ର

Satisfied beyond even his wildest imaginings, Hollywood caught Chad as he shivered and collapsed on his chest. "Holy fuck," he said into the quiet when he could breathe again. Chad's body began to shake, then he heard sniggers and finally the guy rolled off him. His laughter was joyous, exuberant even. He could only hope it meant Chad had enjoyed what they'd just shared as much as he had.

After a few minutes, Chad sobered and turned to Hollywood. "Yeah, 'Holy fuck' is right."

"Is it always like that?"

"How?"

Hollywood felt the blush on his cheeks, but he pushed through it. "Super intense, like nothing else exists."

"Sometimes." Chad looked away. "Rarely."

"Chad?"

When Chad faced him again, Hollywood rolled onto his side, mirroring Chad's position. "You aren't just an experiment."

"No?"

"Definitely no. I..." His voice trailed off into never-never land as he lost his nerve.

Chad laid his arm over Hollywood's waist. "Tell me."

Hollywood huffed out a sigh. "I like you."

'Chad's eyes sparkled. "Oh, you *like* me. Good to know."

"Fucker."

"No. This time, that was you." The grin joined the smile in his eyes. Snuggling closer, Chad kissed him again. It was slow and lazy, and exactly what Hollywood needed. He stroked Chad's dark hair, so different from his own. His fingernails scraped the stubble on Chad's cheek. The sensation was strange, but not unwelcome. In fact... fuck. He really liked it.

"I want to try this."

Chad leaned back a little and bit his lip. The look on his face was so mischievous that Hollywood waited more than a little anxiously to see what the guy would say. He did not disappoint. His voice rising an octave or two, he said, "Why Lieutenant Wright, are you asking me to be your *boyfriend?*"

Hollywood gawped. Was he? He thought about Harry and had his answer. "If that means we're exclusive, then yes, that's what I'm asking."

Chad shook his head. "The look on your face, man. I was teasing. Lighten up."

Hollywood rolled over onto Chad's chest and narrowed his eyes. "I'm not joking. I don't want you fucking anyone else while we're together."

"Hollywood—" Chad started, then stopped and shoved him off his chest. "I don't even know your real name."

"Why do you want to know it? Because we're fucking?" He snorted. None of his previous sexual partners had known his real name, and he'd certainly not known theirs. "That's not a good enough reason."

Chad's eyes closed and his voice was much too soft when he asked, "Does Jamie know?"

"Of course. He's my best friend."

Chad sat up on the side of the bed, and turned his back to Hollywood. "That's why."

Oh no. Hollywood wasn't going to let Chad turn this into another argument. Before the guy could get up, Hollywood knelt behind him and wrapped his arms around his chest. "It's Nathanial."

He rested his cheek on Chad's shoulder, experiencing every breath he took through the intimate contact of their bodies. Intimate. There was that word again. He'd never held anyone like this, not since Isabel.

Chad laid his head against Hollywood's. "It's a nice name."

"I hate it."

"Why?"

"My father named me after his grandfather. When he caught me with Bobby, he said I didn't deserve to carry the name of such a respectable man. That day, he started calling me Nathan."

There was a question in Chad's eyes.

"I hate both those names. My grandfather was a disgusting pastor who terrorized his family. I don't remember much about my childhood before my mom died, but I do remember her tears every time my grandmother came to visit with a black eye or a split lip."

"Oh my God." Chad couldn't help wondering if Hollywood had been caught up in some vicious cycle of abuse handed down through generations. "Did your father ever hit your mom?"

Hollywood shook his head. "Just me. It's only after my mother died that everything went to shit. Before that he was..." His words thickened. "Fuck. He was a regular dad until then. Taught me to ride a bike, took me to ball games. All the usual father-son stuff."

"I'm so sorry." Chad turned until he could get his arms around Hollywood's shoulders.

Hollywood held onto him, taking comfort in the strength of the arms surrounding him. "Even Jamie doesn't know all that," he whispered.

"Thank you for telling me." Chad stroked his back. "Those names will never cross these lips." He sealed his vow with a sweet kiss.

"I'm not used to talking about my feelings." Growing up, Hollywood had quickly learned that sharing his feelings was not in his best interests. But if he wanted a relationship with Chad, he had to do better. Not only did he have to be honest with Chad, he also had to be honest about his feelings *for* Chad. He couldn't keep hiding, not from Chad, not from his friends and colleagues.

Letting out an embarrassing, shuddering breath, Hollywood sat back a little so he could see Chad's face. "I'll come out. I promise. I want this relationship to be real. Just give me a little time, okay?"

"Take all the time you need."

The glitter in Chad's eyes opened the door to Hollywood's next concession. "And you can call me Nate." Hollywood stared at him pointedly. "But *only* when we're alone."

Grinning, Chad saluted him. "Got it, LT."

"You always such a brat?"

Chad shimmied his hips, his expression sliding into a lusty, lazy smirk. "Only in bed."

Hollywood pounced on him, tickling his sides and licking the tattoos that had his cock saluting back. "Then I'll have to do my best to keep you here."

ℬ 🚃 ℭ

An annoying buzzing tore Chad from the best dream, a dream where he was in bed with Hollywood's hot body and hard dick heating his backside. Blinking in the darkness, broken only by the faint glow of moonlight filtering through the blinds he'd forgotten to close last night, he tried to identify the source of the buzzing. Shit. It was the alarm on his phone, which was still in his pants, on the floor.

On the floor.

Just like in the dream.

Reaching over the side of the bed, he fumbled around until he located his cell and silenced the alarm. Then he closed his eyes and snuggled back under the covers, anxious to get back to the dream. Just for a few minutes before he had to get up and go to work.

Warm breath fanned his shoulder, sending goose bumps over his skin. An arm—big and muscular with a light coating of blond hair—wrapped around his chest and tugged him back, and Hollywood's sexy scent engulfed him. Chad glanced over his shoulder and grinned.

Not a dream.

He and Hollywood had really had sex last night. Wow. He'd been expecting Hollywood to end their flirtation, if that was even the right word. What had happened instead had fulfilled his every fantasy. Well, not quite. Hollywood's tight, taut ass came to mind. He smiled and snuggled deeper into Hollywood's hold and pushed his butt against Hollywood's impressive morning wood.

Ouch. Wincing, he let out a groan.

Hollywood tensed and he rose up on an elbow to peer at his face. "You okay? I didn't hurt you last night, did I?"

"Nah. I'm just a little... tender."

For a moment, Hollywood's expression was torn between pride and regret, then pride won out. "You do look well-fucked."

Chad snorted. "Give me a couple days, I'll be good to go again."

Hollywood's jaw went slack. "A couple days?" Rolling Chad onto his

174

back, he gripped his jaw, the aggressive action and the hunger in his gaze making Chad hard. He leaned in closer, so their lips were almost touching. "Now that I've had a taste of you, I don't think I can keep my hands off for that long."

Unable to resist the lure of the man's full lips, Chad arched up and took Hollywood's mouth, possessing and claiming as he began to move under him. "I didn't say we couldn't have sex. Just not anal, at least not with me being the fuckee." Teasing, but not really, Chad lifted a brow.

Hollywood's face paled. He remained immobile, his throat working overtime. "I... I'm not ready for that. I don't know if I ever will be."

Chad forced himself to smile, to stroke the side of Hollywood's face, even as his insides clenched. He'd certainly enjoyed bottoming for Hollywood, and absolutely wanted to do it again. Frequently. But, he didn't think he could turn it into a long-term full-time deal. He was, first and foremost, a top, and his cock wanted inside Hollywood's ass.

For now though, he'd take Hollywood any way he could have him. The guy was scared, confused, yet willing to explore and try new things. Chad had to give him time to adjust to his new reality. That didn't mean he couldn't work on changing the guy's mind.

Using a martial arts move Drew had taught him, Chad flipped Hollywood onto his back and swallowed his pulsing dick. To the root. Hollywood's back bowed off the bed and he let out a gratifyingly surprised shout that had Chad's cock leaking with pleasure.

Chad tortured his lover with his tongue, his teeth, and one hand while the other toyed with his balls, tugging and rolling.

"Oh God, Chad. No one gives head like you." Hollywood's grunted praise was all the encouragement Chad needed. Keeping Hollywood distracted, he slicked his thumb with saliva and pre-cum, and brought it to its destination. He took advantage of the journey to apply a gentle pressure with his index finger along Hollywood's taint, from the area right behind his balls to his hole. Once there, he pressed his thumb against the opening, looking up at Hollywood's face to catch his reaction.

The big man's body tightened, and worried green eyes latched onto Chad's. Slowly, Chad dragged his tongue along the underside of Hollywood's cock until he released the head. Hollywood made a whimpering sound Chad was sure he'd deny, and his cock twitched against Chad's cheek. He smiled gently. "If you want me to stop, say no."

Hollywood licked his lips, then dropped his head onto the pillows. Beneath Chad's hand, Hollywood's stomach quivered. "Keep going."

Not wasting a moment, Chad pointed his tongue and wedged it into Hollywood's slit, lapping up pre-cum, loving the salty taste. When the quivering in Hollywood's abs reached his legs, Chad parted his lips and took Hollywood's throbbing crown into his mouth, stretching his lips wide. Confident that Hollywood was once again relaxed and receptive, Chad went back to work, circling Hollywood's virgin pucker with his thumb. The tight muscles fluttered under his attentions. But before he could do more, he needed lube. Christ, where had they put it last night? Then he remembered knocking it with his feet before falling asleep.

With his other hand, he searched the foot of the bed, almost crying with relief when his hand closed around the tube. He really wanted Hollywood to have something to think about after they both headed off for their twenty-four-hour shifts.

As he swirled his tongue around the underside of Hollywood's crown, Chad flicked open the lube and poured some down Hollywood's crack, eliciting a surprised gasp that was quickly silenced when Chad took Hollywood down his throat. It was hard to control his own excitement at having Hollywood in his mouth, his taste on his tongue, and the broad head of his cock squeezed in his throat. But he had to, because this was the ideal time to breach Hollywood's perfect ass.

Pulling back, just enough so he could breathe, Chad ran his finger through the lube, coating it well, then pushed against the opening. He gently scraped his teeth on Hollywood's shaft, and when the man groaned, he pushed his finger in. The slight resistance soon gave way, and he was in up to his knuckle.

Hollywood narrowed his eyes. "Whatcha doing down there, Caldwell?"

"You saying no, Nate?"

"Fuck you."

Laughing, Chad rocked his finger from side to side, loosening up the tense muscles. Hollywood's frown disappeared and his eyes glazed over. Just a bit. Chad grinned. "You like?"

"Shut up." Hollywood's hips bucked. "Don't stop."

Not needing to be told twice, Chad started to slowly pump his finger, working it in deeper and deeper as he took Hollywood's cock back into his mouth. Immediately, he sensed the difference. Hollywood hadn't deflated at all. In fact, his cock had swollen and by the taste and amount of pre-cum, Chad knew he was close.

His heart pounding in anticipation, Chad pushed in all the way. After locating that small protrusion that could bring a man so much pleasure, he pressed down with the pad of his finger and massaged gently. His eyes wanted to close, to savor Hollywood's sexy sounds and the feel of all that hard flesh in his mouth, but he couldn't risk missing even a second.

Hollywood's reaction to his touch was instantaneous. His back arched off the bed and hips bucking, he came in a glorious explosion of movement and hoarse cries that catapulted Chad into his own release. After a minute or so of silence, punctuated by harsh breaths, Hollywood gripped Chad's hair and dragged him up from where he'd collapsed with his head on Hollywood's thigh. The muscle and soft hair had made a great resting spot.

Resisting the urge to pout, Chad let himself be led until he was draped over Hollywood's chest. That's when he noted the narrowed look, the flat lips. Huh? Hollywood's orgasm had obviously been powerful. Was he actually going to complain?

"What the hell was that?" Hollywood asked.

"That, my friend, was your prostate."

Hollywood ran a hand over his jaw, and the sound of stubble scraping against skin had Chad's palm itching to join in. "Wow. Straight men are really missing out."

Staring at Hollywood's satisfied expression, Chad had to wonder: Did Hollywood realize what he'd so casually admitted?

CHAPTER 18

Hollywood dropped his feet onto the coffee table and sighed in relief. His last shift had been a bitch, then he'd spent half the day at the station catching up on paperwork and the other half dealing with tenant issues.

But now here he was, getting ready to spend Christmas Eve with Chad. It would be the first one since Isabel that he'd be spending with someone he cared about. Usually, he either worked the holiday, taking on shifts for his colleagues with families, or he hooked up with some equally lonely bimbo.

Tonight would be different. Yesterday, Chad had dragged him to a Christmas tree lot. The pickings had been pretty slim, but Hollywood had been happy to buy a scraggly little tree like the one in that old Charlie Brown Christmas special. They'd brought it home and set it up in the corner of his living room. He'd strung a few strands of lights on it and Chad had brought over a box of ornaments from his place.

The colored lights flashed on and off, illuminating the awkwardly wrapped box sitting on the floor under the tree. He smiled. That present was also a first for him.

Rather than buying Chad something tried and true like a shirt or a tie, he'd decided to offer him something more personal, something he'd created with his own two hands. And since Hollywood was working on Christmas, he'd give Chad his present tonight, after dinner, but before they watched the movie Chad wanted them to see together.

His stomach flipped. Would Chad like the present? He'd never made something for someone before.

The sounds of Chad fussing in the kitchen and the scent of the roasted whatever he was cooking made Hollywood think back to his mom. How he'd felt when she'd hugged him, the smell of freshly baked chocolate chip cookies lingering on her clothes. Sometimes, with Isabel, he'd come close to that feeling, but he'd never reached it. Maybe because with her, he'd always been denying a part of himself.

But with Chad, there could be no denial.

The guy, all muscled six-plus feet of him, turned Hollywood on in a crazy lose-your-mind way. If Chad had been a woman, Hollywood would probably have already proposed and whisked him off to Vegas for a quickie Elvis wedding.

The thought of the two of them in tuxes, exchanging vows and rings before a sequined Elvis impersonator should have had him shitting bricks, but it didn't. Probably because it was all so fantastical. Chad was young, still sowing his oats. He wasn't going to pressure Hollywood into "putting a ring on it," or rake him over the coals with a pregnancy scare. Life with Chad was definitely the best of both worlds.

Since becoming official boyfriends, they'd been spending all their free time together, and Chad had been taking care of him better than anyone ever had. While Hollywood watched sports, Chad cooked. While Hollywood took a nap, Chad cleaned, and it didn't matter whose place they were in. Hell, he'd even changed Hollywood's sheets and done his laundry. And the sex? Frequent and phenomenal. Unlike with a woman, there was no need for coaxing, or wooing. They were two horny, hot-blooded men eager to get each other off.

It was fucking heaven. Better than heaven even, because it was so *dirty*. God, the things they'd done to each other. His cock came to life at the memories.

Hearing movement, Hollywood cracked open an eye, smiling when he saw Chad with a beer in his hand. Christ, the guy was good to him. He took the beer and downed a third of it. "Thanks, man." When he noticed that Chad didn't have a beer, he asked, "Didn't you want one too?"

Chad made a face before spinning on his heel and going back to the kitchen. The fridge door slammed, then Chad came back with another beer and flopped onto the couch. Not next to him, but at the other end.

Sitting up, Hollywood set his bottle on the coffee table. Something was off. Chad's shoulders were stiff and the usual spark in his eyes was gone. A vise tightened around Hollywood's gut. "Something wrong?"

"I'm a little tired."

When Chad kept his gaze averted, Hollywood knew his instincts were right. He just didn't know what to do. Trying for levity, he gave Chad his best wicked grin, in case the guy actually deigned to look at him. "Am I wearing you out?"

"Maybe. I think I need to get some sleep tonight."

On Christmas Eve? Hollywood's palms started to sweat. Something was definitely wrong. He slid along the couch and put his arm around Chad's shoulders. "It's tough to keep my thoughts pure around you, but whatever you want."

Chad shrugged his arm off and stood. "I think I need to go home and take care of some stuff." He shoved his hands into the pockets of his black skin-tight jeans. "I'm not used to sleeping with someone."

Although he was disappointed, really disappointed, Hollywood could relate to that. It had been years, thirteen in fact, since he'd spent the night with someone in his own bed. Unlike Chad though, Hollywood found he slept much better with Chad as the small spoon to his big one.

Turning away, Chad headed for the hall closet. That's when the lightbulb in Hollywood's head finally clicked on. "You're leaving *now*? But you made dinner."

"I'm not really hungry. It'll be ready in fifteen minutes."

"What about our plans? We were going to watch that movie together—"

"I'm not really feeling it right now."

Hollywood slammed his mouth shut. His gaze strayed to the gift under the tree, and his throat closed up. *Fuck.*

Chad pulled his leather jacket on, the one that made him look like a sexy badass and always made Hollywood hard. But not this time. His heart was pounding, and not in a good way.

Was this the end?

"I'll see you," Chad said, opening the door.

Hollywood grabbed his arm, and it took him several painful swallows before he could form words. "I do something wrong?"

"No." Chad sighed and rubbed his forehead. "I think *I* did."

Had there been a glitch in the timeline? Chad had done everything right. Everything. "I'm not following."

Chad gave him a sad smile and patted his cheek. "I know, and I'm sorry." He turned to go.

"Wait." Adrenaline was doing a number on his pulse, his brain screaming "Do something!" But what?

He scrambled for something to say. Something to keep Chad with him, or at least have the promise of seeing him soon. "Uh... on the twenty-sixth, I'm hosting poker night again. To make up for last time." His face burned. Fucking poker night? *This* was his grand plan to see Chad again? "Anyway, want to come?"

"I'll think about it," Chad said, stepping out into the hall. It wasn't a promise, but it was better than nothing at all.

With the snick of the closing door still in his ears, Hollywood went back to his spot on the couch. He stared at the tree, at the gift below it. Picking up a throw pillow, he spiked it at the wall. Goddamn. He'd really thought his life was starting to change, but it hadn't.

Here he was, alone again.

Loser. Why can't you man up?

He should have forced Chad to talk about what was upsetting him. But that would have meant cutting open his own chest and letting Chad see what lay in his heart. And he couldn't. He fucking couldn't.

Grabbing the remote, he switched on the television. Might as well watch the movie Chad had been insisting on. When "It's a Wonderful Life" appeared on the screen, a lump filled his throat. And then the tears came. Fucking *tears*. He hadn't cried in forever.

This shit had to stop.

Fuck Jimmy Stewart, fuck this movie, and fuck Christmas.

He wasn't a goddamn kid anymore. He wasn't a boy who needed someone to love him.

And if Chad doesn't come back?

Hollywood wiped his cheeks and changed the channel. He was going to be strong, he was going to get through this, even if it fucking killed him.

෨ 🎬 ෬

H: Hey, beautiful. Have u made up ur mind about tonight?

Today was one of those rare bright and warm December days in Seattle, and Chad was taking full advantage of it. He'd combined his need to confide in someone with his need to run and had bribed Austin into it for the small price of a lunch at the little sushi place he liked.

Chad's phone buzzed yet again. Pointing to it, Austin asked, "You gonna check that?"

Chad shoved the phone further away. "No."

"Guy's sure persistent."

"You have no idea." Hollywood had texted him three times yesterday to wish him a Merry Christmas, then again four more times this morning. The messages were always cheery and hopeful. They were also unusually tentative—not really Hollywood's style. And each one drove home the fact that what he'd done to Hollywood, leaving him alone on Christmas Eve, had been a really shitty thing to do. He'd started feeling bad about it the minute he'd walked out the door, and things hadn't gotten any better since.

The problem though was, what should he do about it? His reasons for leaving had been valid; it was his timing that had sucked. He just hadn't been able to stomach the idea of faking a jolly holiday mood the whole evening.

Yeah, he was a class-A asshole. No doubt about it.

"Come on, darlin'. Fess up."

His eyes fixed on the calm blue waters of the bay, Chad debated how much he should tell Austin. Normally, they told each other everything. This time though, Chad had kept his encounters with Hollywood close to the vest. Too close. His gut burned. Hollywood had gotten him to do the one thing he'd vowed never to do again—go back into the closet.

Austin sat forward and squeezed Chad's arm. "Let me make this easy for you. I reckon this has somethin' to do with our favorite straight lieutenant. He finally admit he's got the hots for you?"

Chad snorted and shoved the closet door wide open. "Let's just say that's not a problem anymore."

"Hot damn! So he took the plunge into the gay pool? Can't say as I thought he had it in him."

Chad's cock hardened at the mention of Hollywood's plunging. Shit. He shifted into a more comfortable position. "Enthusiastically, I'd say."

Austin took a bite of rainbow roll dunked in soy sauce and nodded appreciatively. "He come out to anyone? That's the first step to really acceptin' it."

"Yeah." Chad smiled, still unable to believe Hollywood had had the balls. "He came out to Jamie."

Austin's eyebrows popped. "Seriously? How'd that go?"

"Pretty well apparently."

"He tell your brother about the two of you?"

"No. He seems to think Jamie wouldn't approve."

"Because of the age difference?"

"Because of Hollywood's track record."

"Ah. You gonna let that stop you?"

Chad smiled, remembering Tori's advice. "I'm old enough to make my own decisions." His smile fell as they got closer to the crux of his problem.

"Hey," Austin said. "You've wanted this guy for a long time, and now you've got him. So why do you look like your favorite vibratin' butt plug just died?"

"We had a fight. Well, not really a fight. But, long story short, I walked out on him before we even had dinner."

Austin frowned. "All right."

"It was Christmas Eve."

"Dude. That's cold as a banker's heart."

"I know. I feel like crap about it."

"And what heinous crime did he commit to deserve such treatment?"

Chad cupped his glass of water between his hands and blew out a long breath. "Hollywood is gorgeous and funny in an I-don't-mean-to-be way. He's smart and has a good job. He owns real estate, for God's sake. He's one of the most loyal friends a guy can have, and he totally rocks my world in bed…."

"But?"

Chad's eyes dropped to the cubes of ice melting in the bottom of his glass. "But." He closed his eyes, unable to believe he was going to say this. "He treats me like a woman. And… I don't know. All of a sudden, I couldn't take it anymore."

Stunned silence filled the space between them. When Chad looked up, his friend's face was a dark cloud of confusion. "Like a woman?" His gaze swept up and down Chad's body. "Darlin', there's nothing womanly about any of you, not to mention that fat eight inches you've got in your pants. How'd he miss that?"

Chad couldn't help a chuckle. "You always know just what to say."

Austin's eyebrow quirked and he held up his fist for a bump. "Bros before…"

"Uh… other bros?" Chad laughed and bumped Austin's fist.

"Damn straight," Austin said, slapping his thigh passionately. "Now tell me, he's touched your pecker, right?"

"Yeah."

"Okay. And how did he miss your cock when it was up his ass?"

Chad looked away. "We haven't quite gotten there yet."

"There? You haven't had sex yet? Now I can see how he'd think you're a woman."

"Fuck you." Chad threw his balled-up napkin at Austin, bopping him on the nose. "We've had sex. Just—"

Austin interrupted, his eyes like saucers. "You're bottomin' for him? Wow. You must really be into this guy."

"I thought it would be easier for him to get into the whole"— he rolled his eyes—"gay thing, if I let him top."

"Makes sense. So how exactly has he been treatin' you like a woman?"

Chad threw his hands up as his frustrations bubbled to the surface. "Gah! I don't know. He's so incredibly macho, you know? I bet all his girlfriends fawned over him, and there's this implied—I don't know what—that I'll take care of him. I'm doing all the cooking, cleaning, laundry, while he watches TV or naps. Christ, I feel like June fucking Cleaver."

"Whoa, Nelly." Austin glanced at the nearby tables. "Take it down a notch."

Chad covered his mouth and stared at his best friend. "What am I going to do?"

"He ask you to do any of that?"

"Not really. But you know what happened last time he cooked."

Austin sniggered. "Sure, but is he really that bad? Seems to me he just got distracted. Could've happened to anyone."

Eyes narrowing, Chad glared at Austin. "Why are you defending him? I thought you didn't like Hollywood."

"Ha!" Austin broke into a fit of laughter. "If you weren't so puppy dog in love with the guy, I'd be all over that ass."

"Stay the fuck away from him," Chad warned.

"I don't hear you denyin' the in-love part."

Chad crossed his arms and pressed so hard his chest hurt. "Because we aren't discussing that right now."

Holding up a hand, Austin nodded. "Okay, I'll back off." He finished another crab maki and pointed to Chad's untouched meal with his chopsticks. "You gonna eat that?"

"How the hell do you eat so much and stay so fit?"

He flexed his huge biceps and winked. "Eat big to get big."

"Yeah and then spend hours at the gym."

"Like you don't?"

Okay, he did. Chad liked his body, liked having hard muscles and tight abs, and an ass that didn't quit. *Thank you, squats.* Hollywood seemed to enjoy all of that.

"Hey, cut that sad face. Talk to Daddy."

"I don't know what to do. I've never been super dominant in my previous relationships, but gender roles have never been an issue. We've naturally split the chores up along the lines of what we hated least."

"Dude, the guy's lived his whole life straight. Gender roles are a thing for them. I grew up with a daddy who refused to let any of his boys do women's work. My poor ma and little sister had to do all the cookin' and housework while me and my two brothers did the yardwork, fixed the cars, and watched sports on TV. Wasn't fair, but that's the way it was."

Chad couldn't imagine his mom and Tori slaving away while he and his brothers goofed off. His mom had made sure all her boys did their share of the housework, and Tori learned to change a tire when she was ten, same as him. They'd even traded cooking chores against yardwork because he liked to be in the kitchen, and she liked to have her hands in the dirt.

"So you're saying that this is happening because he doesn't know better? I'm not buying that."

"No." Austin's steady gaze bore into him. "It's happenin' 'cause you let it. Guys love to be pampered. If someone wants to do it, we let 'em."

Had he done that? Maybe.

"And I know you can be a little passive-aggressive," Austin added.

"Me?" Chad shook his head. "I don't play games like that."

"No? So tell me. When the bed was wet with your cum, did you say let's change the sheets, or did you wait to see if he'd do it, and then when he didn't, you got up in a huff, tore them off, threw them in the washer, then put clean ones on before you crawled into bed to stew for hours?"

Heat washed over Chad's face and his ears burned. "Oh God. Maybe I am acting like a woman."

"No. You're acting like a little bitch. Now let me finish my fuckin' lunch."

His appetite returned, Chad laughed and ordered them another round of Orion beers.

ଛ 🚌 ଔ

"Come on, deal those cards, Lieutenant. I'm feeling lucky tonight!" Manny crowed as he rubbed his hands together.

"Lucky?" Jamie smacked him on the back hard enough for the guy, small compared to the other men at the table, to pitch forward. "We've only been playing an hour, and you've already lost half your money to William."

Manny curled his lip. "Speaking of which, LJ, you never told us your brother was such a card shark. A little warning would've been appreciated."

Hollywood snickered every time he heard the guys call Jamie "LJ," short for "Lord James," instead of "LT" or "lieutenant." It had all started one day when Jamie had let slip that he'd been named after his ancestor James Caldwell, the fourth son of Viscount Kensworth. Given Jamie's sometimes autocratic approach to leadership, the nickname had stuck.

"How do you do it, William?" Chad asked, and Hollywood listened attentively to his response, hoping to pick up a trick or two.

William tapped his temple. "It's all about what you've got up here."

Drew grinned. "That counts you out, Manny."

"Fuck off, Caldwell."

To which four Caldwells frowned and shouted, "Hey!" in perfect synchronicity.

Holy shit. It hit him all of a sudden: Hollywood was surrounded by Chad's three brothers. Oh God. What if he said something or looked at Chad the wrong way? Would they guess that he and Chad were sleeping together?

His gaze slid from his study of Chad in all his artfully-ripped-jeans-and-muscle-defining-sweater boxer-tightening glory to the cards in his hand. Sweat beaded on his brow as his belly tumbled. How the fuck was he going to get through the night?

He began shuffling the cards, careful to keep his eyes on the deck, and not on Chad. As he was about to start dealing, the oven timer rang. Hollywood smiled, happy to have something to distract the guys. "Wings are ready." He passed out the round of cards, stopping when he realized no one had moved.

Chad hadn't moved.

The timer was still buzzing. He shot Chad the most discreet look he could. Chad returned it with an arch of his brow. This was new. Ever since they'd gotten together, Chad had always been the first to race to the kitchen, to open the door, or do whatever was needed. Maybe the guy was still pissed. For what, Hollywood couldn't even begin to guess. He was so new at this, and clearly, doing it wrong.

With a resigned sigh, he put down the pack of cards and went to get the wings and turn off the alarm from hell. He didn't leave quickly enough to miss the inquiring looks the brothers were shooting each other.

Shit. Hurry the fuck up, Wright!

As fast as he could, he loaded the wings onto a plate and raced back into the dining room, just in time to see Chad throw his head back and laugh at a comment from Drew.

Every ounce of blood in Hollywood's body rushed south at the sight of the man's gorgeous neck stretched out, his seductive blue eyes shining with mirth, putting the leather choker he wore on display. The whole happy package was really rocking Hollywood's boat.

After dropping the plate of wings on the table, Hollywood turned away to hide the bulge that was growing in his jeans. "Who needs a refill?"

At the same time, everyone said, "Me."

Hollywood groaned as he practically hobbled into the kitchen. Because of the way the apartment was structured, the kitchen was hidden from view of the dining room where he'd set up the poker table. Thank fuck. He reached down and pushed hard on his erection, hoping the pressure would ease up a bit. Because how in hell was he supposed to make and carry six fucking drinks with an eight-inch drill bit between his legs?

Trying to remember what everyone was having, he began to make the drinks: Glenlivet for William—with any luck, he'd leave behind what was left—Jamie's Redhook, Manny's gin and tonic, Gabe's Southern Comfort, Drew's Sky Hag, and his own Grey Goose. He'd loaded everything onto a tray when he heard Chad's smooth voice teasing Jamie about something having to do with their sister. He looked back down at the tray. Shit! He'd forgotten to get Chad something. What was the guy even drinking tonight? Hollywood had been trying so hard not to focus on him that he hadn't even looked long enough to see if he was having wine, beer, or one of those mixed drinks he sometimes favored.

As discreetly as he could, Hollywood peered over the breakfast bar that separated the kitchen proper from the breakfast nook. If he stretched far enough, he could see into the dining room. Unfortunately, his view of

Chad's glass was blocked by Chad's fabulous shoulders, clearly outlined by the snug knit sweater he wore. His hands itched to tunnel under that sweater and feel all those chiseled muscles and warm skin. Chad had come over tonight, but had he forgiven Hollywood for whatever relationship blunder he'd committed?

He cleared his throat. "Chad, could you come over here for a minute?"

"Sure," Chad said, a small frown furrowing his brow when he stood.

"Need rescuing again?" Jamie asked, his tone teasing.

Chad smacked him in the head. "God, Jamie. Let it go, will you?"

The shock on Jamie's face had the guys around the table doubling over with laughter.

As Chad rounded the breakfast bar, Hollywood quickly turned away, trying to prevent Chad from seeing the sappy smile his defense had put on his face, but his feet got tangled. As he started to trip, Chad's strong arms caught him. "Whoa. What's going on with you tonight?"

Once he was steady, Hollywood took a step back. Chad tilted his head. He wore that concerned and confused look dogs got when their humans were acting weird. Feeling stupid, Hollywood stuffed his hands in his pockets. He looked at the wall, at the fridge, at anything but Chad's beautiful, erection-inducing face. "Couldn't remember what you were drinking.

"Why didn't you ask?"

He shrugged. "I just did."

"No. I mean, call it out. Why ask me to come here?"

Hollywood risked a quick glance at Chad, and his gaze was arrested by Chad's crooked smile. He swallowed and forced himself to be honest. "Maybe I wanted to talk to you. You got here after everyone else and we didn't get to say hello." God, the not-knowing was killing him. Stepping closer, he cupped Chad's cheek, enjoying the smoothness of his strong jaw on his palm. "Are we okay?"

"Yeah, I think we're going to be."

The curve of Chad's lips turning into a blinding smile did nothing to help get rid of Hollywood's aching hard-on. All the worry of the past two days coalesced into a wave of relief.

"Merry Christmas, babe." Hollywood's hands went to Chad's back and pulled him close for the kiss he'd been craving ever since Chad had walked through his front door. His knees almost buckled when Chad parted his lips and started kissing him back. Having this man in his arms felt so right, so fucking good, he wanted to stay like this forever.

But that would mean coming out, not only as bisexual, but as a couple. Fear suddenly knotted his stomach. Could he do it?

He bumped his groin against Chad's and barely managed to muffle his moan. Fuck. Releasing Chad's lips, he nuzzled his neck, nibbling on the sensitive skin when what he really wanted to do was suck deep and leave his mark. When he slipped his thigh under Chad's balls, Chad pushed against his shoulders. Hollywood's chest puffed with pride at the dazed look on Chad's face.

Chad took a few ragged breaths—music to Hollywood's ears—and rubbed his cheek. "You planning on talking to them about us tonight?" His eyes flicked toward the dining room where Chad's three brothers were laughing at some story Gabe was telling them.

The thought of their reaction gave him hives... If he lost Chad... If he lost Jamie... Shit. The Caldwells were the only family he knew. Of course, he'd have to come out soon, but not right now. He shook his head and disappointment flitted across Chad's face.

"I need tonight." Hollywood tried to explain the turmoil he was feeling. "Something normal, before I blow my world apart."

Chad gave him a gentle kiss. "I understand."

"Are we still good?"

A hand snaked down his back to squeeze his ass. Chad grinned. "Yes." He turned to go, paused, then shot over his shoulder, "Oh, and I'll have sex on the beach."

Hollywood gripped the counter and looked longingly out the window toward the Sound. "Christ, don't tempt me."

CHAPTER 19

After William had relieved everyone of all their money, Chad got up, unsure of what he should do. He wanted to stay and apologize for how he'd acted, for leaving Hollywood alone on Christmas Eve and ruining his whole holiday. It would look weird if he did though, seeing as he had no reason to linger that the others knew of. Resigned, he joined in the good-natured teasing and bitching as they all pulled their coats on.

"Where're you parked?" Drew asked. "I didn't see the roadster out front."

Because he was still driving the rental and he didn't want his brothers to know why. "I needed a walk, so I parked a few streets over."

Jamie clapped his shoulder. "Come on. We'll give you a lift to your car then."

Chad snuck a glance at Hollywood. Spying the hint of sadness in his eyes cemented Chad's decision. He hugged his brother with one arm and slapped his shoulder. "Nah. I'm a little wired. The fresh air will do me good."

"If you say so," Drew replied. "Thanks for tonight, Lieutenant. I had a blast."

Hollywood shook his hand. "Join us anytime you're free."

Licking his lips, Chad held his hand out, dutifully playing the part. "Thanks for inviting me, Hollywood."

"You're always welcome," Hollywood said, squeezing his hand.

When their palms made contact, electricity raced up Chad's arm, and he struggled not to react. What came out was an odd bark, which he covered up by making a funny face and pointing at William. "Not sure I can compete with Mr. CFO's big wallet."

William's eyes narrowed mischievously and he charged Chad, poking

189

his fingers into Chad's ribs. "My wallet's not the only thing about me that's big."

Laughing, Jamie put their more-than-a-little-tipsy brother in a chokehold and dragged him to the elevator. "Come on, let's get you and your big… yeah, back to Dani before you get yourself into trouble."

As the elevator doors were closing, Chad waved to Hollywood and wistfully watched him shut the door to his apartment. Damn, Chad hated all the pretending to be little more than acquaintances, pretending that he wasn't already half in love with the big blond he'd left with a fucking handshake.

Worse he hated lying to his brothers. His chest tightened as he watched them climb into Drew's car.

"You sure you don't want a lift?" Jamie asked. "It's kind of cold."

"I'll be fine." He slapped his hand on the frame of the open window. "You guys be careful."

As the designated driver, Drew had only had a couple beers before switching to soda. Come to think of it, Hollywood hadn't had more than a couple drinks himself. William, on the other hand, was three sheets to the wind. "I really want to marry that girl," he whined.

Dani had made it quite clear she wouldn't get hitched until her suspension from the fire service was lifted, which had happened a month or so ago. "So when's the big day going to be?" Chad asked.

"I don't know." William leaned his head against the seat and closed his eyes. "I think she's mad at me."

The sound of his voice, soft and defeated, had Chad's heart aching for the guy. "What's going on?"

"She's been really tense lately. And she's never around anymore." His big brother looked adorably frustrated, like a three-year-old denied his favorite candy.

Chad had had a chance to talk to Dani last week about how things were going. The TRT had been really supportive. Some of the other guys? Not so much. But if he knew Dani, and he did, she hadn't told William any of this.

Drew nudged William in the ribs. "Stop being a baby. You just got used to her being home all the time."

William's eyes opened and a corner of his lips curved up. "Maybe. Was really nice having her take care of me."

Chad could only marvel at how accurate Austin had been. His brother, Mr. Independent Bachelor, was all tied in knots, thinking his fiancée was pissed, because she didn't have time to pamper him anymore. "Ever thought about taking care of her a little? You know going back hasn't been easy on her. I'm sure she'd appreciate a foot rub or breakfast in bed every once in a while."

"There you go, William. Grow a pair, then Dani will set a date," Jamie said.

William looked up at Chad. "She's been really upset. Might take more than a foot rub."

"Well." Chad paused. "Do you have tickets for the big New Year's Eve Charity Ball?" It was an event hosted by a volunteer organization that honored fallen firefighters and provided assistance to their families.

William's eyes lit up, making him laugh. "There's a party?"

"Yeah. She hasn't mentioned it?"

He shook his head and grabbed onto the dashboard when he started to lose his balance.

Chad chuckled. It wasn't often any of them saw William drunk. But if anyone deserved to cut loose these days, it was him. "I'll get you a couple tickets. Make a big deal out of it. She'll probably argue she doesn't want to go, but she does. She's just nervous."

"You'll all be there?" William looked around.

"Yeah." To support William and Dani or any other members of his family, Chad would do anything. Including attending a New Year's party alone.

Because even if Hollywood forgave him for being such a petty ass, which he seemed inclined to do based on his behavior in the kitchen tonight, he'd still never go to something so public as a New Year's Eve party with him.

It was just as well. Chad didn't think he could fake only being Hollywood's buddy on such a special occasion, surrounded by his family and friends… It had been hard enough to do tonight.

Jamie said he'd already bought tickets, and Drew asked Chad to pick a couple up for him and Tori while he was at it. "All right," Chad said. "See you guys on Wednesday."

He waved as Drew pulled away from the curb and merged with the traffic. His gaze drifted to Hollywood's building and the Christmas lights he could see through Hollywood's living room window. Chad's heart constricted and he blew out a breath.

It was time to face the music.

ⅎ🚋ℛ

Hollywood was elbows deep in suds when the doorbell rang. One of the guys must have forgotten something. As he dried his hands, he scanned the dining room for any items that might have been left behind.

"Hey," he said, opening the door. He stopped short at the sight of Chad, all pink cheeked and sexy, standing on his doorstep with an uncertain smile on his face.

"Hey."

Hollywood looked left and right down the corridor, then grabbed the lapels of Chad's coat and hauled him inside, quickly kicking the door shut behind them. Chad landed with a thud against the wall, and the last thing Hollywood saw before he took the guy's mouth was a very self-satisfied smile.

He angled his head, deepening their kiss, as the taste of orange juice and spices tickled his taste buds. His fingers fumbled with the buttons on Chad's coat as he desperately tried to get it open. "Need my hands on your skin." His voice had turned to gravel.

Chad's soft chuckle answered him and, seconds later, the coat keeping him from his target fell abandoned to the floor. His hands tunneled under Chad's sweater, and then he was there, the heat of Chad's skin warming not just his hands, but his heart.

"I've been wanting to do this all evening," he whispered against Chad's lips.

He felt them curve. "Just touch? Because, you know, if you're not in the mood, I can go home."

The anxiety that curdled his stomach was ridiculous. He knew Chad was teasing. "You are *not* going home tonight," he growled, pressing his whole body against Chad's. Their erections rubbed together and he moaned in satisfaction.

Chad threaded his fingers through Hollywood's hair in that way that gave him goose bumps. "I wasn't sure you would want me to come back."

Hollywood rolled his hips, making Chad gasp. "You sure now?"

"God, yes. Take me to bed, Nate. And fuck me. Fuck me hard."

Not someone who needed to have things explained twice when fucking was part of the equation, Hollywood took Chad's hand and led him to the master bedroom, stopping beside the bed. "I need you naked."

With a seductive undulation of his body, Chad grabbed the hem of his sweater and pulled it over his head. Every sexy, sinuous muscle was on display for Hollywood's licking pleasure. Bending his knees, he trailed his tongue over Chad's collarbone, first on one side, then the other, as his hands ran up and down the guy's sides, his thumbs brushing Chad's nipples. Nipples that called to him. His tongue flicked one nub, then he took it between his teeth. Chad's whimpers urged him to bite harder.

He loved Chad's chest, all broad shoulders, solid pectorals, smooth golden skin even in the dead of winter. And the taste of it rivaled the best vodka, both in potency and in palate. Hollywood could pay homage to the man's body all night. Dropping to his knees, he followed the thin trail of dark hair that bisected Chad's amazing abs and dragged his tongue over the bold tribal tattoo right above Chad's belly button. His heart warmed at the sound of Chad's chuckles. Ticklish. Good to know.

Gripping Chad's hips, he lovingly bathed the pronounced V that cradled his sharply defined abdomen. It was like a neon arrow that proclaimed: nirvana here!

Chad clutched at Hollywood's shoulders. "You're killing me, Nate."

"I love your body. I want to lick and taste every inch."

Hollywood unbuttoned and unzipped Chad's jeans, slowly lowering them. Already in heaven, he nibbled at each inch of tender flesh as it was revealed. Hollywood didn't want anything for Christmas, because everything he needed was right here, in his arms.

When Chad's cock popped free of his jeans and trunks, Hollywood tongued it teasingly up and down. Chad arched his back, seeking more. "Come on, man. I'm dying."

"What do you want, Chad? Tell me and I'll give it to you." Hollywood blew on the wet skin, and his arousal doubled at the sound of Chad's plaintive moan. It was all a sexy game, but what if Chad said he wanted Hollywood's ass? Could he give it to him?

In a rough-as-nails voice, Chad said, "I want you to suck me." Hollywood opened his lips and tasted Chad's weeping crown, using his tongue to pierce the slit. Chad moaned and gripped his head. "I fucking love that."

Hollywood did it again, then took Chad in his mouth, using his flattened tongue to stimulate the sensitive underside of his shaft.

"Oh fuuuuck," Chad blurted and pumped his hips. "So good."

Hollywood relaxed his jaw and let Chad take over, loving the way Chad was using him for his pleasure. Suddenly Chad stopped and only his loud panting filled the room. Since his mouth was still full of hard, thick cock, Hollywood looked up and raised his brows.

"Sorry. Didn't mean to do that."

Hollywood slowly released him, more than a little pleased to see Chad's pout. "Do what?"

"Take control."

"Do it again. Fuck my face. Fuck it until your cum fills my throat." Hollywood grinned, knowing exactly what his words would do to Chad. What they were doing to him.

"Jesus. When did you get such a filthy mouth?"

The jerking of Chad's cock against his cheek told Hollywood everything he needed to know. "You like it."

"Damn right I do. Now put that dirty mouth to even better use."

His heart lighter than it had been, Hollywood eased his lips over Chad's cock, which had grown even larger, even harder during their brief chat. Then he fixed his gaze on his lover's and relaxed as Chad went to town on his mouth. The unadulterated lust on Chad's face, the almost pained rictus, turned Hollywood way-the-fuck on.

Making short work of his zipper, he soon had his hand wrapped around his own dick, stroking it in time to the pounding Chad was giving his mouth.

"I'm so close, babe," Chad murmured, tightening his grip on Hollywood's hair. The sensation of fingers on his scalp was almost as exquisite as the silky slide of salty flesh on his tongue. God, he really loved this. Loved having Chad fuck his mouth, loved jerking himself off to the sound of Chad's grunts and groans, to the bitter taste of the man's pre-cum, to his cock stretching his mouth wide.

It was just a blow job, but the experience was intense, almost more intimate than sex. He was at Chad's mercy, and maybe that was why. He looked up to see Chad watching him stroke himself, watching the up-and-down slide of his hand.

Chad panted, his cheeks reddened. He'd never looked more beautiful. "Oh yeah." He moaned, the sound low and sexy. "Faster, Nate. Let's come together."

With their gazes locked, Hollywood fucked his fist while Chad fucked his mouth.

The sounds of their raspy breathing and moans mixed together until Chad stiffened and thrust deep into Hollywood's throat. Then the room was filled with shouts as Chad came. Hot spunk filled Hollywood's mouth, sending him crashing into his own orgasm. They both groaned as thick ropes of cum jetted out of Hollywood's slit.

Unable to even pull himself onto the bed, Hollywood slid to the floor and lay on his back. Chad lowered himself and stretched out beside him. His head on Hollywood's chest, he toyed with the button at the neck of his polo shirt. "You're still dressed."

Hollywood snorted. "You drive me crazy." But it was more than that. That Chad had been naked and using Hollywood while he'd been fully dressed and on his knees was part of what had made the whole scene so fucking hot. He supposed a similar thing could happen with a woman, but none of the ones he'd been with had ever been aggressive enough to take control in such a powerful and mind-altering way. No, this was something he could only have with a man. With Chad.

He ran a finger down Chad's shoulder to the tattoo of entwined thorns that circled his bicep. "What does this tattoo mean?"

"I got it when I came out. It was a promise to myself." Chad blinked and looked away, his voice suddenly hoarse. "To always be true. No matter the hardship."

Hollywood's hand stilled. Chad had broken that promise. Broken it for him. It wasn't fair to make this proud man hide himself, to make him feel like there was something wrong or evil about what they did together—how they felt about each other.

As he resumed stroking Chad's arm, he listened to the quiet sounds of the man's breathing and reveled in the feel of having him in his arms. He wanted to be free with Chad, to walk with him in public, maybe even hold his hand, to introduce him as his boyfriend. Just thinking the word made Hollywood's gut clench, but that's what they were. *Boyfriends.* And he needed to be proud of that. There was no shame in it, no matter what his father might think.

"You going to the New Year's Eve Ball?" he asked before he lost his nerve.

"Yeah. William's bringing Dani, and we promised we'd all go to support them."

"It's good that she'll have all of you there." He paused, drawing in a deep breath. His gaze slowly slid to Chad's. "Want to go together?"

Chad smirked. "Sure, that way only one of us has to stay sober."

"No, I meant *together.* As in, will you be my date?"

In a rush of hands and elbows, Chad pushed off his chest. Hollywood grunted and laughed at the same time. The stunned expression on Chad's face was one he'd remember for a lifetime.

"You really mean that? Your dad's going to be there, you know."

"Yeah."

"And Jamie. And your whole platoon."

"I know." He chafed Chad's arm. "You make me so happy, and it isn't right for me to make you unhappy."

"I'm not unhappy," Chad said, even as his gaze dipped to the side.

"I saw how you looked in the elevator, not to mention how you've been acting lately."

"I'll grant you that I didn't want to leave. I hate sneaking around my brothers, but I'll be honest. My being bitchy has nothing to do with your not being out."

Hollywood sat up so they were at eye level. "Tell me. Whatever it is, I promise I'll do better."

"It's not you, sweetie. It's—"

Hollywood slapped his palm over Chad's mouth, trapping his words. "If you say, it's me not you, I'll have to smack you, and believe me, that would make me very unhappy."

Sighing, Chad grabbed his trunks and sweater, put them on, then sat on the edge of the bed. He patted the spot next to him. Hollywood zipped up his pants, grimacing at the cum crusting on his clothes. He'd deal with that later.

As soon as he sat down, Chad took his hand, threading their fingers. "So, I've never spent much time with a guy who came from a conservative family or who used to be straight."

Hollywood's stomach rolled. Chad still hadn't answered his question.

"Have I... Did I offend you somehow?"

"No." Chad smiled that damn crooked smile. "It was me. I assumed some things, and that wasn't fair to you."

Hollywood massaged the back of his neck. "I'm not really following." As far as he was concerned, things had been great—better than great—right up until the moment when Chad had walked out the door.

"I know." Chad put his other hand on top of Hollywood's. "I assumed things would work the way they have in my past relationships with respect to household duties and gender roles in general."

Gender roles? All of a sudden, it hit him, and he pinched the bridge of his nose. "Fuck. I've been acting like my dad, haven't I?"

Chad snorted. "I don't know your dad that well, but if you mean acting like the lord of the manor, then yeah."

Embarrassed, his face burning, Hollywood fell back onto the bed and closed his eyes. "I let you do those things because I thought you wanted to do them."

"I did." Chad eased himself down onto his back and turned his head. Their gazes met in a clash of heat.

"Just not all the time," Hollywood finished for him.

"Yeah."

"Think you can forgive me for being a horse's ass?"

"Only if you can forgive me for not speaking up sooner."

Hollywood pulled a stern face. "Communication is the keystone to any relationship."

"No more assumptions," Chad said.

"No more taking my sexy boyfriend for granted."

"Boyfriend?" Chad asked, his voice that sensual low drawl that always wrapped around Hollywood's dick like a warm, wet mouth.

"Yes," he breathed.

Chad used his shoulders to inch closer until their lips touched. "Forgive me?"

"Yes." The hot breath on his lips made Hollywood shiver. "You forgive me?"

"Damn right."

"And you'll be my date for the New Year's Eve party?" Hollywood asked again.

Chad brushed his lips. "Are you sure?"

"I'm sure. I want this. I want you."

Rolling on top of Hollywood's chest, Chad stretched out, and since their legs hung over the side of the bed, their cocks were pressed firmly together. Hollywood moaned and gripped Chad's ass cheeks as he pumped his hips. "Please say yes. Say you'll come with me."

A grin spread across Chad's face, and Hollywood's heart filled with joy. Chad's white teeth sparkled against his kissable—and very fuckable—lips. "Yes. I'll be there. With bells on."

Hollywood's jaw dropped at the illicit image forming in his mind. "Uh..."

ဆ 🎥 ଔ

Chad followed the progress of the shadows on the ceiling of Hollywood's bedroom while he gently played with his lover's chest hair and listened to the sound of his soft, even breaths as he slept. Everything was perfect, everything except the rock of guilt sitting in his gut.

They'd spent a few hours in bed together, and the sex had been fantastic as usual. They'd talked, they'd managed to iron out the issues that had been bugging Chad, and Hollywood had even invited him to the New Year's Eve Ball. So, why was he still so antsy? Why did he still feel like he owed Hollywood?

Because you treated him like shit.

Yeah, that. And he still hadn't really apologized.

Given his present state of mind, sleep was a long way off. He gingerly extracted himself from the tangle of Hollywood's limbs and slipped out of bed. He tiptoed from the room and entered the kitchen to make himself a cup of herbal tea from the box Hollywood kept for him. So sweet of him to do.

Sighing, he gripped the hot cup in his hands and sat on the living room couch, facing the pathetic little tree Hollywood had selected. It was almost as if he'd brought it home because he knew no one else would. He hadn't wanted the sad little tree to be alone in the tree lot at Christmas.

Alone, like Hollywood had been after Chad had walked out on their plans.

Jesus.

Hollywood hadn't even tried to make Chad feel guilty about leaving that night, which only made it worse. And tonight? Not one word. Not one mention. Not one only-a-dick-leaves-their-boyfriend-alone-on-Christmas-Eve.

Was that Hollywood's plan? To never talk about it and let the remorse gnaw at Chad for the rest of his life?

Austin was right; Chad had to stop getting all up in his head. If he wanted to talk about it, he had to broach the subject. It wasn't fair to leave that ball in Hollywood's court.

His gaze sank from the little tree to the package below it. It was a flat box artlessly wrapped in Rudolf paper and had a big red bow in the middle. Chad smiled, picturing Hollywood's big fingers attempting to gracefully manipulate the stiff paper. He didn't imagine the guy had had too many opportunities to practice in his life.

But Hollywood had made the effort this year for someone.

A deep sadness made his chest ache. He thunked his head back, wishing the couch weren't so soft, wishing it would hurt a bit. Chad had had the opportunity to make this Christmas season different for Hollywood, to make it special—their first Christmas Eve as a couple. Instead, he'd gotten his panties in a wad and had stormed off like some prima donna on the opening night of *La Bohème*. All he'd had to do was smile, eat supper with the guy, and watch a fucking movie. Had that been too much to ask?

Not for someone you claimed to care for.

Not for someone who was supposed to be your boyfriend.

Not for someone you hoped to have a future with.

Resigned to digging the knife in even further, Chad crawled across the carpet to peek at the name on the box.

"Open it," a deep voice said from behind him. "It's yours."

Chad sat on his ass and swung around to stare at Hollywood. "I didn't hear you coming."

Hollywood smirked. "Guess not." He walked farther into the room and picked up the box. Flipping it over, he grimaced. "Sorry for the quality of the wrapping."

"Nate." Chad's voice was little more than a whisper. The vise around his heart was squeezing so hard he could barely breathe.

Frowning, Hollywood knelt in front of him and set the box on the floor. "What's wrong, babe?"

A sob hiccupped through him, escaping despite his best efforts. The frown on Hollywood's face turned into full-blown concern. "Hey," he said, pulling Chad into a hug. "Did something happen? Are you hurt?"

And as if Chad weren't embarrassed enough, Hollywood's alarm turned him into a blubbering mess. Tears burst forth and words spewed out. "How... how can you even talk to me? How could you let me touch you, and kiss you, and fuck you?"

Hollywood's eyes widened and his hold got tighter. "Let you? I wanted everything that happened tonight." He pulled Chad onto his lap and Chad melted against the big warm body, his tears wetting Hollywood's shoulder.

When Chad finally calmed down, Hollywood put the gift on his lap. "Open it, please."

Chad sniffed and dried his cheeks. How could he say no? He carefully peeled off the tape, removing the paper without ripping it. Hollywood snorted and Chad gave him a shaky smile. "This way you can reuse it."

"Sure, whatever you say."

Chad stared at the box. It was rectangular and made of plain brown cardboard. Totally devoid of any store markings. "What is it?"

"You'll have to take the cover off to find out."

"Smartass."

Having finally regained some emotional balance, Chad opened the box. Inside, enveloped in pristine white tissue paper, was a drawing of himself. He was sprawled on his own bed, naked except for a sheet tugged dangerously low on his hips. The precision of the pencil strokes, the accuracy, the detail—it was incredible. "You drew this?"

Not meeting his eyes, Hollywood pointed at the bottom-right corner where he'd signed it with a simple "Nate."

"It's beautiful." He tipped Hollywood's chin up. "When you told me you liked to draw, I thought you might be good. I never expected you to be so amazing."

"The subject helped."

Chad scoffed. "Hardly. I can't believe how talented you are. Have you ever tried to sell your work? I bet you could make a bundle."

Hollywood shrugged. "I do all right."

"Wow." Chad's eyes bugged. "Does Jamie know about this?"

Stroking Chad's cheek, Hollywood leaned in to kiss him. "Just you."

The blush and the smile that erupted on his face were beyond Chad's control. Carefully, he placed the drawing back inside the box and set it aside, then he pulled Hollywood into his arms and peppered kisses all over his face. "Thank you. Thank you. Thank you."

Hollywood laughed and kissed him back. "You're welcome. You're welcome. You're welcome."

And that was all it took to turn Chad's joy into guilt. "Oh God. I'm so sorry, Nate. So fucking sorry."

Hollywood took Chad's cheeks in his gentle hands. "Talk to me, Caldwell."

"I—I walked out on our Christmas Eve plans. I left you alone. And you'd arranged all of this... Shit, you *made* me a present. It probably took you hours to draw something so perfect. And I left you hanging because I got into a little snit. What kind of a boyfriend am I?"

A sweet smile curved Hollywood's mouth as he captured Chad's lips. The kiss was gentle, comforting. One of those kisses that made gray days seem like sunny ones. "You're exactly the kind of boyfriend I want. Just you, Chad. No one else."

"Oh God. I don't deserve you."

Hollywood sank backward, pulling Chad along with him until they were lying on Hollywood's thick new carpet. "Let's not deserve each other together, then. Okay?"

Chad looked over at the man who was coming to mean so much to him and smiled. "I love the sound of that."

CHAPTER 20

Chad raced through the lush lobby of the grandly appointed Fairmont Olympic Hotel where the New Year's Eve Charity Ball was being held, praying he wasn't late. After the trouble he'd gone through contacting all the Technical Rescue Team members and getting their support for Dani, he didn't want to miss a second of her arrival.

Hitching up the jacket of his tux and shooting the cuffs, he rounded the corner to the hallway where they'd all agreed to meet and blew out in relief. Everyone was here, and he hadn't missed anything. As he snaked his way through the crowd, he thanked the members of the Technical Rescue Team and their plus-ones for making it. He spotted Jamie and Erica, who was looking radiant and sporting a cute baby bump. At four months, there was no mistaking that she was pregnant. Next to her were Drew and Tori.

On Jamie's other side was Carlos Dawson, the lieutenant of Platoon C and Drew's boss. Platoon B hadn't been able to attend as they were on shift, but they'd sent along a card and a gift for Dani. Craning his neck, he looked for a tall, broad-shouldered blond. Hollywood had been supposed to pick him up so they could arrive together, but when the guy had been already ten minutes late, Chad had received a text that Hollywood had gotten "caught up" in something and would meet him at the party.

Tori broke away from her conversation and came to hug him. "You look nervous as hell. What's going on?"

"Don't I deserve even a little compliment?" He rubbed a hand over his black silk-lined jacket and pink embroidered waistcoat. "I think I wear this tux damn well."

Giggling, she swatted his arm. "You jerk. You know you look stunning as always. You're the most handsome man here." Chad's gut tightened. He hoped Hollywood would think so too when he finally got here.

Tonight was such a big night for Hollywood. For both of them. Things *had* to go well.

Putting on a more optimistic face, he tugged Tori in to kiss her cheek. "And you, dear sister, are the most beautiful woman here, hands down."

"What about Erica?" she teased. "The mother to be?"

"Our lovely sister-in-law is, of course, in a class of her own."

Tori smiled. "Chad Caldwell, you're too much."

He shot her a naughty grin. "So I've been told."

"You are so bad." Her laughter rang out over the din of conversation and, when he opened his mouth to respond, she smacked her hand over his lips. "Don't you dare."

After a few moments of holding his gaze with a mock glare, she relented. "So tell me why you're acting like a long-tailed cat in a room full of rocking chairs."

"Have you been hanging around Austin?"

Her brows knitted together. "Chad."

"I'm just wondering where Hollywood is. He should be here by now."

"Maybe he's stuck in traffic or can't find parking."

Something told Chad that neither was the reason for the man's tardiness, but he didn't want Tori worrying too. "Yeah." He shrugged. "You're probably right."

Hollywood was scared. Hell, Chad was scared too. They'd talked about tonight several times during the past week and, each time, Chad had tried to convince Hollywood to at least tell Jamie about them before the ball. It would've taken some of the pressure off. But no. He'd insisted on the big bang approach. Chad only hoped they had more supporters than opponents. Shit, if Hollywood didn't get here soon, he was going to lose his mind.

Obviously sensing his mood, Tori slid her arm through his and rested her head on his shoulder. In a low voice she asked, "Are you and Hollywood attending the party together?"

God, *were* they? What if Hollywood backed out? He kissed Tori's head. "That's the plan." But whether he officially came out or not, it would be Hollywood's choice.

"I'm so happy for you," she said, and squeezed him. Suddenly, she straightened and smirked. "Look who just arrived."

Chad's head whipped around in time to see Hollywood skidding into the hallway through a side door. Warmth, like a full-body hug, draped around him at the sight of Hollywood. His formfitting black tux and crisp white shirt set off the intense green of his eyes. His shoulders looked even wider and his legs longer than usual. But his hands were clenched, his jaw tight. Remembering his own coming out, Chad knew how wound up the guy had to be. Until he learned whether the coming-out plan was still on, he couldn't very well walk up to Hollywood and give him the hug he so clearly needed, but he could stand by him and offer him the moral support he deserved.

As Chad took a step in Hollywood's direction, William and Dani arrived. Cheers and applause rose from the gathered crowd. Stunned, Dani's forward progress halted. She gripped William's arm, and tears welled in her eyes. Beside her, William grinned proudly.

Once the crowd quieted a little, Jamie, Hollywood, and Carlos went to greet the new arrivals. As her former lieutenant, Jamie took the lead. "Dani, we wanted to formally welcome you back to the team and to let you know that even though you're temporarily in training right now, you're still one of us, and we've got your back."

Cheers of "Here! Here!" rang loudly.

Hollywood smiled. "K9, I'd be happy to have you and Coco on my team, any time. Captain Starling is working with HR to make it happen. As soon as you're recertified—"

"Soon. I'll be getting the all clear soon."

"—you'll be back on a platoon. Hopefully mine."

She grabbed his hand. "Thank you, Lieutenant."

"My pleasure, Firefighter Harris."

"Hold on, now," Carlos said, coming to stand next to Hollywood. "I've put in a request as well. You're one fine firefighter, Dani, and Platoon C wants you too. Right guys?" he asked, grinning at his team members.

A playful argument started up between the two platoons, and Dani's cheeks pinked adorably. Chad couldn't help grinning at his brother and his fiancée. William had found his perfect match, and Chad felt it deep in his bones that they'd be happy together. William stroked a possessive hand down the open back of Dani's dress, and smiling, she leaned into it. "See, sweetheart. They're fighting over you." His amused expression turned into a playful frown. "Should I be concerned?"

"Ha!" she snorted. "It's Coco they want. I'm just a bonus." Everyone laughed. "Seriously though," she continued. "I've never had much of a family, but you guys, the whole Technical Rescue Team, have been a family to me since I started at 44. You're my brothers and sisters, and I've missed you all so much. Coco and I can't wait to be back."

Everyone smiled and there was more than one pair of teary eyes, including Chad's own. He wasn't part of the elite Technical Rescue Team, but through Jamie and Drew, he'd come to know most of them pretty well. They were an amazing group of men and women. Loyal and dedicated.

"So, when's the big day?" Sawyer, a driver in Hollywood's platoon, called out.

Everyone went silent and the woman next to him smacked him in the back of the head. "Weren't you listening? She doesn't know yet, idiot."

"I meant the wedding!" he cried, clearly affronted at being mistaken for an idiot.

With wide smiles on their faces, Dani and William looked at each other. He nodded, and she snaked her arm around his waist. "We're thinking February or March, depending on when I can get time off."

"Oh!" Erica ran up to Dani and hugged her. "I'm so happy for you." She lifted her head to include William. "For both of you."

Jamie hugged William and kissed Dani's cheek before sliding his arm around Erica's expanding waist. When she turned, the necklace with the locked heart at her neck twinkled in the light of the chandelier above them. It was a subtle reminder of the path they'd embarked on and what they meant to each other. Chad was honored that Jamie and Erica had trusted him enough to share that part of themselves with him. He hoped they accepted his and Hollywood's news in the same spirit.

When Chad finally made his way to William and Dani, he wrapped his arms around his brother, who responded with a bear hug of his own. "I'm so happy for you, bro."

William squeezed him again before taking a step back, leaving one big paw on Chad's neck. "I can't thank you enough for tonight. The support of the team is exactly what Dani needs to get through this transition."

"Hey, she's family." William's hand tightened once more, conveying the emotions his words couldn't. Chad smiled. "So, what decided the date?"

Over Chad's shoulder, William eyes tracked his fiancée. "The police informed us a few days ago that they expect to have the case wrapped up by the end of January and that they'd issue an official press release to clear my name of the charges of embezzlement. We're giving them a couple months leeway. In case."

No kidding. Last August, the Seattle PD had promised to wrap up their sting operation in two months, and four months later, still no arrests had been made. His brother had been living with a pall of scandal and false accusations over him, but by some miracle, he'd managed to keep his head up and keep things running smoothly at Caldwell Fine Furnishings.

Chad hardened his features. "Point me in the right direction, and I'll light a fire under their asses."

William chuckled and small hands snaked around Chad's waist from behind, hugging him close. The sparkling ring on Dani's finger gave her away. "Thank you so much for this, Chad."

"For what?" he asked, playing innocent.

"A little bird told me that not only did you suggest this, but you did most of the heavy lifting to organize it."

"Little bird?"

She slid around him to lean against William. "Okay, he's not exactly little, and he's not a bird at all. Still." A grin spread from ear to ear, lighting up her face.

"God, it's so good to see you happy again." Dani would be a wonderful addition to the Caldwell family.

She threaded her fingers with William's, who looked on adoringly. "Our lives are finally back on track. What about you? We've hardly seen you lately."

Chad fidgeted and kicked the carpet with the toe of his shoe. She had a way of seeing the secrets in a person's eyes.

William snickered.

Dani gasped and elbowed Chad in the ribs. "Oh my God. You have a new man. Who is it?"

Chad tried really hard not to glance toward Hollywood who stood chatting with Jamie, Erica, and Drew several feet away. Jamie was staring at something, a frown between his eyes. Chad followed his gaze to see Tori laughing with Gabe and some of the other guys from Jamie's platoon.

The intense look on his brother's face made Chad's stomach knot. How would Jamie react to the news that Chad and Hollywood were dating? Hollywood was playing brave, but he'd be devastated if Jamie ended their friendship. Jamie could be a hard ass, but he also loved his family and wanted them to be happy. If Hollywood made Chad happy— and he did—then Jamie would want them to be together. Right?

"Hey!" Dani elbowed him again. "Is he here?"

He shrugged, not committing either way. "Maybe."

"You suck."

Chad gave her his best naughty smirk. "Why yes I do. And very well... or so I've been told."

Dani bellowed with laughter while William winced. "TMI, brother."

"Really?" Dani asked, clearly amused. "That's nothing compared to the stuff you say in bed."

William's face turned bright red. His brother, based on the tabloid photos Chad had seen, could be quite sexually adventurous. That he'd blush at the mention of dirty talk was hilarious. As Chad was thinking up some clever way to tease his big brother, he spotted Hollywood slipping out a side exit.

"I've got to take care of something. See you two inside?"

Dani's eyes twinkled. "Something, huh? Don't you mean someone?"

"Rein it in, Miss Buttinsky," he threw over his shoulder before dashing off after the elusive blond, the knot in his stomach burning like a budding ulcer.

છે 🎥 ⚮

Hollywood barreled through the exit door into the small, dark courtyard on the side of the hotel. His hands shook as they clawed at the tie that was slowly but surely strangling him. For some reason, he hadn't expected so many people to show up tonight. Ridiculous really when he'd been attending the charity ball for years. Everyone loved the chance to get dressed up and have fun together and bond in a nonwork setting.

He tugged at his collar again, sucking in great lungfuls of air. The day had started off so well: he and Chad had enjoyed a lazy breakfast in bed followed by amazing sex and a nap, wrapped in each other's arms. Then Chad had gone home.

That's when Hollywood had started to unravel.

He'd put the bottle of Grey Goose on the coffee table and stared at it, craving a drink, but knowing he shouldn't. If he did this—coming out— drunk, it would be too easy for him to backtrack on it later. And it would be an insult to Chad.

Assuming the guy even wanted him after he'd begged off on picking him up. This was supposed to have been a proper date. Their first and most important. *Fuck.* He rested his head against the brick wall at his back.

The door banged open, startling him. Chad appeared, his mouth pulled into a strained half smile. Tension was etched into the deep lines around his lips. "What are you doing out here?"

"Getting a little air," Hollywood said, looking anywhere but at the gorgeous man beside him. "While I still can."

Two fingers touched Hollywood's chin and turned his head slightly until he was looking into Chad's blue eyes, so full of hurt. "Weren't you even going to say hello?"

Hollywood closed his eyes, unable to stand the pain his insecurities were causing Chad. "I was afraid that if I got too close, I'd want to kiss you. I know it's kind of the point of tonight, but I didn't want to take the spotlight off the happy couple."

It was mostly the truth.

Chad nodded. "I'm close now."

As surreptitiously as he could, Hollywood took a quick look around to make certain they were alone, before taking Chad's mouth in a slow, intimate kiss. Chad had the best mouth: pink, strong, and perfect. The taste of minty toothpaste exploded on his tongue, and he moaned, pulling Chad against him, aligning their chests and groins. God, it felt so good. So fucking right.

When they came up for air, Chad rested his head on Hollywood's shoulder, each exhale a warm breeze on Hollywood's neck. The sexiest chills raced up his spine.

"I thought you were going to stand me up," Chad whispered, full of uncertainty.

I almost did. The words formed in his mind. Refusing to let them out, he shook his head. "Nah. Just lost track of time. I still intend to do this."

"Okay." Chad raised his head. "I want you to know that whatever happens here tonight, I'm on your side. We'll get through this."

Hollywood stroked Chad's clean-shaven jaw and filled his nose with the enticing, reassuring scent of Chad's cologne. "That means a lot."

"Just think"—Chad's eyes shone in the lights sprinkled around the courtyard—"after tonight, we won't have to hide anymore. We'll be able to hold hands—"

"Or kiss," Hollywood added.

Chad smiled, that sweet, lopsided curve of his lips that was both naughty and innocent. "Or kiss, anywhere."

"Within reason."

Chad ignored him. "You'll come to Sunday dinners at my parents' as my partner instead of as Jamie's friend."

"I'm not sure if he'll still think of me that way after tonight."

"It's going to be all right."

Hollywood frowned. He was under no illusions about how things could go. There were bound to be some looks, whispered comments, and a few people who'd be genuinely upset. Like his father. And Jamie.

"Okay," Chad conceded. "At first Jamie might go all overprotective brother, or he might be pissed that you didn't tell him about us sooner. But he already knows you're attracted to men, and he's okay with it."

That was true. Since that night at the pub when he'd come out to Jamie, nothing had changed between them. They still joked around and teased each other, and Hollywood was so damn grateful for that. Jamie and Chad were the two most important people in his life, and he didn't want to lose either one. Despite that, he had to own up to the fact that if it came to choosing between Hollywood and Chad, Jamie would always choose his brother. As he should.

"My being his friend is one thing, my being his baby brother's boyfriend is something else entirely. If you were my brother, I wouldn't want you near me."

Chad's brows rose. "I should hope not."

When the guy's shoulders started to bounce with laughter, Hollywood had to wonder if he'd lost his mind. Then he realized what he'd said. "Fuck. I'm so rattled, I can't even speak coherently."

Lips pursed, Chad leaned in and sniffed him.

Hollywood snarled. "I haven't had anything to drink, if that's what you're trying to figure out. I sure as fuck could use one right about now though."

Chad cocked his head. "Me too. But it's not a good idea."

Hollywood sighed dramatically, hoping to ease the tension that had sprung up between them. He had to calm the fuck down before he said or did something stupid. He really wanted to do this. Needed to do this for Chad. Needed to do this if he wanted them to be together. And he did want that. More than anything.

Taking Chad's hand, he kissed it. "Stay with me?"

"I wouldn't be anywhere else."

Steeling his spine, Hollywood led Chad to the door. He could do this. With a little courage, and Chad by his side, he could face anything. But as they reentered the building, he used holding the door open as an excuse to drop Chad's hand.

Christ. He was acting like a fucking coward. Since he couldn't very well make a speech, he'd planned to "come out" in a more subtle way, by entering the ballroom with Chad's hand firmly tucked in his.

Outside the ballroom, a few yards to the right of the door, he stopped and took several deep breaths to slow his racing heart. Moisture beaded on his forehead and dripped down his jaw. He tugged at his collar again Why was it always so hot in these places? A trickle of sweat ran down his back to pool in the waistband of his boxers, plastering his new tailored shirt to his back.

Come on, Wright. Get it over with. Pull the Band-Aid off.

Chad patted his shoulder in silent support. Hollywood wiped his moist palms on his slacks, and held his hand out. Shit. He was shaking. Thankfully, Chad didn't comment on the show of weakness. Instead, he entwined their fingers, and smiled encouragingly, but his blue eyes were filled with concern. When he started to say something, Hollywood shook his head. If Chad even cracked open the door to let him off the hook, he'd take it. He knew he would.

"Let's do this." He pulled open the ballroom door and came face-to-face with his father.

Gasping, he stopped short, and Chad ran into his back.

Hollywood froze, every muscle paralyzed, as he followed his father's scornful glare down to his and Chad's joined hands. His father's red face twisted into an ugly sneer. "What the fuck is going on here? Don't you think you've already embarrassed me enough?"

All the blood drained from Hollywood's head, and he felt sick to his stomach. The people around them started to notice the commotion. Several stepped closer. His vision began to blur at the edges and he stumbled. He'd have fallen if Chad hadn't already been holding his hand.

His father's derision stabbed into him. The words he'd thrown at Hollywood that night at his house pinballed inside his brain. He pressed a palm against his temple. The humiliation of having all these people—his friends, his colleagues, Chad—witness his father's bigotry and hatred was too much.

It was all too much.

Hollywood gripped Chad's shoulders and stared into the face that had brought him so much joy and acceptance. His eyes filled. "I'm sorry, Chad. So fucking sorry."

Chad rubbed his hands up and down Hollywood's sides. "It's okay, Nate." He shot a venomous scowl in his father's direction. "He means nothing."

Hollywood wasn't half the man Chad was. He wasn't half the man Chad deserved. His father was right. Hollywood was a coward. Always had been, always would be. "I can't do this." The words tore from his chest. Letting go of Chad, he took a step back.

Chad mirrored his step and grabbed his arms. "You don't have to say anything. Everyone thinks we're just friends."

Hollywood shook his head. That right there was the problem. They weren't *just* friends, and it was wrong to force Chad to live in the shadows. Wrong to make him live like he was ashamed when he'd always been so proud. Hollywood would rather die than take that away from the man. He took another step back. "I—I can't."

"Can't what? Talk to me, Nate." Confusion radiated from Chad, but beneath the worry and concern, Hollywood saw defeat. Chad was smart, and he'd already seen the truth. But Hollywood would give him the words he needed. The words Hollywood wished with all his heart weren't true.

His father laughed, his eyes mean and hard like they'd been that day when he'd caught Hollywood with Bobby. "Christ, what a disgrace. You're standing there shaking and stuttering like a fucking nancy. Oh," he sneered. "That's right. You *are* a fucking cock-sucking nancy."

Stomach churning, heart shattering, Hollywood blocked out the sound of his father's insults, the sight of people closing in on them, and focused on Chad's stormy blue eyes. He had to let Chad go.

"I can't do this. Us. You. I can't be gay."

CHAPTER 21

Ice slid down Chad's spine and circled his heart as Hollywood's words hit home. He took Hollywood's face in his hands and forced him to meet his gaze. When he had his full attention, he said softly, "It's not a choice, Nate. It's who you are."

Deputy Chief Wright, who was smaller than Hollywood but still bigger than Chad, violently shoved him against the wall. "Take your fucking hands off my son and stop filling his head with your deviant bullshit. Haven't you done enough damage already?"

Like a tank on a mission, Chad advanced on the chief, his mind blazing with millions of truths he wanted to throw in the man's face, but he made himself concentrate on this latest accusation. "*My* damage? I'm helping him undo years of abuse heaped on him because of your small-minded bigotry."

"Abuse? I made a man out of him. I kept him from becoming a depraved sexual deviant like you." He sneered and his gaze slid to Hollywood. "Or is it too late? Tell me, Nathan, have you taken his cock up your ass yet?"

Chad's vision went red. "Fuck you." Without even a thought, he swung his fist, aiming to shut the chief's mouth, to end the hateful spew that would push Hollywood further into the closet. His hand was forcibly halted mid-punch.

"Stop." Jamie held him immobile, his commanding voice freezing everyone. "Someone better tell me what the hell is going on. Now."

Chad lowered his arm, and tore his eyes from Deputy Chief Wright to see how Hollywood was handling what his father had said, only to find him gone. *Shit.* The guy shouldn't be alone after having his coming out turned into a miserable nightmare.

Jamie wanted answers, but it wasn't Chad's place to tell anyone about his and Hollywood's relationship.

I can't do this. Us. You. I can't be gay.

He couldn't tell Jamie, especially now that their relationship was apparently over. Chad rubbed at the soreness in his chest. How would he survive losing the man he'd come to love? Jesus Christ. What a clusterfuck.

Shoving his hands in his pockets, he gave Jamie the Cliffs Notes on the evening's altercation. "Chief Wright was making crude, discriminatory comments about Lieutenant Wright."

"And that's why you tried to hit him?"

"Had to shut him up somehow," Chad muttered under his breath.

Jamie coolly eyed the drink in the chief's shaking hand and Chad realized the chief was already drunk. Was he seeing Hollywood's future? He hoped not, although it was likely if he kept denying himself.

"Sir," Jamie said, all but choking on the word. "I strongly suggest you go home before you say anything else."

"Why? It's the truth." Spittle sprayed out of his mouth. "Guys like your brother and women who think they're better than men are destroying the fire service." Deputy Chief Wright turned to Chad and shook his fist in his face. "I'm going to bring you up on charges. Invoke the morality clause, like I did with that arrogant slut. I'll see your faggot ass fired if it's the last thing I do."

Chad shouldered his way around Jamie. "Oh yeah? On what grounds? My sexual orientation is protected by law."

Deputy Chief Wright scoffed. "Hitting an officer."

Jamie crossed his arms. "I didn't see any punch." He swung around to take in the growing crowd of onlookers, most of them from the TRT. "Any of you see a punch?"

"No, LJ."

"Not me, LJ."

One after the other, everyone denied having seen anything. The chief sputtered and his face grew alarmingly red. Jamie took him by the shoulder and led him to the row of waiting taxis at the front of the hotel. Chad followed at a safe distance. Jamie took the drink from the chief's hand and passed it to the valet. "Good night, sir."

"I'm not done here," the chief insisted.

"For tonight, you are. Go home. Sleep it off."

Deputy Chief Wright glowered at him, then got into the taxi. Watching it drive away, Chad's relief was a live thing, starting in his chest and radiating out to his head and feet, until he could finally breathe again.

Jamie walked back to him, his expression tight, but neutral. "Want to tell me what that was about?"

His brother already knew about Hollywood not being straight, so Chad would stick with that. "The chief wasn't happy that Hollywood intended to come out tonight."

Jamie's brows rose. "To everyone?"

"Yeah."

"Brave move." He rubbed his chin. "How was he going to do it?"

Chad adjusted the jacket of his tux. Jamie's intense gaze pinned him in place. "Something you want to tell me, little brother?"

"N-no," Chad stammered. He tried to avert his eyes, but it was as though Jamie had control of his body. *Holy crap.* If this was Jamie's Dom look, no wonder Erica was so happy. Not that Chad was a sub or that Jamie did it for him—fuck! Even in his head he was rambling. All he meant was that with a stare like that, Jamie could get anyone to do anything. Even admit their deepest held secrets.

"Chad," Jamie growled.

"He was going to enter the ballroom with me. Holding my hand."

"Why you?"

God. Why did Jamie have to be so insistent? He rolled his eyes. "Because I'm his boyfriend."

"What?" Jamie took a small step back as though reeling from the news. As soon as he recovered, he invaded Chad's personal space. "You're dating? This is for real?"

"For real? What the fuck?"

Jamie scowled. "Calm down. I mean were you going to pretend to be together to help him come out or are you really together?"

Maybe it was the adrenaline rush from the fight with Hollywood's father, or maybe it was the disappointment that Jamie was reacting exactly as Hollywood had feared, whatever the reason, his emotions boiled over. "Do you need details, Jamie? Do you want to hear about how Hollywood's cum tastes when he's jetting down my throat or how all that muscle feels against my back when his cock is pounding me into the mattress? Is that clear enough for you? Or maybe you want to know about the star-shaped mole on his left nut?" Out of breath, Chad stood facing Jamie, his fists clenched at his sides.

"You done?" Jamie's tone was low, cold, and Chad was suddenly scared shitless. "Jesus Christ. What a fucking mess." Jamie scrubbed at his scalp. "Why didn't you guys come to me with this? I could have helped smooth the way. At least I could have recruited some of the team to keep Chief Fucktard away."

"You'd have helped us?" Chad's eyes widened before he could control his reaction.

Jamie spun away, hands on his hips, his chest pumping as he breathed deeply. When he turned back, his eyes were sad, hurt. "I must be a pretty shitty brother if you ever thought I'd turn on you."

Chad rushed to clasp Jamie's neck. "No. No. That's not it at all."

"Then why?" Jamie rested his forehead against Chad's. "I can't believe my little brother and my best friend—shit."

"We didn't want to keep it from you. We just didn't think you'd..." Chad trailed off. Damn, no matter what he said, Jamie would be upset.

"Didn't think I'd what?" Jamie all but growled.

"Didn't think you'd approve."

Jamie wrenched out of Chad's hold and went to stand a few feet away. Chad took in his brother's wide back, the shoulders that had carried him at parades and when he'd been too tired to walk. Jamie had always been there for him with a smile, a hug, a joke, or a fist. Whatever Chad had needed.

Placing a hand on Jamie's shoulder, he said, "I'm sorry. I shouldn't have underestimated you."

Jamie snorted. "No. You were right. I don't approve."

Chad dropped his hand and mentally prepared for what he expected to be a long list of Jamie's reasons.

Jamie shrugged. "But you're both adults, grown men, and it isn't up to me to decide what's right for you."

"Wow." Chad's surprise was complete. "Tori will be thrilled to hear that."

Jamie put up a hand. "She's another story."

Deciding that was an argument for another day, Chad smiled and pulled Jamie into a hug. "Thank you, Jamie. Your support means the world to me. To both of us."

"If he hurts you, I'm going to fucking kick his ass."

Chad released Jamie as reality flooded back. His smile fell. "I don't think that'll be a problem. He... Well, back there?" He indicated the ballroom with his thumb. "He dumped me."

Jamie's brows popped.

"Yeah. He said he couldn't do us. He couldn't be gay."

"Idiot."

Tears burned at the back of Chad's eyes. He cleared his throat and forced a smile. "Yeah."

Jamie dragged him against his chest, his hands stroking his back. "I'm sorry, kid. He's probably just scared."

"I shouldn't have pushed him to come out." Chad sniffed and rubbed his cheek against his brother's comforting shoulder. "I'm so fucking stupid."

"You might have encouraged it, but it was his decision. If anyone is responsible, it's his miserable excuse for a father." Jamie's tone was harder than Chad had ever heard it. He was definitely not an admirer of the chief's.

"Should I go after him?" Chad asked. "I'm kind of worried."

"My guess is that by the time you find him, he'll be in no condition to talk," Jamie said, proving how well he knew his friend.

"But what if—"

"Chad, he's a big boy. When he wants to see you, he'll let you know. Give him some space. If he was sincere about everything, he'll come back to you."

Chad huffed. "Patience is so not my virtue."

Jamie pulled him into a chokehold and rubbed the top of his head with his knuckles. Chad laughed and easily escaped. "Thanks, man. Really."

"That's what brothers are for." Jamie slung an arm around his shoulders. "Just don't ever keep something like this from me again. You hear?"

"Yeah, I hear." As soon as the words were in the air, Chad's gut clenched with guilt. What would his brother say if he found out that the harassment had started up again?

છ ₪ ભ

Hollywood rolled over in bed, let out a jaw breaking yawn, and nearly keeled over from the stench. Christ, what had curled up and died in his mouth? Cracking open an eye, he checked his alarm clock. Four PM. Shit. He'd slept all day. Reaching back, expecting to find Chad's hard muscles and silky skin, all he found were cold sheets.

With his hand on the wall for support, he hobbled down the hall toward the kitchen, hoping Chad was there. "Chad?" he called out, stopping short when he spotted the mess in the living room. Empty bottles of Grey Goose, beer, and William's Scotch lay strewn on the carpet. The cushions of the couch were torn and thrown around the room. What the hell had happened here? Chad was too much of a neat freak to leave things this way. The place looked and smelled like a bar, the morning after.

A beeping sound drew his attention. He could hear his phone, but he couldn't see it in all the chaos. Finally, after collecting a few bags of garbage, he located it under the recliner. The first message was from Chad, the second from Jamie.

And that's when it all came back.

The charity ball, holding Chad's hand, his father, Chad and his father arguing, Jamie intervening, people watching—

Oh God. His head spun and his stomach cramped. As best he could, he raced to the bathroom and emptied the alcohol that was left in his stomach. He remembered the rest now too, telling Chad they were over, and coming home and drinking himself into oblivion like the weak man he was. The weak man he'd always been—too chicken to stand up to his bastard of a father.

His phone beeped again, reminding him of the messages waiting in his inbox. He read Chad's first.

C: You okay, man? Call me, please.

He closed his eyes to block out the memory of Chad's sweet face, the lips turned down in confusion and disappointment when he'd told Chad they were over. Tears burned, then spilled over onto Hollywood's cheeks.

He loved Chad.

He knew it now. But, he'd tried to come out, and his dad had won.

Bitter laughter erupted from his mouth. Here he was, thirty-six years old, and he couldn't do what young teenagers did every day. Talk about being a fucking loser. *Pathetic, that's what you are.*

And he was going to end up like his father too—a sad and lonely drunk. He picked up a bottle of beer next to the recliner and threw it at the wall. It splintered, spraying shards of glass throughout the room. One landed on the coffee table in front of him. He stared at it.

For far too long.

He could end it all today. End all these years of misery, and prevent the forty or so that were sure to follow. Picking up his phone, he thumbed to the photo gallery and a picture he'd taken of Chad when they'd gone for a walk around Alki Lighthouse. He traced the bold line of Chad's black eyebrows, his hard square jaw, those firm, soft lips. That fantastic smile that always made him forget everything, except how happy Chad made him. He swiped the screen and a selfie of him and Chad together came into view. They were hugging, cheek to cheek. Big grins on both their faces because Chad had just told him some sexy, dirty thing he was going to do to Hollywood when they got home.

Damn, his chest hurt so badly, aching with an emptiness no one else could ever fill. Chad was his "one." His only one. And he'd lost Chad because Hollywood was only half a man. A sob shook his shoulders and he buried his face in his hands.

A loud banging at the door scared the shit out of him. Adrenaline kicked in, a dangerous mix with his still high blood-alcohol level. His pulse raced out of control.

"Hollywood! Open the fucking door, or I'll break it down."

Jamie. Fuck. He couldn't deal with him now, not when he was so messed up he couldn't even think straight. Maybe if he stayed real quiet Jamie would think he wasn't—

"I know you're in there, fuckhead. I saw you through the sliding door."

Hollywood shook his head and groaned when the room started to spin. Not relishing the damage Jamie could inflict on his front door, Hollywood pushed to his feet and went to let in his friend... assuming they still were, after last night's fiasco. Not looking forward to a lecture or worse a shouting match, he opened the door, and without a word turned around and headed back into the living room.

Jamie cautiously entered the living room, his expression stunned as he took in the torn cushions, the broken glass, and the stained carpet. It was concern, not anger, that filled his blue gaze, so like Chad's. "Hey, buddy. You look like death warmed over," Jamie said, sitting on the coffee table in front of him.

Hollywood chuckled unhappily. "Feel like it too." Jamie's hands fisted on his knees and Hollywood tensed.

Here it comes.

If the man wanted to hit him, beat him up, he'd take it. He deserved it after all. "So, Chad and I talked last night, after you... left," Jamie began.

"Yeah?"

"He told me you two are together."

Hollywood's gut clenched and his temples throbbed a little more. "*Were* together. That's done now."

"What do you mean?"

"Everything. It's over." Hollywood hugged a throw pillow against his chest, the ache growing worse every minute. He plastered on an arrogant grin he absolutely didn't feel. "We will now return to our regularly scheduled program."

Jamie cursed, then peered at him, a furrow between his brows. "Are you still fucking drunk?"

"No." At least he didn't think so. In fact, he was seeing things very clearly. The only way his life worked was if he went back to women. He wasn't cut out to be gay or bi or what-the-fuck-ever.

"That's it?" Jamie shoved to his feet. Towering over Hollywood as he was, Jamie made Hollywood feel smaller, more insignificant, than he ever had before. Like a bug squashed under a shoe. When Hollywood said nothing, Jamie continued. "So my baby brother was just what? Some fucking experiment? And now you've decided you like pussy better?"

The more questions he threw at Hollywood, the lower Jamie's voice got and the more menacing it became. White framed his rigid mouth, and he vibrated with indignation.

"No. I—I..." He what? What could he possibly say that would fix this?

Jamie snarled and started to pace in front of the TV, his big feet grinding shards of glass into the carpet. "I don't know whether to shake some sense into you for being such a clueless dumbass, or pound your face in for acting like a fucking bastard."

Hollywood could see it. Jamie was torn between being a good friend to Hollywood and being a good big brother to Chad. It was going to kill him, losing both his best friend and the only person he'd loved since Isabel, but whatever pain he suffered would be better than seeing Jamie hurting because he was stuck between Chad and Hollywood.

If push came to shove, Hollywood knew exactly who Jamie would choose. He just wanted to make it easier on Jamie, so he wouldn't feel guilty for supporting Chad. Hollywood wanted him to help his brother get past this.

Is that the real reason?

Shut up, he ordered his brain. Standing, he pasted a sly grin on his face and said the most damning words he could think of. "Chad's tight ass is something pretty special all right, and he was a good sport for letting me try it out. But you know me, I'm a ladies' man. Gotta have me some pussy, as much as I can, as often as I can. Although... Maybe in a couple of months, it could be fun to have another go at—"

Jamie's fist interrupted his spiel. *Thank fuck.* Hollywood went down on impact. "Christ, I can't believe I fucking defended you to Chad. Motherfucker." Jamie kicked him in the ribs, hard enough to hurt but not hard enough to do any real damage. The guy was obviously holding back the rage that was twisting his features.

"Don't you go anywhere near my brother, ever again. You got that, Wright? You so much as look in his direction, and I'll end you." He leaned over, his pointed finger going from Hollywood to himself. "And us? Our friendship—that's fucking sayonara too. If it's not about SFD business, stay the fuck away from me and the rest of my family."

With a last kick that sent the coffee table flying into the wall, Jamie stormed out of the apartment and the door clanged shut behind him.

In the devastating silence that followed, Hollywood reached for his phone, lit up the screen, and kissed the photo of him and Chad. Their time together was the happiest he'd ever been, the happiest he'd ever be. Now all he had left were memories.

CHAPTER 22

It had been a week since Hollywood had broken up with him, a week of unanswered text messages and phone calls, a week since his world had turned to shit. Chad would give everything he had to turn back the clock, to steer Hollywood away from the idea of coming out at the charity ball.

He should have counseled Hollywood to take his time, to be sure. To take it in smaller steps. Instead, too excited by the prospect of living openly with Hollywood as his boyfriend, he'd gotten caught up in the plan. It had been selfish and irresponsible, and now he had nothing.

Had he anticipated the ramifications, he'd have willingly chosen to live in that firmly locked closet with Hollywood, because at least then they'd still be together.

With a long finger, Liam poked him in the ribs. "Why so glum?"

Chad had already told Liam about what had happened at the ball and refused to be a Debbie Downer about it every shift. "It's Anna's birthday. You should be home with her."

"Nah. She's feeling tired, so she's having an early night. We'll celebrate tomorrow."

Chad studied his partner for any sign of worry and was relieved when he didn't spot any. Liam and Anna were so excited about this baby, their first. Chad prayed nothing went wrong. Unfortunately, being a paramedic, he knew all the things that could.

His phone rang, making Chad's gut clench. Lately all his phone calls had been either Jamie or Tori calling to check up on him, or they'd been hangups. The hangups were never from the same number, so he couldn't block them, and when he'd tried to do a reverse search on some of them, nothing had come up except a few pay phones. The number on his screen now was yet again one he didn't recognize.

"You gonna get that?" Liam asked.

Chad hit answer, said "Hello," and waited for the inevitable click. And there it was. Sighing, he put his phone back into his pocket.

"Hangup?" Liam asked. When Chad nodded, he added, "You seem to get a lot of those."

"Yeah. Must be something about my number."

"Didn't the same thing happen last summer before we were attacked?"

Chad caught the edge in his partner's voice. "Yes." He kept his answer short to keep from encouraging Liam's worry. But it didn't work.

"Have you told Deputy Chief Conroy or the cops?"

Chad scratched his head. "We've been over this before. The police aren't going to do anything about it."

"Chad, buddy, listen to me. Even though my brother got the guys who attacked you last year, that didn't end this mess. There's a pattern of harassment here that goes beyond mere phone calls. Your car was vandalized, and I'm sure there's a bunch of other things you haven't told me. You're being targeted, and it has to stop."

"No one cares about some fag getting hang-up calls or getting his tires slashed. Look, can we just drop it? I don't want to fight tonight."

"Okay, okay. But you have to let me know if anything else happens."

"I will." As soon as this asshole did something that he could bring to the cops, Chad would.

The radio crackled, and the dispatcher's voice filled the ambulance. "Medic 11. We have a leg injury at 4575 First Avenue South. Fourth floor."

Chad picked up the mic. "Medic 11, responding."

"Copy that, Medic 11."

Liam drove them into the Industrial District. A few minutes later, they stopped twenty yards away from a multistory structure that looked old and abandoned.

"Dispatch, please confirm the address," Chad said.

"4575 First Avenue South."

"Roger and out," Chad said, peering out the side window at the decrepit building. "Looks like this is the right one."

Liam inched the ambulance forward and up alongside the curb in front of the building. "Fucking creepy. Think we should ask for a police escort?"

Maybe he was being paranoid because of the phone calls, but Chad had serious chills. "Yeah." He clicked on the mic. "This is Medic 11 with a code blue. Do you copy?"

"Roger that. Requesting escort."

While they waited, Chad got out the paramedic bag, while Liam found a couple large flashlights in the back. Four minutes later, a patrol car pulled up. "You called for police backup?" asked the driver, a large black officer, whose presence instantly reassured Chad.

"Yeah. Thanks for getting here so fast," Liam said.

The cops climbed out of their vehicle and joined Chad and Liam on the sidewalk. The male cop, who had a good-sized belly, grunted, hitching up his pants. He studied Liam's nametag then his face. "You Karl Parker's brother?"

"Yeah."

"He's one lucky bastard, enjoying the sunshine out there in Hawaii while the rest of us are stuck here freezing our asses off," he grumbled, pulling up the collar of his jacket.

The female cop, an older woman who looked like she could kick some serious butt, rolled her eyes at her partner. "Is this an assault with weapons response?"

"All we got was a medic response, top floor. But the building is creepy as fuck," Chad said.

The male cop groaned. "It's always the top floor."

Laughing, Chad and Liam picked up their gear, then followed the two officers inside. They cleared each floor before allowing Chad and Liam up to the next. On the last floor, they heard faint cries from a room in the back of the building. The officers went in, their flashlights illuminating a young, beat-up white male in his early twenties, who lay sprawled on the dirty floor. The somewhat effeminate man wore tight, colorful clothing and makeup that had now streaked with his tears.

"Oh, thank God you're here," he cried. "Those bastards shot me!"

Chad exchanged a look with Liam and frowned. Normally dispatch warned them of a gunshot wound and police backup was automatically requested. Liam spoke into his radio, "Dispatch, this is Medic 11. We have an assault with weapons response at 4575 First Avenue South. One police unit is already on scene and it's been cleared. Do you copy?"

"Roger that, Medic 11. Relaying assault with weapons response." In no time, two teams of firefighters, a battalion chief, and Medic 34—Chad and Liam's lieutenant—would be on scene.

"What happened here, son?" the male officer asked the victim, his gaze continuously sweeping the room.

After depositing his kit on the ground, Chad started to examine the victim, whose eyes were red and pain-filled. A hole pierced the middle of his right thigh, and a considerable amount of blood pooled on the floor beneath him. Burn marks in the fabric indicated a point-blank shot. With any luck, the bullet had gone right through. Based on the man's state of awareness, it didn't seem to have hit any major arteries.

"I—I was meeting friends over at Boyzville to have one last night out before school starts again. But some guys grabbed me, brought me here,

219

and shot me in the fucking leg!" His voice rose to a shriek at the end.

"What's your name?" Chad asked in his most soothing voice as he carefully cut through the man's jeans.

"Sam. Sam Hoover."

Gently, he lifted the leg to check the back of his thigh for an exit wound. Spotting one, he sighed in relief. "Okay, Sam, other than your leg, does anything else hurt?"

"My nose. I think it's broken. And it hurts to breathe." He put a hand on his ribs.

The officers asked Sam a few cursory questions while Chad wrapped Sam's leg with an Israeli bandage to slow the bleeding, and Liam put him on a cardiac monitor and took his baseline vitals. If Sam's ribs were fractured, they could end up dealing with a pneumothorax in addition to the gunshot wound.

"We're going to call this in and meet up with you at the hospital to take your statement," the male officer said to Sam.

Sam sniffed, grimaced, then nodded. "Thank you, officers."

"I'll go down with them and get the stretcher," Liam said. "You going to be okay?"

"Yeah. Thanks," Chad said.

To keep the guy focused and talking until he could determine the full extent of his injuries, Chad asked Sam for more details. "Those guys say anything to you when they brought you here?"

Sam's shoulders stiffened. "Besides all the smack talk about me being gay? Yeah, they said I'd be great bait. I thought they were going to use me to get some poor closeted dude to come out—I've seen it done before— but then after they shot me, they seemed to lose interest and left."

Bait. Listening to the guy's story, Chad had to force his voice to remain calm and his hands to keep from shaking. Every creak in the old building had him jumping, every shadow cringing. Shit. Where was Liam? He wouldn't breathe easy until they were far away from this hellhole.

℘ 🎞 ℭ

Hollywood sat in the officer's seat of Ladder 27 while Drew drove them back to Station 44. Dawson had asked to switch shifts with Hollywood so he could attend some family function with his wife and kids. Given his lack of a social life, Hollywood had been more than happy to do it. Fortunately, neither Jamie nor Chad had informed their brother about last week's events so the shift had gone well so far.

The call they'd just finished had been ugly. A couple kids who'd had too much to drink had driven their car into a wall that had then fallen in on them. The platoon had worked for hours to get the drunk driver and his passenger out from under the rubble without further injury. Everyone was looking forward to some grub and a little shuteye.

A call came over the radio from dispatch. "Assault with weapons response at 4575 First Avenue South." Everyone groaned. They were only a block or two away. Hollywood picked up the radio. "Ladder 27 and Rescue 21 en route. ETA one minute."

"Roger that, Ladder 27."

As they passed Monroe Street, Hollywood spotted Medic 11 with the cop car next to it. Drew noticed it too. When Hollywood caught his eye, Drew simply said, "Chad's on tonight."

Even though his gut was screaming in protest—or maybe he'd developed an ulcer from all the drinking and not sleeping—he nodded his okay. They'd go make sure Chad and Liam didn't need assistance, then they'd get back on the road. These kind of responses were usually more of a just-in-case measure. Drew parked behind the ambulance and hopped out, leaving his turnout coat on the seat.

"We'll go in first and see what's going on. You guys gather the usual gear," Hollywood said to Manny and Leiderman, who were sitting in the seat behind him.

"Copy that, Lieutenant."

"Thanks, guys." He jumped down as Rescue 21 pulled up behind. He gave Emma and O'Reilly the same message.

Liam walked out of the building accompanied by two cops. Hollywood frowned. Had they left Chad alone? Hollywood walked over to Medic 11 and took the portable stretcher that Liam was pulling out of the unit. "I've got it."

Liam scowled, but after glancing at Drew, he relented and bit out a not very sincere "Thanks."

As soon as they entered the building, unease crawled up Hollywood's spine. "What's going on here?" he asked Liam, wanting reassurance that Chad was okay.

"GSW victim on top floor. Police escort cleared all the floors and asked the victim some initial questions. Seems like a possible case of gay bashing."

"Shit." The beam of his flashlight bobbing in front of him, Drew took the stairs a little faster, with Liam and Hollywood right behind him.

A minute later, they emerged on the top floor and made quick work of joining Chad in the backroom. Seeing Drew, Chad smiled, but his smile turned sharp when he noticed Hollywood with the stretcher. Tilting his head in acknowledgment, Hollywood set the stretcher down beside the victim. His heart rate slowed considerably now that he knew Chad wasn't in any danger.

"What are you guys doing here?" Chad asked Drew.

221

"We were a block away when the call came in," Drew let the words hang.

Chad smiled at his patient. "Sam, this is my brother, Drew."

Sam grinned, then winced. "I'd flirt, but I hurt too much."

"I think you'd have better luck with my brother," Drew joked, and Hollywood felt his hackles rise. Chad was *his*.

Or he would have been, if Hollywood hadn't acted like a damn coward.

"Already tried," Sam said. "He was gracious, but no go."

Drew raised his brows at Chad, who blushed in that way Hollywood really loved. It made the ache in his chest worse. Hollywood forced himself to stand next to Drew while Liam and Chad lifted their patient onto the stretcher.

A small sound, like a pop, came from another room. Hollywood stepped out to investigate. After extricating his flashlight from the belt at his waist, he shined it on the floor, the walls, even the ceiling as he walked down the narrow hallway. His nose twitched seconds before he saw smoke filtering through a vent in the ceiling.

Flicking the switch on the radio at his shoulder, he said, "Dispatch, this is Lieutenant Wright at 4575 First Avenue South. We have fire in building. Ladder 27 and Rescue 21 responding. Do you copy?"

"Roger that, Lieutenant. Engine 13 is on the way. ETA four minutes."

He switched channels and gave his team orders to check and vent the roof and for the others to bring the extinguishers up.

Returning to the backroom, he told the others what he'd found. "We have to evacuate. Now." The words were no sooner out of his mouth than there was a huge boom, and the ceiling exploded in a mass of fire and wood shards. Hollywood, who was wearing his fireproof bunker gear, dove to cover the person closest to him—the GSW victim. Sam's frightened, breathless screams filled Hollywood's ears, blocking everything out as the world fell down around them.

As soon as the echo of the explosion faded, another male's shouts of pain replaced Sam's. Christ almighty, Hollywood needed some help. Before even attempting to move off of the now unconscious gunshot victim, Hollywood radioed the dispatcher. "This is Lieutenant Wright, Ladder 27. Major explosion on top floor. Balancing this to a full response. Do you copy?"

"Roger that, Lieutenant. Additional units are on the way."

In the near total darkness, Hollywood was all but blind. And if he couldn't see anyone, he couldn't help them. After struggling out from under the sizzling piece of drywall on his back, Hollywood searched for his flashlight and spotted the beam a few feet away from him. He dragged himself over to it, dug it out of the debris and scanned the room.

Smoke was everywhere, heavy and thick and already making it difficult to breathe. Getting back to Sam, who remained unmoving, Hollywood pressed his fingers to the kid's neck, relieved to find a slow but steady pulse. He swung the light around and his breath caught in his chest when he saw the burning support beam on Drew's back, and Chad crushed beneath him. "Oh fuck, oh shit!" Hollywood shouted.

Drew's agonized screams were all Hollywood could hear now and the reek of scorching flesh all he could smell. He raced toward Drew and Chad. That's when he noticed Liam, a few feet away from them. He lay on his back, a large steel rod penetrating his abdomen. Liam's eyes were pinched against the smoke and his chest rose and fell in quick, shallow movements. Hollywood blew out. At least Liam was alive. They were all alive, and he was going to keep them that way.

Again, Hollywood radioed dispatch. "This is Ladder 27. Medic 11. We have three firefighters down. I repeat: three firefighters down. Need immediate medic response. Do you copy?"

"Roger that, Lieutenant."

He flicked his mic on to radio his platoon. "Get your asses up here. We've got fire, structural damage, and multiple injuries. Bring the cutting edge saw and my damn SCBA."

"On it, LT," came his team's reply.

He tried to shove the flaming beam off Drew's back with his feet. Drew's arms flailed and he hollered in pain under the increased pressure. Hollywood immediately backed off. "Okay. Okay. Shit."

Sam was stable and ready to be transported out of the building. Chad's eyes tracked his movements, so he was obviously alert. Freeing Liam of the rod would require the team's assistance. But Drew? The threat to his life was immediate and growing.

Quickly, Hollywood did up the ties on his jacket, raised the collar and pulled on his gloves. "Chad, Drew," he shouted to get their attention. "When I say so, cover your faces."

Then, using his covered hands, Hollywood beat the flames on the end of the beam that was in the air so he could grab hold of it. Drew moaned and his cries weakened. *Shit.*

Hurrying, Hollywood anchored his feet in the debris and pushed against the heavy beam with his hands and shoulders. He let out a roar as he raised it off Drew's back.

"Now!" he yelled as he shoved it away from Drew and Chad and raised his own hands to protect his face from the sparks and debris that shot up when the beam hit the floor.

Rushing back to the men, he asked, "Can you move?"

Drew didn't respond. Hollywood shined his flashlight on Drew's back, swallowing hard at the sight of the mangled and charred flesh.

Ripping off his gloves, he pressed his fingers to Drew's neck. Thready. He'd probably passed out from the pain.

"LT!"

Hearing Manny's voice, Hollywood swung his flashlight in the direction of the door. "Over here."

A few seconds later, Platoon C was next to him, awaiting orders. "Leiderman and O'Reilly, get Drew on a backboard. Manny and Emma, take the GSW down. His name is Sam. He was conscious before the explosion."

Leiderman and O'Reilly lifted Drew onto a backboard, taking care not to jostle him. With Drew's weight gone, Chad was able to push up on his hands. Hollywood helped him into a sitting position and waited while Chad finished a bout of coughing. The smoke was worsening. Hollywood had to get all the injured out of the building before something else happened. "Can you walk?" he asked.

"Yeah, I think so."

Hollywood nodded. "Okay. Go with them." He turned back to his platoon. "Once you're done, hurry back to help me with Liam."

"Liam?" Chad grabbed his arm. "What's wrong with him?"

Hollywood knelt beside Chad to block his view of Liam and pointed to his men cinching the straps around Drew. "Go with him," he said firmly.

"I need to see Liam first." Chad's voice had an edge.

"No, you don't."

"Is that an order, sir?"

Hollywood sighed. "Drew needs you now." And Chad didn't need to see his partner's broken body.

"Sorry." Chad wiped a sooty hand over his face and coughed again. Hollywood gripped his arm and pulled him to his feet. Chad's face paled and he swayed slightly.

Hollywood steadied him. "You okay?"

"Yeah." Chad lumbered over and quickly examined Drew's back, which was covered in extensive burns. Hollywood had seen enough burns over the years to know these were bad. Very bad.

All business, Chad kicked through some smoldering ceiling panels and located the medical bag that all paramedics carried. "You'll need this..." His voice broke. Tears welled. He swallowed, once, twice, before continuing. "What I need for Drew is in Medic 11." The message in his pleading eyes as he handed Hollywood the bag was clear: save my partner.

Feeling the weight of responsibility on his shoulders, Hollywood nodded. Then Chad was gone, chasing after Leiderman and O'Reilly with Drew between them on a portable stretcher.

Glad that the man he loved was safe and leaving the unstable structure, he turned to Liam to figure out how to extricate him. Liam's eyes were closed, his head hanging down. His heart in his throat, Hollywood checked Liam's pulse. Thank God. He was still alive.

The air was thick with smoke and ash, so Hollywood put on his SCBA and slipped a mask over Liam's face as well. His vitals weren't the best, but at least he was breathing on his own. Carefully, Hollywood cut through the man's blood-soaked clothes and packed gauze around the puncture wound.

A few minutes later, Manny and Emma returned. "Backup units have arrived, LT."

"Not a moment too soon." While his team ventilated the roof, the additional engine and ladder teams would be setting up ladders and double-checking the building to see if anyone else was inside and potentially injured before they started to hose it down.

His concern right now, though, was Liam. Before they could do more for him, they had to free him from the bar, which snaked from Liam's abdomen to a piece of concrete a few feet away. They wouldn't remove the bar, but they would cut him free. Hollywood covered as much of Liam as he could with a fire-retardant blanket. Then, Emma held the metal bar and Manny began to cut through it, angling the saw so the worst of the sparks flew away from their patient. When the bar snapped, Hollywood checked Liam's vitals again. "Pulse is slow, but still pretty steady. Let's see if we can move him now."

On the count of three, they shifted his shoulders to slide him onto the backboard, and that's when Hollywood saw that the pole went right through Liam and was attached to a larger structure beneath him. "Shit. Manny, hurry. We have to cut it back here, too. Emma, help me hold him up."

Hollywood wrapped the blanket around Liam's back and upper thighs. He and Emma supported Liam's weight while Manny cut through the remaining bar. Hollywood quickly fashioned a donut-shaped pad out of the gauze and placed it around the wound and the inches of piping that remained. Together they laid Liam on his side on the stretcher and strapped him in.

"Okay, get him out of here, guys."

Hollywood scanned the room and headed for the stairs as Engine 13 reached him with hoses. "This floor should be clear, but do a quick scan to be sure," he instructed them. "The fire and subsequent explosion started in the ceiling. No cause as yet determined. Be careful, guys."

"Got it, LT."

Making his way out of the building and toward Chad, Hollywood sent up a quick prayer to Saint Florian, the patron saint of firefighters, that no more surprises awaited them that night. Especially not one in the form of Deputy Chief Wright.

୫୦ ☕ ରୁ

As soon as they got Drew to Medic 11, Chad located his gloves and, using thermal shears, cut off Drew's bunker pants to aid in the cooling-off process. If Drew's pants were wet or even humid from a previous call, or if he'd sweated a lot, he could get thermal or contact burns to the skin underneath them.

As he removed the thick material, Chad examined Drew's legs and buttocks for damage, breathing a little easier when he didn't find any. Drew had more than enough obvious burns to deal with. Continuing up, he slowly and painstakingly removed what was left of Drew's shirt, assessing as he went. Using his mic, he radioed Harborview Medical Center. As a paramedic, he could confer directly with the designated Medic One physician as well as his lieutenant, who was still a minute or so away from the scene. "This is Medic 11. I've got an unconscious burn victim, firefighter, male, twenty-eight, with second- and third-degree burns on fifteen to twenty percent of his body—back, neck, and right shoulder."

As he spoke, Chad used forceps to remove the large pieces of fiber sticking to the wounds, then covered Drew's burns with a sterile dressing that would protect him until they got to Harborview Burn Center.

He relayed Drew's vitals to the doctor, and they negotiated a course of action. Drew's breathing seemed okay. Still there'd been a fair amount of smoke. He didn't think intubation was necessary at this point, but not wanting to take a chance that Drew's lungs had been singed, Chad administered humidified high-concentration oxygen through a non-rebreather mask. Lastly, he found a good vein in Drew's arm and inserted a large-bore IV to begin fluid resuscitation. Drew was ready to be transported to the hospital.

But he needed a driver.

Shit. Liam.

Now that Drew was stable, the tight control on Chad's nerves began to waver. He switched his radio over to the channel that would put him in touch with everyone on-site. "This is Medic 11. I need a driver for patient transport to HMC."

Before he'd even finished speaking, Hollywood poked his head in the back. "How's he doing?"

"Stable. Unconscious."

"Damn. Listen, I would drive, you know that, but I was first on scene and so—"

"You're in charge. I know. Anyone else available?"

Hollywood looked over his shoulder as someone approached. He glanced at Chad, then back to the new arrival. "Henderson, you're in charge. I need to transport these guys to Harborview."

"Sure thing, Hollywood." Lieutenant Henderson, the officer of Engine 13, glanced at Drew, then up at Chad. "Godspeed."

With a nod, Hollywood slammed the back doors shut, then climbed into the driver's seat. "Hang on," he said. "I'll get us there."

"I know."

Chad waited until Hollywood had maneuvered out from between all the fire trucks and hoses crisscrossing the street before asking the question he was dreading. "How is Liam?" Holding his breath, he focused on observing Drew's vitals on the cardiac monitor, anything to block out the worst-case scenarios that tried to take root in his mind.

"We got him out alive. After that, I don't know. Medic 30 was on-site and took off with him a few minutes ago."

"And Sam?"

"Regained consciousness, and his vitals were good last I heard."

Chad let his shoulders relax and kept his hands on his brother's forearm, the touch reassuring him as much as he hoped it did Drew. Drew hadn't regained consciousness yet, but maybe it was a blessing. At least this way, he wasn't in pain.

Five minutes later, Hollywood drove them into the ambulance bay, then came around to open the doors. Together, they lifted Drew's stretcher out and wheeled him into the emergency entrance and straight up to the burn center. The Medic One doctor had a team waiting, and they quickly took over Drew's care, whisking him into a treatment room.

A nurse came to ask Chad some questions, and when he told her Drew was his brother, she handed him a clipboard with a stack of forms to be completed. Resigned, he slumped down into a seat and looked them over, but when he started to write, his hand shook so badly the pen slid through his fingers.

Hollywood picked it up and took the clipboard. "Let me do that."

"I have to call my parents," Chad blurted and suddenly it wasn't only his hands that shook, but his whole body. "Oh God. How am I going to tell my mom and dad about this?"

"Drew was under my command tonight. It's my responsibility," Hollywood said. His voice sounded as beaten as he looked. Guilt shrouded him so completely, Chad found it hard to keep from crying. Because he knew he looked the same.

"I'll call." Chad fished out his phone, surprised it hadn't been crushed, and dialed the number to his parents' house. The phone rang twice before his father's sleepy voice asked, "Hello?"

"Dad, it's Chad. Listen, you and Mom need to come down to

Harborview Burn Center. Drew's been hurt."

"Goddamn," his father cursed, sounding fully awake now. "Caroline, wake up. How bad is it?"

"I don't know. I just brought him in. He was unconscious but stable."

"You brought—"

"Bill, what's going on?" his mother's voice asked.

"I'll tell you on the way. Get dressed, honey." There was a squeak of bedsprings, then his father said, "We'll be there as soon as we can."

"Thanks, Dad."

"Sit tight, son. I love you."

"Love you too," Chad choked out, then ended the call. "Jesus." He closed his eyes and prayed he wouldn't have to make a worse call to Liam's wife, Anna.

CHAPTER 23

Even though Chad hadn't said a word, Hollywood knew what he was thinking, knew he was torn between staying in the burn center for his brother and going down to the emergency room to check on his partner. This, Hollywood could do for him. He handed Chad the completed forms. "I'll head on over to the ER to get an update on Liam's status. I'll text you.

Chad nodded, his eyes burning. "Thanks, Nate."

"It's the least I can do." Literally. Besides, he was certain Jamie would rather not see him when he arrived. As he would soon. The Caldwells stuck together, supported each other, especially in times like these. But he was a Wright, *not* a Caldwell.

Jamie had made that perfectly fucking clear.

Ten minutes later, he'd found a doctor he'd once gone out with who informed him that Liam was being prepped for surgery. After turning down another date, he settled into the waiting room and called the chief of Liam and Chad's battalion.

"Deputy Chief Conroy, this is Lieutenant Wright. It was my team that got Liam Parker out of the explosion."

"Dispatch alerted me. I'm ten minutes away. I've already notified Liam's wife."

"She's pregnant, sir."

"I'm aware. She promised to take a taxi in."

Hollywood rubbed his forehead. He hoped Anna hadn't ignored the chief and tried to drive herself. They didn't need any more shit tonight. "I'm in the waiting room now, sir. I'll keep my eyes open for her."

"Thanks, Lieutenant."

Hollywood ended the call, then texted Chad about the surgery. Over the next several minutes, firefighters and paramedics began filling up the waiting room. Hollywood asked a couple of them to wait outside the emergency and front entrances and to escort Anna in if they spotted her.

His phone buzzed with a message from Chad.

C: Thanks. Room's filling up here.

Hollywood had taken Rescue 21, Ladder 27, and Aid 44 out of service until a replacement lieutenant could be brought in, so everyone on the TRT would be in the burn-unit waiting room. Everyone except him; he didn't dare show his face in there, knowing it would be totally unwelcome by a certain TRT lieutenant. No, he was more useful here, acting as Chad's eyes and ears.

H: Same here.

He heard crying in the corridor outside the waiting room and went to see what was going on. Anna, whom he'd met a couple times, saw him and a sob escaped her. He held his arms out and she fell against him, seeming impossibly small, light, and young, too young, despite her baby bump. Or maybe because of it.

"I'm so sorry, Anna."

"How is he? They said you were there."

"Let's sit down first." He led her into the waiting room and helped her into a seat before sitting next to her, an arm around her shoulders. Calmly and without adding too many details, he gave her an account of the events. The other firefighters and paramedics in the room listened attentively, wincing when he explained about the bar.

"So the surgery is to remove it?" she asked, her eyes red, her cheeks wet.

"Yes. They'll repair any damage as they do it."

"Do you know the damage?"

"No." But he could imagine, and apparently so could she.

"Oh God. How could this happen? I haven't been feeling well, that's why Liam was at work instead of taking the night off for my birthday. We were going to celebrate tomorrow afternoon, when I wasn't so tired."

Hollywood pulled her against his chest. "Shh. None of this is your fault, Anna."

"I—I know," she sobbed.

No, it wasn't her fault. It wasn't even his fault really. But he had been in charge, and Liam had been his responsibility.

"Is there anyone you want me to call? Liam's brother is with the SPD, isn't he?" Hollywood asked. Although the waiting room was packed with Liam's colleagues, no one from either Anna's or Liam's families had shown up yet.

She wiped the wetness off her face. "Karl is on vacation in Hawaii. I'll call him as soon as I know something."

A few minutes later, a doctor entered the room, and all eyes turned to the doorway. "Mrs. Parker?"

When she struggled to rise, Hollywood jumped up and supported her. "May we speak in the hallway?" asked the doctor.

She shook her head. "These men and women are here to support my husband." Her tremulous smile had Hollywood's throat closing up. "I'm sure they want to hear what you have to say."

"Very well." The doctor clasped his hands behind his back. "Your husband is in critical condition. He has internal bleeding from a ruptured spleen, and the bar also caused a gastrointestinal perforation. We need to perform a splenectomy and repair the damage to his large intestine before peritonitis sets in."

"Is he going to be okay, doctor?" She squeezed Hollywood's arm at her waist.

"We'll know more about how extensive the damage is once we open him up."

The doctor hesitated, and Hollywood frowned. "Is there something else, doctor?"

"We're concerned about his left kidney. It's possible the bar damaged it, but we couldn't come to any conclusions with preliminary tests."

"Oh!" Anna sagged against Hollywood. He tightened his hold and led her back to her seat. "Th thank you, doctor," she said through more tears.

"I'll keep you posted." The doctor turned on his heel and hurried out of the room. Anna sobbed quietly into a tissue someone had handed her. Hollywood held her and rubbed her back as they waited. When she'd calmed some, he helped her place that call to Karl. Thankfully, Liam's brother would be on the first available flight out. His family would follow later.

An hour into the surgery, a police officer poked his head into the waiting room. "Lieutenant Wright?"

Hollywood looked up. "That's me."

"I need to take your statement. Can we go somewhere private?"

"Sure." He smiled at Anna. "I'll be right back."

She patted his arm. "They need to find whoever did this."

He nodded and followed the officer into the hallway where it was a little quieter. Hollywood didn't know all the details of what had gone down tonight, but Chad had told him what Sam, the gunshot wound victim, had said, that he'd been bait. As far as Hollywood was concerned, Chad had been the intended target of the baiting. He had no proof, of course, but he knew it in his gut. It was too much of a coincidence that the beam had fallen right on top of where Chad had been kneeling, right beside Sam, who'd been perfectly positioned to ensure the responding paramedics would be hit by the explosion.

Some son of a bitch motherfucker had tried to kill Chad tonight. Would have killed him if Drew hadn't been there—if he hadn't been close enough to protect his younger brother.

Because Hollywood had let his fear control him, had let his fear keep him away from Chad, even at the scene of a call. He'd stayed on the other side of the room so no one would see how Chad had affected him. How much he'd wanted to touch him.

How much Hollywood loved that wonderful, kind-hearted man. And that was the truth.

Whatever he was, whatever label applied, one thing remained true: Hollywood would do anything for Chad.

He knew that now. He'd known it for some time, actually. But he'd been too fucking scared to act on it.

Assuming Chad gave him another chance, Hollywood would come out. He'd tell everyone about their relationship. About how much Chad meant to him, and how much he wanted them to be together.

And for once in his life, he'd be the man he wanted to be, the man Chad needed him to be, and he'd face down his father's wrath.

ⅎ 🚒 K

By three AM, the doctors came out to give them an update on Drew's situation. He had regained consciousness and, as Chad had determined, suffered extensive second- and third-degree burns on his back, neck, and right shoulder. He would require specialized treatment that included excision of the damaged tissue, which the doctors had already begun, followed by skin grafts and rehabilitation. Several muscles in his shoulder had been torn when the beam fell on him, and those would require surgery.

Chad didn't even know how to process the news. Drew would be okay, assuming they could stave off infection, but it would be a long and difficult road. Austin, who'd arrived some time earlier, clutched his shoulder. "He's strong as a bull, Chad. He's going to be okay."

Helplessly, Chad looked at his mother and sister, both red-eyed from crying. Dani and Erica had fared no better. His father, Jamie, and William stood stony-eyed next to their women, looking like they needed the support just as much.

The doctor's gaze passed over them, stopping meaningfully on each person. "Drew is going to need all of you. I won't lie. It's going to be difficult and painful, and sometimes the psychological impact will be worse than the physical one. Burn victims often go through phases of depression, anger, and despair. But Drew is strong, and with your help, your love, he will make it back."

His father nodded. "Thank you, doctor. What's the next step?"

"Drew will have surgery in the morning. It's scheduled for eight AM. I suggest you all go home and get some rest."

His mother's lip trembled. "When can I see my boy?"

The doctor walked over to her and, taking her hand, he patted the back of it. He spoke softly. "Right now, he's receiving hyperbaric oxygen therapy. This maximizes our efforts to keep infection from setting in. We'd like to keep him as isolated as possible until tomorrow morning. You or your husband can see him for a few minutes before the surgery."

The sound of his mother's hiccupping breaths echoed in the silent room. She turned into his father's chest and clutched his shirt. The seriousness of Drew's situation was finally hitting them. Chad pulled Tori to him and held her tightly. They needed each other's support now more than ever.

When the doctor left and no one moved, Chad broke the silence. "There's plenty of good news. Drew is alive, and his prognosis is very good. He's strong, he's young, and his lungs and heart weren't damaged. It's going to be tough, but we'll help him through this. We won't be any good though, if we all get sick too."

Tori sniffled, then patted Chad's chest. "Chad's right." She slipped out of his hold and went to take their mother's arm. "Let's get you home and into bed. We'll come back in the morning."

They all left, two-by-two, until only Chad and Austin remained. "Let me guess. That speech was just for them?" his friend asked.

"Liam's still in surgery." At least according to Hollywood's latest text.

Austin nodded at the phone in Chad's hand. "Who's been sendin' you updates?"

Looking away, Chad shoved the phone into his pocket. "Hollywood."

"So y'all are back together then?" Hearing the strained note in his friend's voice, Chad turned back. Austin's serious expression and furrowed brow matched his tone.

"No..."

"But you're hopin'. Hasn't he hurt you enough?"

"You don't understand."

"Damn right. That jerk threw you away like a used condom."

Chad grimaced at the imagery, his face going hot.

"Sorry, but it's true," Austin added.

"There's more going on than you know." More going on than even he knew. Tonight, there had been something different in Hollywood's voice, in his eyes. He'd seemed less tense, more accepting. Maybe—

"Promise me somethin'," Austin said, interrupting his thoughts.

Chad eyed him uneasily. "What's that?"

"Don't get your hopes up. The guy is fifty shades of confused right now. Emotions are runnin' high, and one look at you and your tight ass in that sexy-as-fuck uniform will be enough to rock his world, if you know what I mean."

Chad rolled his eyes in exasperation. "I'm just going to talk to him."

"Make sure talkin's all you'll be doin'. Okay? That's all I'm askin'."

"Austin, we're in a hospital. I work here."

"Yeah?" He arched a brow. "Like that's ever stopped you before."

"My brother's in the burn unit, and my partner's in surgery fighting for his life. Getting my sexy on is the last thing on my mind."

"It would be a hell of a lot safer than layin' your heart at that man's feet so he can stomp all over it again, which is what I know you're goin' to do." Chad opened his mouth to argue, but Austin cut him off. "Don't you even try to deny it."

Chad blew out a breath and hooked his hands on his hips. "I love him."

"That's what scares me."

It scared Chad too. Scared him senseless. What scared him worse, though, was the thought of spending the rest of his life without Hollywood in it.

ଚ ☕ ର

The sound of a voice on a PA system woke Hollywood from a crazy dream-filled sleep. Thinking he was in a bunk at Station 44, he sat up to get ready to roll out. A hand pressed against his chest. A large, warm, very familiar hand that held a trace of blue nail polish near the cuticle of the thumb.

"Easy there."

Chad's voice, soft and smooth, wrapped around him, snuggling him into its cocoon. He looked up and drowned in that blue gaze, seeing it so close for the first time in a week. God, he'd missed Chad something terrible. He was a fool. A fool for ever letting the man go.

Another voice came over the PA system and Hollywood remembered where they were, remembered the explosion, remembered that Chad had been crushed under the weight of his brother and a goddamn burning beam. There was a cut on Chad's cheek that now sported a butterfly bandage, and his left wrist was wrapped in a clean white dressing.

"It's just a little burn."

Hollywood swallowed the emotions swelling in his chest, fighting for freedom. "How." He stopped and cleared his throat. "How's Drew?"

Chad gave him a quick rundown of what the doctor had said. Hollywood bowed his head and clasped it between his hands. "Thank God."

When he'd first looked up and seen the burning beam, he'd prayed

Chad wasn't the one under it, that it wasn't Chad's back being burned to shit. It hadn't been, and he refused to feel guilty about it. That didn't mean he didn't feel bad for Drew though. Chad's brother was a good man, and a really good firefighter. He hoped like hell the guy pulled through this and was able to return to the TRT someday.

"How's Liam?" Chad asked.

There was a tremor in his voice that Hollywood had never heard before. He laid his hand on Chad's knee, offering his support, and held his breath, waiting to see if Chad would smack his hand away. When he didn't, Hollywood exhaled. He checked his watch. He'd slept for only fifteen minutes. "The surgery ended about twenty minutes ago. A nurse came to take Anna to recovery. Liam's friends and the guys from your house left after that."

Chad smiled. "But you stayed."

"In case she... needed me." He'd stayed for Anna, but for Chad too. He'd have been right there in the burn center with the rest of the TRT waiting on news of Drew, except that he hadn't wanted to push Jamie tonight. His little brothers had been hurt while under Hollywood's command. He'd been the most senior person on-site and what had happened had been his responsibility. If Jamie had laid eyes on Hollywood tonight, he'd have kicked his ass. Hollywood didn't blame him. He wanted to kick his own ass.

So instead of causing the Caldwells more pain, he'd taken Chad's place with Liam's wife and his coworkers, leaving Chad free to concentrate on his family. Chad rested his chin on his hands as he leaned forward. "Thank you for being here. For Anna, and for me."

"It's the least I could do." Chad's eyes watered and, gutted, Hollywood looked away. "You should go home. Get some rest."

"No, I need..." Chad's sentence hung unfinished.

Hollywood turned back. "They're both going to be okay. The doctors managed to stop the bleeding and fixed the hole in Liam's intestines. His kidney is fine too. You can relax now."

"I—we need to talk."

Scrubbing his face, Hollywood leaned back against the uncomfortable couch. They did have to talk. Just not tonight. His emotions were too raw. "I don't think now's the right time."

"I couldn't leave without saying thank you."

Hollywood snorted. "For what? Almost getting you killed? Getting all of you killed?"

"That had nothing to do with you," Chad said firmly. "I was the target. We all know that. If anyone's to blame, it's me." Chad shoved off the couch. "Anyway, you're right. I should go."

He said the words, but his feet didn't move. Hollywood watched him, frozen. Paralyzed by fear, by indecision.

Grow a pair, Wright!

Chad's blue eyes shone with unshed tears and his bottom lip trembled as he shook his head and turned away. It was now or never. Hollywood's hand whipped out and grabbed Chad's wrist. "Wait." He stood in front of Chad, trailed his fingers along Chad's cheek. Chad closed his eyes and leaned into his touch. Warmth pooled around Hollywood's heart. Maybe there was still hope. "I've missed you. So fucking much."

Opening his eyes, Chad asked the question Hollywood had been dreading. "Why'd you end things then?"

"Because I'm a coward. I thought I could be strong like you and not give a shit what others thought, but then my dad showed up, and I was ten years old again." It was a partial truth, and Hollywood hoped it would be enough. The rest was just too hard to admit.

Chad cradled Hollywood's hand and brought it to his lips. "Have you ever talked to a counselor or therapist?"

"About what?"

"Nate," Chad said softly. "Your father abused you emotionally, mentally, and physically for years."

"Because I didn't stand up to him."

"Because you couldn't."

"Maybe when I was a kid. What's my excuse now?" Unable to bear the compassion in Chad's eyes, a compassion he didn't deserve, he looked down at the tiled floor. Hot bile rose in his throat. "He always said I was a poor excuse for a man. Guess he was right."

"Hey, stop that. You're strong, brave, loyal, and dependable. I, for one, am very proud to know you."

"Great. Just call me Lassie."

Chad smiled sadly. "If you talk to someone about the abuse, they can help you deal with it, and maybe you can finally shake the hold your father has over you."

Hollywood's face and ears flushed with heat. His gut churned. "You make me sound like a victim."

"Nate, you *were*, and like any victim of violence, you have scars deep inside that only you and the asshole who put them there can see."

Eyes itching, Hollywood blinked to clear his vision. Chad's face was too beautiful to be distorted by tears.

"Maybe Tori could recommend someone," Chad said.

Panic gripped Hollywood. "Don't tell her it's for me, okay?" He didn't want anyone else to know what a sniveling weakling he was. It was bad enough that Chad knew.

"Of course not." Chad squeezed his arm, then his posture slumped unhappily. "It's my fault that this blew up anyway. If I'd grasped how bad

LOVER ON TOP

things were with your father, I would never have encouraged you to come out at the ball. It was selfish, and I'm sorry."

"No." Hollywood sat on the couch and dragged Chad down with him. "I wanted to do it. I thought if I wanted it enough, I could stand up to my father. Tell him I was gay or bi and proud, and he could go to hell if he didn't like it."

"Doesn't work that way though." Chad's head tilted sympathetically and something stirred in Hollywood's belly.

"No, it doesn't." He kissed the back of Chad's hand, a soft, tender kiss that expressed how sorry he was. His stomach did flip-flops as he looked up into the warm blue gaze that reminded him so much of the bay water on a sunny summer day. "I want to try again. Will you let me?"

ഔ 🎬 ക

Chad barely dared to breathe. What was Hollywood's asking? "Try what again?"

"Being away from you, seeing you almost get killed, I don't know. It made me realize how short life is. How vulnerable we are, how quickly we can lose someone we love. When I saw you bleeding and trapped under that beam, only protected from the fire by Drew's body, I wanted to die. I'd have given anything to be in Drew's place. To be the one protecting you."

Did Hollywood just say he—? Chad's mouth opened and closed, but no sound came out.

"I—I love you, Chad." He looked down at their joined hands. "I know I didn't act like it at the party. I let my fears control me, but I promise to work on it, and some day—"

"Not until you're ready," Chad said, finally finding his voice.

"—I'll come out. With you by my side."

"I'll follow your lead." Chad lifted his other hand and stroked Hollywood's hair, thrilling at the feel of the short spikes on his palm. He'd thought he'd never get to touch Hollywood's hair again. He swallowed and licked his dry lips and admitted the secret he'd kept locked away for so long. "I love you too. I think I always have."

Hollywood leaned in. Their lips met in a gentle exchange of their newly declared feelings. Hollywood scooted on the couch so his back was partially pressed against the armrest. He bent one knee and raised it on the seat, then patted the vinyl between his spread legs. "Stay with me?"

Chad eyed the small couch. "I'm not sure we both fit. Besides, aren't you concerned about who will see us?"

"I only want to hold you. Nothing else."

God, he wanted that too. So badly. A lumpy hospital couch with Hollywood on it was a million times better than his top-of-the-line king-size mattress at home without Hollywood.

Turning so his back was flush against Hollywood's chest, Chad let his head rest on Hollywood's strong shoulder. Hollywood's arms folded around him, one draped across his waist, the other over his chest, holding him tightly. Chad inhaled, deeply filling his lungs with the faint odor of smoke from Hollywood's hair and that manly scent that was all Hollywood. It was better than his favorite cologne. It was the scent of home.

CHAPTER 24

A noise in the distance dragged Hollywood out of the best, most peaceful sleep he'd had in over a week—since he'd been a scared little shit and pushed Chad away. Sighing, he tightened his hold on his boyfriend's waist and nuzzled the curve of his neck, taking a long lick up the stubbled expanse. Nothing had ever tasted sweeter.

Chad chuckled and angled his head to give Hollywood easier access. He never played hard to get. Hollywood really appreciated that about the guy. "Such a slut," he teased, whispering softly.

"And you love it."

Cracking open an eye, he grinned and kissed Chad's smiling lips. "Yeah, I do."

A throat cleared a few feet away from them, and they both turned to see who it was. Caroline stood there, wearing a bewildered expression.

"Mom," Chad tried to sit up and winced. He turned his worried eyes on Hollywood's, searching his face as though looking for a sign as to how to handle this.

Maybe Hollywood was still sleepy enough to be loopy, or maybe it was the softening of Chad's mother's expression, but either way, Hollywood was okay with this. "Good morning, Caroline."

She took a few steps closer, clutching a Starbucks bag and cup in her hands. "I didn't mean to wake you, but..." Her eyes welled, and Hollywood knew exactly how she felt. He patted Chad's chest, then slipped off the couch and walked over to her. "But you wanted to check on your boys." He put an arm around her shoulders. "Believe me, I understand."

Her gaze darted to Chad, then back to Hollywood. "I'm beginning to think that you do."

Chad's face lit up, igniting a fire around Hollywood's heart. "Please tell me that's a triple venti nonfat latte."

She set the bag on the couch beside Chad. "Along with several pieces of that pumpkin bread you keep going on about." She touched his cheek, the gesture full of love and affection. Chad reached for the coffee cup. His eyes practically rolled back in his head as he took a sip. It was the same look of bliss he wore when he came.

Hollywood had to look away. How had he ever thought he could deny his feelings for this man? The attraction, the lust, the love?

Caroline sat on the edge of the couch. "So... what's new?"

Again Chad's gaze sought his. He was trying so hard to let Hollywood lead. Even so, his happiness and desire to share their new relationship with his mother was coming off him in waves—from the sappy grin he kept trying to hide to the jiggling of his feet.

Taking pity on his man, Hollywood walked around to the opposite side of the couch and sank his fingers into the bristly hair on Chad's neck. "Chad and I are dating."

"Dating?" She smiled. "Is that what they're calling it these days?"

"Mom," Chad groaned, his face going beet red, and Hollywood laughed at the giddy sense of freedom. It seemed Caroline's unconditional acceptance extended to him as well.

She reached her hand across Chad's lap to Hollywood as he sat down. He enclosed her small fingers in his large ones. So small yet so strong. This woman amazed him. He liked to think his mother would have been the same way.

"Does anyone else know?" she asked.

"Only Tori and Jamie," Chad answered. "So you can't tell anyone, okay?"

The sadness flickering in her gaze punched Hollywood's heart. With this secrecy, he was caging Chad, like a beautiful, exotic bird forced to keep its glorious wings tucked in tight.

"I promise you, Caroline, it won't be for long. I just need to do this slowly."

She squeezed his hand. "Tori mentioned an altercation with your father at the ball. Was it about..."

Chad's arm hooked around his waist in a silent show of support, his loving eyes telling Hollywood he was there for him. "He saw me holding Chad's hand."

"And went ballistic," Chad added.

"Oh dear."

Hollywood focused on Chad. "I'm done letting him control me."

A slow applause followed his words. Jamie entered the waiting room, his intense angry eyes taking in the cozy scene. His lip lifted in a snarl.

When Jamie's steely gaze settled on him, Hollywood gulped. Chad stiffened and pulled Hollywood closer. Caroline watched her eldest son in confusion. "Jamie?"

Hollywood's gut was a roiling, churning mass. He briefly tightened his grip on Chad's hair, and tilting his head up, he swooped down for a quick press of lips. "I'll be all right."

Chad blinked, his blue eyes darting to his brother. "You don't have to do this alone."

"Yes." He kissed Chad again. "I do."

Jamie had been his best friend for so long, the brother he'd never had. Their estrangement weighed heavily on him, worse than he'd anticipated. He owed the man one hell of an apology.

Hollywood followed Jamie into the hall and out to the parking lot. With each step, his anxiety grew. Jamie was a Dom; he knew a lot of ways to hurt someone, to break them. Was he taking Hollywood outside to kick the shit out of him? And if he did, should Hollywood even try to defend himself? His father had taught him long ago that fighting back only made things worse.

Jamie continued walking through the parking lot until they reached a small wooded area. Hollywood looked around and swallowed hard. Perhaps due to his size, Hollywood had always felt safe wherever he was, as long as his father wasn't around, but right here, right now fucing Jamie? He might as well be three feet tall again.

Jamie stopped walking a few yards ahead and turned to face Hollywood. Crossing his arms, he stared Hollywood down with that piercing, penetrating, ice-cold gaze.

The longer the stare-off continued, the worse Hollywood's apprehension became. He shoved his hands into his pockets so Jamie wouldn't see the tremors. He was such a fucking pussy.

Jamie laughed then, the low harsh sound one Hollywood had never heard before. It was the sound of a man who would do anything to protect his family. "You look ready to piss yourself," Jamie said.

"Fuck you." Jamie had that drop-to-your-knees-on-my-command voice thing going on, but Hollywood was no weakling. He worked out and had done some martial arts. He was bigger than Jamie too. It was time he showed Jamie what he was made of, that he too had someone to fight for: Chad.

"I told you to stay the fuck away from my family. But then here you are, all cozy with Chad and my mom." Jamie's fingers gripped his hips so tightly his knuckles were white. He wasn't shouting, but if the vein pulsing at his temple was any indication, Jamie's legendary cool was about to blow.

Hollywood held his hands out. "Look, you have no idea how sorry I am for the things I said to you at my apartment. I didn't mean any of that shit." Bile rose in his throat just remembering the crude lies, the way he'd put Chad down.

"Why should I believe you?"

"Chad does."

"Chad's in love with you. He'd believe anything you say. As for me? Right now, I'm finding it real hard to be forgiving. Try again."

Pacing a few steps, Hollywood scrubbed his rough cheeks. He'd known this wouldn't be easy, that Jamie would force him to bare his heart. Chad was worth it though. "I was scared," he blurted before he chickened out.

"Scared of what? I already knew you swung both ways, and I even told Chad I was cool with you two being together."

Thinking back to the scene at his apartment, Hollywood remembered Jamie mentioning something about talking with Chad. He'd been so caught up in the drama with his father, he hadn't grasped the importance of it. Would knowing Jamie was on their side have changed his behavior that day? Maybe, although his worry over Jamie's reaction wasn't his only issue, and he had to be man enough to voice all his fears. Starting now.

"I was scared of what other people would say, what they'd think."

Jamie's brows dipped low. "Why the fuck would you care what other assholes think? One look from you and they'd run away with their tails between their legs."

Hollywood shook his head. "It's not as easy as Chad makes it look. It takes a special kind of strength not to let insults and dirty looks get to you. I thought I had that strength. I thought I could take Chad's hand, march in there, and stare down any fucker who dared even think something nasty, but when I walked into that damn ballroom—" His jaw locked shut and the rest of his words stalled, stuck in his throat, choking him.

Branches crunched, then Jamie's hand was on the back of his neck. "Then you saw your father."

Still unable to speak, Hollywood nodded.

"I don't know everything about this, do I?" Concern resonated in Jamie's voice.

Hollywood shook his head and stared at his shoes. Jamie sighed and kneaded his shoulder. "Look, I'm not going to force you to talk about it. You ever want to give me details, I'll be all ears. But for now, tell me one thing: Is your father why you tried to push Chad away?"

The image of his father shouting at him, at Chad. Saying that Chad was turning him into "a depraved sexual deviant" exploded in his mind. His father had definitely factored into his decision. "He said some really bad shit before you arrived. Then you heard him threaten to have Chad fired." Hollywood rubbed the heels of his hands against his burning eyes. "I thought the only way to keep Chad safe was to stay away from him."

"But…"

"Then I almost fucking lost him in that explosion!" Staying away from Chad hadn't helped at all. There were too many homophobic assholes in the world, not just his father. "Now I know the way to protect him is to be by his side."

"Protect him. Hmm. That's not the only reason."

Hollywood stared up at the clouds gathering in the early morning sky. It was time to be the man Chad deserved. He held his hands out, leaving himself as open and vulnerable as his heart. "I'm in love with your brother. I know I'm the last person you'd pick for Chad, but I'm a better man when I'm with him. I want him to be as proud of me as I am of him."

Jamie huffed and ran a hand through his hair. "I wouldn't exactly say the last. But the drinking?" He peered at Hollywood. "It's an issue."

"Actually, I think it might be a symptom." Hollywood crossed his arms. "Chad suggested I see a counselor."

"That would be a good start." Jamie rolled his shoulders back, his face hardening. "Now what about your relationship? Are you going to make him hide it?"

"No." Hollywood looked away.

"I'm hearing another 'but.'"

"Telling people I'm gay or bi is one thing. Introducing my boyfriend to them is another. I'm going to take it one step at a time, one day at a time. Chad understands that I need to do this in a way that I'm comfortable with." His brow arched. "Do you?"

Jamie's smile was wry. "More than you know."

The lightbulb went off in Hollywood's head. "Does your family know about you and Erica? About the BDSM stuff?"

"Chad knows all of it, William knows some. The rest suspect. It's tough to be honest about something that ignorant people could use to have me locked up."

"But your family? They're obviously very open-minded."

Jamie's smile was more genuine this time. "We plan to tell them after the baby's born. Hopefully no one will notice Rickie's collar before then."

Hollywood sputtered, "Collar?"

Jamie touched the base of his throat. "Yeah, the necklace with a locking heart she wears? It's a collar, a symbol of her submission and surrender to me, her master. It's also my vow to honor and care for her, my sl—submissive. We had a private ceremony, just the two of us, about a month ago. It was even more beautiful than our wedding." His eyes took on a hazy quality that matched the reverence in his voice.

Would Hollywood and Chad ever make vows to each other, pledge their love, their commitment? He hoped so, because Chad was already a part of him, the other half of his soul. He'd never felt so connected to someone before—not even Isabel. Not even close.

Hollywood yanked Jamie into a hug. "Whatever you guys are doing, keep doing it, because I've never seen either of you look happier."

Jamie hugged him back. "If you need moral support when you start telling folks, let me know. I'll be there."

After a few back slaps, they stepped apart. Hollywood held out his hand. "So we're good?"

Jamie grabbed it and shook, grinning. "Yeah, we're good." He pulled him closer and threw his arm around Hollywood's shoulders as they started walking back toward the hospital, and for the first time in weeks, Hollywood felt good. Happy. He had his boyfriend and his best friend back. With them by his side, he could face anything. Even his father.

ℴ 🚋 ℭ

Chad's heart warmed when Jamie and Hollywood walked into the waiting room, joking and laughing, arms on each other shoulders, something he'd seen them do countless times before. He was so glad they'd made up. Hollywood would need all the support he could get in the coming days and weeks as he slowly came out to the world about his sexuality and their relationship. But this time, they'd do it right, and Chad would make damn sure they were better prepared when it came time to face Deputy Chief Wright again.

His mom beamed at all three of them. She stood, walked up to Hollywood, and cupped his cheeks. "I've always considered you a part of my family, Hollywood. I hope that now, you will too."

"Thank you, Caroline. That means a lot."

She took Jamie's arm, and her smile dimmed a little. "It should be time for me to visit Drew before his surgery."

Hollywood sat down and hit his fist on the arm of the couch. "Christ, I should have made him wear his bunker jacket when we went into that damn building."

"Hey," Jamie said, sitting down next to him. "There was no real sign of danger or fire when you went inside. You couldn't have known some asshole had planted a bomb."

Chad gripped his fingers. "If Liam and I had had our gear on, no one would have needed to protect us."

"As a paramedic, you can't go into every call expecting a fire or an explosion, Chad. How would you work on patients in full gear? It's just not possible." Jamie sighed, the sound full of sadness. "What happened last night was a tragedy we couldn't have foreseen."

Hollywood's eyes flew to Chad's. Chad gave a very slight shake of his head, but it was enough for Jamie to catch on. "Chad."

Chad narrowed his eyes at his lover. "We don't even know if these things are related."

"If what things are related?" Jamie pressed.

"Chad, dear." His mother patted his knee. "Did something else happen?"

Keeping his eyes locked on his feet, Chad pushed the truth past the tightness in his chest. Since he'd been a kid, he'd always tried to handle everything on his own, because he hadn't wanted his family to feel bad for him, or worse, to feel targeted themselves. Somehow though, eventually, they'd always figured it out. Looked like nothing had changed. "My tires were slashed outside the station."

"And..." Hollywood prompted. Chad shot him a death glare, which the guy chose to completely ignore. "His car was tagged with the same slurs as the ambulance was last summer."

"That still doesn't mean anything."

"Did you tell the police?" his mother asked.

"Not when it happened, but I did last night when they questioned me." He met each of their gazes, his own burning with shame. "This is all my fault. I should've sucked it up and called the cops, told them about my car and the phone calls."

Too late he realized what he'd let slip. Three pairs of eyes widened. Hollywood's voice was impossibly hard. "Phone calls?"

Chad swallowed and picked at a burn hole in his duty pants. "Some hangups. I thought they were nothing."

His mother took his hand. "What do the police think?"

"They're looking at all my incoming calls and trying to trace them. I already know they're from payphones, but they're hoping to find some street or store surveillance footage of the calls. They're hoping it will lead them to whoever set the trap last night."

After glancing at her watch, she patted Chad's knee. "All right, son. You let us know if you hear anything." She leaned down to kiss his cheek, then Hollywood's. "You two go get some rest. I believe your turn to see Drew will be this afternoon?"

Chad nodded. "That's what the nurses told me. You should get going before you miss your visiting time. Drew needs you now."

Jamie nodded at them, then led their mother to the elevators. As soon as they were out of sight, Chad shuddered and Hollywood pulled him against his chest. Chad looked up at the face of the man he loved and lay his guilt at his lover's feet. "Liam almost died because of me. Drew's in for months of procedures and rehabilitation, and who knows if he'll ever fully recover. And you"—his eyes grew moist as he traced the strong bone of his man's jaw—"you could have been hurt too. And all of this happened because of me."

"Hey." Hollywood cradled the back of his head. "You didn't rig that explosion. Jamie's right. The crazy fuckers who did this are responsible for everything that's happened. Not you."

Silent tears spilled over and tracked down Chad's cheeks. He went to wipe them off, but Hollywood stopped his hand, and leaned down to kiss the wetness away.

"The police will find whoever did this, even if we have to go down to the police station every day to kick some ass."

"Maybe if I wasn't so out there, if I played it straight more, maybe—"

"You can't let people like that win. Liam and Drew accept you the way you are. They *love* you the way you are. No one blames you. You're a victim as much as Sam, and Liam, and Drew."

"It's just that sometimes I really wish I were straight."

Hollywood smiled gently and smoothed his thumbs under Chad's eyes. "I don't."

The gravel in his voice had Chad stirring down below. "Why's that?" he asked, breathless.

"Because then I couldn't do this." A gentle finger slid under Chad's chin, angling his face up as Hollywood's lips took his mouth in a burning kiss full of hope, promise, and love.

Chad gave a small moan and deepened the kiss, infusing it with all his dreams for the future, their future together. After several long minutes, he slipped out of Hollywood's hold, stood, and offered his hand. "Come home with me, Nate."

෨ 🚋 ೦ಶ

They awoke around noon, ate, showered, and shaved. Hollywood was stepping back into his dirty uniform, scrunching his nose at the stench, when Chad walked into the bathroom carrying a pile of clean clothes. "You left these here."

Jeans, T-shirt, boxers, socks, everything he needed. Hollywood beamed at Chad. "I could kiss you."

Chad jutted out a hip and struck a sassy pose. "What's stopping you, gorgeous?"

Not needing to be asked twice, Hollywood quickly took the bundle of clothes out of Chad's hands and set it on the counter. His fingers speared through Chad's short, silky hair, the dark strands tickling his fingers as he cupped Chad's head and brought their lips together.

What had started out almost as a joke quickly turned into a blazing inferno. Hollywood slid his hands down Chad's back, down inside his jeans and briefs, to cup the firm flesh of his ass. Almost delirious from the pleasure, he yanked Chad against him, against his aching cock. "Oh God," he said on a groan.

Chad's hands were all over him, igniting trails wherever they touched. He moaned and made small sounds of pleasure as he explored Hollywood's mouth. "I need you so bad."

"Need you too. Always." Hollywood breathed in his man's scent. Yes, *his* man. Chad was his, for as long as he'd have him. He shoved Chad's shirt over his head, his tongue licking at each exposed inch of golden skin. Skin he'd dreamt about every night they'd been apart. Skin he wanted to own.

Chad fumbled with his button and fly while Hollywood walked him backward to the bed, his teeth nipping at Chad's hard nipples. The soft whorls on Chad's broad rounded muscles rubbed on Hollywood's cheek, driving him wild. "I love your chest. Love that you have hair."

Chad stopped at the bed and Hollywood pushed him backward. He fell with a gasp that had Hollywood's dick hardening. And when he saw Chad sprawled on the bed, caressing his chest and tweaking his own nipples, he couldn't swallow back the aroused whine in his throat.

"It doesn't bother you that I don't have boobs?"

The odd question and even odder note in Chad's voice stopped him short. "What?"

"You're bi. You love tits and I don't have any." He dropped his arms on the bed and closed his eyes. "I've never been in a relationship with someone who was bi."

Hollywood chuckled. "Neither have I."

Opening an eye, Chad curled his lip in a rock star sneer. "Wiseass."

Under the humor, Chad's discomfort was evident. Hollywood grabbed the bottom of Chad's jeans and ripped them off, then his super sexy trunks, leaving him gloriously naked. He gripped Chad's knees and, forcing them to bend, set his feet flat on the bed. Now he was perfectly positioned. Sinfully exposed. Hollywood's mouth watered. "God, you're beautiful."

Chad rolled his head to the side. "But am I enough? I mean, I don't have all the equipment you like."

Hollywood lovingly palmed Chad's balls with one hand and his long, thick cock with the other. "This cock," he said, "and these balls." He released Chad's sac and dragged his thumb along the taint to that perfect dusky star. "And this asshole, they're all the equipment I need."

Chad thrust his hips up, then back, his face contorting in pleasure as he fucked Hollywood's fist and pressed harder against the thumb probing his ass. Sucking in a deep breath, his fingers grappled with the bed sheets. "Are you sure?" The question held a hint of desperation.

Damn. Whatever Chad was hung up on, they had to sort it out before things went further. Removing his hand from Chad's crack and letting go of his cock was almost physically painful for Hollywood. Like getting a junkie to leave a line of coke on the table.

Christ no, that wasn't it. Chad was so much more than a drug to him. Chad was a part of him, and right now, he was hurting. Stretching out on the bed beside Chad, Hollywood stroked the chest that had become as familiar to him as his own. "What's going on?"

Twin flags of red appeared on Chad's cheeks and he looked away. "It's stupid."

"Not if it's bothering you. Come on, talk to me."

Chad stared at the ceiling. Hollywood didn't like that Chad wouldn't look at him, but if it helped him talk, he'd allow it. For now.

"So, a few bisexual friends I've had either kept hopping from one gender to another, never satisfied, never settling on one, or they wanted both at the same time."

"Like a threesome?" Hollywood asked, not at all opposed to the idea as long as the third wasn't another guy. Was that selfish of him?

"Like a triad."

Hollywood frowned. "What's that?"

"It's a relationship between three people where each has a relationship with the other two, and all are equal."

"Hmm." Hollywood didn't really know what to say about that. Relationships were difficult enough with two people; he couldn't imagine the mess when three people were involved.

"Is that something you're interested in?" Chad pressed.

"I've never thought about it." Hollywood gripped Chad's jaw and applied a little pressure so he'd turn his head to face him. "What's this all about, Chad?"

"What if you get bored with me?" Chad's voice shook. "What if I can't satisfy all your needs because you want pussy one day?"

"Babe, I don't think that's the way it works for me. I loved Isabel. Now I love you. Maybe I'm gay for you or maybe I just love who I love, regardless of that person's gender."

Chad smiled, and as it spread across his face, it raised sparks in Hollywood's chest, sparks that sizzled down to his cock. "So you won't drool every time you see a busty woman?"

"Hey now. I never said I wouldn't look."

Chad laughed and rolled on top of Hollywood, aligning their straining erections. With each thrust of his hips, his expression grew more serious, his eyes more blissful.

Hollywood loved the way Chad looked, the way he moved, the way his hips rolled in a smooth rhythm as though to music. What would it feel like to have Chad pumping his hard cock into his ass like that? His asshole clenched in response and Hollywood threw his head back. A powerful orgasm punched through him, warm cum slicking both their abs. Chad sat up as Hollywood gripped his ass cheeks and feathered his fingers over Chad's hole.

"Oh God!" Chad groaned and bowed his back. The tendons on his neck stretched and his jaw tightened until he shouted Hollywood's name and came in hot streams on Hollywood's chest.

What a sight.

On impulse, Hollywood scooped up a dollop of their combined cum on his finger and brought it to his lips. It tasted like both of them, and something else. Something beautiful, something he hoped to have forever.

Leaning over him, braced on his arms, Chad grinned. "You're such a dirty dog."

"Oh yeah?" Hollywood scooped some more up and painted it on Chad's mouth. "I dare you to wear this as lipstick." Silently, Chad swiveled his hips and ground against Hollywood's cock, licking his lips in the most sexual way Hollywood had ever seen. Hollywood hardened instantly, like a fucking sex-starved sixteen-year-old. "You like that?" he asked, feeling a little needy for wanting the reassurance.

"Love it."

Hollywood pulled Chad's head down for a taste. "Me too."

"Someday, I'm going to take you to Doymville, wearing this 'lipstick.' We'll dance, and you'll kiss it off me."

The idea was so dirty, so damned erotic, it made Hollywood's aching dick throb. In two seconds, he had Chad spun around in a sixty-nine and the man's cock in his mouth. Chad grunted and gasped as he swallowed Hollywood's erection and ground his ass on Hollywood's face.

This was heaven. This was nasty. And it was exactly what he loved most about sex with Chad. Nothing was too dirty. Nothing was too much. Nothing was off-limits. And soon, he'd prove it.

CHAPTER 25

After another round of quick showers that Hollywood insisted they had to take separately because he couldn't keep his hands to himself, they headed back to the hospital.

Chad stomach was a mass of roiling worms. It would probably be clear to anyone who saw them that they were together. Hollywood's eyes softened and he got this goofy expression every time he looked at Chad and thought no one was watching. If Chad had caught him doing it more than once, others would too. Under other circumstances he'd find it amusing. But what if the wrong person noticed and said something, how would Hollywood react? After everything they'd shared, the last thing he wanted was for Hollywood to have a relapse. It would kill Chad.

When Chad turned his roadster into the hospital parking lot, Hollywood squeezed his thigh. Chad bit back a groan. Even the slightest, most innocent touch made him hard if it came from Hollywood.

"Dude, we're meeting my parents."

"I know."

"You're giving me a hard-on."

Hollywood looked shocked for a few seconds, before bursting into laughter. "Sometimes I forget how fucking young you are."

"Fuck off. I'm not that young."

"You came twice, not even an hour ago, and my hand on your leg gets you revved up again? That's fucking young."

"Your hand was on my thigh! Besides," he added with a grin, "I've always had remarkable recovery time."

Hollywood arched a perfect blond brow. "We'll have to put that to the test."

The sneer, the seductive, challenging tone had Chad's I'm-slightly-turned-on go to I've-got-to-come-now in two seconds flat. "Fucker." Chad wiggled in his seat in the hopes of alleviating some of the pressure. It didn't work. He swung the car into the first empty spot and dropped his head onto the steering wheel. "Jesus Christ. I'm going to die."

"Nah." Hollywood jostled his shoulder. "You're a tough firefighter/paramedic. You'll survive." And with a smile that was way too satisfied, Hollywood got out of the car while Chad stayed behind doing math problems in his head. When he could finally breathe again, he adjusted his semi and got out to join Hollywood.

"Don't," he said when the guy turned to him. "Don't talk to me. Don't even look at me."

Hollywood chuckled.

"And for fuck's sake, don't laugh." That rumbling sound, like water bursting over rocks, always got him going. Frustrated, his balls aching, Chad beelined for the entrance.

They rode up the nine flights to the BICU in silence and when they got off the elevator, Hollywood followed several feet behind. "Too close," Chad called out.

Hollywood mumbled under his breath, "I'll show you too close," and entered the waiting room glued to Chad's side.

Conversations stopped, and everyone looked up. Hollywood gripped Chad's shirt in the middle of his back, where no one could see. "Shit," he said low enough that only Chad could hear.

Chad waved to his family. "Hey, everyone."

Behind him, Hollywood said a tight, "Afternoon."

His mother smiled indulgently, Jamie smirked knowingly, and Tori patted the chair next to her. Thankfully, there were two empty seats side by side. Once they were both settled, Chad scanned the room. Everyone was there. "Hollywood wanted to keep me company, since, you know, the police haven't…"

His father's spine straightened. "Have they said anything to you? I went down to the station earlier, but Detective Wong, who was assigned to the case, was in the field and no one would tell me anything."

"Not since they questioned me last night," Chad said. He glanced at Hollywood. "You?"

"Nothing."

A nurse came out and said two people could go visit Drew for five minutes. In an hour, two more could go. It was going to be a long afternoon and evening.

"Want to get some coffee?" Hollywood asked.

Sensing how uncomfortable he was surrounded by curious Caldwells and significant others, Chad nodded. "Sure. Anyone else want anything?"

William and Dani decided to go for a walk outside, while Erica,

Jamie, and Tori said they'd stay in the waiting area. Because of Erica's condition and the fact that Chloe was at home with a babysitter, it had been decided that she and Jamie would be next to see Drew.

After getting their coffee from the cafeteria, Chad and Hollywood headed back, walking slowly since there was no need to hurry. An out of uniform police officer stopped in front of them. "Lieutenant Wright, I'm Detective Wong. May I have a word?"

"Sure." Hollywood crossed his arms, but didn't move.

"In private?"

Hollywood turned to Chad, searching his face as though for permission. Then like he'd found it, he smiled. "This is my boyfriend, Chad Caldwell. Anything you have to say to me, you can say in front of him."

The detective flipped through his notebook. "Chadric Caldwell, one of the paramedics on scene?"

"Yes. I gave my statement to the officer last night."

"You've been getting hang-up calls and your vehicle was vandalized."

"He was also attacked last August," Hollywood said, anger charging his words and posture. "The trap last night was set for him."

Chad patted his arm.

"Your... uh... relationship, is it new?" Detective Wong asked.

"Why does that matter?" Hollywood shot back hotly.

"We're trying to establish means, motive, and opportunity."

"Motive is pretty obvious. These guys went after Chad because he's gay," Hollywood challenged.

"Why him and not you? Why not any of the other LGBTQ members of the community? Why an SFD paramedic?"

"All good questions," Chad said. "Got any answers? Because this has been going on long enough and now people are getting hurt." It wasn't just about him anymore.

"Sam Hoover, the GSW victim, provided us with a few leads. We caught one of the men who set the explosion."

"What?" A wave of relief rolled over Chad.

"Don't get too excited," Detective Wong cautioned. "The perp and his boys are two-bit hustlers. They don't do anything if it isn't for money."

"What are you saying?" Chad's head started to buzz.

Could someone really hate him so much they'd hire street thugs to kill him?

80 🚆 ⊂Ջ

Face pale, hands shaking, Chad stared at the detective. Hollywood took the cup of steaming coffee from Chad's hands before he burned himself and set it on the floor. Cradling his boyfriend's cheeks, he said,

"Hey, nothing's going to happen to you."

Not as long as I'm alive.

Not caring who might see, he put his arm around Chad's shoulder. "Detective, please catch whoever is behind this before they come after Chad again."

He held the man's gaze, infusing as much of his determination into it as he could.

The detective nodded. "Deputy Chief Wright is your father?"

"Yes."

"If you see him, can you ask him to call me? We've been trying to talk to everyone involved with the Technical Rescue Team as well as Medic One, but some of the higher-ups have been difficult to pin down."

"My father and I aren't exactly close," Hollywood said, stiffening at the mere memory of the man's smug face when he'd been yelling at Chad. If ever there'd been a time to stand up for himself and for Chad that had been it. Given the chance for a redo, he wouldn't waste it. He'd tell his good-for-nothing father all the reasons he never wanted to see him again.

"Still, if you run into him, have him call me." The detective handed Hollywood a business card before walking away.

"Wow." Chad picked his cup of coffee off the floor. "At least they're taking it seriously this time."

"Yeah." But was it only because others were involved?

Chad had grown up gay, out and proud. He'd also suffered through years of being discriminated against and having to choose his battles, because there were so many. Hollywood hadn't. Due to his size and reputation, people had always shown him respect and acted upon his authority. He wouldn't allow his sexual preferences to change that. He was too old to accept being treated differently or, worse, being ignored, as normal. When he came out at work, if anyone sneered at him or insulted him, they'd be dealing with the business end of his fist.

Chad was by far the bigger man. With Hollywood, there'd be no turning the other cheek.

⁜ 🍸 ⁝

They stopped by Liam's room and learned that an exhausted Anna had finally gone home with Liam's brother, Karl, after spending the night and most of the day at her husband's bedside. "You have an amazing wife, my friend," Chad said, pulling up a chair next to Liam's bed.

"Man, don't I know it. I had to send her home though. All this worrying and being around germs isn't good for the baby."

Chad smiled at his friend's concern. Fresh out of surgery, he was more worried about his wife than he was about himself. Chad glanced at

Hollywood lounging against the wall and knew he'd feel exactly the same way. Smiling, he turned back to Liam. "You look a lot better than you did last night. How are you feeling?"

He still had a cardiac monitor and several IVs connected to him, but he was reclining in his bed and alert, even though his eyes looked a little glazed from the painkillers. Best of all, his skin was now a pale pink. "I'm feeling alive, and that's all that matters. When the explosion went off, my life flashed before my eyes, and I thought I was a goner." His voice roughened. "But you got me out."

Chad blushed. "Actually, Hollywood did. He took charge and got us all moving."

"Thank you, Lieutenant," Liam said warmly. He seemed to be thawing a bit with respect to Hollywood. Maybe Anna had put in a good word. "How's Drew?"

"I haven't seen him yet. My turn is in about two hours. But the doctors are optimistic he'll make a full recovery. It'll be a long tough road though."

"I'm so sorry, Chad."

Chad coughed to clear the frog in his throat. "He saved my life, Liam. That beam was coming down right on top me."

"He's your brother. He loves you."

"I know. But look at how much it's costing him. Costing you. Even that poor kid, Sam. None of you had anything to do with this." Hollywood's strong hand gripped his neck. Chad choked back his emotions. He needed to quit complaining and be strong for his friend and his brother. He shouldn't make this about him—even if it was. "Sorry. I'm being a whiny bitch again."

"You get five minutes every shift. Remember our deal?"

Hollywood snorted. "You seriously have a deal about that?"

"Damn right," Liam said. "Before we struck that agreement, he'd go on and on and on… Every shift was like an episode of *Jersey Shore*."

"Hmm… maybe we need a deal like that too," Hollywood teased.

"Fuck you. Fuck you, both." Chad laughed and exchanged a grin with Liam. The bond he had with his partner was similar to the one firefighters on a platoon had, but, in some ways, it was even stronger because shift after shift, it was just the two of them alone, in the ambulance, going on calls and saving lives. Despite how very different they were, their friendship worked.

"So," Liam said, eyeing him and Hollywood. "Everything good with you two?"

Chad felt himself flush, and he shot Hollywood a worried glance. Would Hollywood be upset that he'd told Liam about them? He rose uncertainly, trying to come up with a good way to backtrack on what he'd told Liam, before making a quick exit with Hollywood in tow.

His heart skipped a beat when Hollywood stepped up behind him so his chin rested on Chad's head, his arm across Chad's chest. The move was casual and almost natural and it filled Chad's heart with a joy so deep, it was almost more than he could handle.

"I apologized for being an ass and Chad forgave me."

Chad craned his head around to look at Hollywood and the heat in the guy's green eyes melted his trunks. Hollywood's arm tightened, pulling Chad even more fully against that big hard body, where he could feel every inch of Hollywood's considerable bulge.

Liam laughed, pressing a hand against his side. "From the looks on your faces, I'd say he did more than forgive you."

%) 🚆 (%

Hollywood walked beside Chad as they made their way through the hospital maze to the gift shop, so Chad could get something for Drew. "I don't want to go in there empty-handed, you know?"

"Yeah, I know." Chad was anxious to see his brother. Anxious to see that he'd be all right. Unnecessary guilt was eating at Chad, and Hollywood vowed to do his best to rid him of it.

After Chad had picked out a few bodybuilding and martial arts magazines and selected some candy bars, they headed out Hollywood checked his watch. "There's still a little time before your turn. Want to get some air?"

"That sounds good."

They exited the hospital and located a bench in the sun. Hollywood cracked open the bottle of water he'd purchased and offered it to Chad, who took a long drink before handing it back and resting his head on Hollywood's shoulder. "This is nice," Chad said.

And it was. The morning's clouds were gone, leaving a bright blue sky, and a gentle breeze carried the promise of an early spring.

A few minutes later, the soft sound of Chad's snoring, already so familiar, cut Hollywood to the core. He wanted to hear it every night and every morning. He wanted to hold Chad against his heart as they slept. After taking a quick glance around, he raised his arm and pulled Chad against him. Chad made a snuffling sound, then smiled and sank deeper in Hollywood's embrace.

The moment was so pure, so magical, Hollywood would remember it forever. Remember it as the turning point in their relationship. He loved Chad, and Chad loved him. They'd already made their declarations. Now it was time to put his money where his mouth was. Today, they'd told Liam they were together. Hopefully soon, they'd tell the rest of Chad's family, then their friends and colleagues. It wouldn't be easy for

Hollywood, but to be with Chad, he'd do it. One person at a time, until he was comfortable with it.

Hollywood had told Chad how he felt about him, but he hadn't shown him that publicly. No wonder the guy didn't fully believe or trust that he was one-hundred-percent on board. But that was going to change. The first chance they got, Hollywood was taking Chad on a date. The man deserved to be wined and dined and showered with gifts.

His thoughts screeched to a halt. Was he doing what Chad had accused him of before he'd called things off? Was he thinking of Chad as the woman in the relationship? Well, shit. What did he know about what a guy would like?

It was one of those *doh!* moments, and Hollywood would have smacked his forehead if he hadn't been afraid to wake Chad. His boyfriend—Hollywood's ears burned red at the thought—was a man's man, even if he occasionally wore makeup and nail polish. He enjoyed action movies and dramas, he enjoyed drinking beer and eating wings at the pub, just as much as he enjoyed wine and cheese at a soirée with his friends. Maybe he'd enjoy going to the local art show next weekend. It would be a way for Hollywood to introduce Chad to that part of his life, one none of his friends knew about, not even Jamie.

He laid his cheek on top of Chad's head, taking the scent of his shampoo deep inside his lungs. Sighing, he tightened his hold and kissed the soft skin at the back of Chad's cleanly shaven neck, enjoying this moment of quiet in the midst of all the chaos. That's when he realized that with everything that had happened at the ball and afterwards, he still hadn't wished Chad a happy new year. Unable to resist the draw of Chad's earlobe, he nibbled it and whispered, "Happy New Year, babe."

Chad rubbed his cheek on Hollywood's shirt and cracked open a gorgeous blue eye. "Happy New Year to you too, Nate. We sure blew this holiday season, but we'll do better next time around."

Hollywood's heart swelled. He hoped he'd be able to spend next New Year's Eve dancing with Chad instead of drowning his sorrows in alcohol. Before he could respond further, Jamie raced up the pathway from the parking lot. The corner of his mouth quirked when he saw them. Hollywood wasn't sure whether he should be proud or embarrassed, so he decided to be proud and a grin spread across his face. Looking amused, Jamie shook his head.

"So how is Drew?" Hollywood asked softly.

"He's in a lot of pain from the burns and the surgery. At least that went well." Jamie's face looked haggard and he rubbed his neck. "I wish there was something I could do for him."

"Believe me. I know what you mean," Chad said.

"Hey now," Hollywood jumped in before the brothers could take this conversation down an even more depressing route. "You're both here. That's all any of us can do right now. He's getting the best medical care available, and he has the support of a loving family."

Chad shot him a grateful look and thumped his knee. "You're right. We need to stay positive."

"Buck up, Chad. Your turn's next. By the way, shouldn't you be heading up there right about now?" Jamie said, glancing at his watch.

"Oh crap!" Chad grabbed his bag of surprises for Drew and bussed Hollywood on the lips. The kiss was short but sweet. "Meet me upstairs?"

"Yeah." Hollywood laughed, certain Chad hadn't heard him. He was already through the sliding hospital doors.

Jamie swore, and that's when Hollywood noticed the pale yellow sweater he held. "Damn. I wanted him to bring this up. It's my mom's. She'll need it later when it gets chilly."

"Always the protector." Hollywood smiled at his friend and took the sweater. "Is Erica in the car?"

"Yeah. We need to get home to Chloe. She has a special tea party planned for us."

"Sounds nice, man." It really did. Some days, Hollywood envied his friend's life. Not in the sense that he wanted to take it away from Jamie, just that he'd like to have the same. Did Chad want children? They'd never discussed it.

"Hey," Jamie said, interrupting his introspection. "Doesn't your dad drive an old baby blue Cadillac DeVille?"

Hollywood grimaced at the reminder that his father drove what basically amounted to a pimp mobile. The car was so distinctive that all the cops and firefighters in the downtown and SoDo districts knew it on sight. He stood and searched the parking lot in the direction Jamie was pointing. "Yeah. That's it. I wonder what he's doing here."

"Checking on Drew maybe?" Chad volunteered.

Since his father was the deputy chief for Battalion 5, it wasn't out of the realm of possibility. Fishing out the card the detective had given him last night, he dialed the number. "Detective Wong, this is Lieutenant Nathanial Wright. You were looking for my dad? Well, his car is here at Harborview."

"Thank you, Lieutenant." There was a muffled sound as though the detective had covered the phone, then he came back. "Is Chadric Caldwell at the hospital as well?"

"He's at the BICU, visiting his brother Drew."

"Are you with him right now?"

A tingle of unease began in Hollywood's gut. "No. Detective, what's this about?"

"We've uncovered evidence suggesting that the person or persons who hired the men who ambushed Medic 11 had at least one man on the inside. Someone fairly high-ranking in the fire service who could have arranged to have Medic 11 sent to that particular call."

Each damning word stabbed at Hollywood, until, light-headed, he had to grip the back of the bench to keep from falling. Jamie grabbed his arm to steady him. "What's going on?" he asked.

"Lieutenant?"

The detective's sharp tone brought him back. He shook his head, unable to believe the reality that was cementing with each new bit of information. His father was dating a woman who worked dispatch. "Was Marjorie Delaney working dispatch last night?"

Jamie stared at him, his muscles vibrating as he struggled to understand the one-sided conversation. There was a shuffling of papers in the background, then the detective confirmed his fears. "Yes, she was on from eleven until seven this morning."

What kind of evil tried to kill someone because of who they loved?

His father apparently.

Anger welled from deep within him. His own father had tried to kill Chad. But this shit ended today. Deputy Chief Wright would never get another chance to hurt Chad. "I have to go." Ending the call, he shoved the phone into his back pocket and turned for the hospital entrance. He had to catch his father before he made it up to the burn center.

Jamie caught his shoulder, whipping Hollywood around. Rage radiated off Jamie's tense body. "What's going on? Do they know who did it?"

"Someone on the inside." Hollywood's voice broke. "I think it was my dad."

"Your dad? Fucking shit." Jamie sprinted through the sliding doors of the entrance. Hollywood took off after his friend. People coming for afternoon visitation crowded in front of the elevators.

"Stairs!" Hollywood shouted, taking a sharp right. They raced up the nine flights. Hollywood had never been so thankful for all the training they did wearing seventy pounds of gear. In his regular clothes, he felt like Usain Bolt.

Desperation egged him on, and in record time, he charged onto the burn center floor, dashing frantically left and right, trying to catch a glimpse of his father.

"This way," Jamie shouted. Adrenaline laced with panic spread throughout Hollywood's body when he realized Jamie was headed for the BICU instead of the waiting room. Surely his father wouldn't go after Chad while he was visiting Drew.

Jamie's eyes were narrowed, determined. Hollywood's heart raced and his feet pounded down the hall, his need to make sure Chad was safe overpowering, all-consuming.

Pulling ahead of Jamie, he entered the BICU. The frantic activity at the nurses' station told him Jamie's instinct had been right. "He's here."

"Goddamn motherfucker." Jamie grab an adjustable IV stand. He quickly loosened the knob and yanked out the top half of the pole to use as a makeshift weapon. Hollywood did the same with another stand.

Quietly, they moved down the hallway to the corner room assigned to Drew.

"Shut the fuck up, you goddamn fag."

Hollywood's step faltered. His father was definitely in there. "Wait," he whispered harshly, catching Jamie around the waist to keep him from charging in like a bull. "We have to be smart about this."

"My mom and brothers are in there!"

"I know." Hollywood shoved Jamie against the wall. "And my son of a bitch father wants to kill the love of my life." His voice turned gruff as realization set in. "I know."

A furious Jamie held his gaze, then he let out a breath, and his shoulders deflated. "What's your plan?"

"I'll go in there. Alone. I'm sure he's waiting for me to show up. He wants me to see what he does to Chad."

Jamie's fists curled and his voice grew even harder. "He lays one finger on "

"I'll kill him first," Hollywood said, meaning the words more than he'd ever meant anything. If he'd stood up to his father before, none of this would be happening. He inhaled deeply. "I'll go in. Get him to talk. Maybe get him to let your mom out. I'll signal to Chad. We'll tackle him, then you come in and help us keep him down."

Jamie shook his head. "What if he has a weapon?"

A weapon? Shit. "New plan. I'll go in. Cause a distraction. You sneak in and knock him out. Better?"

The muscles in Jamie's shoulders rippled. "Okay."

Hollywood loosened up his tense arms by shaking them out, then pasted what he hoped passed for a friendly smile on his face. With a casual stride, he walked into the hospital room. "Hey, Drew. How're you feeling, man?"

He forced himself to keep walking, even after seeing Chad standing in front of his father with a gun pointed at his chest. Caroline was bent over the bed, protecting Drew with her body. Her face was white with fury. Drew seemed to be sleeping. Thank God.

The room smelled like a distillery, and it was obvious who'd been indulging. Tightening his abs to keep from puking, Hollywood inserted himself between Chad and the gun. "Dad. What're you doing here?" After this, he'd deserve an award for his acting skills.

"Came to finish the job." His father spat on the ground. "Can't find decent help these days."

"What job is that, Dad?"

His father went to shove him out of the way, but Hollywood refused to budge. Chad was not getting hurt again on his watch.

"Move," his father barked.

"Talk to me, Dad. What's going on?"

His father lifted up onto his toes and raised the gun high, waving it in Chad's direction. "I have to take care of everything myself."

"Take care of what?" If he kept his father talking, it would be easier for Jamie to sneak in. Chad came to stand beside him. His features were hard and angry, but when their eyes met, Chad also seemed very much in control. That's when Hollywood remembered Chad's own martial arts training. Chad's gaze flicked to the gun, and he stepped in front of Hollywood.

No, no, no! He'd rather die than let his father hurt Chad.

"Come on, Chief. Whatcha got to say to me, huh?" Chad taunted.

"This is all your fault. You turned my son into a fag."

Chad snorted. "I'm pretty sure that happened a long time ago." He moved a few feet to the left, away from Drew and his mother, forcing Hollywood's dad to follow.

"Stop moving!" his dad yelled.

"What's the matter? Can't keep up with the homo, Chief?" Chad laughed, then he sneered. "You need a gun to face me. Who's the pussy now?"

Hearing Chad challenge his father took ten years off Hollywood's life. His father's hand was shaking and the gun waved wildly. He had to do something.

"Dad, you know none of this is about Chad. You said so yourself. You and Mom knew I was different even when I was little."

At the mention of his mother, his father's eyes started to glisten.

"You miss her, don't you, Dad? I miss her too."

"She was so beautiful. The kindest woman, even after she got sick." He wiped at his eyes with the back of his hand. "She was so proud of you." Hollywood stepped closer. His father didn't even seem to notice. "I wanted you to grow up to be the man she wanted you to be: a husband and a father."

Realization dawned. "That's why you beat me?" Hollywood asked.

"If I could make you normal, her dreams for you would come true."

Christ. All these years of fighting, of hating each other, simply because his father wanted to see his dying wife's wishes fulfilled. But his father's memory differed from his own. "Before she died, Mom told me she'd love me no matter what. That she was proud of me and always would be."

"She didn't know what you are," his father spat, his voice growing hard again.

"I think she did know. Remember she bought me the drawing paper, the pencils, and watercolors? We used to dress up and dance to Boy George and Elton John. She *knew*, Dad."

"No. You're lying. None of that ever happened." He pointed the gun at Hollywood's chest. "I can't save you now. It's too late."

Before Hollywood knew what was happening, Chad jumped up into the air and kicked the gun out of his father's grip. Hollywood lunged for his legs and tackled him to the ground. Jamie sprang up out of nowhere and landed on his father's chest at the same time. The old man struggled for a moment, then Jamie rolled him over and quickly tied his hands behind his back with a belt.

Hollywood watched, then nodded in approval. "I guess that kinky stuff comes in handy sometimes."

Jamie ground his teeth. "If I'd known you were going to be a dick about it, I'd have let him shoot you."

"Well, I wouldn't have," Chad said. "You okay, babe?" He pressed against Hollywood's back, wrapping his arms around him, and kissed his neck. "I was so fucking scared when I saw him turn that gun on you."

Hollywood covered Chad's arms with his own and turned to kiss his man, his hero. "You didn't look scared, Mr. Lee."

Chad laughed. "I noticed Jamie by the door. That's when I knew we could take him down without anyone getting hurt. I just had to get that gun away from him."

Hollywood stood and pulled Chad into a hug. "I love you so fucking much." He squeezed him really hard. "But never do that again."

"Can't. Breathe."

Everyone laughed. Chad's mother embraced them both and Jamie joined in. Until they heard a croaky voice from the bed. "What about me?"

The group hug moved to the bed where they carefully included Drew.

"You all make me sick," Hollywood's father muttered from where he squirmed on the floor.

Chad stiffened next to him. Hollywood patted his arm. "I've got this."

On the table beside Drew's bed was a roll of surgical tape the nurses had used to secure his dressings. Hollywood grabbed it and went to kneel beside his father. "You know what I think? Mom would be proud of me. Proud that I found a family like the Caldwells to show me how to love. Proud that I found a guy like Chad to show me how to be a man. Those are all the things Mom wanted you to do, Dad. She loved me and she loved you. But I doubt she'd care for the man you've become. Think about that while you're sitting in prison doing time for multiple counts of attempted murder."

When his father opened his mouth to respond, Hollywood slapped a piece of tape over his lips. "Save it for the cops."

CHAPTER 26

Drawn by the great view outside Chad's floor-to-ceiling windows, Hollywood leaned against the glass and sighed. They'd had a hell of a week. Chad had taken time off work to be with Drew and Liam, while Hollywood had spent every nonwork hour supporting Chad and Jamie. But Liam would be going home in a week or so and Drew's prognosis was good, even though he'd have to spend several more weeks, maybe even a month, at the hospital.

Tonight though, it was only the two of them. And Hollywood meant to take full advantage of their first evening alone in forever. He was going to give Chad a surprise. The thought of turning the tables on the guy had been with him all week. Longer than that, if he were being honest. He just had to be brave enough to do it.

When he heard the shower turn off, he plugged his iPod into the docking station of Chad's stereo and selected one of his favorite songs. As the first smooth beats came over the speakers, Hollywood closed his eyes and remembered how Chad had danced when he'd performed at Bar None. He raised his arms above his head and did his best to mimic Chad's slow sexy sway, undulating his hips in time with the music.

A groan interrupted his thoughts.

He opened his eyes to find Chad standing before him. The towel at his waist tented over his growing erection. Hollywood smirked and began playing with the lyrics to Ria Mae's hit, "Clothes Off."

"What're you doing, Chad? We're wasting time."

Chad's pupils dilated. His chest heaved. "Take your clothes off."

Hollywood smirked, loving the effect he was having on his man. He grabbed the back of his T-shirt and slowly pulled it up.

Licking his lips, Chad advanced on him. "Why are you taking so long?"

The sound of Chad's singing voice, deeper and gruffer than usual, had Hollywood's cock aching. "Care to help?"

Immediately, Chad was on his knees, undoing Hollywood's fly and tugging his jeans and boxers down his legs. Hollywood's erection sprang out, almost touching Chad's shiny lips. The heat of Chad's breath hit the tip of Hollywood's cock moments before he took it in his mouth.

Sensation flooded Hollywood as he sank further into that delicious warmth. The sight of Chad at his feet, his gorgeous lips pulled tight around Hollywood's cock, nearly did him in. His balls drew up and Hollywood had to pull Chad off him before he came. He gripped Chad's shoulders, panting harshly as he tried to regain his control. Tonight, he wanted more, so much more.

Chad shot him a confused look.

"Bedroom." Hollywood's voice was raw with arousal. He kicked free of the tether of jeans and boxers around his ankles and took Chad's hand, helping him to his feet. The towel slid off Chad's hips, revealing his thick cock. The mushroom head was dark and pre-cum dribbled from his slit.

Hollywood couldn't resist. Bending down, he gripped Chad's shaft and swallowed the crown, licking up every drop and moaning at the taste he'd never get enough of. Again, he had to remind himself of his goal. He pulled back, and after placing an open-mouthed kiss on the tip, he stood and led Chad to the bedroom.

But as they approached the big king-size bed, apprehension began to knot his stomach. Could he go through with this? Hanging his head, he rubbed the back of his neck.

"Hey, babe." Chad ran a hand over Hollywood's chest. "What's wrong?"

Fuck. Hollywood was going to ruin everything if he didn't man up. He'd accused Chad of not being frank about his needs, and now he was doing the same thing. If he wanted this relationship to work, he had to communicate.

He kissed Chad, then held his cheek, forcing himself to focus on Chad's concerned blue eyes. "I want..." He broke off and swallowed. "I want to bottom tonight, but I'm... a little..."

"Scared?"

Hollywood nodded.

"That's a pretty normal emotion to have when you're considering letting someone stick something as big as"—Chad palmed his cock and shot Hollywood a salacious grin—"this up your ass. If you weren't at least a little scared, *I'd* be worried."

"Jesus." Hollywood barked out a laugh. "You're a sweet talker, aren't you?"

They exchanged a smile, then Chad's expression turned serious. "You don't have to do this, you know. I'm happy to be the bottom in this relationship."

Hollywood ran his tongue over Chad's lips, lapping at the corners. "I know. But I've—" He broke off as memories of his dreams swamped him. Dreams of Chad slipping into him, using his powerful hips to drive into Hollywood, filling him, taking him. Owning him. A shudder wracked him. *Christ.*

"You've what? You can tell me anything, Nate."

"I've dreamt about it. I want it. I want to know what it feels like to take someone—you—into my body like that."

Chad flushed and his cock jumped against Hollywood's thigh. "Keep talking like that and this thing won't be happening at all."

"So." Hollywood hated how hesitant he felt. He stiffened his spine. "I want you to fuck me. You good with that?"

Chad pushed him down onto the bed. "Fucking A." Like a panther closing in on its prey, he moved up Hollywood's body, nibbling at his flesh, tasting it with his tongue, before lowering his weight completely on top of him.

Hollywood sucked in a breath. *Christ,* he loved that feeling. Loved how big Chad was. How strong. How *heavy.* All that warm naked flesh sliding on his own, that hot hard cock grinding on his, was pure heaven. He gritted his teeth against the fresh wave of arousal that washed over him, but a low moan slipped out anyway. Chad made his fucking head spin. "I need you, man."

"Patience, young padawan."

Hollywood groaned. "Bastard."

Chad pulled open the drawer of the nightstand beside the bed and pulled out a tube of lubricant and a condom. Hollywood eyed the shiny package. "We need that?"

"The lube?" Chad held up the tube. "Yeah, man. I don't want to hurt you."

"I meant the condom."

Chad's brows shot up. "You serious?"

"I've always used condoms, and I get tested every couple of months. The last time was in November."

"Me too."

Looking up into the eyes of the man he loved, the only man he would ever love, Hollywood nodded. "I'm serious about you, Chad. I don't want anyone else."

Still straddling his hips, Chad straightened. "Giving up condoms is a big deal. A commitment. Are you ready for that, Nate?"

"I'm about to let you put your giant cock in my ass. I'd say I'm committed." Hollywood squeezed his stomach muscles and sat up so he was at eye level with Chad. "I want to be with you *all* the time. And not just in bed." When Chad continued his dubious stare, Hollywood drew Chad into the circle of his arms and kissed him tenderly, trying to express everything he was feeling. "This is more than sex. I love you, and I can't imagine a future without you in it. I want to be your boyfriend. Hell, someday, I hope to be your husband and even fucking have babies with you."

Chad laughed and choked on a sob. His eyes glistened as he leaned his forehead on Hollywood's. "We'll need help with the babies part, but, hell yeah, I want that too."

"So no condoms?"

"No condoms."

Hollywood felt Chad's smile against his lips before he was pushed back onto the bed. Chad sat between his legs and pushed his feet closer to his butt, forcing him to bend his knees. "This part, you're a little familiar with," he said, as he dribbled some lube on his finger and smoothed it over Hollywood's hole.

The lube was cold at first, but quickly warmed up with Chad's rubbing. "Oh, man." It felt so fucking good. Instinctively, he pushed against the finger and it slipped inside. The slight burning sensation he remembered from the last time Chad had done this was quickly replaced with the joy of being stretched.

Chad pulled out, applied more lube and returned. "Two fingers now." The burn was stronger, but so was the stretch. He crooned soothingly, fucking Hollywood's hole. When Chad leaned over and took his mouth in a dirty kiss with lots of tongue, shivers raced up Hollywood's spine. Kissing had never been his thing before, but Chad's demanding, dominating assault really turned him on.

"You're doing great, babe." Chad slid down his body a little and teased Hollywood's nipples with his teeth.

Hollywood writhed, grunting and moaning. Chad slid his fingers in deep and Hollywood felt a zing go through him as Chad found his prostate. "Oh fuuuck." His entire body erupted with goose bumps.

The stretching sensation increased, the burn grew. His gaze flew to Chad's.

Chad's hand stopped moving. "Too much?"

"N-no."

"Good, because my cock's a lot bigger than three fingers."

Three. He hadn't even noticed when Chad had gone from two to three. He'd only noticed the pressure, which even now was giving him more pleasure than pain. Chad rotated his fingers as though seeking out every inch of Hollywood's passage. Each touch sent sensation pouring into Hollywood's cock.

Lifting up his head, he took in the sight of Chad intent on preparing him for what was to come. Lust-filled eyes were focused on Hollywood's ass, on where Chad's fingers scissored and worked to opened him. The chiseled chest heaved with each deep breath and starkly defined abdominal muscles rippled with each movement of his hand. When Hollywood's gaze dropped lower, he was nearly overcome by the stream of pre-cum that leaked down the side of Chad's shaft, making it glisten in the dimmed light on the nightstand.

He wanted that beautiful cock. Wanted it driving into him. Wanted it pounding him into the mattress.

"Now…" he ground out through clenched teeth.

Chad's gaze snapped to his face.

"Need you."

Nodding, Chad squeezed more lubricant from the tube and slicked it over his straining erection. Hollywood's mouth watered. He dropped his head onto the pillow and dug his fingers into the sheets on either side of him. He couldn't keep his hips from rocking in anticipation.

"Relax, Nate." Chad's voice, so sure and confident, eased Hollywood, and his hands loosened their grip on the bedding. The fingers rubbing more lube into his hole didn't hurt either. Chad pushed up onto his knees, gripped Hollywood's thighs and lined his cock up. "Last chance to change your mind."

Hollywood bared his teeth.

Chad chuckled. "Right."

A presence at his hole made itself known. Skin soft as silk. A cock hard as a pipe. Chad shifted and the pressure grew. Hollywood's chest tightened as he tried to suck air into his lungs.

"Push out and breathe."

Doing as he was told, Hollywood let out a long breath. The burning increased. Christ, it hurt worse than he'd imagined. Sweat beaded on his forehead.

Chad snapped his hips, and as soon as he was inside, all motion ceased. "You okay?" His face was tense, his voice rough. Each muscle held immobile by the sheer strength of his will. Hollywood had never appreciated the guy more.

He filled his lungs several times, focusing on the stretch instead of the pain. On the alien sensation of being filled. Of having Chad inside his body. Of being one.

His hips lifted, and Chad, smart man that he was, got the message. With small thrusts, he inched his way in deeper and deeper until their balls were snuggled together. Hollywood almost laughed at the thought.

Christ, he was such a sap.

Once he was fully seated, Chad lowered himself onto Hollywood and smiled. "How do you feel?"

"So fucking full."

"In a bad way?"

Hollywood arched a brow. Chad had to feel the throbbing of his cock against his abs. Abs that were ridged like a washboard. Ridges that rubbed along Hollywood's shaft with every breath the guy took. Hollywood hissed and Chad grinned wickedly. Oh the guy knew all right.

Two could play that game. Hollywood tensed his glutes and was rewarded by the reddening of Chad's cheeks and his suddenly ragged breathing.

Chad grabbed Hollywood's wrists and slammed his hands onto the bed at shoulder height. His lips closed over Hollywood's and his tongue searched out the depths of Hollywood's mouth, exploring every nook and cranny. When he was done, Hollywood was breathless. Boneless.

"Fucker."

"After tonight you're going to know why I take that as a compliment." Eyes glinting, Chad rose up on his knees. He began rocking his hips. The pace was slow at first, something for which Hollywood was grateful. But soon Hollywood's hips were pushing up, grinding against Chad as he sought to rub his cock on those hard muscles. Chad shifted and increased the pace. He drove into Hollywood, deep strokes that proved who was the boss, who was in control, and it sure as fuck wasn't Hollywood.

"You're mine." Chad punctuated his words with a hard thrust that pegged Hollywood's prostate just right.

Hollywood arched his spine, seeking more of the exquisite pleasure that had his eyes rolling back. "Oh God." Chad changed his rhythm. That's when Hollywood became aware of the music. His playlist had completed and Ria Mae's song was playing again.

Chad was dancing.

His hips undulated and rotated, lifting, lowering and swirling, in a sinuous motion that never started and never ended. The tension in the pit of Hollywood's belly grew, whirling and tightening with each note, with each slow thrust. Their eyes met and held.

Chad wasn't fucking him anymore. They were making love.

"You're mine," Chad said again.

Hollywood smiled, more certain than he'd ever been of anything. "I'm yours."

When he tugged lightly on his restrained arms, Chad immediately released him. Hollywood grabbed Chad's head and pulled him down into a heated embrace. They kept their eyes on each other. Hollywood held out as long as he could, but when Chad leaned down and whispered,

"Now," just before biting his earlobe, Hollywood could do nothing other than give in to the pleasure. Chad snapped his hips, hitting him exactly right, and Hollywood's world exploded.

Chad continued to move in slow easy strokes, increasing the duration of Hollywood's orgasm until he lay limp, completely spent. "Christ, you're good at this."

"It's my turn now."

"It's your—?" Hollywood's eyes widened, and Chad laughed.

Rising up, he slid his hands under Hollywood's knees and lifted his ass up higher onto his thighs. With biceps bulging, he grinned. "Hold on."

As Chad pistoned into him, shoving him higher and higher on the bed, Hollywood grabbed hold of the headboard and pushed back. Testosterone flared and unbelievably, his cock twitched and began to fill again. Jesus.

He freed his legs and wrapped them around Chad's hips, impaling himself on that fat cock he'd grown to love almost more than his own. Sweat dripped off Chad's chin and landed with a plop on Hollywood's stomach, mixing in with his cum from earlier. It reminded him of the dare he'd teased Chad with last week. He swirled his finger in the mix, but this time, he painted his own lips.

Chad groaned. "Oh fuck."

He pried Hollywood's legs from around his waist, then flipped him onto his stomach.

"What the—?" Hollywood gawped, not used to being manhandled by his lovers. Before he could gather his thoughts, Chad pulled him up onto his knees.

His hands gripped Hollywood's ass, spreading the cheeks. "I fucking love this ass." He blew on the tender skin.

"Oh God." Hollywood moaned at the sensation of cool air hitting his hole. His arms shook as need consumed him. "More. Holy fuck. Give me more."

Chad's hand came down in a firm swat on his butt cheek. Yelping, Hollywood glared at him over his shoulder. Chad only grinned. "No bossy bottoms." Then with one swift push of his hips, he entered Hollywood from behind. Keeping Hollywood impaled with a strong grip on his shoulder, Chad reached around and grabbed Hollywood's now rock-hard cock. He started to jack him off with a firm hand.

Hollywood had never been at the mercy of anyone in bed, but Christ was he ever loving it. In Chad's arms, he was finally safe. "Faster," he shouted as unbearable pleasure tore through his body. Chad increased both his thrusting and his stroking. Hollywood felt the pulse of Chad's cock deep inside him. The foreignness of it, the *rightness* of it, sent him over the edge. Again.

Powerful hands gripped Hollywood's hips, holding him steady as Chad thrust twice more, then shouted. "Nate! Oh fuck...!"

Seconds later, Chad collapsed onto Hollywood's back, pinning him down on the mattress.

For several long minutes, Hollywood reveled in the sound of Chad's heavy breathing in his ears, the tickle of Chad's lips pressing small kisses on his shoulder, and the scent of Chad's cologne invading his senses. He hid a smile in the pillow, knowing what was coming.

Soon Chad rolled off Hollywood's back and settled onto his side, propped up on an elbow. He grinned proudly. "So, on a scale of one to ten?"

Hollywood couldn't hold it in anymore. He burst into laughter. Roared even harder when Chad's grin morphed into a disgruntled frown.

Chad huffed. "You don't have to be an ass about it."

Hollywood howled, stopping only when Chad tried to smother him with a pillow. He rolled over onto the guy, loving that they could roughhouse like this. That Chad was big enough and strong enough to take his weight. He cupped that stubbled jaw between his hands and smiled. "Twelve. It was a fucking twelve." Anyone who could make him come twice in one hour deserved to gloat.

Pride filled his lover's eyes and his lips curved into that sexy half smile. "So, should I get you that 'I would bottom for you so hard' T-shirt we saw at the sex shop on Pike Street?"

"Fucker."

Chad blew on his nails and rubbed them on his shoulder. "Like I said—"

Hollywood sat up and tossed the pillow at his head, then grinned. "Fuck yeah. Get me that damn shirt."

Harry's story continues in *Going All In*, the first book in the Men of Boyzville series. Read on for a special scorching hot preview!

A NOTE TO READERS

Thank you for reading *Lover on Top*. I hope you've enjoyed it!

Are you a fan of gay romance? If so, you may be happy to hear that I've launched a spin-off series called Men of Boyzville, starting with Harry's story. Be sure to read on for an excerpt of *Going All In*! Psst: Austin's will be next.

If you want more of Chad and Hollywood, be sure to read all about their first Valentine's Day as a couple in *Baby, Be Mine: Valentine's Day with the Caldwells*!

If you enjoyed *Lover on Top*, please consider writing a review to help others learn about the book. Every recommendation helps, and I appreciate anyone who takes the time to share their love of books and reading with others.

I've started a reader group for fans of my books on Facebook. If you enjoy talking about books, reading sneak previews, and playing games, then this is the place you want to be!

www.facebook.com/groups/FansKristineCayneBooks

If once-in-a-while emails are more your style, you can sign up for newsletter:

www.kristinecayne.com/Newsletter.html

Thank you for your continued support of me and my stories!

ABOUT THE AUTHOR

Kristine Cayne's books have won numerous awards and acclaim. Her first book, *Deadly Obsession*, was an *RT Book Reviews* Top Pick and won Best Romance in the 2012 eFestival of Words Best of the Independent eBook Awards. Her second book, *Deadly Addiction*, won two awards at the 2014 eFestival of Words and 1st place in the INDIE Awards, Romantic Suspense Category (a division of Chanticleer Book Reviews Blue Ribbon Writing Contests).

Her book *Under His Command* won Best BDSM Romance at the 2012 Sizzling Awards and was a finalist in the 2013 eFestival of Words and 2013 RONE (Reward of Novel Excellence) Awards, and her book *Everything Bared* was a finalist in the Erotic category of the I Heart Indie awards.

www.kristinecayne.com

Kristine Cayne Proudly Presents

GOING ALL IN

Book one of the Men of Boyzville series

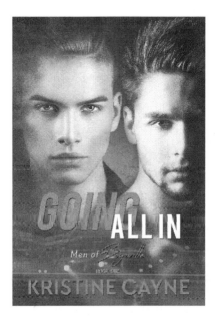

What happens in Vegas doesn't always stay in Vegas.

After a night of partying in Sin City, struggling musician Harry Cooper and his best friend Melissa wake up in the same bed, only to realize that they've both been a little naughty—and that they're not alone. When a gorgeous man comes out of the bathroom, their only question is: Who did what and who with?

But that's not the question they should be asking.

They should be asking why they can't remember anything... and why Mr. Gorgeous, aka Ashton Montgomery, filthy rich heir to a famous perfume company, shows up in Seattle a week later and picks up with Harry right where their raging chemistry left off.

What game is Ashton playing?

And why is he hiding the wedding rings he found in Harry's room in Vegas?

Praise for Kristine Cayne's *Going All In*

"What an awesome book, I loved every bit of it, I really don't have any negative thoughts at all, it had everything, romance, hot sex, great secondary characters, but the chemistry between Harry and Ashton was bouncing off the page, poor meets rich, closet meets out and proud, older meets younger, successful meets floundering.. can they make it work?"
—Karen Lane, Amazon review

"This book is such a fun read! It's light-hearted, laugh-out-loud while tea comes out your nose funny, and well-paced. It deals with heartbreak and trust issues, but Ashton and Harry work things out. Harry is a friend of those sexy firefighters in Six-Alarm Sexy; all of them have his back when things get tough with Ashton. … *Going All In* has tons of sexy men and their friends. They have a lot of fun and troubles on their way to happy ever after. I'm looking forward to more of this series."
—Amazon reader review

EXCERPT – GOING ALL IN

Ashton Montgomery let out a huge sigh of relief as he and his cousin Charlie entered the packed auditorium. They'd purposely timed their arrival between the opening act and just before the Red Hot Chili Peppers were expected to take the stage. The lights were already dimmed and the audience worked into a near frenzy.

No one would recognize him here. And after the debacle with Stephanie, an escape from his life was what he needed. Ditching his bodyguard might not have been the wisest decision he'd ever made, but, for his sanity, it had been a necessary one. And besides, he wasn't completely alone. Charlie was with him.

Yeah, that would totally reassure his parents.

Charlie raised his red Solo cup of beer and grinned. "To negative pregnancy tests."

Ashton laughed, finally giving himself permission to let go of the tight hold he'd had on his emotions. "Christ, yes. To negative pregnancy tests."

It wasn't that he didn't want to have children someday. He just didn't want to have them with Stephanie. Their families had been longtime friends, often vacationing together when he'd been younger, and he'd thought she'd understood his predicament. Thought she'd understood that he'd dated her to shut their parents up. He'd always gotten along well with her and considered her a good friend.

Now? After the scheme she'd pulled, he wasn't sure what she was.

Charlie bumped his shoulder. "Snap out of it, man. Leave that shit in New York. This is Vegas. Sin City. Red Hot Chili Peppers. No one's here to tell you what to do or what *not* to do. For two nights and two days, you're free, man. So let it all hang out!"

He waggled his eyebrows suggestively, making Ashton snort. Still, the idea had merit. Not the letting it all hang out part. That would get him arrested, but the being free part. How long had it been since he'd gotten laid?

Although his parents knew he was gay, they persisted in pressuring him to date women… for the tabloids, of course. They claimed that the media learning he was gay would ruin the family business, Montgomery Aromas. He wasn't sure he believed them, but the last thing he wanted to do was endanger the company. Too many of his relatives depended on it.

He followed Charlie through the crowd. The tickets they'd purchased from a scalper had cost a fortune, but were well worth it. They were in a standing-only section right in front of the stage. About fifteen feet in front of them, he spotted a man and a woman whose party had clearly already started.

The man couldn't be more than five eight or five nine, but he was deliciously packaged. His blond hair, swept to the side, reflected the stage lights and drew Ashton to his big brown eyes, artfully made up with liner and mascara. His form-fitting black T-shirt revealed a slim body, but defined biceps peeked out of his sleeves. Ashton licked his lips as his gaze strayed further south to the firm ass encased in tight red jeans.

If it were ten years ago, even five, Ashton would have readily concluded that the guy was gay. These days, it wasn't so clear.

Charlie tossed an arm over Ashton's shoulders. "See something you like?"

Ashton tilted his head toward the younger blond man. Charlie whistled between his teeth. "Get a load of that redhead."

"No, I meant the blond—"

"I know. Duh. But check out the girl with the curly hair next to him."

Ashton winced. Damn. "Think they're *together* together?"

Charlie clapped Ashton on the back. "Not a chance."

"Hey, just because a man wears makeup that doesn't mean he's gay."

"Relax, dude. The guy's shirt makes it plenty clear, even to those of us with broken gaydar," Charlie said with a smirk.

"What about his shirt?"

The redhead moved to speak to a girl beside her, and Ashton got a

275

clear view of the front of the man's T-shirt. As he read it, his smile grew. *I'm like 104% gay.*

Now there was a man with confidence to spare. Ashton was rich, had a good education, a great job as director of research for the New Scents labs. He was just shy of six feet and weighed one-eighty. Yet, the blond had way bigger balls than Ashton. Not that he was in the closet, well, not exactly, but there was no way he'd have the guts to announce his sexuality so visibly or blatantly.

Just then, the lights went out and a single spotlight illuminated the center of the stage. Music started, a deep thumping bass that stirred Ashton's blood. When Flea, the bassist of the band, walked out, Ashton's gaze returned to the blond, who wore a look of such ecstasy that Ashton's cock decided to join in the fun.

There was something about the guy's total abandon that really did it for Ashton.

During the band's opening number, Ashton had to keep dragging his gaze away from the man. The show onstage was good, but it was the show taking place a few feet ahead of him that commanded his attention.

The blond danced to the music, his arms in the air, his hips swiveling enticingly. Ashton thanked God he'd listened to Charlie and had worn jeans. Dress pants didn't do much to trap an erection.

The band segued into their second song. Charlie shouted in his ear. "Let's move up."

Assuming Charlie wanted to get closer to the stage, he followed, only to realize that Charlie had wanted to get closer to the redhead. Not that he minded. The move put him within arm's reach of the blond.

So close, in fact, that Ashton could make out the smell of his cologne, a scent he'd recognize anywhere, because he was the one who'd created it. Although he had to admit Risqué had never smelled so damn sexy.

Charlie whispered something to the redhead. She smiled and took his beer.

A hand closed around Ashton's. He jerked his gaze back and found himself sinking into brown eyes, the exact shade of creamy, milk chocolate.

"Hello, handsome," the blond said.

Normally a pretty smooth talker, Ashton found himself tongue-tied. Since he couldn't form a single thought, much less a word, he presented his untouched beer.

The guy's eyes widened, drawing attention to the beads of sweat decorating his forehead. "Oh God. You're a life saver." He took the cup and downed half. "Oh, shit." He wiped his mouth with a sheepish look on his face. "I didn't mean to drink so much of it. I'm just so hot."

Something about his genuine embarrassment put Ashton at ease. No one knew him here. He could be himself. 104% himself, like the guy's T-shirt said. He quirked his lips and said exactly what was on his mind. "Yes, you are. *Damn* hot."

A blush stole over the blond's cheeks, making him even more flushed. He really was too cute.

Cutting the guy some slack, Ashton held out his hand. "I'm Ashton." He had to lean in close and shout, giving him another chance to fill his lungs with that incredible scent.

"Harry. Aren't they great?" Harry asked, facing the band again.

Honestly, Ashton was barely aware of the Red Hot Chili Peppers onstage, or of the people screaming and dancing around him. All his awareness was focused on one person, one person whose name he now knew. Harry.

He answered something meaningless that was lost in the thunderous applause marking the beginning of a new song.

"Oh, I love this one," Harry said, starting to dance again. Ashton's chest felt like it was going to explode. He could barely catch his breath. Why was it so hot in here? Everything Harry did had Ashton thinking of sex. What would Harry look like naked? How would he move in bed? All questions that demanded answers. Sooner rather than later.

Taking a large gulp of beer, he tried to cool his thoughts. But Harry had other ideas. He danced around Ashton, bumping and grinding, driving Ashton crazy with the need to touch him. Finally, Harry stopped in front of Ashton and interlaced their legs. Placing his hands on Ashton's hips, he coaxed, "Come on, gorgeous. Move with me."

Ashton wanted to move with Harry all right. Against a wall, on the floor, leaning over a couch. Jesus. He wiped his forehead and had another sip of beer.

Whether it was the heat, the loud music, the crushing crowd, or Harry himself, Ashton started to relax. He allowed Harry's hands to direct his movements, and soon, they were swaying together, like two figure skaters. Okay, not quite. But he was trying.

Harry looked up, his eyes hot and lust-filled. Ashton could no longer control himself. Lowering his head, he pressed his lips to Harry's, savoring his first taste of man in months. And not just any man. No, a beautiful, bold Adonis. A man Ashton wanted to taste a lot more of.

Angling his head, Ashton played his tongue over the seam of Harry's lips. Cautiously, at first, drinking in the other man's sexy little moans. When Harry's lips parted, Ashton swept his tongue inside, exploring that sinful mouth. Their tongues wrapped around each other, twirling and swirling until Ashton was dizzy.

His hands slid down to grasp Harry's ass, and that's when he realized he was still holding the damn cup of beer. Harry chuckled, took it from him, had another big gulp, then raised it to Ashton's lips. Once the cup was empty, Harry let it fall.

Ashton wasted no time in finding Harry's ass again, while Harry's hands dug under his T-shirt and rubbed along his spine, up and down in a hypnotizing rhythm. Their mouths crashed together, one tongue seeking out the other.

Jesus Christ. Ashton couldn't remember a time when another person's touch had been so arousing, so freeing. He felt high, like he could just will it, and they'd float up into the air.

Harry wrapped himself around Ashton, his legs around his waist, arms around his shoulders, kissing and sucking at his neck. Ashton increased the pressure of his thrusts and Harry moaned beautifully.

Was this a dream? Was he actually having stranger sex—albeit fully clothed—in a concert venue packed with people?

He hoped to Christ there were no paparazzi around. This town promised that whatever happened here stayed here, and it had damn well better. If word got out, his parents would never forgive him.

www.kristinecayne.com

Continue reading for a special preview of Kristine Cayne's first Deadly Vices novel

DEADLY OBSESSION

When an Oscar-winning movie star meets a department-store photographer...

Movie star Nic Lamoureux appears to have a playboy's perfect life. But it's a part he plays, an act designed to conceal a dark secret he carries on his shoulders. His empty days and nights are a meaningless blur until he meets the woman who fulfills all his dreams. She and her son are the family he's always wanted—if she can forgive a horrible mistake from his past.

A Hollywood dream...

Lauren James, a widowed single mother, earns barely enough money to support herself and her son. When she wins a photography contest and meets Nic, the man who stars in all her fantasies, her dreams, both professional and personal, are on the verge of becoming real. The attraction between Lauren and Nic is instant—and mutual. Their chemistry burns out of control during a photo shoot that could put Lauren on the fast track to a lucrative career.

Becomes a Hollywood nightmare

But an ill-advised kiss makes front-page news, and the lurid headlines threaten everything Nic and Lauren have hoped for. Before they know what's happening, their relationship is further rocked by an obsessed and cunning stalker who'll stop at nothing—not even murder—to have Nic to herself. When Nic falls for Lauren, the stalker zeroes in on her as the competition. And the competition must be eliminated.

An excerpt from *Deadly Obsession*

Lauren rolled her eyes. "Fine. Do it."

Nic bent down and brushed his lips against hers. For the first few seconds, she didn't kiss him back, but she didn't push him away, either. Then, on a sigh, she leaned into him and her arms locked around his neck. His tongue darted out to taste her bottom lip. Mmm… cherry—his new favorite flavor. When her mouth opened, he didn't hesitate.

He dove in. And drowned.

He'd meant this to be a quick kiss, only now he just couldn't stop. His lips traced a path to her throat. Cupping her bottom with his hands, he lifted her up, grinding against her. She moaned. It was a beautiful sound, one he definitely wanted to hear again.

A loud noise pierced the fog of his lust. He raised his head from where he'd been nuzzling Lauren's apple-scented neck to tell whoever it was to fuck off, but as the sexual haze cleared, he swallowed the words. The paparazzi had gathered around, applauding and calling out crude encouragements. Some snapped photos while others rolled film. Shit. He'd pay for this fuck-up and so would she.

www.kristinecayne.com

Continue reading for a special preview of Dana Delamar's first Blood and Honor novel

REVENGE

A woman on the run...

Kate Andretti is married to the Mob—but doesn't know it. When her husband uproots them to Italy, Kate leaves everything she knows behind. Alone in a foreign land, she finds herself locked in a battle for her life against a husband and a family that will "silence" her if she will not do as they wish. When her husband tries to kill her, she accepts the protection offered by a wealthy businessman with Mafia ties. He's not a mobster, he claims. Or is he?

A damaged Mafia don...

Enrico Lucchesi never wanted to be a Mafia don, and now he's caught in the middle of a blood feud with the Andretti family. His decision to help Kate brings the feud between the families to a boil. When Enrico is betrayed by someone in his own family, the two of them must sort out enemies from friends—and rely on each other or die alone. The only problem? Enrico cannot reveal his identity to Kate, or she'll bolt from his protection, and he'll be duty-bound to kill her to safeguard his family's secret.

A rival bent on revenge...

Attacks from without and within push them both to the breaking point, and soon Enrico is forced to choose between protecting the only world he knows and saving the woman he loves.

Praise for Dana Delamar

"Here is to a WHOOPING 5 Stars. If I had to describe this book in about four words, it would be action-packed, sexy, romantic, and adrenaline rushing...." —*Bengal Reads* blog, 5 stars

An Excerpt from *Revenge*

Enrico raised a hand in greeting to Kate, and she returned his wave and started descending the steps.

She headed straight for him, her auburn hair gleaming in the sun, a few strands of it blowing across her pale cheek and into her green eyes. With a delicate hand, she brushed the hair out of her face. Enrico's fingers twitched with the desire to touch her cheek like that, to feel the slide of her silky hair. A small, almost secretive, smile crossed her features, and he swallowed hard. *Dio mio*. He felt that smile down to his toes.

She stopped a couple feet from him. "Signor Lucchesi, it's good to see you, as always."

He bowed his head slightly. "And you, Signora Andretti." He paused, a grin spreading across his face. "Since when did we get so formal, Kate?"

She half-turned and motioned to the doorway behind her. And that was when he noticed it—a bruise on her right cheek. *Merda! Had someone hit her?* Tearing his eyes off the mark, he followed her gesture. A tall, sandy-haired man, well-muscled and handsome, leaned in the doorway, his arms crossed. "My husband, Vincenzo, is here."

Enrico's smile receded. He looked back to Kate. "I'd like to meet him." *And if he did this to you, he's going to pay.*

www.danadelamar.com